MW00831780

Acknowledgments

Roni would like thank her loving family, and every generation, past, present, and future, who braves the diaspora through this ever new world.

John would like to recognize the sometimes annoying prodding and support of his family: parents John Sr. and Mary, sisters Felicia and Frances, children John Cody, Lucia and Jesse, and his "nephew" Justin.

To Ray Bradbury, whose *Martian Chronicles* and other brilliant inspirations opened our hearts and minds to the wonders of this world and let us know we were not alone.

To the many teachers and authors who inspired our love of the arts.

"Anything you dream is fiction, and anything you accomplish is science, the whole history of mankind is nothing but science fiction."

-Ray Bradbury

"Wonder rather than doubt is the root of all knowledge."

-Abraham Joshua Heschel

CHAPTER ONE

THE JEWISH QUARTER OF PRAGUE,
THE YEAR 1589

Evie was a good girl. She made the fire in the grate when her father, the esteemed old Rabbi Loew of Prague, was cold. She brought cool water when his throat was parched with the Word of God. This night she made the fire and brought a pitcher of cool water to the study where her father and two of his most devoted and unquestioning students, young men of the Yeshiva, conferred. This night they pored over charts of the moon and the stars. Outside the true state of the heavens was obscured by a dark and stormy night, the rain falling as if dropped from buckets, the lightning flashing as if unleashed by *shemot,* demons that would storm the heavens, the *Gan Eden,* if they could. She, her father, and the two students, wore white. This was not a normal state of affairs.

"It's nearly time, Evie," said Rabbi Loew. The two Yeshiva students would have looked to her for an enthusiastic response if they had dared. But they did not dare. Evie was female. Evie did not care if they looked at her or not. If they did not look at her, it was probably for the better. She was not about to give an enthusiastic response. She was too busy trembling. "Tonight is the night," said Rabbi Loew, finishing his thought. Either in agreement or warning, depending on who made the interpretation, the elements responded with a brilliant bolt of lightning followed with a blood-curdling rumble of thunder that shook the building. The disturbance in the sky was that close.

Since her father had first told her of his plan, she had lost weight. The normal shadows scooped out under her eyes had darkened to black. Her usual pale pallor had succumbed to a white that made her look as if she had been powdered with the refined flour the women of the *shtetl* reserved for their Passover cakes, cakes that had to rise without the use of yeast. Nobody liked cake that was flat and hard as matzoh, even on *Pesach*, the Passover holiday of the Jews. No woman liked to deprive her family of a good dessert on such a special holiday. For eggs to work in lieu of yeast the flour had to be light as a feather and shed of any trace of the dark, heavy wheat husks. What remained of the grain was bleached white as Evie under the mammoth stress she was carrying. The contrast with the foreboding, black circles under her eyes made her look unnatural as a wraith.

Her father, on the other hand, had gone from a shrunken elderly widower to a wild man—his overgrown white mane was uncombed and stuck out at all angles, his face had taken on a red ruddy glow, his arms had coarsened with old but ropey muscle from carrying mud up from the riverbank to the attic in the middle of the night. From the look of him, so overcome was he with passion, it seemed he had fallen in love though in the winter of his life and was about to take a wife, not mess with the furies and the very hand of Yahweh.

The difference was that if he had been about to take a wife, his youngest daughter Evie would have been happy. As it was, he was bursting with a snot-wrenching fury that was not befitting a man of God, and he knew it and his daughter knew it, but his people who loved him were so glad to see him recovered from the loss of his wife that they overlooked that he was full of an anger they had never known. The truth is that they were angry too. Evie was wary of anything born of anger, especially a full grown giant with superhuman strength. She had tried to talk him out of it, tried to abandon him. As it was, she was stuck.

"The time is now," said Rabbi Loew as thunder exploded on top of lightning, making the house and the windows quake and tremble in their panes, as if kneeling before God.

Rabbi Loew and his two students laughed, jubilant. "See," said the older of the two students, "we have agreement from above!"

If any of the three men had looked to Evie they would have seen her eyes roll back in her head as she swooned. They all heard her fall to the ground behind them. Only the old Rabbi Loew looked to his youngest daughter, his eyebrows knit with fury. "Will you mar this sacred night with your histrionics? I'll go get the butcher to take your place, he'd do better."

But Edie did not answer him. Rabbi Loew, realizing he had been a prick, even a *schmuck,* grabbed a glass of water that she had poured for him not five minutes before and knelt next to her, raising her head onto his thigh. As he wet her face, and brought the water to her lips, the color returned.

11

She took a sip and sat up of her own volition. She looked the Rabbi in the eye and would have met the others too, if they had dared to meet her gaze. "I will go before and light the candles," Evie said, straightening and untying her apron as she stood. She left the room.

The old Rabbi Loew shrugged and stood with the help of one of his students. "She has a point," he said. "This is nothing if not risky. A single slip in pronunciation, perhaps we all die."

Flanked by his two students, thoughts racing through their bowed heads, the old Rabbi Loew left the comfort of his study and started up the stairs, following Evie to the attic where preparations had been made in anticipation of this night.

Arriving at the top of the stairs first, Evie drew the key from her pocket and turned it in the lock. Her father, the esteemed Rabbi Loew, soon stood just behind her on the landing. She could feel his breath on the back of her neck. He was winded from the steps and his hard-earned age. Worse, she could hear his two young students behind him, more winded than her father from their indolent habits. Yes, they engaged in *midrash,* studying day and night, and engaged in great debate. But such activities alone did not a *mensch* make.

As a habit, Evie had poured herself into her work in keeping the Rabbi's home and disdained the idea of ever getting married. The flock of scholars that would be her suitors, far from lighting her passions, made her eyes roll up in boredom. They lacked what she called practical magic. In her dreams such a man came to her with strong arms to share the labors of the world and a nature born of awe and wonder. Such a man would be capable of love, not just lust. The scholars seemed to see women as objects designed for their satisfaction, so that they could return to their studies renewed. Lust, not love.

But she was a practical girl and knew that the man she dreamed of was just that, a dream. And not just a dream but her dream, the dream of a virgin. She had curiosity and thought she would have given up her virginity some day in exchange for the knowledge of what all the fuss was about. She loathed being naïve about anything. But her being the daughter of Rabbi Loew, no one had approached her yet for so much as a kiss. And the way things were going, she was not getting married anytime soon, if ever. These boys had plenty of prettier and younger, ready and panting virgins eager to stand under the *chupah* with them and make their babies. And her father needed her, at least now, and certainly tonight. He was crazy with need. Impatient, as she worked to coax open the door, he reached under her arm to paw the knob of the door and make it turn. The door to the attic was not often used and was prone to being stuck. It jammed.

Evie stepped out of the way as the two scholars helped her father get the door open, proving her belief that a woman was as good as three men. She would have had no trouble finessing open the old door but no one had asked her to do it. When finally they got the door open, she stepped in before them and began lighting the white candles that she had earlier placed all around the room.

When the idea had awoken in her father to make a Golem, Evie put herself to the task of preparing the attic. First, she carried down the dusty tomes, the reams of rabbinical notes, and the old garments shredded to rags by time and vermin that had been stored there. Then she swept up the rat feces and the dust balls and carried them outside. Next she dusted from top to bottom, being sure to sweep away the cobwebs from even the highest rafter. After she was done, her father and his two scholars had toured the attic, walking its floorboards, hands clasped behind their backs, until they turned to one another and nodded. Yes, they said, this place was good. No one clapped her on the back. No one said, *great idea, Evie, this is just the place*. But it could have been that Rabbi Loew did not want to waken any jealousy in his scholars, who were challenged enough by the fact that a woman would be helping them make the Golem, a task that would have surely been reserved for men, if the Torah had discussed it.

At any rate, next she had whitewashed the attic—floor, roof, and all four walls. No one else was allowed in the attic except the four of them so the task had fallen to her. She wondered if her mother would have let her father put her to such masculine work. Evie, though, cherished it. She loved the time alone, and put that love into doing sacred tasks that would create a sacred place. She put the same love into her cooking and that was why she was such a good cook (as had been her mother) and was why her father was living such a long, robust life, though he cursed God for his longevity these days. Evie did not take it personally. Not taking it personally was another of her gifts. *Oy*, she was a very gifted child.

Notwithstanding her gifts, by the time she completed her tasks, Evie was unclean, and they had to wait while she completed her time of the month.

Next they all had bathed themselves, separate and apart, spiritually as well as physically, engaging in a ritual cleansing privately prescribed by the Rabbi Loew, according to the need of each person. Rabbi Loew did not pull any punches, and it was a regular blood letting of the soul. Evie herself had to give up both her intellectual and spiritual arrogance and allow that she did not know everything, though fortunately only before God. Without her cloak of condescension she felt naked and began to see the world and the people around her for the first time. The potent nature of her emotional prostrations, exacerbated by the fasting that her father mandated, left her trembling. But this did not spare her father's scholars from her private castigations. Some things could not be denied.

It was then that they began to *daven* in earnest. As they recited their prayers, they carried up mud from the banks of the river Moldavka, a river that ran through the mountains and sloughed down mud that had never been plowed. When her father first announced the plan to Evie and the scholars, the idea had been that the four of them would be transporting the virgin mud. Just like me, had thought Evie with a smirk, I have never been plowed, mounted, or rutted rudely like the cows in the fields and the wives in their defiled beds. But as the thought crossed her mind and the smirk met her lips, she fell to the ground as if struck by lightning. She curled in a ball troubled by tremors until the smirk was wiped off her lips and her mind and spirit was once again cleansed. *Oy vay,* she would think as she recovered, *this being a rabbi's daughter was quite a curse.* But then she would remember herself and recover her forced humility, which she was beginning to carry like a cross. *Before long, I'll be cowed enough to be a wife,* she would think, and then she would fall again to the ground and shake like a *grekkor* on Purim. Her new frailty, perceived by the scholars as weakness, limited her ability to carry the heavy mud the distance required. Her father, the rabbi, therefore wisely put her to the private task of receiving the mud in the attic, kneading it free of rocks and twigs, and molding it into the shape of a man.

15

Of the three of Rabbi Loew's co-conspirators, Evie was the only one who had studied the art of sculpting. Actually she was self-taught, running her eyes and hands over the statues of Prague, their curves and lines, and kneading breads into decorative shapes suitable for the Christian holidays and selling them to the local burghers. Her Lamb of God and Cross of Our Savior were favorites. She carved violets of dough to adorn the Cross that were so realistic that her customers swore they had a floral fragrance. The little Lambs wore such endearing expressions that little Christian children had to be persuaded to eat them. For her special customers, like the wife of the Chief of Police who swore her Easter table was not complete without one of each of Evie's creations, Evie would tie a pink bow around the Lamb's neck.

The other Jews in the *shtetl* gossiped about her odd talent, muttering about her *goyim* breads and her work with leavened bread during the Passover. And they were right. Secretly, Evie had a crush on Jesus, the handsome young Jewish man who defied tradition and inspired the wise and lunatics alike. Sometimes she would peer inside the churches of Prague to catch a glimpse of the different Sons of God on their crosses to see which splendidly endowed young specimen, cloaked only in a loincloth and sometimes not even, most captured her imaginings. But the monies she earned from her breads she did not spend on herself, instead stepping in where need demanded in the *shtetl*, and so the whisperings against her shapely loaves did not go far. Besides, however odd and crazy she was, she was Rabbi Loew's daughter.

Now, this night, when her father and his two scholars had gathered and the door to the attic was locked again, now behind them, Evie removed the cloth from over her mud sculpture. The men gasped, in spite of the solemnity of the moment and the prayers rumbling off their lips. The body was handsome and shaped according to Evie's taste, and why not? It was well endowed in every respect. She was gifted — it's true. In the first moment, a flash of jealously sparked in the men, for which man has never wished that he himself embodied the masculine ideal? The power over other men and women alike that a pleasing aesthetic gave was a thing to be envied, as well as the satisfaction of being coveted. Evie was pleased to see her work so well received. She did not care if the men liked it or not, only if it awed them. And they were awed.

The next moment the men were wary of such perfection. How could they hope to control such a being? In that moment Evie was also pleased, as if somehow she had challenged the men and defeated them by something as simple as being true to her art.

But in the third moment, the men reminded themselves that the being before them was only made of mud shaped by a strange girl and that they were, in fact, all powerful, naturally superior by virtue of their calling and that they would be standing in place and stead of God for this being. A surge of testosterone thus boosted through their seed-born flesh and bone bodies. Men were simple, thought Evie, watching them go through their responses in unison, like trained horses. But in the next moment, her smugness was again shattered.

Evie had expected that in the fourth moment the three men would now turn to her and commend her work. She had strived for Michelangelo. If her work had somehow fallen somewhat short, it was still going to be pretty damn good, certainly for an effigy made of mud. Instead her father rolled his eyes. "Evie, for crying out loud. You couldn't make him a little less handsome, more like a Semite perhaps?"

"Yes, for God's sake, make him look like a Jew, or he too may turn against us."

Rabbi Loew, more gently, said, "He is very good looking, in a strange *goyisha* kind of way."

"Like some kind of Greek god," said one scholar.

"Or an Emperor, " said the other.

"An angel," said the first, "or a painted Christ in the church."

"Jesus was a Jew!" said Evie.

"Oh yeah, and a regular Adonis!" The two scholars clenched their biceps, feigning muscle. They clapped each other on the back and burst in to laughter, but catching a look from Rabbi Loew they tried to suppress themselves. Still they hiccupped with glee.

"We want to solve problems, not cause more," said Rabbi Loew to his daughter, putting a hand on her shoulder. "It would be good if he were more plain, more simple. But if you like him the way he is, I suppose we can work around it."

Evie turned to her perfect creation and smashed the heel of her palm into his still wet face. Rabbi Loew gasped. His scholars gulped their laughter and succumbed to dread. Were they going to be blamed for Evie's actions? They should not have had such a good time at her expense, or at such a serious moment. Perhaps the strain of what they were about to try to accomplish was too much for any of them. Well, not them, but for Evie at least. She was a frail egg, the very definition of *tsedoodelt*.

The rain, already wailing down, took on new life and pounded as if with a thousand fists on the rooftop overhead. "Evie, give him a face, whatever you like. Just make sure he

18

has all the parts," said the old Rabbi Loew. "Then we will give him life."

After old Rabbi Loew and his students failed to appreciate her stunningly handsome Golem, it took Evie a while to come up with a face for the Golem. Locked away in the attic while the storm raged on outside, she worked alone, fitful against time. Time augured that this be the night, so she had a deadline. Being a good girl, or so her father thought, she worked to meet that deadline, come hell or high water. That meant she had no more than a few hours. Angry, she made the Golem ugly. Sad, she made him frown. Bereft, she made him stern. The bells tolled in the clock tower as time went by. Her frustration built in her like steam in a kettle.

She grit her teeth and clenched her fists. She would have screamed to vent her rage but knew that the men lingering downstairs would not have understood it. But she did allow herself to imagine how good it would feel to scream right then and there. And then she did allow herself to imagine how panicked her father and his students would be if she did scream right then and there. And then and there, just like that, she broke into laughter, great peals of laughter. The laughter was manic and hysterical. The laughter shook her whole body. The laughter made her whiney like a horse and hiccup like a frog, but it was laughter and it was good.

What had dawned for Evie was the realization that if she'd had the backing of women, preferably the giggling and giddy girls she had known as a teenager before she lost them to their marriages, the Golem would have been allowed to be handsome. Homely had been passed down from one generation of men to the next in the *shtetl*. Here and there a girl blossomed bright, but any beauty was extinguished as soon as possible by hooking it up to a yoke of duty that would have reduced an ox to tears. Evie's girlfriends would have swooned over the Golem's good looks, the likes of which was not to be seen in their dreary little village, and petitioned her father for the Golem to stay handsome. And old Rabbi Loew would have listened.

And what had dawned for Evie was the realization that the old Rabbi Loew and his two students would have listened because, while Evie and her three girlfriends had all undergone the same obligatory course of study of sewing, cooking, and childcare, there had been no course in feminine wiles. If there had been such a course, Evie would have flunked it. It was why she remained unmarried. But her girlfriends could wrap men around their little fingers like the Snake around the Tree of Knowledge. They could have and would have twined the old Rabbi Loew around their little fingers with a few choice words and sighs, and so saved the Golem to enjoy the good looks that Evie had first endowed him with.

And what had dawned for Evie was the irony that the guileless condition that that had prevented Evie from marrying, had also led on her path of destiny, one solitary step at a time, day after day, year after year, to the attic of old Rabbi Loew that night and the creation of the most handsome Golem ever conceived. But that guileless condition had also made it impossible for her to fulfill her promise as an artist and deliver her Golem as designed and sculpted to represent all that was sublime about the male gender. Instead the Golem was plain.

Edie laughed until she peed. No wonder the world was so bereft of art. Men got what they deserved, the fools. But in the next wave, in her next dawning of realization that night,

Evie realized that God must have meant the Golem to be plain. And therefore, he was. And she saw that it was good.

That being said, old Rabbi Loew and his students had heard Evie laughing and thought she had lost her mind, which she had in a way. They bounded back up the stairs and knocked on the door, which Evie had locked behind her when they had left a few short hours before. When the night became darkest, the storm became its fiercest, and the dawn threatened to show her livid beauty, Evie swung open the door triumphant to her father and his cohorts who leaned against it. The men stumbled in and collecting themselves, gazed on the Golem's new face. And behold he was plain. Not ugly, not handsome, not angry, sad, or anything. The Golem would be nothing if not plain, so plain that there was nothing more to complain about. The Golem was ready; everything was ready for whatever came next—except perhaps the quaking hearts of the old Rabbi Loew's students.

CHAPTER TWO

EASTERN EUROPE, 1942

THE SHTETL AT ZEBRAK

"A girl?" asked Samuel, a freckle-faced red haired boy. "What's a girl doing in this story?"

"Girls can make monsters too!" said Myrtle, a pretty raven-haired child. She was ready to give Samuel a shove.

"A Golem is not a monster! It's a... Golem."

Everyone laughed. Embarrassed, Samuel thought to shove Myrtle but his friend Asher stopped him.

"*Shtuss,* be quiet," said Asher, "Who cares? We're going to learn how to make a Golem."

Rachel, an earnest young woman, and the children of the shtetl sat beneath the budding willow tree on the knoll overlooking the Moldavka River. Though clouds gathered in the distance, it was springtime. Sunlight glinted off the flowing river below. She told a story that took place on a dark and stormy night long ago.

"It was the very night that had been selected!" she said. "All had been prepared. The rabbi's daughter had swept and cleaned the attic. And so she climbed the stairs with her father and two of his students in order to fulfill the Rabbi's plan."

"I know what happens next!" said Myrtle, jumping to her feet. "The Golem gave them such a beating, a real *shlogn!*"

Samuel jumped up too. "Those bad guys were whipped but good!"

"*Shlogn?* What about his *shlong?*" asked Gil, a gawky, fair-haired boy joining them. "It must have been huge!"

"Maybe he beat them with his *shlong!*"

Rachel put a finger to her lips and gestured for all of the children to sit back down. Speculation about the Golem's organ was not something she could allow, not if she were going to be allowed to continue teaching.

When the children had settled down, Rachel continued, "The old Rabbi Loew and his two favorite students from the *yeshiva* had brought up load after load of mud from the riverbed."

"Into the attic?"

"From our river? From the Moldavka?"

"No, from someone else's river!"

"Of course from our river! The same river that flows through Prague."

As long as they sat near her on the knoll, Rachel let the children chatter while she spoke, "And while the clay was being shaped and the words were being spoken, all the while outside thunder crashed and lightning followed."

As if in answer, a rumble of thunder rolled across the sky from a distance. At least, Rachel wished it were thunder.

Another rumble came now, like the thunder but at ground level. Out in the street an armored Panzer "Tiger" Tank rolled into view, the Iron Cross of the Third Reich emblazoned on its side. The children shuddered at the sight. At the acrid smell of the diesel fuel.

"Old Rabbi Loew should have kept the Golem around," Asher said, "He could have been a big help!"

"Especially now," said Gil, his voice dropping low, although now there was no need. More German tanks continued to rumble past, making it difficult to be heard, even among themselves.

"Perhaps," said Rachel. "But maybe even the *Kabbalah* couldn't have foreseen this enemy."

"Why do they hate us, Rachel?" asked Myrtle.

Rachel pulled her attention back from the passing militia to the upturned faces lit in the sunlight. Some faces were freckled, some alabaster, some olive, and some darker. Each face was the face of a Jew adrift in their centuries-long *diaspora*.

"I don't know," said Rachel. "Maybe they are scared."

"Of us? They have all of the tanks and the guns and the soldiers."

"While others can choose their religion, we are born into ours, and so we are called the chosen people," said Rachel. "Maybe they are angry, and even scared, that we are different and apart."

"Maybe they are scared because they think we have the Golem," said Samuel.

"Maybe," said Rachel, doubting it.

As tanks continued to pass, they were joined by ranks of marching German soldiers.

"Will it always be this way?" asked Myrtle.

"Always? No. God would not allow it." Rachel stood and brushed off her dress. "What is important to remember is that this too will pass. For now we can trust and believe and do what we do whenever a storm comes. Which is?"

"Go home?"

"Gather around the hearth with our families?"

"Right," said Rachel, "Hurry home, now, and mind the streets as you go."

THE JEWISH QUARTER OF PRAGUE

Forty miles Northeast of Rachel and her charges, Isaac, the younger Rabbi Gottesfurcht, was surrounded by his own young students. They sat around him on the steps of the ancient synagogue of Prague. Before them lay the Old Jewish Cemetery where, three centuries before, the great *rebbe*, old Rabbi Loew, had been buried.

On the other side of the cemetery wall, a German *Schutzenpanzer* idled. Half tank, half truck, Isaac studied it, wondering what it would take to blow up such a vehicle. He might even have the necessary materials if only he had the scientific training. He often daydreamed about stealing weapons from the Nazis but whenever he shared the plots he dreamed up, his father asked him if he was crazy, did he want the whole *shtetl* to be wiped out in revenge? Isaac thought it would be better than being sealed in the ghetto, waiting to die.

"Just how big is he?" asked Levi.

"He?" said Isaac.

"The Golem! The Golem!" said the boys, laughing, believing that Isaac was just pretending to be distracted.

"Are you asking me about the Golem again?"

"What else?"

"Your studies?"

"My *zeyde*, my grandfather, says that the Golem has to stoop down and lean over sideways to get through even the highest doorways of the synagogue!" said Kel. "My *zeyde* says that his arms are as big as the haunches of a bull!"

"Just look at the statue of the Golem outside the Town Hall," said Levi.

"And they had to shrink the statue in size, says my *zeyde*. The Golem is way bigger than that!"

"The Golem is that big? He could toss a tank in the air, easy!"

"They say the Golem is hidden in Rabbi Loew's attic in a coffin!"

"Let's go find him!" The boys scrambled to their feet.

"Sit, sit," said Isaac.

"Come with us! And while we are hunting for the Golem, you can teach us the words that the old Rabbi Loew spoke to make the Golem," said Levi, pulling on Isaac's coat sleeve. "So we can bring him back to life!"

The boys leaped in to help Levi. They tugged on Isaac's sleeve, even as he tried to dissuade them. "Sit, sit!" said Isaac. But the old coat, a hand-me-down from the older Rabbi Gottesfurcht, gave at the shoulder. The arm of the coat separated from the shoulder with a rip. The boys gasped. Levi's face dropped. He let go of the coat sleeve. It hung from the remaining threads at the underarm. The other boys stepped back.

"Sorry, Isaac," said Levi, looking at the ground. "I mean, Rabbi Isaac."

But the ripping sound had torn something open inside of Isaac. He began to laugh. If today was his day to die, so be it.

He would wait no more. He reached across his chest, tore the sleeve off his coat, and waved it in the air. The boys shrunk back in surprise.

"No need to call me Rabbi, Isaac is fine! Why not call me by my name! I am Isaac. Who is this rabbi you speak of?" He looked around for the Rabbi. "Who is this wise man who can explain our dilemmas to us?"

The boys laughed and pointed at him. "It's you, it's you!"

But Isaac would not surrender. "Me? Not me!"

The boys backed him down the stairs into the cemetery and wrestled him to the ground. "You! It is you! You are the Rabbi!"

Isaac resisted, giving the boys a good match. He broke a sweat. The sun came back out. For a moment, he forgot everything else and it felt like spring. The boys shrieked with enthusiasm.

But as two more tanks rumbled into view, Isaac conceded the battle in order to calm and silence the boys. "Okay, okay. Yes, I am a rabbi," said Isaac. The boys fell backwards on the ground, panting. Isaac fell back too, feeling the cold earth under him as he looked up into the sky.

Birds scolded each other in the branches of a budding birch. Clouds scudded across the sky.

As Isaac caught his breath, he sighed. "But some day when some young boy looks to you as if you were wise, you must remember me and realize then what a dilemma I am in now. I know nothing. And yet you need me to know everything."

The cemetery was ancient. The memorial stones marking the graves rested flat on the stubborn grass that refused not to grow. Winter after harsh winter all signs of life died. Water wore over the stones so that the words carved in them grew soft and faded. Water caught in the crevices of the stones expanded as it froze, cracking them. But as the stones grew worn, the fresh green seedlings reappeared immortal. Century after century, spring after spring, they pressed up through the hard frozen earth.

Isaac sat up and looked at the young faces. So young they still believed a good world was possible. He could not crush that. "Okay, for today I will say this much about the Golem. Just when all had seemed lost for the Jews, the great clay monster that resembled a man, only in form, rose and cast his mighty shadow over Prague, on those who were their tormentors. The wicked Captain and his awful horsemen who tried to destroy the Jews by burning down their shtetls? When they were driven away, the Golem was no longer needed. Old Rabbi Loew gave thanks and released him, allowing the great monster to turn back to clay."

The boys looked to each other.

"Not back to clay," said Levi. "Where is he?"

Isaac shrugged. "Back in the river?"

"The attic then!"

"There is no Golem in the attic," said Isaac. "I have looked."

"You have looked?" said Kel, his face fallen.

"Why don't we make our own Golem?" said Dagan.

"My sister says that it is just a story," said Kel.

"It is just a story, isn't it?" said Dagan.

"When I get back from Zebrak, we can talk more about this," said Isaac, "I promise. But for now, come on, class is over." Isaac watched the end of the Nazi military parade disappear.

"If there is no Golem in the attic, he must be buried in Rabbi Loew's grave. Right over there." Levi pointed toward an aging stone tablet beneath which Rabbi Loew's body had centuries before been buried. The stone tablet had been engraved with the Star of David drawn with two triangles, six points, and so pointed both up to heaven and down into the earth. The four centuries of harsh weather had worn away at the stone but the Star was fresh and deep as if carved the day before.

Isaac tapped the yellow Star of David sewn on the left side of his coat with the fingertips of his right hand. As above, so below, he thought. That the Nazis forced all the *Juden* to wear the yellow Star did not rob it of its glory.

A few weeks before, Isaac had been returning from the river through the woods with fresh-caught fish. Shafts of sunlight poked down through the trees. The rhythmic drip of the rain from the night before slid off their branches. His nostrils caught the rich smell of the loam. A gypsy child, looking backwards at the *shtetl* as he ran into the woods with a chicken under his arm, had run smack into Isaac. Rather than turning him into the authorities who he detested, Isaac returned the child to the caravan with the chicken, a few loaves of bread and some cheese, all of which he could scarce afford. Isaac meant it as a *tzedakah*, a good deed for which he sought no reward.

An old gypsy woman with rough-shorn grey hair that stuck out in all directions would not allow Isaac to leave the caravan without a reading of Tarot cards. More than willing to be distracted on such a morning, Isaac sat on a tree stump across from her as she spread her shawl on the ground and took out her dog-eared hand-drawn deck of cards. The old gypsy grinned toothless when The Magician card appeared, pointing to the sky with one hand and pointing to the ground with the other. "As above, so below," the old gypsy had chuckled. The old gypsy woman had touched the yellow Star of David pinned to Isaac's coat, and tapped his heart. "As above, so below," she had repeated, looking into his eyes.

"As above, so below," said Isaac now. According to the old stories, the old Rabbi Loew had risked everything—heaven, earth, and even his own soul—to bargain with God for the safety of his people.

Kel stood behind Isaac. Overhearing Isaac's whisperings, he asked, "As above, so below?" he asked. "Does that mean that there are Nazis in heaven?"

Isaac looked at the boy, "It means that *Yahweh* is here. See how He makes the grass grow?" said Isaac, pointing out the new seedlings breaking through the thawing earth besides the gravesite. Isaac stood.

Kel sighed and ran a hand through his hair, "Instead of making the grass grow, *Yahweh* should make the Nazis go away."

Isaac added, "Before God will permit the Nazis heaven, they, like the rest of us, will have to face the gravity of their acts, and that, my young friends, will be their hell." But as Isaac spoke, his words sounded hollow. A little introspection offered after the fact did not seem like a fair punishment for inflicting hell on earth. The eternity of hot coals and agony from never-ending tortures inflicted by screeching demons, as described in other religions, seemed more like it.

In raising this issue, Isaac thought to plant a question of debate, and so further the boys' education, but they were on to something else. Two squirrels were chasing each other, looking to procreate. Dagan and Levi nudged Kel and pointed out the happy pair. The boys grinned and elbowed each other as the second squirrel caught the first and mounted. Levi tried to chase the squirrels apart, waving a stick. The sound of a burst of gunfire did what a stick could not. The squirrels separated and darted to safety.

Levi dropped his stick. "We're all going to die, aren't we?"

Another burst of gunfire but more distant. The fading sound of feet marching. The fading rumble of tanks. The Nazi parade had passed.

"Enough, go home now," said Isaac. Isaac walked the boys out to the street and with a wave and the exchange of *shalom* – peace be with you – they dispersed.

Isaac sighed as he turned and went back to the synagogue. He entered the room set aside for Torah Study, and put his book away in a cabinet. Hearing voices from down the corridor, he stepped to the door and listened.

"It is not an order," said a German voice.

Isaac opened the door a crack and saw his father and a uniformed German officer at the end of the hall, entering the sanctuary. "It is a request, Herr Gottesfurcht," said the German officer.

From the far end of the hallway, Isaac saw his father, Yakov, the older Rabbi Gottesfurcht, and the officer enter the sanctuary. Isaac followed them at a short distance as they went into the sanctuary, and stood at the entry unnoticed.

"But you have all the power. Why come to me for help?" said his father. Rabbi Yakov was not tall, but stood straight. His white hair curled out from under his yarmulke. He spoke in measured tones. But with his animated hands, he seemed boyish. He loved well, and was loved in return. He stood before the Ark of Holiness carved from oak that held his beloved Torah, facing the German officer who was the military governor of Prague.

31

The German officer was impatient to deliver his message and leave. He had only a faint awareness of the sacred nature of the room where he stood. Jews had been *davening* in this sanctuary since the earliest days of Prague. The German officer felt a sacred presence in his own Cathedral back in his Berlin when he sat with his baby daughter on his lap, her head resting against his chest, while the local bishop intoned, wreathed in the smell of incense. But here, none of those familiar cues were present. This room was plain, adorned mostly with a sense of timelessness. From the perspective of the German officer though, the air in the room was old, stubborn, and stale. He could not know that the Torah had been inscribed on parchment that had been pressed from papyrus generations before the German officer could even begin to name and count his own ancestors. He was undirected and uninterested, and so unable to sense the love and worship that saturated the walls.

"Your people listen to you," said the German officer. "Just make it clear it would be best for them to observe the curfew." He did not notice how Rabbi Yakov's hand clutched the edge of the table on which the Torah was spread on the holy days. He did not notice how Rabbi Yakov's knuckles turned white. He did not notice how Rabbi Yakov covered his revulsion at the thin smile that curled the edge of the German officer's mouth. Instead, in the mind's eye of the German officer, his newest mistress was lying on her back on his bed and spreading her legs open. He was thinking how with this good Rabbi's swift cooperation, he could be in her arms before dinner. The German officer misinterpreted Rabbi Yakov's silence as concession. "Think of it as a Sabbath every night," the German officer said.

The spring afternoon, laced with the hypnotic hum of newly hatched insects and the rumble of tanks, broke when a rapid-fire chorus of gunshots burst out in the near distance. The echo of the gunfire melted into a squabbling of disturbed crows. Rabbi Yakov found himself hoping that the gunfire had come from the next *shtetl*, not his own. He caught and cursed himself for wishing ill on his neighbor. His shame caused his mind to jump like a rat in a trap to familiar territory.

Many times a day, Rabbi Yakov chewed over the blight that was spreading across Europe. Of all of the ideas that had arisen in men's minds, the idea that killing all of the Jews could be a final solution was among the most irrational. What was the problem that any ethnic cleansing could solve? The thinker of such an idea would still have to deal with his own demons once every man, woman, and child lay buried in a mass grave. His mind was exhausted but he could not stop it from wrestling with such thoughts. He sighed. The evil that lay in the hearts of men arose by mystery, just as the good arose by miracle. "I can remind the members of the congregation about the curfew at *tefilla*, at prayer time," said the older Rabbi Gottesfurcht, growing older every moment. He was too aware that he was bargaining for the precious breath of each and every person in his *shul*.

The German officer sighed with relief. His value to his superiors in the Reich was his ability to coerce cooperation. He rarely, if ever, failed to get peaceable agreement to any of his proposals to the local people. Had this old Rabbi refused, he would not have known how to explain it to the fierce and iron-fisted Colonel Kohl, a career soldier who years before the war had earned his rank. Had this old Rabbi refused, Colonel Kohl might have ordered the German officer to take this disheveled old Rabbi out into the fields and shoot him. And if he had refused or delegated the task to one of his soldiers, the German officer himself might have been ordered to the front lines.

Among his fellow officers there were those who preferred to entertain themselves in the evening by exercising their vicious might against shabby, unarmed Jews. But the German officer was at heart a peaceable man and preferred to spend his nights dining with friends and having a good Cognac. Of course, under orders, the German officer had led his soldiers in the trampling of Jewish ghettos as they advanced across Eastern Europe from Berlin, but it bored him. Not only was it like shooting fish in a barrel, he also, in his heart of hearts, knew it was wrong. He was truly grateful to the older Rabbi Gottesfurcht for his cooperation. "Thank you," he said and meant it.

"But I can't be responsible for the actions of everyone. Many are not happy with your presence here," Rabbi Yakov said. His thought was that if he could not save all of his congregation, maybe he could save some. He was thinking of the children, the innocent children. He did not know that Isaac, his own son though no longer a child, hovered unseen at the door.

"Rabbi, trust me, I want to be here even less than you want me to be," said the German officer. Rabbi Yakov tried not to shrink from the hand of the officer as it reached out to pat him on the back. Isaac was revolted to see the German officer touch his father.

"Really?" said Isaac. Rabbi Yakov and the German officer turned to see Isaac stride into the room.

"Isaac!" said Rabbi Yakov.

Ignoring the warnings he had given the boys not long before, Isaac said to the German officer's face, "I find that hard to believe. Why don't you prove it and leave?"

"Forgive my son, Colonel," said Rabbi Yakov.

But Isaac held his ground with the German. The German officer looked back into Isaac's face, into the dark eyes that sparked with rebellion. The German officer held his gaze, pumping his right hand closed into a fist and open again near the butt of his pistol, a gesture that was not lost on Rabbi Yakov. After what seemed to Rabbi Yakov like hours, the German officer closed his fist and dropped his arm.

"Do you see what I mean?" the German officer said, turning to Rabbi Yakov so he could ignore Isaac. "This attitude of the youth of Prague. This is why your influence is needed." The German officer tried to sound casual. He needed to get this over quick in order to have time for his tryst with his mistress. Otherwise, she might go out to the clubs and find a younger, more handsome soldier to buy her dinner and satisfy her sexual needs. And at that moment, Colonel Kohl was speeding closer and closer to Prague on a train from Poland. It was said that he had been meeting with the Fuhrer himself, or that at least he had been in the Fuhrer's presence. The German officer could be called away to meet with Colonel Kohl at any time. Before that happened, he needed to see her.

Rabbi Yakov glared at his son, but Isaac ignored his father. "What do you expect of a people under occupation?" said Isaac. The older Rabbi Gottesfurcht put a hand to his chest. Isaac was his only son, a child who had caused so much pride and so much pain. He could not bear to see him struck down for this – a shallow opportunity to say a few angry words to a meaningless officer.

The German officer, playing his part, pounded his fist onto the Torah's table. "I expect you to appreciate that we have not leveled your city." Isaac watched his father wince with each blow. The German officer continued, "I expect you to appreciate that I continue to allow your father to conduct his religious activities."

The German officer's mistress said that she found him sexually adept, a man who made her feel alive again. He believed her, and why not? Life was short. He could not let such a woman slip through his fingers. He had gifts for her of cheese and butter, spoiling outside in his car. He was in a hurry to leave. He would push the Jews for compliance, or the hell with it, he could just have a few Jews shot, like this shiftless boy who dared defy him, and then everyone would fall into line.

Rabbi Yakov held himself up by tightening even more his white-knuckled grip on the back of a bench. He could feel his nails sink into the grain of the wood. Isaac, seeing his father's reaction, hung his head. The German officer banged his fist against the table one last time and stepped back. He straightened his jacket. "I expect you to cooperate," he said.

"I am sorry, Sir," said Isaac, grabbing his exposed arm, catching himself from striking out. In that moment both the older Rabbi Gottesfurcht and the German officer noticed that Isaac was wearing a jacket with a sleeve torn off. The older Rabbi Gottesfurcht noticed it with shame, while the German officer with disgust. These people had no pride, the German officer thought. They were dark skinned or just dirty, and belonged in the gutter under a good boot. His bile rose but he caught himself. He looked at the ceiling, thought again of his mistress, and took a deep breath. "We are both being forced into unacceptable situations," he said and, lowering his eyes, met the blank look that Isaac forced to cross his face. "Don't make it worse."

The German officer took a cigarette out of his pocket and lighting it, inhaled. He studied both of the Rabbis, father and son, and felt assured. He could leave now. Even if they would not cooperate, he had done his best. It would be their own fault, and not his, if their village had to be leveled by soldiers.

When the door of the sanctuary closed behind the German officer, Isaac turned to the older Rabbi Gottesfurcht. "*Tateh*, Father, are you all right?"

"No, of course not," said Rabbi Yakov. "Why do you provoke these people?"

"Why do you bow and scrape before these people?" said Isaac.

"I repress my desire to spit in their faces in order to save lives," said Rabbi Yakov. "Now you tell me, why do you provoke them?"

"I cannot help myself," said Isaac, looking at the floor.

"Well, learn to," said Rabbi Yakov. "We have to get through this."

But Isaac was not satisfied. "Get through this? What makes you think that we are getting through this? Just what are we are getting through. This, what?"

"Isaac, how can you say this?" said Rabbi Yakov. "Thus far, through my efforts, we are still in our *shul*, and here in our Temple, we may still practice our rituals and worship our God."

"To cower like this, it is better to have never been born at all, or at least, to die defending ourselves," said Isaac. "When and how does a man recover from having given up the fabric of his life?"

Rabbi Yakov did not know what to say.

Isaac met his father's silence. He grabbed it and studied it, turning it over in his hand as if it were an artifact brought back from a distant shore. And then he said, "If we are so abandoned by God as to be helpless, why are we even trying to survive?"

Rabbi Yakov sighed and shrugged. "Remember, we are the Chosen people," he with a wry smile. He lifted his hands up, "We are chosen for this, we are chosen for that. Some day maybe we'll get to choose." But then he threw an arm around Isaac's shoulder and pulled him close. "I choose this crazy life here with you as my son. Together we will find a way. We owe this much to God, to at least survive. How would it look if God were wrong?"

Isaac allowed a half-smile to cross his face. Yakov slapped his son on the back and went to a window looking out on the road. Isaac joined him. Together father and son saw the German officer talking with his driver.

Rabbi Yakov knew that his son was right; the situation was intolerable with no end in sight. His people needed something more than patience. Patience was killing everyone, even him, but most of all, his son. "What lesson was that I heard you teaching your students?" Asked Rabbi Yakov. Isaac did not reply. "The Golem, again?"

"They asked for it. It's a dark time. They're just children. I give them fairy tales because it is better than telling them the truth," Isaac said.

"And what is the truth?" asked Rabbi Yakov.

"That they will always be victims, always be hated," said Isaac.

"You don't believe that," said Rabbi Yakov. "Have faith."

Isaac shook his head, and turned away from his father. Outside more German tanks rolled by. To Isaac, it seemed that more German soldiers, more German artillery, more German tanks, were ever arriving, always taking pains to circle the *shtetl* and send chills through its residents. When would enough bone-crushing weaponry be enough against the unarmed?

"Isaac, my son, look at me." As Isaac turned back to his father, Rabbi Yakov remembered the features of his wife reflected in his son. Both had the same warm brown eyes that opened to the soul. "Faith can move mountains."

"But can it move tanks?" said Isaac. "And what good is faith if we cannot believe in the old stories, in the miracles?"

Rabbi Yakov answered, "As long as you don't lose your faith, you can help. As long as you do not try to be a politician, you can help. Let me take care of the Nazis."

Isaac clenched his jaw and shook his head. "When I walk through my own town, I slump over. I do not smile or look up. I stop myself on every street corner from confronting these Nazis. And even before they came here to fester, I gave up my dream to study the stars and planets. All for what? For them? For a few crumbs of survival? I cannot even walk out on a Spring evening, smell the blossoms, meet a girl in the orchard, and steal a kiss under the moon. This is life for which I am to have faith?"

A barrage of gunfire echoed in the distance. "If you do not believe in the story of the Golem—if for you it has become just a fairy tale—stop dwelling on it," said Rabbi Yakov. "The boys must be made sturdy for whatever is ahead. Teach them the wisdom of the Psalms, how to walk in dark times. Steady their souls." About this, Isaac realized his father was right. But then again, Isaac had never seen himself as a rabbi. Of course, he himself should have known that it was just a matter of time before he would fail his students.

Isaac allowed his eyes to gaze out the window at the birds twittering and bickering in the still fallow apple tree. The buds were still so subtle they could barely be discerned from the stick-like branches. What a miracle that every Spring those sticks exploded in to first, flowers, then fruit. He trusted his father, and had often agreed to study what his father called the wisdom of patience. On the other hand, he was furious at the platitudes that worked to suppress the impulse to action.

"We should make a Golem," said Isaac.

"What?" said Rabbi Yakov.

"Our own Golem," said Isaac.

Rabbi Yakov said nothing.

"Oh forget it," said Isaac turning to walk away, shaking his head.

Rabbi Yakov stopped him with a hand on his shoulder. "Now it is time for your lesson," he said.

Isaac smirked and gave a laugh. "And this isn't a lesson?" he said.

"Over how many weddings have you presided? A dozen? Half a dozen? Even one?" asked Rabbi Yakov.

"None," said Isaac, abashed. He was disturbed to hear his voice come out sounding like that of one of his schoolboys.

"You want to do well tomorrow, don't you? We'll go over everything again," said the older Rabbi Gottesfurcht.

Isaac shrugged his shoulders. "Yes, *Tateh*," he said.

Outside the German officer's driver opened the door of the car for him. Before getting in, the German officer turned back and stood looking at the Temple as he finished his cigarette. The Rabbi's son angered him with his lack of gratitude. The boy who probably thought himself a man was

40

too indignant for his station in life. He overlooked entirely the risk that the German officer was taking in protecting this community of Jews. To be honest, the boy had hurt his feelings and so terrified him. To be unappreciated by a Jew, it made him feel weak and vulnerable. To be demeaned by the lowest of the low. As a ranking officer of the Nazi Socialist party he could ill afford to feel this way. Now he knew what Herr Hitler meant when he spoke of the Jews as the Devil. Here he had come to delve out compassion and mercy, and he had left demeaned by one of their children, a young boy who had only just left off wearing short pants.

Then he laughed. This lowly Jew boy and his father were trying to intimidate him and it had almost worked. He laughed again. *Heil Hitler!* What genius was Hitler was to have discerned this! Any interaction with a Jew, however Christian an Aryan might try to be, was detrimental and even dangerous. He had come full of mercy and the dirty boy and his father had been working him like a puppet! They had brought him to doubt himself and his Fuehrer. This was the way of this evil domination the Jews worked — the tentacles of their superiority were a mind-game that worked to control the world. He dropped his cigarette to the road and ground it out with his heel, then got into the car. His driver closed the door, got into the driver's seat, and started the engine.

The German officer looked back at the Temple through the rear window of his car just before the car turned the corner. It would be the fault of this Rabbi and his uncontrollable son if their neighborhood had to be leveled by soldiers and its properties redistributed to those who supported the Reich. This very building was serviceable though musty, and could make a grand villa. The stones the Jews had outside in the graveyard, allegedly to mark graves, though scribbled with Jewish carvings, could be carted away and laid with mortar together to make a manor. The Jewish demons! Do the demonic actually die he wondered? This temple, this synagogue, was all a front, a Jewish front. A sanctuary for the unsanctified. His brother-in-law had been a well-regarded mason before the depressed economy had engulfed Germany. Perhaps he would be interested in renovating this land and these buildings into something more useful than housing Jews.

The more the German officer thought about it, the more he realized that no matter what he did, the days of the Rabbi and his son, and their inconvenient community were numbered. He would leave off trying to be civilized and be the one who sent them to their inevitable fate. This would likely please Colonel Kohl and restore his own sense of dignity. He would give the orders that night. But first he would see his mistress.

When his car pulled up beneath her apartment she was sitting beneath her window, in her dressing gown waiting for him. What a good girl. As the German officer climbed the stairs, with his gifts of cheese and butter gathered in the crook of his arm, he thought about how she would open the door and take his hand, pulling him inside. She would take his gifts and kiss his cheek. She would pull out the pins that held up her dark hair, and it would fall heavy and in waves to the small of her back. He would slip off her dressing gown and kiss her breasts as she undressed him, unbuttoning his jacket, loosening his gun belt and placing it gently on the floor. She would run her hands over him as she slid to the floor. Kneeling, she would open his trousers, take out his manhood, and bring it to her lips. He felt the urge climbing already and was eager to enter her.

All went as he imagined, and as she knelt before him, he shared with her the insights he had grown to about the Jews that afternoon. He told her that she had been wrong, and that the Jews did not deserve his Christian mercy. He bragged to her about the orders he was about to give to ravage the *shtetl* and how it was sure to lead to his advancement. She moaned in appreciation and reached a hand down to his Luger that lay on the floor while her lips were wrapped around his shaft. Lifting the pistol, she shot him through the base of his chin. The bullet angled up through his mouth, his pallet, behind his nasal passage, and into his brain.

She ducked the spray of his blood and pushed his body backward onto the bed. She called down to her lover, the German officer's driver, waiting in the car below. He had heard the gunshot and took the stairs up two at a time. Together they stripped the body and slid it, wrapped in bedclothes, under the bed. They pulled her cache of cash from the mattress and emptied the drawer of jewelry given to her by the German officer into an empty pillowcase.

He drove her to the edge of the forest where they left the German officer's car in a ditch for stripping later. Together, hand in hand they darted gleeful through the trees, celebrating the cooing of the evening doves and the swooping of the early owls. Piece by piece they kicked off their civilized clothing, and ran hand in hand, barefoot. Naked they slipped through the woods, disguising their tracks, climbing through along tree branches, making circles in the wet loam to throw off any pursuers. In this way, they made their way back to their caravan, to the old gypsy woman with rough-shorn grey hair that stuck out in all directions.

The old gypsy woman was busy cooking their dinner of roots and cabbages. That morning she had foretold the return of her daughter and her daughter's man in the cards. The old gypsy woman was looking forward to their company, to sitting by the campfire and hearing their stories and telling her own from days gone by, to sharing their plunder. She laid out new garments for them knowing they would arrive as unclad as Adam and Eve.

OSHWIECIM, POLAND

That night the Polish Metaphysical Society convened in order to meet with a different young man named Isaac. His name was Isaac Kronski. While Rabbi Isaac Gottesfurcht had brown hair that fell in curls and the open face of a friend, this Isaac Kronski had straight black hair that fell over piercing dark eyes. He had a fierce tension in his rangy body. Kronski, like Rabbi Isaac, wore the Star of David on his coat.

The meeting was in a temple sanctuary. The windows were draped. The room was lit by only a few candles. Kronski sat on a bare wood chair in the center of the sanctuary, holding his body still. His eyes were closed. His hands with their long pale fingers rested on his thighs. He appeared to be in a trance. "I see fire, leaping flames," he intoned. "Castles fall, temples rise. North becomes south, day becomes night."

A *minyan* of men, the ten or more required for prayer service, gathered around him, watching. Micah and Ira, old friends of many decades, sat together on a wood bench meant for prayer. Yarden stood arms crossed while his brother, Yoel, sat legs crossed. Dov, the candle maker, and Zev, his apprentice, leaned up against a windowless wall. This congregation's *rebbe*, Rabbi Eisenman, elderly and white-haired, lingering at death's door, sat in a chair, blind and nearly paralyzed by arthritis. He was there in form but not substance, his cane leaning against the wall. War torn

44

Europe was bereft of rabbinical students, able to step in and lead a congregation. Hillel, the *hazzan* or cantor who sang in the temple, had been at Rabbi Eisenman's side for years. Now Hillel found himself suddenly in charge.

"The Black Spider on the red flag. Its legs stretch across the land, from sea to sea," Kronski said. Then he took in a deep breath of air and rose to his feet, eyes still closed. He cried, "The eternal victory of the Third Reich is sealed in your hands!" before he collapsed on the floor. First one eye opened, and then the other. He sat up. He allowed his hands to lift off of his thighs and stretch, clenching and opening his fists. Then he exhaled and looked around at the gathered men. The men exchanged glances with one another.

A burly man named Mendel, the local butcher, leaning against the wall, righted himself and walked toward Kronski. A floorboard creaked. Kronski stood and faced him. The two nodded at each other. Kronski smiled.

Mendel said, "And they pay you for that?"

"You'd be surprised," Kronksi said. Almost everyone in the room laughed.

"If only this were a laughing matter," muttered Hillel, the cantor. He had recited services in song as a *hazzan* for all of his adult life. He had devoted his entire life to lifting his voice in prayer. Yet here, in these darkest of times, when he and his people needed prayer the most, when he was thrust into a position of leadership, he was suffering a crisis of faith. He had relatives in Germany from whom he had not had word in eleven months. He feared the worst. Among them were his sister and her family. He was not so lighthearted as to allow the ridicule of Nazi pastimes to entertain him. He was nagged by the thought that old Rabbi Eisenman, elderly and white haired, would still know what to do.

Glancing around the room at the faces of the men gathered, his longtime friends and neighbors, Hillel the cantor wondered who among them would survive these times. According to their faith, as the Chosen people, at least some would survive to carry humanity to the End of Days when the Messiah would come. But he was having trouble holding onto any of the truisms of his religion, including that one. The annihilation of the Jews was one of the primary objectives of the Nazi occupiers, and from the perspective of the overtaken, the war was going well for the occupation.

Hillel continued, "I don't have any place left in my heart to laugh at the Nazi regime. We're men, not children. We don't need to be humored. It's time for action."

Kronski answered, "Exactly right."

Now as the room fell into silence, old Rabbi Eisenman began to laugh. Everyone tried to ignore him. Spittle came to his lips he laughed so hard. He laughed so hard he might die.

Hillel spoke to Kronski over the laughter of the old rabbi. "So, we are placing our trust in you, Kronski. After all, you say you are a rabbi's son. What is your proposal? Do you bring us weapons, a plan of attack? What is it you are offering, and be straight about it."

The old *rebbe* laughed as he had never laughed. The other men in the room stirred uneasily. Yarden exchanged a look with Yoel, who shook his head, and shrugged.

Kronski answered, "I do not brings weapons. Not yet."

"Then we're leaving," said Hillel. "The tanks are in the streets. Our families are in our homes, alone." The men who were sitting got to their feet. The men who were standing put on their coats. Dov stood by the old Rabbi Eisenman, ready to help him to his feet.

Kronski stood before the door, stopping the men from leaving. "But as long as the Germans believe these things of me..."

"These things, what things?!" said Hillel.

"That I have powers, that I can help them see into the future," said Kronski. "They call me the Paranormal Pole."

The old Rabbi Eisenman wailed with laughter, tears streaming down his cheeks.

Hillel let out a snort of laughter himself. "God in heaven, *Gut en himmel*, such garbage," he said, shaking his head. He hated the strutting of this admitted charlatan, this Isaac Kronski, who blithely mirrored the cynicism that Hillel struggled to fight off. This Kronski person might be a pretender for a good reason, but Hillel wished better spiritual advisors for his enemies to inspire them away from the evil that wracked their souls. He wondered if Kronski's well-motivated antics could backfire and invite the wrath of God, who preferred humility and integrity over insolence and mockery. He hoped that in his faux sessions, Kronski did not invoke God by name and so take that name in vain. "We are facing extermination. How can you make light of this?" he asked Kronski.

The old Rabbi Eisenman stopped laughing. He was limp now with exhaustion. His white hair stood out in wild, untamed tufts. Sweat ran down his brow. Still he struggled to speak. Mendel, the butcher, leaned his ear close to the elderly Rabbi's mouth, and spoke out what the rabbi had to say, "And then a note fell from heaven. *Po-lin*." The few words the dear old *rebbe* had left were thus delivered, and he fell back in his chair. He wheezed, spent, and let his head fall to his chest.

Everyone in the room from the Polish Metaphysical Society knew of what Rabbi Eisenman spoke. In 1348 A.D., the plague

47

of the Black Death had appeared in Europe. The Jews were accused of poisoning the wells and springs and so causing the deaths that were, instead, the result of disease. The Jews were tortured and burned to death in large numbers. Their belongings were distributed. The townspeople and nobles rejoiced in their sudden wealth only to die soon after of the plague.

The Jews who still lived, who were not killed as scapegoats or by the plague, wandered eastward through the forests. It was said that on the leaves of the trees were inscribed Hebraic sacred names. In the branches of the trees, errant souls sought deliverance from the Jews who, in passing, would stop to say their twilight prayers below.

As the hard, cold journey of the exiled Jews wore on, it was said that a note fell from *shamayim*, the heavens, on which were written two Hebrew words, *po* and *lin*. Those two words meant *live here*. And so the Jews stopped and stayed, naming their way station after the note from heaven, and so *Po-lin* became Poland. The Jews built their temporary homes, their *shtetls*. A moment to breathe, catch hold of their lives, give birth, raise their young, and die, along the way of their *diaspora*, their journey back to the land promised to Moses. The Jews who had wandered in the time of the plague had stayed now in Poland for nearly four hundred years, forgetting or falling asleep as to where they were headed, or even the fact that they were going anywhere at all.

To the men of the Polish Metaphysical Society, the message of Rabbi Eisenman was clear. Here was the moment that ended their Poland. The Jews, forced by the hand of Hitler, had taken up their *diaspora* again – some migrating through the valleys of death, others wandering again into the forests, and others scattering still further across the oceans of the earth. Kronski, playing the fool, could pretend to draw notes down from heaven for the Nazis. The mystic Jews would take up their journeys and trust that there would be notes from the heavens, the *shamayim*, along the way. They did not need a Kronski for that. They *davened* and were alert to the whisperings of the *Elohim*.

There was a relief in knowing that it was time again for the Jews to wander. There was a lessening of the grip to this home, this Poland, and a reaching to *Yahweh* as their spirits were freed in flight. The Nazis were clowns who dreamed they had the upper hand, who relied on this Kronski for their divination. So the old Rabbi Eisenman laughed.

"What else do we have against this enemy? My so-called powers are my passport through these dangerous times," said Kronski. "How else could I, a son of Hebrew blood, be able to move across occupied territory, through checkpoints and past armed German troops, to pass along messages and unite our insurgency?" If the old rabbi had the strength, he would have laughed again. This Kronski was so earnest that he showed himself a fool. Even so this was a desperate time.

More candles were lit. "Perhaps this is true," Dov said.

"Perhaps you are the one," said Ezra, a tall thin man who had been standing in a corner listening with his hat over his eyes. Something he heard had moved him to push back the hat and speak. Other men, impressed that Ezra had been moved to speech, nodded.

"Perhaps you are the one to unite us," said Dov. Mendel nodded as well.

"What is the plan?" said Hillel, the cantor. "The passing along of messages alone will not accomplish our goal. United we will fall, unless we gather might and strength to our side."

"There is power in numbers," said Kronski.

"There is power in the One," said Hillel. He took a deep breath, closed his eyes and lifted his face upwards. He wished for a sign, something to tell him whether he could trust this man. But his newfound cynicism raged within, telling him that he was alone. Frustrated, he knew that in this state of mind God would not help him make a decision. Besides he seemed to be the only man in the room who doubted Kronski. He wished he knew what his rabbi, now so still and silent, thought not just about the Nazis, but also about this Kronski in particular.

Kronski cleared his throat. Hillel opened his eyes and studied Kronski's face. The Nazis had trapped them in their *shtetls*, and like demons, hungered for their deaths. Some *dybbuck* had fed Hitler and the rest of them with the belief that vengeance for the fictitious crimes of the Jews could somehow staunch the rot in their Aryan souls. The cycle of illogic could not be broken except by the death of the Jews... deaths in the millions... deaths which would disprove the twisted logic by failing to make even a single Nazi a better man. This Kronski was a ray of hope in a hopeless situation. What other choice was there?

"You're asking us to trust you with not just our lives, but the identities of those who trust us," said Hillel.

"I am only here because those senior in the resistance have studied me, found me worthy, and sent me to you," said Kronski.

The two men stared at each other, neither backing down from the gaze of the other.

"I will die to protect your trust," said Kronski.

Hillel relented, nodding his approval. Mendel crossed to the brick wall and pulled out a loose stone, revealing a cache hole. He reached in, withdrew a sheaf of papers, and brought them to Hillel who in turn offered the papers to Kronski.

"With *Yahweh* and those before you as witness, you will die if you violate our trust," said Hillel.

Kronski nodded and allowed his gaze to sweep the room, looking into the eyes of each man, communicating the earnestness with which he undertook his given task, before he took the papers.

It should have been a moment of great satisfaction, as it always is when one man extends his trust to another and the other accepts, brother to brother, but behind the gathered men the wooden door flew inward with a crash, a metal battering ram having blasted it off its hinges. The men in the room froze as Nazi *Sturmtruppen*, Storm Troopers, attempted to crowd all at once through the narrow doorway. "*Verlassen sie eine weise! Idioten!*" shouted their commander.

Mendel took up the old Rabbi's cane, the only weapon in the sanctuary, and turned to face the soldiers. Panicked he thought of his son, a young boy who waited for him in the old Rabbi's study. He prayed that hearing the noise, his son would slip away into the woods. He thought only of his son as he thought to divert the soldiers.

Behind Mendel, Hillel slipped the papers inside the waistband under his jacket. He grabbed Kronski by the arm and shoved him through a back door into a tiny storeroom. Seeing Hillel escape, a soldier opened fire on him. Two bullets stung Hillel. Turning, he closed and bolted the door. He shoved Kronski out of the way and grunting, he tried to open a small, greasy window. It would not budge. He put his fist through the window, pulling the shards out of the frame without regard for his bleeding hand. "Out!" he ordered, and helped Kronski to slip outside unharmed. Only then did he look down at his blood soaked lower garments. He had taken bullets in his abdomen and thigh.

"I cannot leave you," Kronski said.

"Go! You cannot be caught! From among us, you are now the only hope," said Hillel.

"But where should I go?" asked Kronski, reaching his hand back inside, offering to help Hillel out through the window frame.

"The Underground will hide you. Go to a temple north of Prague, a village called Zebrak!" Hillel said, rejecting Kronski's offer of help. "Leave now, without me, without us." Hillel reached into his waistband and handed Kronski the now blood soaked papers.

"I will not forget you," said Kronski.

"Let the papers be your guide. Take them to the old Rabbi Chaim Jecobs of Zebrak. He will protect you and make sure you get to the others," said Hillel the Cantor as he began to bleed to death. "I will buy you time, now run!"

Kronski ran toward the dark woods. Hillel watched him disappear, swallowed into the night. Behind Hillel, the storeroom door splintered open. He backed away from the window and turned around hands raised. The storm trooper racked the bolt on his MP-40 Schmeisser submachine gun. Hillel dove at him but was thrown back by a storm of bullets. The sound of gunfire echoed out of the temple and into the woods.

Kronski turned back to look when he reached the brush beyond which lay the forest. The flames arching high above the ravaged synagogue lit his face. He saw storm troopers back out of the building—their guns raised and ready to obliterate any strays. He saw other German Soldiers, with torches, setting fire to the outlying buildings. He looked from the burning buildings to the red stained papers in his hands. The men of the Polish Metaphysical Society had died to give them to him. He set a grim expression on his face and ran deep into the tangle of trees that made the forest.

Colonel Kohl had his driver pull around in the front of the temple. His vehicle, a *Kuebelwagen 82*, the German Army's version of an American jeep, shuddered to a stop. A tall, imposing man, he climbed out of the passenger side, and stood before the burning building. Hands on hips, he watched emotionless, as the roof collapsed and sparks flew high in the night, carried aloft by the heat of the flames.

A Storm trooper ran to the Colonel's side. "Herr Kohl, we have gathered up everyone who was in the building," he reported with a salute.

The Colonel looked over and saw the remaining men from the *minyan* kneeling in the road. Their hands were on their heads, a line of Mauser 98 bolt-action rifle muzzles at their backs. "And?" said the Colonel.

"He is not among them," said the storm trooper.

Colonel Kohl grimaced in thought. He looked back at the wreckage that had been a synagogue. "Let one live to tell the story of this night and so put an end to this business of an underground resistance," he said. The idea that a handful of unarmed, untrained Jews could take down the Nazi empire would be funny, if it was not so unnerving that some of the Jews seemed to believe it.

"*Javohlt!*" said the storm trooper. He left the Colonel, silhouetted against the remains of the temple that were now not much more than burning embers. The storm trooper went back to where the Jews were being held. He pulled Dov, the hapless candle maker, and sent him wounded to limp back toward his village, his *stetl,* so that he could warn others not to be so foolish as to oppose the Nazi mission. Dov heard behind him the sharp crack of rifle shots and wept.

The old Rabbi Eisenman found peace from his tortured body that night. Of those who escaped with their lives that night there was only a boy named Aaron who had been waiting in the small library of the *schul* for his father, Mendel, the butcher, and Isaac Kronski, the last and best hope held by the dying members of the Polish Metaphysical Society for their cause.

Dov died of the cold and loss of blood before he made it to his home on this earth. In his heart he knew it was for the better. He did not want to be the one to tell the story of the Polish Metaphysical Society and sap others of the courage to go on. As he entered the valley of death, a note floated down from heaven, fluttering as it spun through a veil of golden light, and landed in his open palm.

THE JEWISH QUARTER OF PRAGUE

Isaac, the younger Rabbi Gottesfurcht, loaded a satchel of books onto a single horse-drawn cart, next to a blanket roll.

"It is in your blood, so do not worry," said his father, Yakov, the older Rabbi Gottesfurcht, watching.

"Fine," said Isaac, loading a suitcase of neatly folded garments on top of the satchel. He had laundered them carefully and folded them neatly. It would be important to make a good appearance. To that end, he had allowed Rabbi Yakov to take him that morning for a long overdue haircut from a neighbor woman. She had known Isaac since he was a little boy and was good enough to give him a good trim without shirring off the curls that his mother had loved.

Her cooing over this detail had both warmed Rabbi Yakov's heart, and made Isaac nauseous, or anxious, or both.

"You have the map?" asked Rabbi Yakov.

"Yes, I have the map," answered Isaac.

"You have your cloak? It will be cold," said Rabbi Yakov. He had traveled the route his son would be traveling to Zebrak often enough as a young man, but in times of peace, and had known how bitter the forest could get at night. "And don't stop for any reason. Until you get there."

"Yes, Father, please. Who is the one doing the worrying?"

"It's your first wedding," said Rabbi Yakov, searching for a reason he was willing to speak out loud. Some fears required that you bite your tongue for fear that evil would otherwise seize on the spoken word and form a curse.

"Yes. You're so nervous you would think it was your own," said Isaac.

"My wedding? And who would I be marrying?" asked Rabbi Yakov.

"We could use a wedding," said Isaac. "I'll marry you. Any of the widows would have you," said Isaac. As Isaac reached adulthood, he looked back and felt sorry for his father, that he did not remarry after his mother had died.

"Yes, and your point? My son is about to perform his first wedding, and jokes he is making about his poor old father."

"No need for fear, Father. I will make you proud," said Isaac.

"You have, every day. I will have no fears about leaving the congregation in your hands when the time comes," said Rabbi Yakov. Mortar fire reverberated in the distance. "If there is still a Temple left standing."

"And if there is not, we will hold services in the fields and in the forests of our diaspora," said Isaac.

"You are my son," said Rabbi Yakov. "Now go, and be well. *Sholem.*"

"*Aleichem sholem,*" answered Isaac, "And to you peace." He embraced his father, and patted him on the back.

Often throughout Isaac's childhood, his father had been asked to neighboring *shtetls* to officiate over one of the many holidays or ceremonies honored by the Jews. Whenever his father had to travel to perform a wedding, a funeral, or a *bris*, Isaac would stand by while his father loaded his horse-drawn cart. When the last book and bag were stowed in the cart, his father would turn back to little Isaac and ask him to be the man of the house while he was gone. Isaac would agree, and his father would pat him on the back. Isaac had always been proud to be the boy who would someday be a man who followed in his father's footsteps. That was not, however, the same thing as wanting to be a rabbi. Still, it was a more than honorable trade and a chance for a night away from the troubles of Prague.

"If God is willing, someday soon I will be at your wedding," said Rabbi Yakov, slipping an apple and a cheese sandwich wrapped in paper into his son's pocket. Isaac tried to protest but his father insisted. "Your mother would be furious if I let you leave empty handed," the older Rabbi said.

Oy, thought Isaac to himself, my father is becoming like a little old *yenta*, pushing food in my pocket as if I was traveling to the edge of the earth. Still Isaac accepted the apple and cheese, and the pretense that everything was okay that came with it. Times were eerie and brutal.

Rabbi Yakov watched his son Isaac climb into the cart. He waved as his son Isaac took up the reins and nodded as the horse-drawn cart started away. He knew that it was better anyway for his son to be out of town after so angering the German officer. He wondered if Isaac knew that as well.

When the cart and his son disappeared from sight, Rabbi Yakov nodded to himself and turned back the other way on the cobblestone road, walking home to his *shul* past the hulking shell of an idle German Panzer tank.

KRIVOKLAT FOREST AND THE TEMPLE AT ZEBRAK

The forest was thick and dark. Sunlight darted through the trees in small doses. Drops of water fell from the branches throughout the day, whether it rained or not. Pockets of fog curled around the trunks. Deep among the trees, the young Rabbi Isaac Gottesfurcht tasted freedom. He allowed the horse to clip along. But when night fell, the forest was black. No moon, no stars. It felt unnatural to move forward. He stopped and dismounted. Leading the horse and cart, he maneuvered his way into a clearing just off the path. Holding the reins, he sat, leaning against a tree, drew his hat down over his face, and fell asleep, thinking to nap until dawn.

Some time later he awoke, disoriented in the dark to the sound of approaching horses. He held his breath, not that he could be heard above the rustle of the wind through the trees. To his dismay, the horses stopped nearby. Isaac heard men's voices. He thought he should do something but did not know what. In moments, two German soldiers, reeking of alcohol, stood over him. One held a flashlight, and the other kicked Isaac's hat back off his face. Isaac scrambled for his hat.

"*Ein Jude*," said the soldier with the flashlight.

"Search his belongings," said the other soldier. "Jew," he said to Isaac, "what are you doing out here?"

"What are you looking for?" said Isaac watching the soldier searching the cart open his satchel and toss his precious books out of the cart onto the forest loam, one by one.

"Answer me, *Jude*," said the first soldier. "You have come a long way?"

"From Prague," said Isaac. "I am going to a wedding."

"Friends? Family?" asked the soldier.

"I am to perform the ceremony," said Isaac.

It had not taken long for the soldier searching the cart to tear apart every item he had found. "There is nothing," he said to the other.

"We will leave you, *Jude*," said the soldier questioning Isaac, crunching into one of Isaac's apples. "Tonight we hunt for murderers, not Jews. It's your lucky night."

"Who is dead?" asked Isaac.

"Our commanding officer was found in his mistress' apartment, stripped of his belongings. Do you know something of this?"

"No, nothing," said Isaac trying not to blink as the flashlight shone in his face. He wondered if this news would turn out to be good for the Jews of Prague, or if, as his father feared, the next German officer would be worse.

"You're sure you know nothing? Because if it turns out you have lied, we will make you eat the shit of a pig and then skin you alive," said the soldier who had searched the cart.

"Before we kill you," said the other soldier.

"I am sure," said Isaac.

"You are fortunate that we have found none of his belongings on you."

"And that he was detested by his men and fellow officers," added the other soldier.

"The only friend he had was his mistress, the whore!"
Both soldiers had a good laugh over that, clapping each other
on the back as they left Isaac to himself.

In the receding light, Isaac gathered up his satchel and
suitcase and their contents, and put them back in the cart. He
found his books, brushed off the dirt, and straightened their
pages as best he could. He kissed their covers and tucked
them back into the satchel. He found his shirts, shook them
out and folded them, and put them back in his suitcase. He
found his blanket roll, brushed it off, and unfurled it.

When the sound of horse hooves retreated and the
darkness returned, Isaac crouched again against the tree,
his blanket drawn around him. He drew his hat back down
over his face, and tried to gather what sleep he could, before
the sun came up. He thought he heard muffled cries in the
darkness, but also thought he might be dreaming. When the
sun began to lighten the sky, he was glad.

CHAPTER THREE

THE JEWISH QUARTER AND CITY
OF PRAGUE, THE YEAR 1589

The old Rabbi Loew was proud to be born and raised in the city of Prague. Over six generations and two hundred years before, his ancestors had slipped into the city, with prayers on their lips, hoping for asylum. The *diaspora* had begun many more centuries before with the exit of the Jews from Babylon and Palestine for the colder climates of the Balkans, and Central and Eastern Europe, lit from within by the promise that some day they would return to Jerusalem. But small comfort had been the *mythos* of the Promised Land during the thirteenth century, the time of the Black Plague, while escaping by foot and cart, east through dank, cold Europe.

Roving gangs of *goyim* had sought to wipe out the Jews, who were said to have poisoned the public water supplies causing the quick and gruesome deaths which were all the rage. Foreigners, beggars, and lepers were persecuted too. It was a regular field day for xenophobes who wanted to spend their last days on earth raping, pillaging, and beating other people to death. The truth was that a flea vacationing from the mystic Orient on the back of a stowaway cargo rat had brought the plague, but as it has been from time immemorial, why be rational when you can blame other people for your ills? So it was that flagellants, barefoot in sackcloth, sprinkled with ashes, weeping, praying to the mercy of the Virgin, tearing their hair out, carrying candles and ransacked church relics, wearing nooses around their necks, and beating themselves with whips, walked the streets, always on the ready to serve the higher purposes of terror and genocide. Not everyone was like the flagellants, but everyone had their own problems to deal with in such an era. Only the flea confronted the flagellants, felling them in their tracks whenever possible. For this could the Jews be grateful, even as the insect felled their own. It was a stretch as a comforting thought, but it was what was available.

Once out of the cities, Rabbi Loew's ancestors had knelt in the frosty-rimmed forests of Eastern Europe, gnawing on bread crusts. There among the trees, the question must have crossed their minds as to why, if the Lord wanted to spread pestilence and disease, He could not do it in his own Name instead of allowing the blame to fall on the Jews. Out there in the threadbare cold, the temptation must have been to see God as a schoolyard bully, a clown who created mischief only to let someone else go to the principal's office to take the heat. The temptation must have been to ask why *Yahweh* refused to take full credit for His own natural disaster. *When was He going to come forward and let them off the hook?*

But century after century, God the Ancient Prankster was loathe to step forward, and whenever luck turned for the worse, someone else was blamed. Not just the Jews and the other misfits, but also hapless government officials, random do-gooders, and anyone else who stuck their necks out far enough and long enough, went down for the count in the name of God. It was enough to try one's faith. Why would it be any different in the time of the Plague? But century after century, the Jews shrugged their shoulders, sighed *oy vey*, and rejoiced in being Chosen. They made whole celebrations out of it, no less. *Meshuge* full of *khokhme*, crazy full of wisdom.

This morning, this glorious crisp morning in March, Rabbi Loew was out for an early morning walk. Dawn was just coming up over the horizon and snow crunched under his feet. He was congratulating himself, not consciously of course, on beating God to the punch. He was proud of the strong ties he had created between the Jews and the other communities of Prague, ingratiating himself and his people, and inspiring lessons of tolerance for all people to be imparted from the pulpit and the lectern, anywhere that someone in power spoke. Miracle of miracles, it had become politically correct to not hate Jews. Yes, it would be a beautiful Spring. Once again, at the Passover, God willing, the Angel of Death would pass over not just the Jewish homes, but also the homes of all faiths, except here and there a natural death that would not be blamed on anyone in particular. No more plagues, prayed Rabbi Loew. The Jews were just getting over the reputation that they had acquired in ancient Egypt as a rough bunch you did not want to mess with unless you were ready for everything from locusts and red seas, to the spontaneous dropping dead of your favorite child—your first-born son, no less.

Old Rabbi Loew stopped to catch his breath, hanging in the air before him like a magician's trick, white as the shock of hair on his head. He adjusted his overcoat and wrapped his scarf tighter around his neck. His daughter Evie had knit it for him. She preferred brilliant colors of yarn, magentas and oranges. While he would have preferred a simpler color, he wore whatever she made him with pride. What father would not have wanted a daughter like his good Evie, he thought.

As old Rabbi Loew's breath slowed, something on the ground caught his eye—the first blade of grass of the season, breaking the hard ground with a superhuman strength. He believed that to come forward year after year, the plants had to have a perfect faith. To spend a whole winter shrouded in the dark dirt, and then to burst forward into the air, even before the thaw, was no less than a celebration of will, an act of perfect trust, and an accomplishment he did not hope to rival.

Old Rabbi Loew bent over to examine the hearty sprout when something cold, wet and hard, a snowball no doubt, hit his *tuchas*, knocking him forward, flat on the ground. The sound of merry schoolboy voices, shouting insults about his Jewish faith in the native tongue, disappeared behind him. By the time he was able to push himself back onto his haunches and turn around, the pranksters, who no doubt imagined themselves to be real *tummlers*, the life of the party, had vanished. He lifted his hands off the cold ground and brushed them together. To his dismay, he discovered that he had crushed the sprout, broken its tiny spine. He said a short *Kaddish*; a brief prayer of mourning, both for the tiny blade and for his own pride, as he walked home, his shoulders slumped forward, where his Evie waited with his breakfast.

Late in the afternoon that early Spring day, the old Rabbi Loew left Evie to her laundry. He wandered through the Jewish Quarter, passing the Kosher butcher selling his fresh plucked chickens.

"*Sholem aleichem, Rebbe*, how are you?" said the butcher.

"*Aleichem sholem*," answered the old Rabbi Loew, "And unto you peace."

As the butcher watched, the old Rabbi Loew passed the tailor who was measuring a new suit for a boy who was turning thirteen years old and about to have his *bar mitzvah*.

"*Sholem aleichem, Rebbe*, how are you?" said the tailor and the boy who was about to have his *bar mitvah*.

"*Aleichem sholem*," answered the old Rabbi Loew, "And unto you peace."

As the butcher, and the tailor and the boy who was about to have his *bar mitzvah* watched, the old Rabbi Loew passed the tinker who was negotiating the price of a kettle with the blacksmith's wife.

"*Sholem aleichem, Rebbe*, how are you?" they said.

"*Aleichem sholem*," answered the old Rabbi where people who were not Jewish lived and worked, and passed through the big, rusty gates that locked the Jews in at night and left the Jewish Quarter.

The butcher, the tailor, the boy who was about to have his *bar mitzvah*, the tinker, and the blacksmith's wife, all looked at each other. The old Rabbi Loew was a *mentsch*. The old Rabbi Loew was a *mentsch* among *mentsches*. The old Rabbi Loew was even a *mentsch* among the non-Jewish people of Prague, the *goyim*. He knew what he was doing. The kosher butcher, the tailor and the boy who was about to have his *bar mitvah*, and the tinker and the blacksmith's wife looked to each other, then shrugged, then nodded, and then turned back to what they had been doing.

But the boy who was about to have his *bar mitzvah* broke away from the tailor and ran up to the road at the far end of the Jewish Quarter, and standing there, right in the middle of the road, dwarfed by huge gates that kept his people from the rest, through which the old Rabbi Loew had just passed, and watched the old Rabbi Loew disappear into the rest of Prague. Someday, maybe someday soon, when he was a man, he too would venture out of the Jewish Quarter of Prague and mingle with the *goyim*. He would have great adventures and learn of many things. He would discourse regarding matters of great importance with the people of the world, just like the revered old Rabbi Loew. It would be a great day, and he would make his community proud. Some day, some beautiful day when the skies were blue and there was music in the air. Not today, not today when storm clouds gathered.

The old Rabbi Loew crossed over from the Jewish Quarter into the rest of the city intent on his destination but enjoying the scenery. He was like a voyeur, sampling the different sights and smells of the greater part of Prague. He could enjoy the odor of a pig roasting in a local eatery. Ham might be not Kosher, it was definitely *trafe*, but to smell its rich fragrance was nowhere forbidden. Candies that would delight any child, spun of sugar and painted in bright colors for the upcoming Easter celebration were displayed in the shops. He was all for experiencing new things, and was not afraid to listen to a midnight Mass now and then.

When his Evie was little, the old Rabbi Loew took her on his shoulders to see the great Easter processions. The candles flickering in the moonlight, the abundance of flowers, the mysterious Latin incantations of the priests in their purple robes set with silvery embroidered crosses, and the smoky incense pricking at her nose and lungs, had all caught her young heart and mind straining to catch a hold of the world in all its glory. In the early hours of the morning, as dawn sent its light up through the dark clouds of night, the old Rabbi Loew could see the mystery in her eyes as he tucked her into her bed and pulled the quilt up to cover her. She fell right to sleep, full of peace and wonder. She was too young to hold any fear of the *goyim*. The mystery of God was the mystery of all; the old Rabbi Loew felt, and loved that faith could be pricked forward in a child by all things wonderful. The eras of fear were over, declared old Rabbi Loew to himself. The people of the world would henceforth live together, starting with tolerance, building to compassion, and culminating in love. *The Lord Our God, the Lord is One.*

As the old Rabbi Loew neared his destination, the local jail and courthouse, he leaned on his cane to catch his breath. He smiled and nodded to a man about his age, hobbling toward him from the opposite direction. The man, in a hurry about something, did not acknowledge the old Rabbi Loew other than to land a wad of spit on the street next to the old Rabbi Loew's right foot. The old Rabbi Loew looked at it for a moment, and decided it was just a coincidence. The other man was likely suffering from a later winter cold and needed to expel some phlegm. The old Rabbi Loew had the misfortune of being there at the wrong place and time. When the old Rabbi Loew looked up, he noticed a fruit seller watching him. He nodded to the fruit seller and the fruit seller nodded back. All was right with the world, or could become so with a little *heymishe* direction. The old Rabbi Loew was in a very fatherly mood, and thought to himself that if the time was right; he would invite his old friend, the local Magistrate, to his Passover Seder. It would be a first, but it would be a very good thing.

The old Rabbi Loew helped himself up the steps to the courthouse using his cane one step at a time. He heard shouting from inside, but that did not dissuade him from entering. His friend, the Magistrate, was attempting to comfort a wailing young woman wrapped in a black cloak. He knew that the Magistrate, a slender, high-strung, hand-wringing type, was not the type of man to comfort a woman, and it was all the more awkward in that she was clutched by a another woman, older, likely her mother, also in black, standing behind her, also wailing. The sound was enough to test any man. The old Rabbi Loew noticed the local priest, tall and wrapped in his black hassock, standing in a corner, somber, head bowed, looking at the floor.

"*Shalom Aleichem*," said the old Rabbi Loew. No one seemed to hear him. "*Shalom Aleichem!*" shouted the old Rabbi Loew, adding after, "May I be of help?" But as all eyes turned to the old *Rebbe*, the door behind him burst open and two uniformed soldiers in the service of the Magistrate dragged in Yizhar, the candle maker, and threw him on the floor. The small man, who had devoted his simple life to braiding of wicks and the pouring of wax, lay where he had crumpled, daring only to lift his head. Blinking, he was glad to see the old Rabbi Loew. His face was scraped on one side with some blood from his nose, but the old Rabbi Loew was glad to see that Yizhar looked to be in one piece.

"Yizhar, what is this?" said the old Rabbi Loew. The old Rabbi Loew looked up and stared into the eyes of his friend, the Magistrate. "What is this?" he said. "What is this?" he said, turning to everyone else in the room: the soldiers, the priest, and the two women. "I know my Yizhar to be an honest man." Only the soldiers met his gaze.

But now, again behind the old Rabbi Loew, the door opened and a third soldier entered, holding a small burlap sack of the type in which it was known that Jews bought and stored their flour. "What is this?" said the old Rabbi Loew. The magistrate nodded to the soldier. The old Rabbi Loew, leaned on his cane with one hand, and with the other hand pulled back the opening at the top of the sack. He recoiled to discover the ghost-pale bluish face of a dead baby, eyes wide-open, staring back at him. "What is this!" said the old Rabbi Loew.

Sunlight through the window fell on the young woman who shrieked, making her look, in her loose and flopping black garments and matted hair, like some kind of crazed dark angel. She grabbed the burlap bag from the soldier, cradling it awkwardly in one arm, she pointed at the two Jews in the room, Yizhar and his old Rabbi Weinberg, with her other hand, and cried,

"Murder! Murderers!"

KRIVOKLAT FOREST AND THE TEMPLE AT ZEBRAK

The sun had risen but the morning chill, like mist, still hung in the air. Eager to make up for lost time, Isaac allowed his horse to trot. It was only when the trees began to thin and he knew he was close to the town of Zebrak and Tocnik Castle, high on a nearby mountain, that he slowed the horse.

Isaac had been to Zebrak once before, as a boy traveling with his father. It was the one time he was permitted to go. His mother was busy helping his favorite aunt who was giving birth. His mother needed him to be out from under foot. She gave him a big hug and a kiss as he was leaving. She promised to bake *kichlach*, his favorite cookies, when he returned. But Isaac had looked forward to the trip with excitement and needed no reward for venturing out with his father. Now Isaac caught glimpses of the Tocnik Castle in his memory looming on its mountaintop over the lush farmland in its shadow.

As a boy Isaac had wondered about the lives of the aristocrats it housed. No doubt they had cream instead of milk and extravagant parties with fancy dress and dancing. But now, commandeered by the Nazis, the Castle invoked different thoughts. In their advance on the road to Bavaria, the Nazis had met little opposition in the farm villages along the way. Any resistance remained weak and without resources. Still the Nazis had grown paranoid and insecure, and often engaged in random acts of violence to assure themselves of their local supremacy. He had heard that the Nazis held prisoners in the Castle. Men were tortured though they had no secrets and women were also darkly used.

With a shiver Isaac remembered that when he and his father had returned to Prague after their trip from Zebrak, his favorite aunt was dead from childbirth and his mother was in mourning. After that trip, he did not travel with his father anymore. It became important for him to be a comfort to his mother when his father had to leave Prague to administer to another *shtetl*. His mother never recovered from her sister's death, but now the two women were together with God.

With these thoughts pressing against each other in his mind, Isaac jumped when he felt something graze his shoulder. Looking back over his shoulder he saw the bodies of the two German soldiers, flies already crawling on their faces. They had been hung from branches, nooses tightened around their necks. Cascading cloaks of new leaves camouflaged the bodies from immediate view. The soldiers' horses grazed nearby calm and focused on the tender spring grass. Isaac fought back the impulse to vomit. He focused his attention on Zebrak and fought the urge to force his horse into a gallop. If anyone asked, he would have seen nothing of this. He wondered if he should head back to Prague, but decided against it. His father would send word if he needed him.

Isaac urged his horse forward toward the village synagogue, careful to tuck his chin down and maintain an inconspicuous pace as he passed a group of German soldiers enjoying themselves at a sidewalk cafe. When he reached the Temple, he climbed off his cart and began to unpack. As he pulled down his satchel of books, the front door opened. Rachel emerged, and held the door for an older man, wearing the traditional side-curls and prayer shawl, *payess* and *tallis*. The older man leaned on a cane. Isaac knew he was the village Rabbi, recognizing his comfortable air of authority.

Isaac would have spoken to the Rabbi about the German soldiers, but for the sight of the young Rachel. She was tender, doe-eyed, and altogether beautiful. The effect of her presence shocked his entire body. He could suddenly think of nothing but her. His heart beat too fast, but instead of contracting, his chest felt as if it opened up to contain the entire universe. Isaac, shocked, realized that he was feeling what was meant by the expression, love at first sight. He opened his mouth to say something but could not think of what to say. He stood there, searching for words. He thought that he thought about things too much and knew that he had to say something, anything, when she said, "*Rebbe?*"

Isaac realized that she meant him. "Oh, me. Yes, uh, I am the *rebbe*. My name is Rabbi Gottesfurcht, but please call me Isaac."

"But you are so young," said the young woman.

"Um yes, you sent for my father, but I have come in his place."

"Oh," said the young woman, gazing at Isaac and almost forgetting to fret over her ailing father for the first time in weeks.

"You do not sound so sure," said the village Rabbi. Isaac knew without asking that he was the old *Rebbe* Chaim Jecobs of Zebrak. His father had described him, leaving out the part about him being old. But that was of course, because they had been young men together.

Isaac laughed. "I haven't had a lot of practice introducing myself as a rabbi."

"Soon you'll forget you ever weren't a rabbi. 'Rabbi, what can I do about my husband? Rabbi, please my wife, she's driving me crazy. Rabbi, please my daughter, I'm so worried,'" said the village Rabbi. He started to laugh, but pain jerked through his chest and he turned pale white, clutching the hand that did not lean on his cane, to his heart.

The young woman grabbed him, supporting him. Isaac felt awkward and concerned. He moved to help too. The village Rabbi waved both young people away from him. The color began to return to his face.

"You must be Rabbi Chaim," said Isaac with a respectful nod.

The old Rabbi Chaim Jecobs cleared his throat and caught his breath. "Your father must have told you, we were boys together in the Yeshiva," he said.

"He speaks of you warmly and sends his best regards, and he wishes you a quick recovery so that you are able to resume your rabbinical duties," said Isaac. A look passed between the old Rabbi Jecobs and the young woman. Isaac could not read its full meaning but it spoke of conflict.

Rabbi Jecobs noticed Isaac looking at the young woman with him. "And this is my daughter, Rachel."

Isaac bowed to Rachel, "I am pleased to meet you."

Rachel, averting her eyes, said to Isaac, "We're grateful you could come." Isaac wondered whether she was shy or displeased with him in some way.

A group of German soldiers, laughing with one another and smoking, came from around a corner and began walking down the street toward the *shul*. Rabbi Jecobs leaned on his cane, and took Isaac's arm. "Come, let's get you inside."

Isaac sat in the Rabbi's kitchen and tried not to watch Rachel make the tea. But when she reached into the cupboard to pull out the tin of leaves, his gaze lifted from the floor to her slim waist and the reach of her slender arm. He watched as she laid the tin next to the teacups and pried the lid off of the tin with pale delicate fingers. He watched as she bent into the flames to take the boiling teapot off of the fire. And when she turned back and brought the teapot back to the table, she saw him watching her and tilted her head to the side, a hint of a smile on her lips. Isaac was as if hypnotized. Rabbi Jecobs, his lungs soothed by the warm tea served to him by his daughter, had to cough to get Isaac's attention.

"Your trip here was uneventful?" asked Rabbi Jecobs.

Isaac choked. He wondered if he would just be endangering them by telling them what had happened. "No, it was not," he said, leaving it to the Rabbi and his daughter to ask what they needed to know. They chose not to ask.

"But you have arrived, God willing," said Rabbi Jecobs. "That is what matters. When it is time for you to leave, we will consider what precautions may be taken. For now we will speak of the wedding!" He reached a frail hand over and slapped Isaac's knee. Isaac realized that the Rabbi must have once been a very strong man.

That night Isaac's dreams of the beautiful young woman overshadowed the nightmares of his days. He wanted to tangle his fingers in her hair, and kiss her soft lips. Her skin had the fragrance of flowers. He imagined her breath, sweet and soft on his face.

THE JEWISH QUARTER OF PRAGUE, THE YEAR 1589

The widow woman took up sobbing again. Her wailing quickly reached a feverish pitch that filled the room. She looked as if she would have collapsed in her hysteria had not the older woman held her up.

Yitzhak pushed his face into the floor and quivered. The rest of the men resisted the impulse to cower.

The older woman hissed at the old Rabbi Weinberg, "You steal our babies' blood for your bread! We will see you all burn in Hell!" And with that she turned on her heels and escorted the young woman with her macabre bundle out of the jail.

Through the open door, the old Rabbi Weinberg watched the two women huddle as they scurried away. The older woman turned back and yelled, "The Devil take you!" over

73

the ever louder crying of the younger woman. The women gathered a sympathetic crowd as they scurried away, a crowd that seemed to sweep the women away from the stunned old *rebbe*, glaring back at him as they went, shaking their fists at him. The spittle that had landed earlier at his feet was well explained now. He allowed the door to whine closed. It made a creaking noise that the old Rabbi Loew had not noticed before. He closed his eyes and tilted his head up toward the ceiling.

"Help me, *Rebbe*," said Yizhar. "They say that I killed her baby for the *matzoh*."

The Magistrate said, "They found the baby's body in a sack on his doorstep." The soldiers crowded in closer reaching down to pull the quivering mess of a Jewish man, poor Yizhar, the candle maker, to his feet. The Magistrate held his hand up to stop them.

The old Rabbi Loew used his cane to kneel down next to Yizhar. The old Rabbi Loew put a hand on Yizhar's back to try and still his quaking. The old Rabbi Loew had known Yizhar since birth, presiding at his *bris*, helping him with his studies for his *bar mitzvah*, marrying him off, and watching his wife's belly grow as he became a father. "Did you, Yizhar?" said the old Rabbi Loew.

"No, no, of course not! Why would you even ask me, *Rebbe*?" said Yizhar and began to cry.

"It is for their sake I ask, Yizhar. Not for mine," said the old Rabbi Loew and looked up from where he knelt to his friend, the Magistrate.

"He stands accused with evidence," said the Magistrate. "I will have to convict him and he will have to die."

Hearing this, Yizhar lost awareness of everything, the men in the room, the way his body shook, the wetness of his tears. All he felt was the roughness of the ground pressing into his scraped cheek, and then not even that. He thought of his wife, her good cooking, the smell of a chicken boiling in the pot when they could, nestled among carrots, turnips and quartered onions, and his three daughters who themselves would someday marry. He longed for the smells of the chicken, of the wax as it melt in his shop, and of his daughter's freshly scrubbed faces when he kissed their cheeks good night.

Yizhar felt rough hands reach under his armpits as two of the soldiers brought him to his feet, but his feet would not catch the ground and stand. The two soldiers dragged him along, the tops of his shoes scraping the floor. The third soldier went ahead of them and opened a cell with a key. The soldiers threw Yizhar in the cell, where he fell once again to the ground, and closed the door shut, locking it. Yizhar clung to thoughts of his family and ignored the smells of urine and vomit that tried to close in on him.

"I can give you until Sunday, that is all," said the Magistrate.

"You hang people on your day of rest?" asked the old Rabbi Loew.

"We prefer our citizens to be productive. It would not be good for people to have to leave their work," said the Magistrate.

"For something as entertaining as the hanging of a Jew," said the old Rabbi Loew.

"Not just Jews, they enjoy it whenever anyone is hung," said the Magistrate, realizing as he spoke how awful it sounded.

When Rachel, daughter of the old Rabbe Jecob, woke in the morning, she lingered in her bed, trying to prolong her dream. It concerned the young Rabbi sleeping scant meters away at the other end of the corridor, and it wasn't the first such dream of men she'd had, but it was different from the others. She felt no shame. Perhaps if she closed her eyes, she could return to it. But from the sounds in the street below she knew it was time for her to get up. She began her morning prayers of thanks, grateful to *Yahweh* for allowing her to wake to another day of life. She wondered if the young Rabbi from Prague was thinking about her now too.

At the other end of the corridor, young Rabbi Isaac Gottesfurcht woke with a fluttering beneath the flesh of his belly. Today would be his first day as a working rabbi and the second day he laid eyes on Rachel. He had hung the clean suit he had brought with him over a chair the night before. He slipped it on and straightened it. He pulled on one shoe at a time. He took time to smooth his hair before he put on his hat. The deliberation with which he dressed was like a prayer, and was a way of dealing with the nervous queasiness in his stomach. He did not think he would be able to eat until the ceremony was over. He had been at many weddings, and hoped to recreate the necessary rhythmic flow.

As a teenager, before he had begun his rabbinical studies, he had gone into the study of his father, Yakov, the older Rabbi Gottesfurcht, to tell him that he had helped a young man and woman in the *shtetl* move into their new home, and that they had shown him the blessing ceremony for putting up the *mezuzahs*. A *mezuzah* containing a small piece of paper on which a prayer of protection was written was nailed onto the door frame of every front door in the *shtetl*. "Father," Isaac had said, "I know how to place a *mezuzah* now."

Rabbi Yakov, the older Rabbi Gottesfurcht, had tapped his pencil against the desk at which he was working thinking, before he answered, "You mean, you have the proper words in your memory." Knowing the words was one thing. Another part was getting the music and rhythm of the words and silences between them just right. Bringing the heart and soul of the words into the room was another part still. Then there was the being able to awaken the longing for Divine Union of the souls of those present. And there was the invoking and summoning up the great compassion of God. And then came the art of introducing the longing of Man to the great compassion of God. This introduction had to be made like the introduction of a practiced matchmaker. With a good introduction, man and God could become intertwined in comprehension and commitment. Only then could the act of placing the *mezuzah* be as if by lovers making a plan to meet in the apple orchard at midnight.

With his father's patience, over the years Isaac had studied it all. Then the study had collapsed into the man, and he was as if overnight transformed. He had gone to sleep a child and here he was, waking up a *rebbe* on the first morning of the first day that would not end until he had performed a wedding, waking up to his adulthood, waking up to the laughter of children playing outside this Temple at Zebrak.

Isaac walked down the creaking stairs and found his way to the threshold of the main sanctuary. Sunlight fell in a pool at his feet but beyond him the room was empty and unlit except for a single flickering wick burning in oil representing the Eternal Flame. In the shadows a *chupah*, constructed of fine white cloth hung on a tall narrow wood frame, stood beside the ark. Soon enough it would be dark outside and the room would be fully lit. The groom and bride would stand framed beneath the *chupah*, following his cues and entering vows to live a married life. He imagined this room filled with strangers both younger and older than him, looking to him for inspiration. He felt so far from home. He rubbed his palms, slick with sweat, on the seat of his pants. He heard a woman's voice behind him and turned.

Outside, through the open back door of the temple, Rachel oversaw the children stringing flowers to decorate the *chupah*. Isaac wondered if she had seen him wiping his hands on his pants. Rachel was threading a needle for a little boy who was having trouble getting the thread through the eye. A little girl pricked a finger and ran to her. Rachel showed her how to press on her finger to stop the bit of blood. She was so busy that it was unlikely she had noticed him yet that morning. The bigger question was whether Rachel had noticed him in the way that he had noticed her the night before. Rachel knelt, sorting through the baskets of spring blossoms the children had collected that morning, making sure the petals were all fresh and not browned. Isaac cleared his throat and went outside.

He walked up behind her, and stood without speaking. He let his eyes run down her long back to her waist. He wanted to put his hands at her waist and lift her in the air. Her thick hair was swept up off her neck. Her neck was slender and sweet. Sensing him, she lifted her head from her work. In that moment, she reminded him of a doe he had seen paused in a clearing of the forest. The doe had not run when he and his clumsy cart had driven by. He had thought she must have a fawn nearby. Either that, or he had seemed harmless compared to the things she had seen. He had wanted to shout to her to run from him. It did not seem natural that she did not. He did not mean her harm and rumbled past. Later he encountered the two German soldiers who, he remembered, were now dead with flies crawling under their eyelids. He shuddered and stuffed his thoughts.

"The *chupah* should be out here," he said.

She turned and looked up at him, "Good morning, *Rebbe*," she said.

"Isaac," he said. "You can call me Isaac."

"If you want people to respect you, you should let them call you, *Rebbe*," she said.

"What if you want to be their friend?" he asked.

"You want to be my friend?" she asked. *God, she is beautiful,* he thought. The sunlight played through her hair, bringing out the red asleep in the rich brown color. She went back to the blossoms continuing to speak as she worked, "Respect first, friendship later. It's a practical approach for a traveling rabbi, don't you think? People need to be able to rely on you straight away. Later, in time, you can make a friendship."

He was distracted by the dance of her hands, wrist deep in flowers, and by the sound of the words as they slipped off her lips, but realized she had paused and he needed to speak. "Later in time, you can make a friendship," he echoed, nodding and mouthing her syllables so he could form a thought. "And if there is no time?" he asked, wanting to steal the taste of her lips on his. He met her gaze and savored his desire.

Rachel thought that the young Rabbi from Prague, this Isaac, was wonderful to look at. That was why she averted her eyes and changed the subject. She avoided the attentions of men. She required focus for what she needed to do, whether or not others approved, without a husband giving or withholding his consent. "The *chupah*?" she said. "Of course it should be out here. But in these times, we marry indoors to avoid the attention of the soldiers."

"It's the same way in Prague," he said. "And when it is not in the course of official duty, for a pastime, they get drunk and look for trouble, they look for us."

"We're grateful to you for coming all this way. I'm inspired by your dedication. Traveling alone though the forest in a time like this," she said.

"A time like what?" he said. "The Jews still marry, give birth and die. And for that, they need a rabbi. And for the moment, I am that *rebbe*. You can call me *rebbe*, or anything you wish."

A breeze came up, causing the trees to whispering and a tendril of Rachel's hair to fall across her cheek. Without thinking, Isaac reached out and drew the hair away from her face. The touch moved through both of them. He could not breathe while he waited for her response.

Her eyes met his, and she smiled. It felt good to smile. This man made her feel like smiling. It was good he would be leaving after the wedding. She could not afford something like this, not at a time like this and maybe never.

The young Rabbi Isaac chose to help decorate the sanctuary and the *chupah* in order to get to know everyone. Instead of retiring to his room to quiet his thoughts before the wedding, he did what he could to make himself useful. Besides, he would be leaving the next morning and he wanted to make the most of any time he could be with Rachel. He joined her at the *chupah* where she was winding the vines draped in her arms around its beams.

The children had come inside, and with the help of a few older women, were hanging their strands of blossoms on the *beemah*, what in a church would be called an altar or pulpit. When Rachel had finished with the vines, strands of blossoms would be rested on them.

"How can I help?" he asked.

She poured a few tacks into his hand and handed him a hammer. "I'll show you where." Other villagers filtered inside to lend a hand or watch as the sanctuary was readied for the celebration. The smells of food cooking in the next room and the sound of laughter, gossip and debate filled the room. Rachel's father, the Rabbi Jecobs, hobbled into the room and sat on a bench with some of the older men. He nodded at Rachel and Isaac.

"What kind of illness does he have?" asked Isaac.

"He is younger than he seems, older than he was," said Rachel, returning to her work. "My brother was dragged away shortly after the occupation. The Nazis found him too outspoken. His body was discovered in the forest. After performing the service over his grave, my father would not come in at nightfall or the next morning or the night after that. He fell ill soon after and complication followed. Some days he is better, most days he is worse. But he has not spoken about retiring, at least not to me."

"But your village has grown to such a size since you last called for my father. Your father must have taught someone to take his place as rabbi?" asked Isaac.

"You were surprised that we had to send for you," Rachel said. She pointed to a place on a beam and Isaac hammered in a tack.

"My father has always been called to *shtetls* too small to support enough rabbis," said Isaac.

81

"Many men have been taken away or killed," said Rachel, finishing her task. "But my father may have a plan that he chooses not to discuss with me."

"Or not?" asked Isaac. "But would he leave his own village without a Rabbi?"

"It is not an easy question for him to confront," she said. "There is almost no one now who is close to completing their studies."

"Almost? Then there is at least one rabbinical student. I should like to meet him," said Isaac his eyes scanning the room.

She hung the end of the last vine in her arms on the nail Isaac had placed and turned to him. "I would like to be the Rabbi," she said.

Isaac choked and it came out of his throat as a guffaw. Rachel narrowed her eyes and stormed from the synagogue. Isaac sighed. How did she want him to react? How did she expect other people to react? He helped an older woman perch a small child on her shoulders. He watched as the child laid his string of blossoms on the vines that Rachel had just hung. He chewed his lip. It was not that he did not like women. It was that a village had to be able to follow their rabbi, to trust and lean on him. Therefore, by tradition, rabbis were men who had vested some adult years in life. Even he, who was a man, was too young to be a rabbi who led a village. What she was suggesting was unthinkable in these precarious times when tradition was all that people had to guide them from one day to the next. He noticed that in his thoughts he sounded stale as an overlooked bread crust left in a corner. The din inside the sanctuary, as preparations reached their conclusion, separated him from his thoughts. The time for him to officiate his first wedding was coming near.

He stepped outside to collect himself. Dark clouds huddled as the day grew toward dusk. The sun slipped below them into a clearing in the sky and sunlight shot across from the horizon and blinded him. Instead of turning away, he closed his eyes and allowed the last rays to embrace him. The angelic voice of an *elohim* rose up from inside of him and whispered, "Suppose there's a place where ground never was and foot never stepped." As crazy and complicated as Rachel's idea was, he realized that he had to follow her. He walked toward the knoll. Half-slipping on the wet grass, he came up behind her. Below them, tendrils of the Moldavka River slipped by in its gray riverbed, carrying with it chunks of the ice breaking up now that it was spring.

She heard his clumsy approach and knew who it was. She had not misjudged him. She knew he had a warm and open heart. She said without looking back at him, "I know the *Mitzvot*. I know the *Halacha*. Where is it written in the Torah that a woman should not be allowed?"

Isaac smiled and rested one hand on the branch of a willow beside her. "Nowhere," he said.

"My mother died when I was six years old. My father knew how to lead his congregation but it wasn't easy for him to be a father and a mother both. So he was just *Rebbe* to me. And I just assumed, the way you can when you are just six years old, that I would be just like him. I studied the Torah, the ancient texts by day, and with a candle near my bed by night."

Isaac said, "Like my father, like your father."

"I am like my father, stubborn," Rachel said. "It wasn't long before I figured out that I could never be a Rabbi. I just wish I hadn't wasted my childhood. I should have been studying what women do."

"You are still young," said Isaac.

"What would you know of this?" she snapped. "You are allowed to follow in your father's footsteps."

"It was expected of me," Isaac said.

"Right! Exactly," she said, turning away from him.

"He never asked me if I wanted to," Isaac said. "From that moment I came into the world, I was fated to be just one thing: my father's son. I had no more choice than you did." He took his hand off the willow branch and stepped so close behind her that he could smell the scent of the soap she had used in bathing that morning. "I have read the old texts too. You are right. A woman teacher is not specifically forbidden. Some day you may yet be *Rebbe*."

Rachel uncrossed her arms and turned back to him. "It is kind of you to humor me."

"No, it is your dream. It is not foolish. The world is ever changing," said Isaac. "And maybe someday there will be women who attend the Yeshiva. Maybe."

The light from the day faltered and darkness gathered. A night bird called. They studied each other without speaking, forgetting for the moment about the wedding. The whole village was gathering not far from where they stood.

CHAPTER FOUR

EASTERN EUROPE, 1942

THE CZECHOSLOVAKIAN RAILWAY

The private railcar swayed with a comfortable rhythm as it approached the Castle. The train was German and had most recently come from Poland. Illuminated by the dying light of the setting sun that angled in between the window blind slats, the wood paneling gave off an amber glow.

The imposing Colonel Kohl sat deep in thought at a table. The lines of light streaming in from outside flowed over his face. His size and demeanor contrasted with the delicate china cup rimmed with gold from which he sipped tea. Other men of his rank took the opportunity lent by the position to drink the finest liquor available as frequently as possible. Most of the time and particularly while on duty, Kohl preferred the nourishment of a strong cup of tea made gentle with a slash of local cream.

An aide in uniform entered the car. Before the door had closed behind him, he had clicked his heels, saluted Hitler, and begun to address his commanding officer that sat in silhouette, a flicker of dimming light and shadows. "Herr Kohl, we are almost there," he said briskly. His name was Heinrich, a name he was proud of. It meant "strong ruler," and was given to him by his mother who had always assured him, through even his darkest days in school when the other boys had bullied him, that some day he would show them all.

"Is all prepared?" asked Kohl, his voice deep and authoritative. The impression in the darkened car was that his mouth had not even moved, that his voice had sprung from his body as if he were a mere conduit for a power beyond the ordinary. On the one hand Heinrich was awed by Kohl. On the other hand, he hated that even though he had served as Kohl's aide for over ten months, Kohl still had never once called him by his name.

"The men have their orders," said Heinrich. He turned on the lamp in the car, noticing the half-drunk cup of tea in the Colonel's teacup and the half-eaten biscuit that sat on his plate.

While waiting for Colonel Kohl to speak, Heinrich averted his eyes to the floor to show his respect. He admired the intricate weave of the plush Turkish carpet that ran the length of the car and the elegant floral designs that had been carved into the legs of the table and chairs. Before the war he had never imagined such riches but now in service of the Reich, he had seen spoils beyond his imagination amassed by those who had risen up through its ranks. The tablecloth was hemmed with the finest Belgium lace. Even he could discern its quality. Better these items belonged to an honest German officer like Colonel Kohl than to a fat Jew who had come into them through usury, sucking dry the economies of the world so that an honest man could not live by an honest day's work.

The Colonel cleared his throat. Heinrich dared lift his head. But the Colonel had just been clearing some phlegm. "Then all is ready," Colonel Kohl muttered to himself, and exhaled wearily.

Heinrich stood by and waited, but still the Colonel did not acknowledge his presence. Not even a thank you for turning on the light. Heinrich had expected a compliment, an exhortation of "well done," or a pat on the back of some kind for managing the preparations at the town up ahead. He was disappointed, even irritated, at his commanding officer's lack of acknowledgment which resonated for Heinrich as disapproval. As the Colonel's aide, Heinrich had done everything asked of him and had done it well. He deserved at least a crumb of praise, even just a morsel that one would throw casually to a trained animal. The train car continued to rock from side to side as night fell in earnest. He decided to press the matter with Kohl, even though such boldness could backfire.

"Colonel, I am afraid that I have grown accustomed to your gratitude. Have I somehow erred?" he said.

"No," said Kohl, nothing more.

"Then is something the matter?" said Heinrich, pressing in like a weasel, pretending to brush crumbs off the table into his white-gloved hand. Kohl was a tidy eater.

"I grow tired of these games," said Kohl.

"You consider the Fuhrer's plans to be games?" said Heinrich, thinly disguising his rising disgust. These officers were given everything, luxury upon luxury and the power to command, and instead of being grateful to the Fuhrer, they grew fat and moody. This would not happen to him when the aide was promoted, which was sure to happen if he was able to get a convincing report on Colonel Kohl's indolence to the appropriate authorities. Colonel Kohl was not fat. It might be difficult to prove his indolence.

"I consider them to be jokes. I have little time for jokes," said Kohl. He was not interested in the response of this aide who he considered little more than a puppet, a marionette dancing on strings of the brutal fantasy of the Reich. The aide who stood before him had never lifted a gun. He had never experienced the excruciating toll exacted from any gunman who took a human life. He was not a soldier. He was only a puppet.

"The orders are from Berlin," said Heinrich, the aide, pointed out. He made no pretense of his disdain. This Kohl's days were numbered. It was only a matter of finding the proper evidence.

"The war is not being fought in Berlin, not yet," said Kohl. He thought about his wife and children, staying with her parents in their villa overlooking the Berlin Garten. The nineteenth century botanical garden was where he and his wife had their first kiss. It was July, and the smell of night blooming flowers was overwhelming. They were both home, she from school and he from the service of his country. Two months later, he asked her to marry him and she said yes. Kohl wondered now if he could get word to his wife and his in-laws to change their identities and those of the children, and leave the country. If he managed to be on the prevailing side when the war subsided, he would find them when he got home. If the Nazis were vanquished but somehow he was able to survive, he would find them later.

"We are winning this war," said Heinrich.

"Perhaps. But the war is not being won by chancellors, it is being won by soldiers," said Kohl. To him it seemed that the Reich had lost its compass, lost touch with reality, and was playing out a dance of death.

In Auschwitz, a portable oven had been loaded onto a freight car intended to boost the rate and expedience of the exterminations in the countryside of Czechoslovakia. The idea was macabre and distasteful to Kohl who felt that if you took a man's life, you should be man enough to face him. If indeed the war was won, the world would fall into the hands of out-of-touch sycophants like the man before him, a mere aide, an idiot who found it important to polish his black boots until they glowed. But if the war was won, thought Kohl, it would only be a matter of time before the real victors, the soldiers, revolted. On the other hand, if the war was lost, it would be because the Reich's leaders were preoccupied with jokes—jokes like parties with psychics who claimed to predict the future, jokes like his aide, this puppet who stood before him.

As the train car lurched forward, Kohl noticed that his aide's boots caught the lamplight and seemed to smirk. But Kohl knew that, for now and only now, he needed to appease the boot-polishing ninny who stood before him. And so Kohl put on a smile and said to his aide, "We will follow orders and pray for the best result."

Heinrich shook his head from side to side. "Pray?" he said. "They say there is no place for prayer in the new Reich. We need not scrape for pity before our God who anoints us forward."

What a fool, thought Kohl. He had given his aide an opportunity to back down and instead he had persisted. Kohl knew now that he would have to find a convenient way to dispatch of the aide. Kohl knew the aide had an elderly mother, but no wife and children, so it would not be much of a loss. Kohl would personally make sure that the aide's mother received her son's pension if the Nazis won the war. "They are wrong, we need prayer more than anyone," said Kohl.

THE TEMPLE AT ZEBRAK

Isaac stood at the *beemah* before the village. Everyone who was able had crowded into the small synagogue to attend the wedding. Oz and Neria, a young man and woman, the groom and his bride, stood radiant under the *chupah*.

As the end of the ceremony neared, Isaac felt elated. Apart from the birth of a child, the happiest celebration was the union of two people. To have been privileged to officiate the wedding, to have all go so well, and to be so welcomed and buoyed by the love in this tight knit community was an experience beyond even his dreams of being a *Rebbe*. He continued, "We praise *Yahweh* for His creation of the world, and creation of the human being. In His infinite wisdom, He made the human being a two-part creature, woman and man. One can never truly be happy or complete without the other."

Isaac glanced over at Rachel. She caught his gaze, felt her face warm, and looked away. "The couple will share one more glass of wine," he said, handing the glass to Oz. The groom held the glass to his bride's lips and she drank what she could before he finished the wine himself. Everyone in the room clapped with delight, a few even giving a whoop of joy. Everyone knew what was coming next but in accord with tradition Isaac spoke it out, "The wedding is nearly over, and the marriage is about to begin. The *cheder yichud*, the 'room of privacy,' has been prepared." Happy couples remembered their first union while the children, hungry for the wedding meal, jostled each other. Food had been rationed out over the weeks before in order to afford a feast to celebrate the happy couple.

"But first, the groom will break the glass," Isaac said. "This custom dates back to Talmudic times, to keep Jerusalem and Israel in our heart at this time of our joy. As the Temple in Jerusalem was destroyed, so we break the glass, living the sorrow of the Jewish exile."

Rachel looked over at her father. He leaned on his cane, even as he sat. All of the weddings he ever performed were passing through his mind. He was thankful in his heart that he had been able to be a *rebbe*. When this groom was a baby, he had conducted the *bris*, naming him, Oz, meaning strength. When this bride was a baby, he had named her, Neria, meaning angel. His eyes swam with grateful tears. It was time now that the village had a new Rabbi. He looked back at Rachel and nodded. This young Rabbi, this Isaac, was discharging his job well. Rachel smiled, and her father was pleased that she was happy. The elder Rabbi Jecobs thought that maybe the father of this young Rabbi, this Isaac, would be willing to let him move to their village and be the new *rebbe*, maybe his daughter would have a husband, and maybe, despite her ambitions, she would be content with that. He wondered if her mother could have talked some sense in to her if she was alive.

Isaac intoned, "If I forget Thee, O Jerusalem, let my right hand forget its cunning. If I do not raise Thee over my own joy, let my tongue cleave to the roof of my mouth," and placed the glass wrapped in a cloth napkin under the *chupah* before the groom. Isaac nodded at the groom and asked, "Ready?" Oz nodded and raised his foot. All grooms resolved to succeed the first time, but sometimes it took a less auspicious second.

To stretch out the suspense of this anticipated moment as his father had always done, Isaac put up a hand delaying the anxious groom and said, "Enjoy it, it's the last time you'll get to put your foot down!" The crowd laughed and clapped, young and old, though they may have heard the joke dozens of times before.

Oz stomped on the glass. It shattered under his foot, the shards caught in the napkin. The noise of the breaking glass drove away evil spirits. Oz pulled his foot back and a smile broke on his face. He turned to his Neria, his bride, who now dared smile back at him. He took her hand. "Mazel tov!" and "Siman Tov!" shouted the villagers in unison, again clapping for joy, this time louder than before because the ceremony was complete. Like the broken glass, the world was broken and in need of mending. But still in this world, a couple could come together in union. The mood was overwhelming *nachas* or joy.

The village musicians, a fiddler in a scruffy jacket, and a flutist in her flowery dress, struck up the music for the dancing that would accompany the couple to their wedding bed. Excited conversation, full of blessings and good memories, broke into laughter and song, but all turned to screams when the windows of the Temple shattered inwards. Nazi soldiers poured in, leveling their *Schmeisser* submachine guns at the villagers. Their squad leader entered last, his soldiers gathering around him at the center of the room, facing out. The cowed wedding guests pressed away up against the walls, all except the new Rabbi Isaac, the young Rabbi Isaac who had just conducted his first wedding. He stood before his bride and groom, shouting, "No, not here! What do you want?!"

All Jewish eyes turned away from the young Rabbi from another town, the Isaac who refused to bend for their Nazi occupiers. The Jews knew it was likely that they all would be killed. But in that moment, it became most certain that the young Rabbi would be killed. In a split second his body would be wracked with gunfire and the synagogue stained with his blood. Adults bent over children and pushed them behind them to shield them from stray bullets and the spatter of the body.

The Nazi squad leader narrowed his eyes at Isaac and asked, "Where is the Rabbi's son?"

"Here," said Isaac.

"You are Isaac?" asked the Nazi Squad Leader.

"Yes," said Isaac, wondering how they knew he was there and that he was not just a Rabbi but also the son of a Rabbi. He wondered why they cared about such things, and him in particular. He wondered whether his father's diplomatic approach with their local Nazi officer had failed and he, the older Rabbi Gottesfurcht, had met trouble, and that trouble had followed Isaac through the forest and now to this innocent *shtetl* at Zebrak. Guilt and worry shuddered through him.

"Good," said the Nazi Squad leader. He turned to his troops. "Take him, and kill the rest." Two soldiers reached up under Isaac's arms and dragged him out by the shoulders, his heels scrapping the floor.

"No!" said Isaac. "No!" But the Nazis ignored him.

The Nazi squad leader was already barking other instructions to his men. "Radio Herr Kohl. Tell him that we have him." A third soldier saluted and left the Temple to carry out his squad leader's order.

"What is this?" said one of the remaining soldiers to another, suddenly waking to his surroundings. He held a slender woman in his gun sight, her eyes wide with terror. The rosebud pattern of the shawl which she pulled tight around herself reminded him of something that nagged at him, he could not think what.

"A wedding," said the other. "From the looks of it, the whole village is here."

"A wedding?"

On his way out, the Nazi squad leader passed the wedding couple at the door. Oz stood in front of his bride but the squad leader looked over his shoulder to drink in the fear in her eyes. His childhood had been impoverished, and his frustrated father had beaten him and his mother when there was no food on the table. He, in turn, had become a bully and fed his trembling soul on others' fear. He knew from what he had been taught in school that the bruises on his psyche were in fact the fault of the Jews, and as he and his troops scourged the countryside, he relished the last moments of his victims when they had to admit he had won. He did not need to pull the trigger himself. Others did that at his bidding. Satisfied as if he had just enjoyed a fine meal, he shut the door behind him and strode out to where his car and driver waited.

Inside the sanctuary, the sound of the door closing seemed to echo. Children whimpered. The soldier who could not remember remembered. The woman's shawl reminded him of a dress that his mother had worn when he was a child. He remembered clinging to her rosebud-strewn hem, following her through the marketplace. Those were better times, when there was money for sweet buns at the end of the shopping trip. He dropped his gun to his side, shocked by the vividness and sweetness of the memory at this unlikely moment.

Outside, a night bird called and the squad leader lit a cigarette.

Inside, the soldier closest to the door pulled back his bolt and fired off his whole magazine. The bride and groom fell first. He slumped against the door and slid to the ground. She crumbled after, wafting as if in a breeze from the bullets that struck her slender body, and died in his already lifeless arms. They had been a beautiful couple, with roses blooming in their cheeks. Rachel shielded her weakened father as much from the sight of the dead couple as from the bullets to come. He struggled free of her grip.

Outside, the squad leader pulled on the cigarette and exhaled a cloud of smoke smiling, reassured by the sound of gunfire. His way of being had become a hunger, and he knew it. But he was not worried. There were lots of Jews left to satisfy his craving and beyond them, the world was filled with people who were not Aryan. The dark-skinned and swarthy bred like flies.

Inside, the silence broken, all of the soldiers began emptying their weapons, all except the soldier who had remembered. Bodies fell backward and suffocated the living pressed behind them. Bullets shattered the ark, the *beemah* and the benches. "Stop, who are we?" said the soldier who remembered, shielding the rosebud shawl and what was left of his humanity. The bullets ripped through the silk lovingly wrapped around the parchment onto which the Torah had been inscribed and shredded the parchment itself. The bullets tore through the soldier who remembered, falling first to his knees. When his body found the floor, the bullets tore through the rosebud shawl and the woman who wore it. The bullets tore through living bodies, and when those were in short supply, they tore through dead and quivering flesh. The bullets tore through the body of the woman in the rosebud shawl as it lay face down in blood, next to the body of her soldier. The ceiling was broken by the bullets and spattered with blood. The wood cracked and twisted like broken bones. The gunfire fell quiet, punctuated only by shots leveled at a whimper or a twitch.

When the silence was perfected, the soldiers slung their submachine guns onto their backs, opened the doors of the Temple, stepped out over the bodies that had fallen back against it, and went out into the night. The last soldier out, a young man conscripted by his cronies, afraid for himself and his family to refuse, took a last look around. He held down most of the bile that came up from his stomach, and wiped away the vomit at his mouth with his sleeve. He picked up a candle and set fire to whatever tinder would take, prayer books fallen open, the hand sewn cloth hangings lovingly draped on the walls, the shattered *chupa*, then swept any candles onto the blood-drenched floor before he left.

Outside, the soldiers piled into the waiting truck or slung themselves onto their squad leader's car, according to their assignment, and sped off into the night.

Inside, in the dark stillness left behind, the few Jews that were still alive waited in shock under the bodies that had belonged to their friends and family, gasping for air and listening to their own heartbeats. Assured by silence that they were alone with the dead, they fought up from under the flesh that spirit had left behind, and fainted in body or mind. Flames licked the garments of the dead, and then rose up walls and the ceiling, and pieces of the building fell. A light rain began to fall through the broken roof that began to staunch the fire. Smoke hung in the air.

Rachel found that her father was gasping on the edge of death. She could not find his wound—he was covered in his blood and the blood of others—but he was beyond healing. The waxing moon slipped down through the night sky. She held him as his body grew cold. Then she grew conscious of her own pain until she slipped and found herself floating in a dark place beyond tears.

The young Rabbi Isaac had been dragged out of the Temple, his eyes wild, struggling until the butt of an officer's P-38 nine-millimeter pistol to the back of his head rendered him unconscious. Now he woke in a fetal position, his hands tied together behind his back, pushed into the corner of the flatbed of a truck rumbling over a cobbled road. The drone of the motor told him that the truck was moving fairly fast. The stock of a submachine gun bumped absently against the side of his head. Peering up, he saw under the chin of the soldier who held the gun loosely, its strap slung over his shoulder. He was surrounded by soldiers, dried mud cracking on their boots. The truck was full, a transport truck, taking them where? In the dark he could not see well but had no reason to believe there were other Jews. It was likely that the others from the wedding party were all dead. He wondered whether Rachel had found a way to survive. If lucky, he would be held for questioning. While there would be torture involved, as long as he was alive there would be a possibility of escape, and if he escaped he vowed to wreak justice.

He tried the bonds on his wrists. To his surprise, the rope slipped off easily just as the truck slammed to a stop. He lurched forward and lost his balance. Soldiers were already jumping off as his forehead slammed onto the truck bed. He was frozen cold, his limbs stiffened. Two soldiers dug their hands under his armpits and pulled him up out of his sprawl. They tossed him off the truck and leaped down after him. Isaac landed face first, choking on dirt. A train idled nearby on a track.

"Now," thought Isaac. "Now is the end." He knew his body did not have the fight to overpower the armed soldiers but he knew he would try. He slipped into a peace beyond fear, bringing forth the people of Zebrak who had come for a wedding. Anger ripped through his muscles bringing him to his feet. He landed a punch in the face of the nearest soldier who, clipped solidly on the jaw, fell back. Panting and dirty, full of adrenaline, Isaac jumped on the fallen soldier. Isaac shouted into his face, "There were women and children in there!"

The second soldier watched with interest. He liked a good brawl far better than the executions he had been participating in. A simple man, it was clear to him that going out and shooting helpless peasants every night was not drawing anyone closer to a Final Solution. In spite of himself, he imagined the face of his aging parents in the crowd and thought about what it would be like if the tables were turned and Jews were shooting Nazis instead of the other way around. But the consequences to his family would be dire if not lethal if he withdrew from the *Einsatzguppen*, the specialized execution troops of the Reich, however quietly. This Jew was not large but he was full of fight. Under other circumstances, the second soldier would have wagered on him.

Isaac struggled to maintain his grasp on the throat of the soldier struggling beneath him, and glanced around. He wondered if he could bolt into the clutch of trees just over his left shoulder and disappear without being shot in the back.

"...Women and children," coughed out the soldier beneath him. Isaac, craving even further justification for his rage, loosened his grip, ever so slightly so the soldier could finish his thought. "A waste of ammo," said the soldier and spat in Isaac's face. Isaac clenched his teeth, closed his hands tighter, and began banging the soldier's head on the ground.

The second soldier realized that he was right and the slender Jew really was too much for his companion. He shook his head, allowing one corner of his mouth to smile. The men of the Reich were going soft with advantage. With one beefy arm, he pulled the Jew up and off his companion. He cocked the other arm back, ready to handle the Jew, when a stern voice yelled, "Halt."

The soldier on the ground scrambled to his feet. The second soldier froze and took a step back.

Isaac turned. The voice belonged to the squad leader. "You killed all of them," said Isaac. "Women and children."

"Not all of them. Not you," said the squad leader. "Though we could have easily, Kronski."

"Kron --? I'm not Kronski. My name is Isaac --"

"No need to deny your identity. We know who you are." The squad leader nodded, and the two soldiers took hold of Isaac and led him, stumbling and deflated, toward the train.

THE CZECHOSLOVAKIAN RAILWAY

Isaac was stunned to discover it was not a boxcar train, but rather a well-appointed passenger train of the kind on which he had traveled years ago with his grandmother. She had dreams for her first grandson beyond the *shtetl* and had wanted to show him the city. Years later what he remembered most were the spires of the University and the basket of home baked sweets she had carried for them to eat, tucked under her arm, that had inexplicably smelled like lilacs.

The two soldiers watched Isaac ascend the narrow iron ladder into the train. They watched as a porter handed him a pile of folded clothes. They shook their heads baffled and turned back to the canvas paneled truck. In a few minutes they would be carted off to a shoddy barracks and their next assignment. An owl swooped past them overhead, carrying the limp body of a dead rabbit. A shudder went through the bigger German, knowing this to be a bad omen. Since when had a bird of prey become so careless as to flaunt its prize?

Isaac, his hands holding the pile of clean clothes, was led into the train car where Colonel Kohl waited. "You'll find those more comfortable than that costume you're wearing," Kohl said. Isaac, baffled, knew that it was to his benefit to say nothing. "All the preparations are in place at the Castle. Herr Gemlinger and his contingent arrive soon. Once he's satisfied, then it's off to Berlin."

"Berlin," echoed Isaac, trying to make sense of this.

"From what he's told me, the Fuhrer is quite excited to meet you," said Kohl, repressing the urge to roll his eyes.

"Castle, yes…the Fuhrer…" mouthed Isaac, trying to make it look as if he understood what the Nazi colonel was talking about. A wave of exhaustion overtook him.

"Rest now. You will be expected to perform," said Kohl with a hint of sarcasm. This boy, this Isaac, was witless but it was none of his business. If he was so psychic, if he was such a favorite of the Reich, why had he been unable to avoid arrest? Kohl would deliver the boy to the Castle and then go into the nearest town, get drunk, and find a girl who reminded him of his wife when they were young and first in love. The irony of this need to go back in time to before his rise in the ranks of the German military, to lose himself in imaginings that dated back before his enviable success, was not lost on him.

Rays of the approaching sun made the sky turn purple and then pink. An elderly woman who had been unable to get out of bed the day before woke with an urgency she did not understand. As she went from room to room with her candlelit lamp, she discovered that her home was empty. Her son, his wife and their three little boys were not asleep in their beds. Soon they would come home, elated from the wedding celebration, she told herself. All the same, she wrapped herself in her warmest cloak, took up her cane, and went to the Temple. Perhaps she would not be too late to catch the last of the celebration, she told herself. But even as she neared the Temple, there was no one on the road. She tried to hurry but her aged muscle and bone would not let her. She struggled open the heavy doors of the Temple, and walked down the too quiet hallway to the too quiet sanctuary. She did not realize that all was quiet because she had a few years before gone deaf. But rivulets of blood met her feet, and she heard the howl that escaped her lungs. Using all her meager weight she wrenched open the doors to the sanctuary. In the last of the moonlight that fell in through the broken-out back wall, she could make out bodies fallen one upon the other, bullet-shattered and blood-stained.

The howls of the old woman brought Rachel back to consciousness. She watched the old woman as she moved around the room, trying pulses and checking for the warmth of breath, not caring that blood was smearing her clothes and her cheeks. Rachel was glad when a passing shepherd, hearing the old woman's keening, left his flock and came to help her. Together they found the bodies of her daughter-in-law and three grandchildren fallen together. The middle grandchild, a boy, still drew breath and the old woman with a strength she had not known in years, clutched him to her.

Other villagers who, for one reason or another, had missed the wedding entered timidly. They had heard gunshots the night before and had been waiting for the safety of daylight to verify that the Nazis were gone and enter the Temple. The keening of the old woman had given them courage to creep forward. Rachel watched from above as the rescuers found first her father's body, and then her own. It was then that she realized her soul had left her body and that she was hovering between life and death. She felt a great curiosity, nothing more. A golden voice entered her awareness and told her that she had more to do. Before she could turn her head to see the *elohim*, for only an angelic presence could have such a voice, her heart was shot through with excruciating pain and her eyes flew open. She found herself looking up at the ceiling of the sanctuary with the body of her father, the late Rabbi Jecobs of the village of Zebrak, in her arms. The shepherd tried to take her father's body from her, but she clutched his bulk tighter and began to wail. That's how the rescuers discovered she was still alive.

THE JEWISH QUARTER OF PRAGUE

A bevy of ravens took flight at the piercing cry, the inhuman wail of grief that came from within the Temple.

Inside the synagogue, a villager, an elder of an outlying congregation, leaned on his cane and stood before the older Rabbi Gottesfurcht, Yakov, who had cried out upon hearing of the tragedy in Zebrak. The villager had gotten word and asked if he could come speak with his dear Rabbi Yakov. It was the least he could do for his old friend and spiritual mentor. The villager looked at the floor, hands clasped, and his heart heavy. "I am so sorry, *Rebbe*," he said.

"A slaughter in the Temple, the entire wedding — guests, bride and groom, women, children, of course the men," repeated Rabbi Yakov. The villager nodded yes.

Rabbi Yakov did not ask the next question, but that question hung in the room. The villager answered it. "And the *rebbe*," said the villager. "Everyone, I am told."

Rabbi Yakov buried his head in his hands. To be polite, the villager studied the clock in the den, an antique passed down from the family of Rabbi Yakov's deceased wife. It ticked off a minute, and then two. The older Rabbi Gottesfurcht looked up then and said, "They will need a *rebbe* to perform the *levaye* for the dead. Will you send word I will be there?"

The villager bowed his head and retreated, leaving Rabbi Yakov with the ache in his chest and his need to grieve. The villager went down the hallway out into the shattered sunlight of Prague, the rays of the sun struck apart from one another by the dark storm clouds through which they shone. He knew what he had to do next. Leaning on his cane, he went to share the news with anyone else who had not yet heard. No one would know what to do. Everyone would panic. The villager would go back to his village and speak with his old wife last, and they would sit and cry for the dead young Rabbi and for themselves, and try to come up with a solution. They had no place to go. Rabbi Yakov had kept the Nazis at bay so far. Likely the villager and his wife would stay in their small village on the outskirts of Prague and hope for the best. But first there would be tears.

Rabbi Yakov dropped onto a bench, facing the ark that held the Torah within, and believing himself to be alone, allowed himself to sob. "My son, my Isaac," he wept. This

Sho-ah, this calamity, was no longer news from distant villages. It was no longer something he had to work to keep like a virus from spreading to his town. This *churben* had reached his doorstep, and into his home and into his heart, as his Isaac had feared and spoken of.

The thoughts came fast without warning or reason, flooding Rabbi Yakov's mind and choking his heart. He felt like a fool for not listening, he should have done something to address Isaac's warnings, but he did not know what he should have done, what he could have done. The one thing he could have done, he did not—he should have listened to his son while he still could, while his son still breathed. He should have defied the German officer and then what? They could have died together. Now he was sentenced to walk the earth without his child. "My Isaac!" he cried into his hands. "My son…"

"…Was not among the dead," said a voice behind him. Rabbi Yakov turned to see a young man, dressed in black, standing at the side door of the sanctuary.

"Who are you?" asked Rabbi Yakov. "What do you know of my son?"

Kronski dropped his gaze to the floor. "He was alive. He was the only one."

"Why him? Why did they spare him?"

"Because they thought he was me," said Kronski.

TOCNIK CASTLE

The other Isaac, the younger Rabbi Gottesfurcht, approached Tocnik Castle climbing the mountain on foot, accompanied by Colonel Kohl and flanked by an escort of soldiers. He wore the clean gray pants and the white dress shirt given to him by the Nazis on the train. The sky was blue and the sun shone bright but he had shivered as he entered the shadow of the medieval Castle that had dominated the region for nearly six centuries. The mountain, crowned with the Castle, towered over the valley below, through which ran the train on which Colonel Kohl had arrived recently from Germany. Villages could be seen small and distant below. One of them was the village or *shtetl* of Zebrak, from which the other Isaac, this younger Rabbi Gottesfurcht, had been taken hours before.

Vaclav the IVth, had ascended as one of the four heirs of Charles the IVth during the 14th century. Vaclav's father, Charles, had ruled Luxemburg, become the King of Bohemia, the King of Germany, the King of Rome, and later the Holy Emperor of Rome. In his spare time, Charles also founded the University of Prague, corresponded with Petrarch, constructed the Charles Bridge and the Radschin, completed Saint Vitus' Cathedral, and issued the Golden Bull, a document establishing the accepted procedures for imperial elections. Vaclav, though, had been content with lesser projects like making sure that he and his friends had places to carouse. For that reason, he built the magnificent Tocnik Castle, a hunting lodge. It became his favorite stopping point on his journeys from Prague to Nuremburg.

Though built for the pursuit of luxury and pleasure, the Castle had been outfitted with all defenses necessary to survive dark times. Gothic, it had the appearance of a vulture perched on the highest point of the region, studying Central Bohemia for its prey. The walls of the Castle were over a hundred feet high. The Castle was much the same as it had been during the Middle Ages except that now it was occupied by Nazis who had turned it into a prison camp.

Isaac was not tired, thirsty, hungry, or ill-clothed, thanks to the generous hospitality of the Nazis. He knew there had been a mistake. He knew that his life depended on figuring out what that mistake was as quickly as possible. He knew his odds were not good. But he vowed that, if spared, he would exact justice for the slain Jews of Zebrak.

Birds twitted in the trees, building their nests. People declared wars, fought them and died, but the birds never faltered from their mating habits, raising their babies spring after spring as if nothing was happening. It was disquieting to think that he could be killed then and there, and the birds would go on with their cheerful habits without missing a beat. Being young, he had never faced his own death before, with time for deliberation, as he did that bright morning.

Isaac was escorted past sentries who stood on guard along the mountain trails until he passed through a wooden sentry post and found himself on the stone bridge that led to a stone road that led directly into the gates of the Castle itself. He looked over the stone wall that ran along the bridge and found himself looking down into a castle moat. Within the moat, between the two walls that encircled the castle there was no water, no moat filled with crocodile from Africa, a vain aspiration he had heard Hitler entertained for all of his conquered castles. The moat was only a circular field of grass. But he saw something move, and when he focused, he realized that it was stocked with bears and a shudder of fear ran through him. He knew the Nazis loved gaming, and worried that he might become fodder for the bears. In fact, he might have been saved just for that purpose, based on his defiant nature.

"Crude but effective for dissuading unwanted guests," said Colonel Kohl, joining Isaac. The overture startled Isaac, the fact that Kohl would take the time to stop and talk with a Jew. But Isaac decided to take it in stride.

"I can see that," said Isaac.

"Come," invited Kohl.

Isaac fought the bizarre sensation that he was a guest and being given a tour of the Castle. He knew that he needed to remain on guard for whatever horror the Germans had in store for him. Kohl led him past the bridge. Isaac found they were crossing a drawbridge. He studied its design. He looked for the lever that controlled the mechanism that lifted and lowered it on its hinges in the unlikely event that he was able to attempt an escape. He thought for the hundredth time of Rachel, and hoped without reason that she had found a way to survive.

At the end of the drawbridge, he passed under a stone arch beyond which lay the lower courtyard of the Castle. Isaac realized that in happier times centuries past, the courtyard might be crowded with vendors and their livestock, perhaps even gypsies juggling and performing magic. Instead the courtyard was full of soldiers, all of whom turned to watch him pass. He became convinced now that he was the evening's entertainment. He imagined the betting that was going on behind his back, and knew that the bears were the odds on favorites.

He turned and looked back. The view of the forest and surrounding farmlands was grand and spectacular. He could see how a king could develop a casual and unfeeling perspective toward his subjects. From here, the sweep of the world made human suffering seem insignificant. Living here in the Castle was unlikely to be an experience that enlightened the Nazis who were already given to a grandiose perspective of their place and purpose in the universe.

Guards opened the heavy wooden gates that led into the Castle itself. Isaac crossed the threshold with his captors and stood in the main courtyard where the more awful truth of the situation was revealed. Shackled prisoners wearing gray sackcloth uniforms with yellow stars sewn on shuffled slowly around the parade grounds shoveling mud and struggling to carry stone blocks. The sentries watched them from their posts atop the surrounding walls. The sentries wore black leather gloves and clutched Gewehr 42 semi-automatic rifles. The guards patrolling the courtyard carried riding crops and rifles as well. They stood ready to give the prisoners incentive to struggle on, as necessary.

Isaac felt the eyes of the prisoners on him and on the yellow star on his sleeve. Isaac knew that the prisoners would all be wondering what he, a Jew himself, had done to deserve his preferred treatment. He realized, as he saw their eyes narrow, that they would believe that he had done something heinous, something traitorous to his faith and people, something collaborative with the Nazis. He wanted to tell them that he did not know what he was doing there. He did not say anything though, fearing that if he tried to speak with anyone they would all be killed. But he realized as he looked around that the Nazis had plenty of bear fodder. They would not have saved him for that.

Isaac forced himself to look away from the prisoners and look straight ahead as he walked with Kohl and their guards. It was then he saw the gallows just ahead — a wood scaffold raised ten feet above the courtyard. He stopped where he stood, arrested by thought. The gnarled, knotted rope swung in the breeze. Its shadow skipped back and forth over the muddy ground. His mouth was dry. This all made sense now. His father had warned him about being a dissident. The prisoners did not envy him except his soon-to-be escape from this world of sorrow. He tried to swallow but saliva would not come.

Colonel Kohl noticed that Isaac had stopped before the gallows. It made him smirk. Building a public gallows had been a stroke of genius for its ability to conjure up fear and coerce cooperation. Kohl let Isaac register his horror before he said, "Plenty of time for that, keep moving," and nodded to a guard who shoved Isaac forward. Recovering his balance, Isaac wisely averted his eyes and watched the ground as he followed Kohl inside the Castle, which was constructed of stone. They went down a stone corridor, up a stone staircase that wound around in a spiral, and down another stone corridor. Isaac followed Kohl into a small stone cell with a narrow bed in a corner. The cold, dank stone made Isaac feel as if he was buried deep in the mountain.

"Less pleasant than the train, but far better than the other *Juden*," Kohl said. "You are either a very smart man or a very lucky man. I haven't decided which." Isaac did not know what to make of this but did not dare disagree. Kohl spoke again. "Will you need anything?" he asked.

"Need anything?" Isaac said. "For what?"

"For your performance," said Kohl.

"My performance?" said Isaac, realizing a split second too late that his frank, impetuous response was inappropriate and dangerous. Being raised by the older Rabbi Gottesfurcht to fear no one but God could turn out to be the death of him.

Kohl misinterpreted Isaac's surprised response as vanity. How dare this Jew object to his little show being called a performance, he thought. Some part of him had started to like this scrappy Jew. He liked that, even in his presence, Isaac had shown honest, if restrained, dislike of the Germans with whom he came into contact, including Kohl himself, and also had not hidden the curiosity and awe he had felt as he entered the Castle. Kohl himself had felt the same way when he first entered Tocnik Castle when he began rising in ranks through the Reich. He had been a poor child, and had never traveled in the realms of the rich until the War. Kohl was disappointed when Isaac turned out to be so arrogant, objecting to his little show being called a performance.

"That is what you call it, isn't it? A performance," said Kohl. "I mean, you wouldn't say it was a religious or educational event, would you?" not bothering to hide his disdain. Did the Jew think that he was little more than a puppet to be put on display for the Fuhrer? Did he really think he had some intrinsic value beyond mere entertainment? Kohl was honest with himself about his own intrinsic value. He knew that anyone could rise to his position and become a lackey of the Reich as he had.

"Um, yes. My performance," said Isaac. He panicked. His time was limited.

"Rest. We will come for you when it is your time," said Kohl, not waiting for or asking for any more questions.

Isaac was left alone with a view through his small barred window of the prisoners working in the courtyard. He would not be killed, at least not right away. He did not have any virtuoso music talent. He had heard of prisoners, even Jews, saving their lives by performing. Maybe he was expected to wrestle, maybe another prisoner or a bear. But he was slight of build, why would they have wanted him above another. He should have kissed Rachel when he had the impulse and then died in the Temple with her in his arms. Now he was going to have to die on a cold mountaintop. *But if God had spared his life, it must have been for a purpose.* He laughed at his

110

vanity and was struck cold by the afterthought, *if God was bothering with purpose these days.*

THE JEWISH QUARTER OF PRAGUE

Rabbi Yakov, the older Rabbi Gottesfurcht, invited the Isaac who was not his son, this Kronski, into his personal quarters. He wanted to buy time to see if he could discern whether Kronski was telling the truth, that his son was still alive.

"Tell me this again," said Rabbi Yakov, as he put up water to boil for tea and searched the cupboards for biscuits.

"As I said, I had come from Poland hoping, among other things, to attend the wedding in Zebrak. The bride and groom were distant relatives of my mother with whom she hoped I would rekindle a friendship," said Kronski.

"So, you were there and you met my son?" said Rabbi Yakov.

"I arrived for the wedding late, after the soldiers, and hid in the woods. I saw them take the young *rebbe*, who I learned later was your son." Kronski dropped his gaze to the floor. "He was alive. He was the only one at the wedding that they spared."

Rabbi Yakov poured the hot water into the teapot and placed it and a plate with a few stale biscuits on the table. It was better than nothing and maybe better than this Kronski deserved. Kronski may have brought good news, or at least decent news, but Rabbi Yakov guarded his heart.

This Kronski was young. He looked like he had two good feet and two good arms. Rabbi Yakov did not like how this Kronski sat like a lump and let himself be served as if he were elderly or crippled. Rabbi Yakov pulled out two cups, one chipped, and two spoons, and put them on the table. He

111

watched to see which cup Kronski took, and did not like that he took the one that was not chipped. Rabbi Yakov sat down across the table from this Isaac Kronski and tried to meet his gaze.

Kronski, for his part, looked around the home of this Rabbi Yakov of Prague, of the Rabbis Gottesfurcht. The home was both simple and something of a mess. Kronski believed that these *rebbes* knew how to keep the house tidy enough but that their minds were always somewhere else. And likely this Rabbi Yakov had not had the heart to move or change things, preferring to leave his home the way his wife had left it years before when she died. Therefore, one of the cups was chipped, the teapot sitting between the two men was cracked, the lace tablecloth was yellowed, and the brass candlesticks for the *shabbat* were unpolished and tarnished green. Not to mention that the biscuits were stale and the tea was watery. No doubt this Rabbi Yakov had seen better days, or at least a time of youth and a time without war. But the state of the home had more to do with Rabbi Yakov's inner landscape than the state of the world outside. If Kronski sorrowed, it was because he had been without a home for long enough that he did not reminisce. He had no anchor. He had no cracked teapot to remind him of the past.

"Who are you?" Rabbi Yakov asked.

"I am Isaac Kronski. I was born in Oshwiecim, Poland. My father was a Rabbi at the Temple Beth-Al, a synagogue that no longer stands, thanks to the soldiers who have your son, but it lives in our hearts. Some day we will return and rebuild it and it will be better than ever."

Rabbi Yakov nodded. He had heard what had happened to the synagogue in Oshwiecim and the villagers in its congregation. It was not far from there to Auschwitz from where his wife's cousins had disappeared. "Then you are an orphan."

"Yes, or as good as. I do not know with certainty," said Kronski.

"I wish that you be reunited with your family," said Rabbi Yakov. Kronski did not answer. Instead he looked at the floor. Rabbi Yakov picked up his spoon and turned it between his fingers, watching it distort the light and shadows of the room. He shook his head, thinking.

"Yes," said Kronski, "I'm afraid the coincidences are the reason they took your Isaac instead of me. Because his name is also Isaac and he is a rabbi's son." Apart from their age, Isaac Kronski and Isaac Gottesfurcht did not resemble each other.

"So, a mistake," said Rabbi Yakov. "They took him by mistake."

"And the Germans do not like to make mistakes," said Kronski.

Rabbi Yakov rubbed his forehead. "They took my son Isaac by mistake?" he said.

"And if they haven't discovered the mistake, your son is still alive," said Kronski. "*Rebbe*, we've got to get to him before they find out."

"Why do they want you? What makes you so valuable to these Nazis?"

"I'll show you. Do you have any cards? Playing cards?" said Kronski.

Rabbi Yakov opened a drawer in a cupboard. He pulled out a deck of well-worn playing cards. His son Isaac had learned to play cards on that deck, beginning with the game, *pisha paysha*. And Isaac had liked to play by himself, spreading the cards out all over the floor face down and picking matched pairs. Rabbi Yakov had taught his son to add and subtract with the cards.

"Shuffle them," said Kronkski.

"Where did they take him?" asked Rabbi Yakov.

"A military command center set up in Tocnk Castle, north of Zebrak. Shuffle the cards, I'll show you what they want."

Rabbi Yakov shuffled as he was told. "I was in Zebrak many years ago as a young man, and I've seen the castle on the hill. He's being held there?"

"Now cut." said Kronski. Rabbi Yakov did.

"And look at the card," said Kronski. "Don't let me see it." Rabbi Yakov looked at the card that had been revealed by the cut, the queen of spades.

"Put the deck back together," said Kronksi. Rabbi Yakov took the last stack of cards taken and put it on top of the first.

"Good," said Kronski, "Now put the deck in the center of the table." Rabbi Yakov put the deck down next to the brass candlesticks that were turning green, so thick with melted wax from *Shabbats* past that they were stuck to the tablecloth.

Rabbi Yakov watched Kronski put his hand over the top of the deck. Never once had he touched the cards since giving them to Rabbi Yakov. Kronski raised his eyes and met the Rabbi's gaze. "The queen," said Kronski.

"What?" said Rabbi Yakov.

"Your card was the queen of spades, right?" said Kronski.

"Yes, but how did you know?" said Rabbi Yakov.

"I am what they call a psychic," said Kronski, running the fingers of one hand through his hair, brushing it back.

"A what?" said Rabbi Yakov.

"At least the Germans think I am," said Kronski. "I learned some parlor tricks traveling here and there. I had a professor who considered himself a naturalist."

"They want you because you know what card they already drew?" said Rabbi Yakov.

"This professor, he taught me exercises so I could appear to have powers," said Kronski. "At first I used these 'powers' to impress girls, but word got around. I got a reputation. So, he wants me."

"He?" asked Rabbi Yakov.

"Hitler," answered Kronski.

"Hitler? *Gut in himmel*," said Rabbi Yakov.

"In spite of the news coming out of Berlin, braying of victory, the German leader is terrified he will lose the war," said Kronski. He had picked up the deck and was idly shuffling them from hand to hand, skilled as any card shark. "Hitler has declared the war against the Jews, all the while fearing in his heart of hearts that it may be true that we are God's Chosen People. He wants the forces that oppose God and religion on his side. For the last six months his men have kidnapped every person believed to have psychic powers, so that he and the Reich might be in thrall with the darker side of all existence."

"But you are a fake," said Rabbi Yakov.

"An actor," corrected Kronski. "I knew you drew the queen by the look on your face, the dark queen." And because he had searched the Rabbi Yakov's house and studied the Rabbi's deck even before meeting the Rabbi, but he did not admit that to the Rabbi nor did the Rabbi care to ask.

"Okay, so now, my son, Isaac?" asked Rabbi Yakov.

"We've got to get to him before they find out their mistake in taking him," said Kronski. "When they find out that he is not me, they will not keep him alive very long."

"What was I thinking in sending him to Zebrak?" said Rabbi Yakov.

"Nowhere is safe," said Kronski. His eyes met Rabbi Yakov's eyes. Rabbi Yakov drank in Kronski's truth and relaxed. Rabbi Yakov sighed.

"And you know this because you are so psychic?" said Rabbi Yakov.

"Let me help bring him back," said Kronski.

"How?" said Rabbi Yakov.

"I'll need the help with the underground resistance of Prague," said Kronksi. "I cannot do this alone."

"But I know nothing of such thing," said Rabbi Yakov. "Familiar with our limitations, we are practicing peaceful cooperation with this occupation."

"It's no time for secrets, *Rebbe*. You are the spiritual leader of your community. You must know how to contact them," said Kronski.

"I am a man of peace, not war," said Rabbi Yakov.

"Don't you want your son back?" asked Kronski, pulling his chair in closer so that it scraped the floor. He leaned into Rabbi Yakov and put a hand on his shoulder.

"Of course I do," said Rabbi Yakov, "And I will get him back." He felt the sincere desire to comfort and help coursing through Kronski's grasp. It awoke in the Rabbi a desire to shrug him off. This Kronski felt like trouble, well meaning but full of trouble. Lacking subtly, skill, and wisdom, Kronski would try his young man's might against the German army, nothing but trouble. He was worse than his own son, his Isaac.

"Then you will need the help of the Underground," said Kronski.

"I cannot ask others to risk their lives for my family," said Rabbi Yakov. "If there is such an underground resistance, they must use their efforts to resist the German army in the ways they know best."

"You are going to get your son back from a squad of the Gestapo's best storm troopers by yourself?" asked Kronski.

"I will ask no man's help," said Rabbi Yakov.

"You cannot do this alone," said Kronski.

"Thank you for the information about the whereabouts of my son. Far be it from me to bother you further. I will take matters from here," said Rabbi Yakov. This Kronski had searched his house without asking and studied his life down to his playing cards so he could impress him with his so-called psychic abilities. Rabbi Yakov remembered when his son Isaac had bent the upper right corner of the queen of spades when he was first learning how to shuffle. Over the years, most of the cards in the Gottesfurcht deck had developed identifying scars. Such a foolish trick, still he admired this Kronski's determination and thoroughness.

"I will find the Underground myself. Then we will rescue your son in spite of your pigheadedness, old man," said Kronski, shaking his head and slipping out a side door, allowing in a short-lived burst of afternoon sunshine before the door slammed behind him.

Rabbi Yakov was left standing alone in the middle of the room. "I did not say I would do it by myself," he said to himself. He was ready to draw at straws to free his son, rather than trust this Kronski. Besides, maybe his son was right, maybe he needed to have more faith than he did and so trust the old stories, the old fairytales. And if his plan failed, he would free his son with his own bare hands, or die trying. *Chas vesholem*, heaven forbid, his son should depart this earth before he did.

Turning back into the inner recesses of his home and sanctuary, Rabbi Yakov sent up a prayer for the safety of those who held in their hearts the highest good, and as an afterthought, prayed that he was among them.

As he hastily packed his bags, he prayed that his home and *shtetl* would still be in tact when and if he returned. A compassionate man, he also sent up a prayer for their now deceased German officer, whose death seemed to have nothing and everything to do with what was going on. Or maybe the world was just falling apart and everything was descending into death and chaos.

THE CHARLES BRIDGE OF PRAGUE

Kronski ran his hands through his hair with one hand as he strode past the Panzer tanks parked at the towers on either end of the centuries-old Charles Bridge. His coat was draped over his other arm. He glanced without staring at the German soldiers who sat on the Panzers. They continued their conversations as he passed, almost not noticing him. One unarmed man, no matter how agitated, was no threat to them or their mission.

The bridge that led into the heart of the city, named for the King whose son had built the Castle Tochnik, was the only way across the Moldavka River into the city of Prague. Beyond the bridge, untouched by war, lay the Town Square of Prague.

In the late 12th century, the Town Square was the central marketplace of Prague. Over the intervening centuries, wealthy merchants erected Roman, Baroque, and Gothic buildings around its perimeter, giving the Town Square distinction and grandeur. But the business at its center was the simple barter and trade of the stuff of daily life.

Even during times of war, the life of a merchant went on. There were goods to be sold to those who had money. Townspeople flocked to the square, comforted by what normalcy the stench of livestock and the bickering of tradesmen had to offer. They bought what they could and admired the rest, dreaming of more peaceful and prosperous times, free of the occupation. The mighty Roman Empire had come and gone, and so in time would the Germans.

Kronski searched the merchant's booths. His eyes fell on a young woman carding spun wool. A sheep and her two lambs grazed nearby. He was not prepared for what came next. The young woman lifted her face and beamed Kronski a broad smile that revealed a gap between her front teeth. Instead of awakening criticism and rejection from Kronski, a man so selective he was born to be alone, he found that her gapped teeth and loopy smile only enhanced her beauty. She had milky skin and jet-black hair. She seemed Czech, but Kronski wondered if she was feigning and was really gypsy. Something about her struck him to the quick and threatened his focus, a focus which had been relentless and impenetrable until now. She woke the ravenous part of his body and soul, a distraction he could not afford.

"Wool?" she said. "The highest quality, hand spun with care." Annoyed, Kronski shook his head. He pulled his attention away and glanced back over his shoulder at the German soldiers. One soldier leaning against a Panzer took a deep drag on his hand-rolled cigarette and allowed his gaze to wander over the Town Square. Kronski could feel her looking at him. He turned back to the girl.

"Or if you'd prefer the mutton," she said, "The sheep itself is also for sale. But you must buy her quick before she is taken to feed them." She tossed her head toward the bridge, indicating the soldiers. The dying sun caught her thick mane of hair as it swung.

Against his will, Kronski allowed his eyes to drop. The image of her naked body flooded his senses. The attraction was brutal and compelling. They would make love for days once they got started. He met her eyes but said nothing. She smiled and held out a hand. His heart pounding in his chest, he forced himself to turn away and moved on through the marketplace.

A few stalls away from the girl and her sheep, he was able to swallow and catch his breath.

A few moments after that, he became annoyed with himself. He forced the mutton girl from his mind. It was easy. She was nothing.

"Wine, fresh from the vine," said a man's voice at his ear.

Kronski found himself standing next to the booth he had been looking for. "Actually I would like some sherry," Kronski said, and turned to look at the merchant who had broken his thoughts.

The wine merchant wore a yellow star on his coat. It made sense to Kronski that a man who knew the craft of producing alcoholic beverages would enjoy a special immunity from the Nazi ground troops. As much as any soldier in the German army, these troops would suffer the stress, angst, and loneliness of men stationed far from home in service of a brutal cause. The merchant of a good wine, regardless of his ancestry or allegiances, would be allowed and even encouraged to ply his craft, so long as he did not take sides, was not choosy about his customers, and was liberal with his bribes.

No longer shaken, Kronski said again, "Do you have any sherry?"

"I'm not deaf," said the merchant, looking Kronski over. What the merchant saw was a man dressed in black, looking more vagabond than either a servant or master. A vagabond could ill afford his sherry. "It's not cheap," the merchant said. "May you want a local squeezing? Only two months old but good enough to ward of the cold at night, and the price is right."

"That's okay. I'll take the sherry," said Kronksi. "It's important."

"Important sherry?" asked the merchant. "The local girls are hardly that particular." He was prying to see if the vagabond had any good information. Perhaps the vagabond had discovered a German officer willing to take a bribe, an officer not already known to the wine merchant.

Kronski pulled a fistful of German marks from his pocket and thrust them at the merchant. "No more conversation. How much?"

The merchant raised an eyebrow but pulled the necessary bills out of the vagabond's hand, pulled a bottle of Sherry out from under his counter, and handed it to the vagabond. From the look of the money, the vagabond was either a friend of a German officer or the murderer of a German officer. Either way, the merchant could ill afford to refuse him service and was grateful for the business. Enough of the German currency could get a person across borders and into unoccupied territory if luck was also on his side.

Kronski pushed the remaining bills into the merchant's hand, took the bottle and pried its wax seal off with his teeth. "Important and in a hurry," said the merchant, raising an eyebrow. It was not unusual for someone desperate to forget to uncork their goods and take a few swallows before they left his stand. That is, unless they bought his pricey sherry.

But Kronski pulled his shirttail out of his trousers and tore off a thin strip of material. So this is what the vagabond was up to. The merchant watched for soldiers over Kronski's shoulders. Regardless of the value of the merchant's skills to the occupiers, he could not be caught witnessing the vagabond's behavior if he ever wanted to see his family again.

Kronski shoved the end of the strip of material into the end of the now open bottle and pressed the wax back around it, leaving a strand hanging out. He looked up at the wine merchant and smiled. "I just know some fellows who look like they could use a drink."

The wine merchant nodded and with a single motion reached over and pulled his label off the bottle. Kronski concealed the bottle under his coat and nodded back. The merchant caught a glimpse of the yellow Star shrouded in the wrinkles of Kronski's coat as he turned away and headed back toward the stone bridge. Kronski slipped his arms into his coat as he went, shrugging it onto his shoulders, careful to keep the bottle hidden.

The wine merchant went back to tending his wares. He allowed the slightest of smiles to appear at the corner of his mouth.

The German soldiers sitting on the nearest Panzer looked up as Kronski approached and tightened their grip on their Mauser 98 bolt-action rifles. The closest soldier jumped off his tank and raised his rifle, focusing his site on Kronski and his yellow Star.

Kronski raised his hands in the air. "No. *Fruend*," he said. He plucked a pack of cigarettes out of the thin air and held it up. "*Rauch? Zigarette?*"

122

The closest soldier lowered his rifle muzzle and stepped forward, curious. His two companions jumped off the tank too, and crowded up behind him, their rifles tucked under their arms.

Kronski extracted a cigarette from the pack. *"Haben sie ein licht?* Do you have a light?"* he asked the soldiers.

The closest soldier held out a hand.

"Of course," said Kronski, and handed over the pack.

The closest soldier turned back to the others and handed out cigarettes to them before putting the rest of the pack in his pocket.

Another of the soldiers pulled out a lighter and lit his companions' cigarettes.

Kronski put his cigarette in his mouth and motioned to the soldier with the lighter. *"Wie uber mich?* How about me?"

None of the soldiers moved. They looked at Kronski. They owed him nothing. They didn't have to do anything for him. If anything, he should have already fallen to his knees begging for his life, the pitiful Jew, at the sight of a rifle raised in his direction.

The soldier with the lighter closed his eyes as he drew on his cigarette allowing the smoke to curl inside his chest and fill his grateful lungs. Exhaling, he opened his eyes to see Kronski, a pathetic look on his face. A moment of pity flickered and the soldier clicked open his lighter, offering Kronski a light for what could be his last cigarette. A Jew this bold would run afoul of some officer and be dead before long. He himself would shoot the Jew but it was not worth the effort or within the mandate of the moment, which was to guard the bridge. But if the Jew caused any trouble – boom, he would get a bullet between the eyes, smokes or no smokes.

Cupping his hands against the breeze, Kronski leaned in and accepted the light. But when the Jew straightened up, the soldier noticed that he had lit, not a cigarette, but instead the end of a strip of cloth stuffed in a bottle. "*Danke*, thank you," said Kronski, holding the bottle. He no longer looked pathetic with the burning Molotov cocktail in his hand.

The soldiers dropped their cigarettes and fumbled for their guns, too late to stop Kronski from throwing the lit bottle of sherry against the tank's turret. The bottle smashed open and the flaming liquor from within flashed across the tank's shell. The soldiers dropped their guns and patted the flames out with their hands.

A moment later, they remembered Kronski. "*Finden sie ihn!*" shouted the soldier who had taken the pack of cigarettes from Kronski.

Panting, Kronski stopped and drew back into the shadow of the stone wall that ran on either side the Town Hall Tower with its great astrological Clock. He caught his breath beneath the great face of the Clock that foretold the will of the heavens. Its many hands, shining and engraved, did not tell the time but rather told the location of the stars and planets relative to this puny Earth. A plump, near naked bronze angel sat atop the clock, blissfully unaffected by the travails of mortal life.

Kronski, however, was preoccupied with avoiding his pursuers, and ignored the ancient Clock. He could not afford to be affected by anything, or anyone. Instead he scanned the crowd, concerned that he did not see the German soldiers who he knew had chased him from the bridge. But he heard, "*Dort ist er!*" and snapped his head to see the soldiers, joined by six others to make nine, at the end of the street. A sweat on his forehead, Kronski slipped back into the midday crowd on the square. Moving as fast as he could, he weaved away from the soldiers, until he could break into a run.

The German soldier who had the pack of Kronski's cigarettes still in his pocket saw him. "*Anschlag! Stoppen sie diesen Juden!*"

Not recognizing where he was, Kronski backed into the space just behind the wine merchant's stall. The nine German soldiers ran past. Relieved, he let out the breath he had hardly been aware of holding.

A hand reached out and grabbed him by the shoulder, whirling him around. "Now that could have been expensive, the cost of the sherry be damned," said the wine merchant.

Shock and recognition flooded Kronski's face. "Please do not give me away!" he begged in a hushed voice.

Three more German soldiers ran up but they did not see Kronski. The merchant had already yanked Kronski behind the folds of the curtains that shrouded his booth. There, in the dark of the wine merchant's tent, Kronski and the wine merchant crouched, watching the soldiers turn in circles before choosing a new direction for their fruitless pursuit.

"Thank you, I cannot thank you enough," said Kronski, helping the wine merchant stand.

"Crazy boy," said the wine merchant, brushing off his trousers.

"These are crazy times," said Kronski. The angular jut of his jaw suggested to the wine merchant a life of hardship and anger.

"These are miserable times. If I had known what you had in mind I would have suggested something with a little more kick – like petrol. A sherry burn is not going to hurt a Panzer tank," said the wine merchant.

"I was trying to send a message," said Kronski.

"A message?" said the wine merchant. "What message? That you should be arrested and hung by your neck as an example?"

Kronski leaned toward the wine merchant, lowering his voice, "I need to contact the Underground."

The wine merchant studied the vagabond, looking into his eyes. There the wine merchant saw a deep and insatiable need for revenge, justice, and resolution. This need, no doubt, drove the vagabond's brash behavior. He did not know or need to know the event or events that were the source of the vagbond's want and its urgency. Whatever it was, it would suffice.

"You must understand," said Kronski, his urgency building, "I need to contact the Underground."

"You already have," said the wine merchant, putting his hands on the shoulders of the vagabond. He felt the young man flinch under his touch in the way of the lonely. He wished that he could provide comfort to this young man and his broken soul but knew that in these troubled times such comfort was the province of *Yahweh* alone. "Tonight you disappear. Find me after sundown tomorrow."

The vagabond and the wine merchant studied each other. The air cracked with the sound of gunfire and the shouts of German soldiers. Both men noticed that neither flinched.

"My name is Nahman," said the wine merchant. "And yours is?"

"I'll tell you tomorrow, if I find you."

Nahman nodded. The vagabond slipped out into the early twilight. Nahman leaned over and locked up his cupboard of sherries and fine liquors. By the time he looked up a moment later the vagabond was gone. The market place was deserted.

Nahman shook his head and went back to closing up his shop. He knew with the disruption on the bridge the business day was over. Anyone who lingered in the market might bear the brunt of the soldiers' frustration. Besides, wine merchant or not, it never hurt to be home early and shut the doors and shutters tight these days.

THE TEMPLE AT ZEBRAK

The shepherd had gone for other villagers, from neighboring *shtetls* and from outlying farms. The Temple at Zebrak, where hours before the young Rabbi Isaac Gottesfurcht had conducted his first wedding between Oz and his shy young bride, was in ruins. Local people, Jewish and people of other faiths or of faith and no religion at all, exhausted of emotion, carried the dead from the Temple and dug their graves. The bride and groom were laid beside each other in their blood-drenched wedding garments.

Rachel leaned against a wall and slumped to the floor, pulling a wailing two-year old girl into her lap. The child's limbs were rigid and flailing but Rachel patted her back until the girl snuggled against her chest. The wailing diminished to sobbing, and the girl began to hiccup. Rachel gave her a sip of rainwater, saved in a tin cup. The hiccups gradually subsided to the gentle sighs of sleep. Rachel had known the child's mother, a sweet and tender woman, and had often looked with longing and wonder at the bond the mother and child had shared.

The Catholic doctor who had slipped away in secret from the Nazi field hospital to tend whoever had managed to survive the massacre at the Temple of Zebrak tended Rachel. He told Rachel that she was very fortunate that it seemed that the bullets had only grazed her. She doubted his diagnosis—her pain was lodged in her heart, deep and insurmountable. The narcotics he gave her did not take away that pain. She shamed herself by wishing for death. She could not cry though, and that seemed to be a blessing, that and the beautiful day that God had unfolded. The sun was out and the birds were singing.

Rachel watched the Catholic doctor probe her skin with his scalpel, searching to make sure there was no buried ammunition. It felt odd that his digging did not hurt. She looked into his face, his knit eyebrows, and wondered how he survived, his own family dragged off to camps, living under the roof of his Nazi captors. No answer came, but she observed that it seemed he had learned to live for others. Maybe he had forgotten altogether that he too existed. Maybe she could also forget that she existed. Maybe that would ease the pain.

THE CATACOMBS BENEATH TYN CATHEDRAL OF PRAGUE

The twin towers of Tyn Cathedral, the Church of Our Lady, and their many gothic spires, reached into the stormy sky above the Old Town district of Prague. Over the Cathedral's grand entrance, flags bearing the Swastika flapped and snapped in the same wind that churned the storm clouds overhead. The last daylight gave a fiery background to the darkening clouds. The sky looked as if it were boiling. In moments the day would end and another cold wet night would be heralded by lightning and thunder.

The Cathedral had been first constructed in the eleventh century in the style favored by the Romans. Then it became Gothic. Later, for a while it was controlled by the Hussites. Lightning brought a fire that destroyed much of the Cathedral but it had been restored. The oldest pipe organ in

Prague constructed in the seventeenth century was inside the Cathedral, as were the remains of the great Danish astronomer Tycho Brache who died while serving as Imperial Mathematician under the Emperor Rudolph the Second.

German staff cars lined the street in front of the Cathedral. Officers of the Third Reich stationed in Prague made themselves at home inside. They smoked cigars and suckled the breasts of whores beneath the statue of the Madonna, while spinning grandiose plans. The Nazis supposed they had conquered the Cathedral, but in the end their presence would be brief like the life span of an insect. The officers had no idea that at that twilight moment their enemies were right under their feet.

Kronski followed Nahman, the wine merchant, through the ancient tunnels dug deep in the earth beneath the Cathedral. "Unnerving, isn't it?"

"What?" asked Nahman, holding his lantern before him to avoid stumbling on the uneven path in the pitch dark.

Kronski inhaled deep the rank smell of the Catacombs. He reveled inside at having been invited into this mystery. Still it was strange. "To meet here, hearing them above, moving around overhead in their headquarters. Do you think that they know of this place?"

"Perhaps," said Nahman. "Perhaps not."

"But knowing there is a chance that they could so easily find you here, why would you choose such a place?"

"For two hundred years, the Jews have foresworn this part of Prague. Do you not know the story?" asked Nahman. He stopped a moment to catch his breath and turned back to look at Kronski.

"No," said Kronski. "Should I?"

"In the 17th century a widespread fire in the Jewish Quarter, fierce, sudden, and voracious, leveled many homes. The Jews were relocated to this part of the city. Suddenly freed from his ghetto, a young Jewish boy named Shimon Abeles, went exploring his new neighborhood, and came upon this Cathedral. He was so enthralled with its trappings that he went to the priests. At first the priests wanted to turn Shimon away, but Shimon begged them not to and asked to convert."

"And did he?" asked Kronski.

Nahman nodded. "And when his father, Lazar, discovered Shimon knelt in prayer to Christ, Lazar was so overcome with shame that he beat his own son."

"Yes," said Kronski. "Anger follows shame like a starving dog and for good reason."

Nahman stopped and cocked his head.

"Well, it does, doesn't it?" asked Kronski.

Nahman had to admit it sounded rational. He had never thought of this, but there were many things he had never thought of. It made him wonder what this Kronski knew of shame. It made him wonder what Hitler was so ashamed of that he could be so furious at the Jews of Europe. It made him wonder if there was something he was so ashamed of that he would be driven to such fury. When he was young, he was ashamed of his poverty, the poverty that made his body hungry and scrawny. So he became a wine merchant, and grew old and fat.

"Shouldn't we be going?" asked Kronski.

"There's more."

"They must be waiting."

"There's time."

"Tell it, and quickly," said Kronski.

130

Nahman wondered, had he made a mistake. This Kronski was so brash, so uncomfortable in the moment, so uncomfortable in his own skin. It would make him act without thought and could make him a liability. But Nahman also knew himself to be an old man and not urgent enough. He remembered being impatient in his youth. The Resistance needed youth.

"It is a story I need to know," said Kronski.

Okay, this made more sense. Nahman was reassured of his original assessment of Kronski. Yes, he was urgent, but for good reason.

"Shimon would show no remorse," continued Nahman. "No matter how hard Lazar beat him, Shimon persisted in his choice, choosing, even in the final blow, Christian martyrdom over his own family and his birthright. The beating ended in Shimon's death."

"So Jews don't come here to avoid the temptation to turn away from their faith, or is it to avoid embarrassment over this story?"

"No, there's more. The soldiers of Prague arrested Lazar for the crime but they did not turn him over to a magistrate to be tried for assault, or homicide. With the encouragement of the Church, the soldiers took matters into their own hands and tortured Lazar for attempting to impede his son's conversion to Christianity. Shimon was a martyr in heaven, his death did not need to be revenged by law. Lazar could have struggled on in life, bearing it the way an ox bears a yoke, and living his repentance. But this torment that Lazar underwent, not just the loss of his son, his part in it, and his son's choice of Christian martyrdom over his family and birthright, but the twisting of his personal tragedy into a public mockery of his faith and all of his people, drove him to suicide.

"But even after Lazar's death, the priests were not done. At their instruction, soldiers accompanied the priests to the Jewish cemetery. They shoved aside Shimon's keening mother, and exhumed the child Shimon's body from where it had been buried by the rabbis. The same priests who had tortured this family when alive, made a great ceremony in moving the body of the child. Shimon the Martyr, they call him. His remains were entombed here, within these very vaults.

"Jews do not come here because this story is faith at its worst, Christians patting themselves on the back for having enticed Shimon, a young boy awash in wonder and curiosity, away from his home and family. Were Jews intent on stealing Christian children away from their parents, how would it be received?"

"So none of us would ever choose to enter these tunnels," said Kronski. "Or even this part of the city."

"The rabbis forbade it, until now. Through our actions, Shimon and his father can now be reclaimed from judgment by providing a cloak for us, a secret place where we can meet. No one would suspect Jews of gathering here, of all places. God works in mystery, the fullness of which will not be made clear until the end of time."

Nahman put a hand on Kronski's shoulder and together, the two men began to move forward through the tunnel again. Not only did the Catacombs harbor insult, they were also revolting. The place smelled of rodent piss. Droppings were everywhere. Grotesque and slippery outcroppings of algae hung off the wall. This alone would have kept Nahman away. But to be a part of the Jewish Underground, Nahman would have traveled through hell itself. "Your elders must have spared you this story?"

"I wish they hadn't. It strengthens my resolve," said Kronski, taking the lantern from Nahman, trying to help Nahman move forward more quickly toward the light up ahead. Yes, there were places to stumble, but Nahman picked his way along as if he were not just older, but elderly.

But Nahman still shrunk back though, doing his best to linger in the dark behind Kronski, following and wondering what this vagabond, this Kronski, meant. He himself was not moved by the idea of reclaiming Shimon and his father, Lazar. Let them stew in their own juices and resolve their differences before God. Nahman would not risk his life for them, but rather for the Jews that still lived in Prague and beyond Prague, for the liberation of the people of Eastern Europe and beyond. In telling the story, he had only wanted Kronski to know why this hiding place was safe. But, thought Nahman, if this crazy story strengthens this Kronski, in his wild-eyed resolve to wrest the world back from the Nazis, so be it. He picked up his pace to match that of his urgent companion.

Up ahead of Kronski and Nahman, a group of men were crowded into a cavern lit by the torches they held. As they neared the lit opening of the cavern, Kronski allowed the older man to pass first. Nahman nodded to the young man standing guard just inside the mouth of the cavern and joined the waiting men. Kronski stopped at the threshold, leaning his hands against the narrowed entrance. The young guard studied his features.

Like Kronski, the young guard had also been at the *schul* in Oshwiecim, Poland on its last night. He had been there the night that the old Rabbi had laughed at death. He had been there on the night of the final meeting of the Polish

Metaphysical Society. He had been there on the night of the slaughter of all of the Society's members. He was Aaron, the boy who had been in the old Rabbi's study waiting for his father, Mendel, the butcher, who had been a member in good standing of the Polish Metaphysical Society, which was in fact a squad of fighters in the underground Resistance against the German invaders. The Nazis had not known that Aaron too was in the *schul*, or he might not have escaped.

Later that night, Aaron had returned to the ruins of the *schul* after the Nazi soldiers had gone. Searching through the rumble, he had found his father's body. As he dug his father's resting place and said his father's prayers, Aaron, now an orphan, had decided to fill in his father's place. He travelled to Prague and joined the Resistance. Within the span of a few days, he went from being his father's child to being a man.

Though neither showed any sign of recognizing each other, Aaron and Kronski had been the only ones to get out of that *schul* alive. And so a ghost of familiarity passed between them, making Aaron feel as if he knew Kronski though unable to place from where or when.

Looking back at the doorway, in the dim and flickering light there was little that any of the men could make of the vagabond's features. And all that Kronski had to recommend him was the single incident on the bridge from the day before. But now that Nahman had brought him here to meet the men in this cell of the Resistance, his admission to their purpose was a foregone conclusion. There was no turning back.

These men of the Resistance in Prague, were also willing to fight against all odds against the occupiers. For their cause they had to live for the most part outside of what was left of society. Resources were slim all around and they were underdressed against the bitter damp chill of the Catacombs.

They warmed their hands by rubbing them together or tucking them under their arms or in pockets. A strength rose from the men, given by resolve. Their faces tended toward hardened and angular. For the most part, their bodies were made tough and muscular by the training demanded of those who would be a member of the Resistance in Prague.

Nahman, the wine merchant, was the most tender of the men due to his age and station in life. He was there because he provided funds, information, and strategy for the group, living the most public of daily lives among them. He had lost word of his wife and children when he sent them away from Prague for their safety, and now could only pray they were safe. He was looking forward to finding and reuniting with them when Hitler was vanquished.

"Here is the man I have told you about," said Nahman.

The men stared into the shadows where Kronski lingered but could see little of his features.

Kronski spoke to the men from his shadowy place, "I was told that you would be able to help me."

The men stirred in disbelief.

Nahman was abashed and aghast, "Us, help you?"

"I have information on an action that can be taken, that must be taken, and that will further our cause greatly," said Kronski. "A Rabbi's son has been taken–"

"You want us to rescue a Rabbi's son?" asked a hollow eyed man named Iphraim. In better times he had worked in a mill. His wife had baked bread. They had two sons and a baby daughter. Now he was bereft of family, thanks to the occupiers. Nahman had found him wandering, crazy with grief, and adopted him as if a younger brother. Iphraim recovered a purpose in life by training himself in explosives. He carried a knife and slit Nazi throats whenever the opportunity arose. His only reasons for living were to see the Nazis dead or ousted, preferably both — and to sit with his friend, Nahman, on the rare occasions when there was a *challah*, or something like it, for Shabbat, and speak of the means to liberation.

"Not just a Rabbi's son. I also want to help you rescue freedom fighters held by the Germans," defended Kronski.

"But first, you want us to risk our lives for this one rabbi's son, a single person?" asked a square-framed man with clenched fists. His name was Cseba. He was the informal leader of this squad. His wife and children still lived, and he meant to keep it that way, at any cost to himself. He abhorred favoritism, and while he loved his people and even his religion, he had grown distrustful of the rabbis, some of whom seemed unwilling to take risks against the occupiers.

"The son of Rabbi Gottesfurcht of Prague. Do you not know him?"

Nahman, the wine merchant, had never imagined that Kronski had come to the Resistance with a demand. As he had found and brought men to the Resistance, all but Kronski had come, not just broken, but also seeking purpose, and not seeking to give orders. He urged Kronski to be reasonable. "Many sons have been lost. We have learned the hard way to focus on large-scale operations directed at frustrating Nazi movement if we are to oust the occupiers. Otherwise we will be picked off and have no effect at all."

The candlelight flickered on Kronski's features. In the daylight, he had looked vulnerable and alone. Here, in the shadows, his face looked cold, impassive. Nahman, the wine merchant, shuddered at what the world was doing to its people. Like everyone else in the cavern, he wondered what this Rabbi Gottesfurcht had offered this Kronski to rescue his son. Was this vagabond, this Kronski, a mere bounty hunter? Nahman regretted his misjudgment. He continued on the off chance that he could salvage the situation, "We cannot help you rescue the Rabbi's son, but you are welcome to join us," he said. He used emphasis, knowing that the Resistance would not hesitate to kill Kronski if he turned out to be a liability instead of an asset, an intruder who had penetrated their secrecy for his own personal gain. The stakes were too high.

To the wine merchant's relief, Kronski relented. "I have joined you, here I am," he said. But Kronski continued to speak, "And here I have the plan that brought me here." Kronski pulled a folded map from his pocket and spread it out on the ground. "Rescuing this Rabbi's son will disgrace Colonel Kohl, the officer that Berlin has put in charge of restricting the Jews and rounding up the resistance in Prague and its outlying areas. Getting rid of Kohl will cripple Hitler's apparatus and allow families to get out of Prague and Poland."

While Kronski spoke and pointed at his map, unfurled on the ground, the men looked to the wine merchant. Nahman, the wine merchant, scanned their faces and silently prayed for advice from God. A decision came to him. He sucked in a deep breath and knelt down next to Kronski, using one of Kronski's shoulders for support, and kneeling, leaned in to look at the map that Kronski had brought.

The men of the Resistance looked to one another. One, then another, and then the rest, crouched beside Kronski and Nahman, the wine merchant, or crowded over them, to look at the map also. The life of this vagabond, this Kronski, was thus spared. If he knew it, he showed no sign.

Kronski pointed at the town of Zebrak on the map, "Kohl and his men are forty kilometers west of here. They've set up a prison within the walls of this Castle and that's where they are holding the Rabbi's son."

The wine merchant already regretted his decision to trust the vagabond. "You want us to storm Tocnik Castle?" he said. "There are only a handful of us."

Kronski answered, "Over a hundred members of the Resistance are being held there! Once we get in – "

"Tocnik is a fortress!" said Cseba.

"And there is a moat," said another man.

"A moat?" said Kronski. "Filled with water?"

"Filled with bears," said Cseba.

"Bears?" said Kronski.

Nahman, the wine merchant, explained as if to a child. How could his vagabond plan to storm the Castle without knowing about the bears? "It's too cold up there to keep water in the moat. Three hundred years ago an imperial guard thought of bears. You climb over that wall, the ursine carnivores, starved and captive, will tear you limb from limb."

"So we won't go over the moat," said Kronski.

"That's right, because we won't be going," said Cseba, getting a rumble of agreement from the other men in the room.

"You don't understand, do you? Have you not heard?" said Kronski.

"Heard what?" asked Cseba.

A dark look crossed Kronski's face. He bowed his head. "The Germans cannot afford to fight this war against the Allies on one front and the Russians on another front, and feed the men, women and children that fill the concentration camps that they have built in Poland. So they are –"

"Wait, quiet!" interrupted Aaron from his post at the mouth of the cavern. He had been chosen, both because he was the youngest and had little to contribute to the conference of the older men who met and planned the action of their squad, and because being young, his hearing was acute.

The older men waited a moment in silence, and then heard the approach for themselves—the rumbling and squealing overhead of the treads of Panzer tanks on the cobblestones in the street above them. The cavern shook. Men braced themselves against the wall. Worse, the noise and the shaking came to a sudden stop. Every man below imagined Nazi soldiers disembarking and entering the Cathedral above their heads. The men snuffed their torches and their faces faded into darkness.

THE JEWISH CEMETARY OF PRAGUE

A bolt of lightning split the night sky, darkening even the pearly moon in contrast. It rained like hell on Rabbi Yakov, the older Rabbi Gottesfurcht, as he worked away at prying aside a heavy stone. The stone marked the grave of his most esteemed predecessor from centuries past, the old Rabbi Loew.

As the stone fell aside, the ground released a rush of stale air. Rabbi Yakov reached into the muddy void, which had been under the stone. With his fingers, he found and pulled out a box coated with dirt and twined with roots. The rain washed away the dirt and Rabbi Yakov tore away the roots. There, in his very hands, was the foretold copper box embossed with the six-pointed star, the Mogen David.

Rabbi Yakov looked up into the torrential rain at the heavens. "Do you rage for me or against me, *Yahweh*? May You forgive me." He put the box aside for a moment. With a strength he had not known in years, he tumbled the stone back onto the gravesite, and disappeared into the rain, the box under his arm.

THE CATACOMBS BENEATH TYN CATHEDRAL OF PRAGUE

The men huddled in the dark listening to the near-deafening sound of the tanks rumbling through the streets above. They tensed, jaws clenched, hands wrapped around the knives and guns wrested from the dead fists of the enemy that they carried, ready for anything. Then there was quiet, but then rumbling again as the tanks passed away into the night, and all that remained was a sound that each man became aware of, the accelerated thrumming of their own hearts. Then soon even that calmed, and the men sighed and stretched themselves by standing if they were sitting, or sitting if they had been standing.

"The Angel of Death has passed over us again," sighed Cseba. A chuckle echoed through the chamber. It was good to know that irony was not dead, even among the Jews of the Resistance, who labored in their own pocket of sorrow, isolated from the rest of the world.

"So, you were saying, Kronski?" asked Nahman, the wine merchant.

"Yes," said another man. "You were saying what the Nazis are doing now that their resources are divided between two Fronts."

"They are roasting Jewish children and serving them as meat to their soldiers," half-joked another.

"This is not a joke," said Kronski. "This is too close to the truth. Rather than feed them, the Nazis are exterminating the Jews in the camps, all of them."

"The Final Solution is really here then," said Cseba. His breath caught at his throat.

"Killing all Jews, without secrecy or shame, as many as rapidly as possible," said Kronski. "They use ovens, the skies are full of ash."

"All of us have friends and family who have been taken," said a man. "It is our hope that we work for their liberation."

It grew so silent that the drip of water seeping though a crack in a wall could be heard.

"*Halevay!*" said a man, and others echoed with, "*O-mein*, A-men."

"We do work for their liberation!" said another. "I cannot give up hope that we will save them."

"And at Tocnik, your fellow citizens of Prague are being interrogated. New means of torture are being dreamed up daily," said Kronski.

"Interrogated? What do they want to know from us? Where Aunt Yetta's brass candlesticks are buried?"

"The locations of any Jews, the places they hide and the means by which they escape."

"And the women?"

"Murdered," said Kronski.

"And children too," said young Aaron, the picture of his three year-old brother, splayed on the floor with his throat slit, forever at the forefront of his memory. His mother and sisters had been taken, his brother slaughtered, early in the occupation, while his father and he were at his father's shop, closing up. Driven mad with grief, his father lost himself in the Resistance, taking Aaron with him to meetings, but always making him wait outside and never allowing him to join. "You are too young and besides there has to be someone left to carry on the family name," his father had said. So Aaron had known that it was only a matter of time before he was alone. With the death of his father, it was just him. With his new freedom he chose for himself to join the Resistance. Even though he did not know if his mothers and sisters still lived, he was as good as an orphan and lacked even a sibling. The Resistance was his life, and represented any hope he dared hold for the future. Life or honorable death, he would not be herded to the slaughter like a stupid beast, the fate of many Jews, if the rumors that were being spoken were true.

"Yes. The Fuhrer has a blood thirst for the Jews," said Kronski. No one offered even a black joke now, but this strange Kronski could not hold back a dark laugh. "Now you will want to know my plan," he said, confident he had their attention.

CHAPTER FIVE

THE JEWISH QUARTER AND CITY
OF PRAGUE, THE YEAR 1589

Evie fussed with boiling the water and straining the tea while the wife of Yizhar, the candlemaker, sat at the rough hewn table, staring at her rough, red hands that lay there like dead fish. Yizhar's wife had been no more than a slip of a girl when he had married her, and now, three daughters later, she was a beefy woman with a ruddy complexion and sad eyes. The sun had gone down hours ago. It was the middle of the night but Evie did not have the heart to send Yizhar's family back to their home, and none of them showed an inclination to go.

Yizhar's two older daughters sat aside, arms entwined, leaning on each other, with tears squeezing out of their swollen eyes and running down their faces. They looked exhausted of grief, but had lost none of their taste for sorrow.

"Poor papa, what will we do?" In the next moment, they caught a glimpse of one another and began howling again. Evie grit her teeth, and after a bit the girls had to catch their breath and stopped to rest.

Yizhar's third and youngest daughter was too young for sadness. Precocious, she could tell anyone exactly what had happened, "Papa's gone to jail and the *goyim* are going to hang him," but to her it did not mean a thing. She could not conceive of life without her Papa who let her stay with him while he worked in his shop, and sometimes let her choose the colors for the candles he made. She played with the neighbor's cat, a ginger who lived on the rodents she caught and the occasional fish head she found. The cat was game and willing to entertain the ignored child by pouncing on the strand of yarn that unraveled from her mitten. Her mother might have scolded her youngest daughter for letting the cat ruin her mitten on a better day, so the fun was double.

Between the youngest daughter's laughter and the oldest daughters' howling, the noise was formidable. Evie correctly pictured her father, the old Rabbi Loew, upstairs in his study, his elbows on his desk, his hands clutching the sides of his head, unable to think for the noise, and compelled to try. He only had until Sunday morning to rescue Yizhar. The additional pressure of the approaching Shabbat grated against him.

Time and time again the old Rabbi Loew had spoken to his congregants about the blessing of Shabbat, and the need to take a day and put worldly cares aside with gratitude and without resentment to the God who required it of them though commerce might call and children needed food, shelter, and clothing. But this moment, were he honest with himself and he tried to be, Shabbat hung over him pointless and infuriating. If he had been completely honest with himself in that moment, he would have realized that he was angry, in fact, not with the Shabbat, but with God Himself, King of the Universe, who would allow such a thing to befall His hapless Yizhar and his helpless wife and daughters. Three daughters and no son, that alone could be considered a curse in better times. At the moment, however, Yizhar and the old Rabbi Loew on Yizhar's behalf, had bigger fish to fry with their God.

As Evie poured the tea and placed a cup before the soon to be widow of Yizhar, she was surprised to see her father crack open the door. No one else in the room saw him, which was just as well. The two older girls launched into another fit of howling and he vanished again.

Yizhar's wife ignored her tea. Evie stood behind her. After a moment, she rested a comforting hand on her shoulder and the two women listened to the three girls shrieking with sadness and joy.

Yizhar's wife raised her hands and slammed them down on the table face down. The sound brought all three girls to silence. "This never should have happened!" Yizhar's wife said.

All eyes were on Yizhar's wife except those of the cat. The cat had silky long hair though which ran stripes of black, white, and the shades of grey in between. The cat was full of growing kittens, thanks to the tom who lived four doors down the street. While she did not mind the yowling of Yizhar's daughters one bit, she did not like the sudden bang that their mother's hands had made against the table. She had shot behind the wood pile, and bunched up as small as she could considering her growing burden, crouched there, blinking.

Evie did not know what to say, so she said, "Yes, it's terrible."

"Yes, Mama," said the oldest daughter. "Horrible."

Yitzhar's wife said, "No, I mean, I should never have married him."

"Never married Papa?" said the middle sister, stunned.

"Never married Papa," echoed the youngest sister, earnestly mimicking her mother, shaking her head from side to side just as her mother had done.

The two older girls began to cry again. "Stop it!" said their mother. And they did. Their mother had a fierce temper and no one wanted it unleashed on them.

"Stop it," said their youngest sister, and stomped her foot on the ground. Being four years old had its benefits, leniency and freedom being two of them, and she was committed to sucking the marrow out of life and enjoying every minute of it.

"Now listen," said Yizhar's wife. "Your father is a fool." Tears were rolling down the older girls' faces. The youngest daughter was busy unraveling her mitten all the way, and the cat was watching her, tempted. "What kind of a candle maker is he? More often than not, the wicks slip into the hot wax. The candles are good for what, half, a third, of the time they should be. Not even candles can he make. I cringe when someone comes to him because they want to make a *zarzheit*. What kind of memorial can you make with a candle that stops burning before the sun goes down?"

"Soon we will have to make a *zarzheit* for Papa," sobbed the oldest daughter, hiccupping from her hysteria. "Because he will be..."

"Dead," said the youngest daughter, playing with her mitten, its unraveled yarn and the cat. The two older

146

daughters grabbed each other and set about howling again, though now punctuated by the oldest daughter's hiccupping for air. *"Mame,* where will *Tate* go when he is dead?" A moment of shocked silence followed this question. The oldest daughter hiccupped. Then, if it can be imagined, the two older daughters' howling got even louder.

Evie leaned down and whispered in the ear of Yizhar's wife, "Maybe we should talk about this another time."

"No, now is the time," said Yizhar's wife. "Listen to me," she confided to Evie. "The blacksmith too asked for my hand in marriage. Such a good man he is. Do you see them leaving dead babies on his doorstep? No. He is the best blacksmith in Prague. Even the *goyim* come to him in secret, shunning their own because he is the best!"

There were prohibitions against commerce with the Jews, which in these lenient times thanks to the efforts of the old Rabbi Loew, could be circumvented. "The blacksmith is a *mensch* and so beautiful to look upon, even now. My father would not give his permission because he was uneducated. But my father was wrong as it turns out."

Yizhar's wife fell silent. Evie was full of thoughts about the wisdom of a girl blindly listening to her father in matters of marriage. She herself had shunned many suitors who her father favored. She wondered if her father had been right about any of them. It was too early, though, to see how they would turn out. Time would tell but by then it would be too late and life would have passed her by. Had she been too difficult? Too cautious? Too scared? Evie was about to say something to Yizhar's wife, something like, "But look at your lovely daughters," but when Evie turned to look at them, the two oldest girls were puffy-eyed and red-faced from mewling with self-pity, and the youngest was picking her nose and pulling the hissing cat's tail.

Evie could think of nothing else to say that would match the occasion. She wondered at how her father did it, always at the ready with something comforting to say to his congregants. But as it turned out, she did not have to say anything because Yizhar's wife turned to her daughters and said, "Your father is a *schlemiel*." With that, the youngest daughter let go of the cat and they all fell silent, contemplating what it would be like to be the lucky family of the village blacksmith. A white frost collected at the windowsills as snow fell, quiet and peaceful outside.

Yizhar's wife took a sip of her tea. The two oldest daughters blew their noses and the nose of the youngest. Except for the lingering hiccups of the oldest daughter, it was as if nothing had ever happened.

Evie took advantage of the moment and slipped out of the room. She began upstairs to check on her father who she knew was suffering the anguish of the spiritually perplexed. For once in his life he felt powerless, and that was not likely to sit well with him.

In the attic, the old Rabbi Loew lay wide-eyed on his back staring at the ceiling. The attic was filthy with dust but it was the furthest he could get from the kitchen and the interminable yowling of Yizhar's family.

Evie reached the top step, her hand on the banister, when she and her father both heard it – the unmistakable creaking of the great rusty gates that separated the Jewish quarter from the city, the great rusty gates that the *goyim* of Prague used to lock up their Jews at night. Someone with a key, someone from the other side, was opening them.

Hearing the gates open though it was the middle of the night, the old Rabbi Loew bolted to his feet and threw open the door nearly knocking Evie down the stairs. They were both startled. "Out of my way, *kinderlach*," said old Rabbi Loew, but Evie did not step aside. If she could have, she would have locked him in the attic.

But Old Rabbi Loew squeezed past her and dashed down the steps with a speed and agility he had not demonstrated in years. Evie turned and followed him, brushing attic dust off the back of his old jacket as they went, raising a cloud. "It's them, it's them. It's the ones who framed Yizhar!" said the old Rabbi Loew, choking on the dust.

"And what do you mean to do about it, *Tate*?" asked Evie, standing in front of the door while the old Rabbi Loew, pulled on his boots, threw the scarf around his neck that Evie had knitted for him when she was nine years old, and took his overcoat from where it hung and shrugged it on.

"I mean to confront them," said the old Rabbi Loew. "And if possible talk reason into them."

Evie stood before the front door. "And if they will not be reasoned with?" she asked.

"Then I will not be reasonable either!" said the old Rabbi Loew. He reached for his cane and the doorknob. In doing so, he gave Evie a nudge, or more like a shove.

Evie stepped aside knowing that there were times when her father could not be reasoned with. So it came to pass that they both stood in the open doorway, reaching for the *mezzuzah* at the same time, touching it, and kissing it to their fingertips. They looked into one another's eyes a moment. Their prayers slipped up to heaven. The old Rabbi Loew kissed his daughter on the cheek, and stomped off into the moonlit, snowy night.

Evie went back inside for a lantern. She meant to follow right behind the old Rabbi Loew. As far as she was concerned, he was not about to go about the darkened streets alone, not while there was someone or a gang of someones skulking about outside. It did not seem possible that anyone from the proper part of Prague would enter the Jewish quarter after dark filled with good intentions.

But when Evie went back into the kitchen to light her lamp, Yizhar's wife needed sugar for her tea, and her daughters needed bedclothes, the better to curl up together in a corner and ride out the first night of their lives apart from their father. By the time Evie left the house, there was no sign of the old Rabbi Loew other than his footsteps trailing off into the distance, filling up with the snowflakes that whispered down from heaven. Evie followed in her father's tracks.

The old Rabbi Loew meanwhile tromped through the *shtetl* toward the gates. His reasoning was to follow the tracks left by whoever had opened them and then spy on whatever mischief they were up to. He would then report that mischief to his friend, the Magistrate, and everything would be made right.

But as he grew closer to the gates, the moon withdrew behind cloud cover and he was enveloped in darkness. He heard rough footsteps. No one answered when he barked out, "Who's there?" his voice raspy and cracked from the cold.

Rough hands grabbed his shoulders and spun him around. A fist landed square in his abdomen, leaving him no air to make a sound. He fell back into a bank of snow and felt a cold heavy package land in his lap. He knew what it was.

He felt the short life that had lived within in it and could not cast it aside.

He worked to catch his breath and struggled to stand with his one free arm. His cane fell aside, out of reach. He was no more than a fish pulled from the river, flopping on the ground. Lantern light flooded his face. Strong hands caught him and pulled him up. As he was lifted he tightened his grip. He felt cold tiny limbs, torso, and head through its wrap. He felt the child had been loved in life. Here they would find their end together, the baby as a gruesome prop for a horrible task, and he as an over proud fool who had thrown himself in harm's way without a plan. Now that he would be the accused instead of an advocate, he doubted he could make a difference for the hapless candle maker, himself, or whoever else was framed in this ugly light. The men, grumbling to each other, complained that he was a fat old Jew. The description struck him as oddly accurate. The men dragged him toward the gateway to the other part of Prague, backhanding him with their fists when he tripped or when the package threatened to slip. They were bound and determined to deliver him in tact, with the goods in hand.

Through the chaos of jostling lanterns and men's voices, the creaking sound of the big rusty gates being pushed closed, and the clanking sound of the gates being locked, he heard Evie's voice cry, "*Tate*, no!" As he was dragged away he tried to raise his voice in prayer to inspire her, but the bitter cold in his wet bones and the fear chattering his teeth had now taken from him the power of speech of which he had been so vain. God worked in mysterious ways to teach us our faults, he thought. He had been so proud of his words, and perhaps neglectful of action.

Evie ran up to the locked gates. Holding her solitary lantern in one mittened hand and clutching at a strut of one of the gates with her other mittened hand, she peered out into the dark that was the other Prague. In the receding distance, the dark silhouettes of men dragged her father away, disappearing into Prague proper. *"Tate!"* she called again but not even an echo came back. Using all of her weight and strength, she tried the big gates but they withstood her.

Evie waited until all fell silent. After awhile she could hear the muffled thud of snow hitting the ground again. The light in her lantern died out as she waited for the first brilliant streaks of dawn to cut the horizon. Then she turned around and headed home to go to work in her kitchen.

In a few hours the sun would be up. She hoped and believed that the gates would be opened as usual in the morning—as if nothing had ever happened, as if her life had not been dragged away from her in the middle of the night. She would pass through the gates as though nothing had happened. She would deliver her morning breads as she did every day. Then she would go to see her father's friend, the Magistrate, and pray for her father's release.

She felt sure that the old Rabbi Loew was being held, still alive. With his prominence both within the Jewish Quarter, and as its liaison with the larger, proper part of Prague, he was too big a catch not to be used for public spectacle.

CHAPTER SIX

EASTERN EUROPE, 1942

THE JEWISH QUARTER OF PRAGUE

Rabbi Yakov, the older Rabbi Gottesfurcht, looked around trying to peer into the night to make sure he was not being watched. He could not make out anything or anyone suspicious, but that did not mean anything in the storm. He would just have to trust. He parted the canvas that covered his wagon and slipped in the copper box that he had taken from the ancient grave of the old Rabbi Loew.

Two borrowed plow-horses waited in the wagon's harness. As much as they may have wanted to stamp and snort to warm themselves in the rain, they bid their time. They must have sensed the urgent focus of the driver or the distance they had to travel, and so conserved energy and reserved judgment. They waited ready to pull the cart down the cobbled road and into the dark verge of Krivoklat Forest just ahead, just beyond the old city. Looking ahead to the black mouth of the forest alone could have sobered them.

Rabbi Yakov hauled himself up under the canopy onto the driver's bench at the front of the wagon. He put his lantern beside him on the bench, picked up the reins, and clucked to the horses. Whatever their misgivings, they needed no encouragement, only the word, to move forward. Once the wagon slipped into the forest, he gave them a slap of the reins. The horses trotted without hesitation, the sooner to get this journey over with. Rabbi Yakov was grateful.

THE JEWISH QUARTER OF PRAGUE, THE YEAR 1589

Evie ducked her head as she made her way through the others, the *goyim* of Prague proper, toward the shop that stocked her morning breads, careful not to bump anyone with her wicker basket full of her still warm and fragrant goods. She did not dare look up for fear someone would read something in her face that would get her into trouble.

She overheard the others making pleasantries as they greeted each other.

"*Dobre jitro*, good morning," they greeted each other.

"*Jak se mate, kamarad*? How are you, friend?" they asked each other.

Evie wondered what it was like to feel so comfortable, so at home on the streets of the proper part of Prague as to be able to stop and chat.

Evie had felt the prick of sorrow so deep that morning it was a wonder, there in her kitchen, surrounded by the slumbering, snoring female kin of Yizhar, that she had been able to bake anything at all. Only the need for a pretense to get through the gates to the other part of Prague so that she could plead for her father drove her to produce her baked goods as usual. Here and there a tear had fallen into the dough as she kneaded it into its rounded shapes. Almost by itself the design rose out of each piece, guided by Evie's nimble fingers. She worked off inspiration, so it was no wonder, with her feelings being so full of despair, that her breads that morning resembled nothing so much as a crown of thorns. She had seasoned the dough with anise, a spice that reminded her of the soulful sound of a bow being drawn across a violin in a minor key, a rich cadence but not without its bitter tang. Though these breads were not for Jewish tables, she prayed her Hebrew prayers as she baked. It was the only language of prayer she knew, and she trusted in God to translate the prayers for those for whom the breads were intended. She blessed her customers and wanted her father back. God would know what to do.

This morning of all mornings, as she made her way down the busy streets, she felt the urge to peer in through the doors of the church at the corner and lay eyes on the comforting face of her favorite Jesus, the handsome one with the friendly face and outstretched hands, but she did not dare. Instead she took comfort in what she remembered of his features. Blue eyes, wavy blonde hair to his shoulders, skin white like snow. All he wore was a cloth to cover his loins, revealing a slender but sturdy build. She wondered how a Jew could be so lucky as to look so Slavic. It could happen, of course. God's only Son could look any way he wanted. And how fortunate that His features made it possible that he could speak to the Others as if He were one of their own. She imagined His voice speaking to her in soothing tones that harsh early spring morning, "Evie, be strong. You do not walk alone." She imagined His touch, a comforting hand on her shoulder in this time of her need. He was young. He was Jewish. He was loved by all. He was the perfect Man.

Evie had just about reached the shop that was the destination of her and her breads, but she was so deep in thought that the horrible happened. She bumped into someone. *"Prominte! Pardon!* Sorry!" she cried, keeping her eyes on the ground. Looking at the cobblestones all she saw were feet. She was relieved to see that no one had fallen as the result of her carelessness. It allowed her to hope that there would be no trouble, that her apology would be accepted without debate, insult, or arrest, and that she could duck down the alleyway that would take her to the back entrance of the shop. There she could unload her bread as she did every morning, accept her payment, and be on her way to see the Magistrate and find her father.

No answer to her apologies came, but no insult followed either. Evie turned, still stooped, eyes still lowered toward the ground. She meant to escape down the alleyway when she felt a hand grab her shoulder. Her heart leaped into her throat. The hand pulled on her shoulder and turned her around. She looked up into the face of the most beautiful mortal she had ever laid eyes on. She blushed and wrenched away, tripping over herself and her big basket, and dashed as best she could for the shop's back door. As she opened the door and let herself in. She glanced back over her shoulder. He was standing there at the mouth of the alley, watching her, munching a bread he had taken from her basket. The fact that his mouth was full explained his silence, the thief. She felt violated, knowing that while she was not aware, he had slipped a hand under the cloth that kept her breads warm and safe, and taken one. She felt relieved that there had not been trouble. And titillated, yes she felt titillated.

The bread thief was young, maybe her age, no more than two years younger. And he was handsome with his pale skin, blue eyes, and blonde hair. Yes, he looked like her friend Jesus, the one in the church on the corner. And she imagined that he probably had a warm comforting voice like the one in her head. And she imagined that under his coat and sweater and whatever else he wore to keep warm, he had the same strong but slender build as her favored icon. Without a flicker of guilt or remorse, he kept munching the bread that he had taken from her basket. Therefore he did not speak. Instead, he lifted her bread, now his, with a grin, saluting her. His smile flashed so broad that it shone like a thousand suns, illuminating inner recesses of her heart and soul that she had never dreamed existed. Evie blushed and darted inside.

"Evie, where have you been?" said the shop owner behind the counter, a robust, friendly woman. "I was afraid you wouldn't come." Evie set down her basket and closed the door behind her, breathing a sigh of relief, glad to be safe in the little shop that sold all manner of foodstuffs, from milk and eggs, to lamb shanks and cheeses, even the now familiar pigs' feet floating in brine. She set down her basket, and pulled back the cloth that had kept her breads warm and safe.

"But of course you are here," said the shop owner, answering her own question. "You're a good girl. You do not make the *matzoh* like your father."

Stunned, Evie clutched the hand of her basket, her knuckles turning white. She allowed the saliva to gather in her mouth. Words of anger rose up and drew toward her mouth. She decided to remain silent and swallow. Jews did not win arguments in Prague proper and she was on a mission to find her father. As she swallowed, her throat was so tight with fear that she could feel the tiny bundle of spit pass downward by pushing against the muscles braced in her neck. She blinked, and kept her gaze on her breads.

The shop owner watched Evie for her reaction, but Evie did not look up. The shop owner knew that soon her husband would return from his morning rounds. If they needed new stock or supplies, he would go negotiate for them. Then he would go to the tearoom and take his breakfast, often with an ale or two, with his pals. He never came back in a good mood. He found the little shop confining and was embarrassed that it was the source of their bread and butter. If he could he would do something big and manly, but had never figured out what that would be.

Anyway, the shop owner wanted to see Evie react and be gone before her husband returned. On top of everything else that he did not like, he did not like that she allowed a Jew in the shop. Needing to goad Evie to respond, the shop owner repeated, "You know what I mean. You do not make the *matzoh* like your father."

Evie looked up and met the eyes of the shop owner who Evie had always found to be so kind. The shop owner had always paid her in money and in compliments, as well she should have. Evie's magic breads flew off the shelves into the hands of happy customers. The shop owner felt sure that wherever Evie's breads were sold, there the trade would go. Thus, the shop owner had always been glad that Evie was a Jewess. That way the shop owner never had to worry about Evie realizing how good her work was and so negotiating for more money, or worse setting up her own shop. Evie was a second-class citizen, without rights of commerce. For that reason, she would settle for whatever she got from the shop owner.

For her part of the bargain, Evie had always assumed that the shop owner was just a generous woman who did not care that she was Jewish. But as Evie looked into the eyes of the shop owner, they both realized that Evie had just figured out that the shop owner, far from being generous, merciful, and tolerant, was just another bigot. And at that, a bigot who had figured out how to use the prejudices of her neighbors to her own financial advantage. A bigot who most often knew enough to keep her mouth shut and her biases and judgments to herself around Evie so she could use her. Evie felt shame that she had been catering to this shallow woman who had used her without apology. Evie felt shame that she had embarrassed her own faith by being such a fool.

The shop owner knew that now she had revealed her truth, she could no longer manipulate the girl. Still the truth did not change anything and the shop owner was not about to apologize for how she and the rest of the proper part of Prague felt. She raised her eyebrows, pinched her lips, and shrugged. As she did every day, though usually with Evie's help, she took Evie's fresh and fragrant breads out of the basket and laid them out for display. "They smell even more wonderful today than usual, if that is possible," said the shop owner, but Evie did not answer. Instead Evie grabbed her now empty basket and backed out the door. "Evie, your money. Here, let me pay you," said the shop owner, reaching into her till. But by the time she looked up, Evie was gone.

The shop owner stepped out into the alleyway, waving her hand full of coins in the air. "Evie!" she called, "Your money!" But Evie did not turn around. She was darting down the alleyway, her empty basket swinging on her arm;

her eyes stinging with tears, focusing on escape, and had almost reached the street.

The shop owner shrugged her shoulders and went back inside to set out Evie's richly decorated breads for sale. Evie would be back. No one understood her like the shop owner. Besides Evie would need a way to earn a living, unless she too hung from the gallows with her father.

THE TEMPLE AT ZEBRAK

Rachel collected prayer books. The fact that it was the middle of the night and a raging storm did not stop her. Instead she thanked conditions that made it a fair bet she would not be accosted by unwanted marauders. She worked by the light of a smoldering candle. A drop of rain dripped off the edge of what remained of the roof and landed in the hot tallow that floated around the candle's wick. The candle hissed.

She rummaged through the ruins of the synagogue for whole, dry texts. A wall and part of the ceiling may have been missing from the sanctuary, but the building still stood. Not if, but when, thought Rachel, the world was restored to its rightful order, so would the Temple at Zebrak be restored. The survival of the old prayer books would be a reminder and a testament to the survival, once again, of her people. Besides she could not leave the Temple. She was not ready to rest and surrender to her grief.

She reached down and pried her fingers under a thick plank of polished wood. By its feel she recognized it as part of one of the prayer benches. No doubt she had sat on it many times. She tugged hard and turned it over. Its broken edge scraped her leg. She felt along the floor under where it had been. Her fingers stumbled on the broken spine of a prayer book. She raised it and found it overall whole and dry. She touched her lips to this sacred reminder of divine providence. It was as if she could kiss God. She cradled the whole, dry, if broken, prayer book in the crook of her injured arm and rose. She made her way through the rubble and placed the broken prayer book with the others she had rescued in the safe, dry nook she had made for them.

The next book she found was not so lucky. It was splayed open against the floor. Its pages were clammy with blood and water. Where it was drying, it stuck to the floor. It tore apart as she tried to lift the spine. She decided not to disturb it and left it where it lay. Another book had fallen next to it though, and it was closed. As she wrapped her fingers around its whole spine, she heard the rhythmic splash of horse hooves. Worse, in the next moment she heard silence intermingled with rain when the hooves stopped right outside.

She deposited her newest find in the safety of her nook, blew out the candle, and tried to lift the sword with her one good arm. It was a rusted Cassock cavalry sword a boy had found in an old barn when the Jews had been herded into the ghetto of Zebrak. His father had confiscated it for the boy's safety and it had been passed from hand to hand, and finally to the Rabbi, her father. Rather than turn it in to the authorities, her father had hid it under a trapdoor in their living quarters. Rachel had once tried to question him about it. What good would a sword ever do them and why would he risk his life for this sword? He would not discuss it with her and warned her never to speak about it with anyone.

In the end, the sword had done her father neither harm nor good. She had pulled it from its hiding place that afternoon as something of her father. Even if just symbolic, she needed something that would offer her a means of fighting back against a world that had collapsed. But now, using both her good and injured arms, she lifted the blade of the sword in the air, and tried to swallow her heartbeat. She used the sting of pain in her bad arm to feed her rage.

Thunder and darkness, then lightning. The cloaked shape of a man was illuminated as it entered what had been the sanctuary where there had been a wall. The same flash of lightning also illuminated the vast form of the Castle crouched on the mountain behind him. Both seemed ready to pounce on her. The cloaked man carried a lantern. Even though the world had fallen dark again, he would see her. Rachel tightened her grip on the sword and stepped forward toward his light. "What do you want?" she said. She was not pleased by the weakened sound of her voice.

Rabbi Yakov, the older Rabbi Gottesfurcht, newly arrived from Prague, his body chilled by the cold and his soul chilled by sight of the temple at Zebrak in bloody ruins. Disaster had been foreshadowed by the hangings he had happened on in the forest, Nazis, but still men, hung as if adornments for the trees. It was as if he had entered another world, a hellish realm where all was now as evil as it had once been good.

He clutched a bundle of his good rabbinical clothes under his arm and turned his lantern on her. "Who are you?" he said and took another step closer before he saw the sword in her hands. He was surprised to hear his own voice, strong from years of *davining* prayers from morning to night, echo off the walls of the hollowed-out shell of the sanctuary.

She could not tell his age or his purpose from the sound of his voice. "The person with the sword asks the questions," she said, willing her voice stronger. She wanted to see the cloaked man's face, to ask what he was doing there. Instead, cloaking her fear, she said, "It may be a relic, but it's still sharp enough to do its work."

Rabbi Yakov tried to focus his eyes. He could not imagine what a young woman would be doing cowering in the shell of the synagogue with a sword in her hands on this stormy night. Even in the worst of times, there would be a better place to shelter. Any place would be less vulnerable to attack than a synagogue. Still he understood. If he was trying to hold onto his last shred of sanity in a time of unutterable darkness, he too would take shelter in a synagogue, any synagogue, and there hold fast, as fast as he could and God would allow. Rabbi Yakov decided to try and talk her to safety, and took a third step toward her through the rubble.

"I ask you again, what do you want?" asked Rachel, trying to tighten her grip on the sword. Her injured arm began to quiver from the effort of holding it in the air. She leaned the tip of the sword against the wall behind her to stop her arm from shaking. She hoped the cloaked man did not notice.

"I am looking for Rabbi Chaim Jecobs. This is his *shul*."

"This is my *shul*," said Rachel.

"Yours, his, or *Yahweh's*?" said Rabbi Yakov.

"It was my father's before he was murdered," she said, kicking at the rubble at her feet. "Now the *shul* is mine by descent and I will be its *rebbe*. I am Rachel Ben Jecobs, Rabbi Jecobs' daughter."

"I am sorry, *mizinke*, my dear daughter, so sorry, for the loss of your father," said Rabbi Yakov. "It is a loss for all of us. I held him dear myself." He held out his hand and ventured another step toward her. It was a mistake that caused Rachel to bristle.

"You should have been protected, you should have been safe," said Rabbi Yakov, taking still another step.

"You'll be sorrier if you don't start answering my questions!" said Rachel. "Starting with, who are you?"

"I'm Rabbi Gottesfurcht of Prague."

She allowed her sword to lower. "Rabbi Gottesfurcht?"

"The older Rabbi Gottesfurcht, I am an old man," said Rabbi Yakov.

"You're Isaac's father?" said Rachel.

"Then you know my son. He arrived here?" said Rabbi Yakov.

"I met him," said Rachel. "We all did. He was performing the wedding ceremony when the soldiers came." Now she took a step toward him. She wanted to see his face in the light cast by his lantern. She wanted to see if she would recognize Isaac there.

Now that Rachel stood in the light, he saw how very young she was. She was just his son Isaac's age. No, even younger. All the color had drained from her skin. Her hair was tangled. She was spattered with dirt and blood. "Tell me what happened," asked Rabbi Yakov.

"The groom had just broken the wine glass. Isaac told me that you always said, and so he said—"

"Enjoy it, this is the last time you'll get to put your foot down," said Rabbi Yakov, his voice breaking.

"Everyone laughed," said Rachel. "The groom grinned, the bride blushed. And in the next breath, the soldiers came, the German soldiers."

"And did this," said the older Rabbi Gottesfurcht. As he turned, he scanned the room with the light of the lantern. It was a horror, a shambles, broken and battered. Blood spattered up the walls and swirled down into the intruding rainwater, coloring it rose. Rachel stood in its midst, the sword lowered at her side, her beauty shining through her wretched state.

"They came in without firing," she said. "In that first moment, I dared to think that we might not be killed. Isaac stood up to them, and I feared for him. Then, as they dragged him away, the orders were to kill all of us. They shot my father dead. They shot everyone dead. Except Isaac, he was taken. And those they missed in the haste of their blood lust, like me."

"Maybe in God's eyes it was not a mistake," said Rabbi Yakov, looking into her eyes. Rachel's lips began to quiver. "Maybe you were spared so you can continue your father's work." She slumped back against the wall and slid to the floor. She began sobbing for the first time since the Nazis had invaded her sanctuary.

Rabbi Yakov knelt beside her and held her. At first the sobs were so violent that her body slammed against the wall. Then the sobs took up a rhythm. Then her breath began to make demands. He listened for her gasps, which slowed as the rain stopped outside. Finally, she was breathing again and her breath became almost silent. He released her.

She sniffed. He stood and pulled a handkerchief from a pocket. She accepted it, and blotted her face. She blew her nose. Outside one of the Rabbi's horses whinnied. Rabbi Yakov offered Rachel a hand. She took it and allowed him to draw her to her feet. They dropped hands and walked out of the sanctuary into the night.

Was the storm clearing or rolling in? It was all the same under these dark skies. Rabbi Yakov comforted his horses.

"Why didn't they shoot Isaac? Why did they take him?" said Rachel.

"They have mistaken his identity," said Rabbi Yakov.

"You know this?" said Rachel, turning to look at the *rebbe* and his horses. "Why have you come?"

"To trace my son's way. I've been told he is held captive in the Castle."

"Then he is dead too," said Rachel. "Tortured to the collapse of his soul, or soon worked to his death."

"No, he's alive," said Rabbi Yakov. "He is being held for a purpose. So I've been told."

"But it was a mistake that they took him," said Rachel. "You said so yourself."

"Isaac is not dead. If he was I would know it," said Rabbi Yakov, his voice trailing off. But what if he was dead, he thought. He looked up and glimpsed the pregnant moon behind the increasing cover of dark clouds. The moon was full and ripe like his anger. Isaac had told him it was wrong to try and appease the Germans. Isaac was right. The moon vanished and all was dark.

Rabbi Yakov turned back to Rachel. "Isaac is alive. And I'm going to bring him back."

She gestured toward the back of the cart. "And did you bring an army with you to help, hidden under this canvas?"

He threw back the tarp, revealing the gray mud that he had taken from the riverbank at home.

"Dirt?" she said.

"Clay, taken from the shores of the Moldavka River."

"This is your weapon to fight your way into the Gestapo stronghold?"

"Yes," he said. "Yes it is," and tucked the tarp back over his precious secret, so strange that it was hidden even when in plain view.

She shook her head. "Come back in," she sighed. "Let me see if I can make you some tea."

Heavy raindrops hit his shoulders. It felt to Rabbi Yakov as if the sky had begun to fall. "Go back inside," he said to Rachel. "I will come along soon."

Rachel shook her head from side to side. When all was lost, God had sent her a *meshuge* rabbi. God was not without a sense of humor. She would take care of this *meshuge* rabbi as she would her broken books. He would be her company in this purgatory that she was living.

She ducked back under what was left of the Temple eaves. On the threshold of the great doorway, tall enough for any man of great stature to enter without stooping, she turned back and called to Rabbi Yakov, "I know what you are thinking."

"You do? You've guessed my plan?" Rabbi Yakov allowed himself to look up into the pouring sky. "And I know what you are thinking. That I am *meshuge*."

"Crazy, yes," she said. "Like your son. Do you, like him, defy Nazi soldiers to their face?"

"No," said Rabbi Yakov. "The sad truth is, I am not that crazy. Such insanity belongs only to my son, remarkable that he is."

"But you are thinking something crazy. You do have a plan."

"Yes, I have a plan."

She raised her palms to heaven. "He has a plan." With a sigh, shaking her head again, she slipped back inside the temple.

Rabbi Yakov looked upward, raising his palms. "I have a plan."

With that pronouncement, the heavens began to pour in earnest.

The good *rebbe* offered himself to the sky for drenching, surrendering as if a prodigal returning to the fold.

TOCNIK CASTLE

Isaac looked out from his cell into the dank night. Searchlights swept the parade grounds in slow motion, illuminating the pale, angular faces of shivering prisoners trying to draw warmth from the thin blankets they had been rationed. Over the patter of rainfall, he heard a scrapping sound that would start and stop, then start again. He realized it was the sound of shackles against the cobblestones as the prisoners shifted their bodies seeking rest. He smelled a thin trail of awful smoke that he wanted to believe was curling off an aged hearth, greasy with the roasting of forest venison.

Heinrich, the aide, strode across the muddy courtyard, a telegram clutched in his hands. Some of the prisoners lifted their heads to watch the aide pass, but most, exhausted and seeking their own thoughts, ignored him. Isaac thought the aide looked strangely like a marionette puppet, his body jerking as he moved, as if strings led him forward and he had no will of his own.

Upstairs in the Castle proper, Kohl lay awake in his richly appointed room under thick quilts that captured his own warmth and returned it to him for his comfort. If that had not been enough against the cold night, a fire burned in the grate. It was a royal room, with gold threaded tapestries of hunting scenes to cover the stone walls against the cold. Against all appearances though, Kohl could not shake the sense of being the hunted, and not the hunter. Therefore he could not sleep, and was awake when the knock came on his door.

"Herr Kohl," called out Heinrich.

Kohl stood and put on a dressing gown. Despite the obvious impatience of his aide who dared to knock again, Kohl took the time to stoke the fire. He also lit the candles in the sconces on either side of the door. There would be no sense in admitting his aide into a dark room. Besides he needed to see the little weasel's face. He did not trust him. He opened the door. "*Vas ist?*"

Heinrich burst past Kohl into the room. "Herr Kohl, a telex from Berlin. Perhaps from the Fuhrer himself!"

Kohl took the telex and ripped it open. As he read it, his face darkened. "So it's come to that." The Fuhrer and his Final Solution. Well, Kohl thought, the Fuhrer was a fool.

"What, Sir? What has it come to?" said the aide.

Kohl hated the sound of the aide's voice, like a parrot. He crumpled the telex and picked up the field phone on his desk. "Strasser, get in here," he said into the phone, ignoring his aide.

"Is it a problem, Herr Colonel?" said Heinrich, watching the crumpled telex in his commanding officer's fist. If Kohl had tossed the telex aside, it would have taken every ounce of Heinrich's strength to avoid swooping down on it so he could read it himself. As it was, he had to content himself with following the telex with his eyes and trying to pry the information out of his commanding officer discreetly. Heinrich longed for the day when he was in charge. He would punish Kohl for his terse rein on information. He would teach Kohl how well he could handle important data. Why did not Kohl see how helpful he could be, if given a chance? He hated being a lackey but knew the Reich would reward

169

him for his unflinching and obedient service. He needed to be better positioned before he began stepping forward and speaking his mind.

"No, not really. Nothing that affects our assignment," said Kohl. Their assignment was to be murderous and mindless. Kohl hated that his Reich asked this of him. That he did not crack under the strain of disappointment and despair was a testament to the strength of his will and the impeccability of his training.

Strasser, head of the camp guards, entered through the open door before he stopped to salute Kohl. His large frame filled the doorway behind him. He had been on duty on the parade grounds when the Colonel had called. The long coat over his uniform dripped with rain. "Yes, *mein* Colonel?" he said.

"Don't get mud on my floor," said Kohl.

With one step, Strasser stepped back across the threshold. "Forgive me, *mein* Colonel." Men like Strasser had no problem with respecting their commanding officer. Strasser did not allow obedience to either detract from his manliness or chaff his delicate ego. Strasser saw service as part of his job.

God in heaven, Kohl hated this aide, this Heinrich. At some point Kohl knew that the two of them would part badly. Kohl would have to see to it that Heinrich got the wrong end of the stick. It would be a matter of survival.

"Strasser," said Kohl, "Alert your men and the train crew. Prisoners may need to be transferred."

"Which prisoners?" said Strasser.

"All of them eventually," said Kohl meeting Strasser's eyes. They both knew what this meant for the men outside. Strasser allowed his jaw to clench. "The new apparatus brought on the train does not consume bodies fast enough to satisfy the Reich."

"The new apparatus, you mean, the oven?" blurted Heinrich who knew that the Reich was very proud of the portable ovens. He was very excited himself to be stationed at an experimental outpost where such an oven was being tried out. Kohl and Strasser ignored him.

"Prisoners will have to be transported to the camps in order to get rid of them in the numbers ordered," said Kohl.

"I will post guards to man the device round the clock," said Strasser.

"The smell is sickening," said Kohl. "What man would do this to another man?"

Heinrich thrilled over the list of treasons by Kohl that he was beginning to accumulate in his mind. The worse he could make it look as if Kohl had behaved, the greater the reward Heinrich would be afforded for turning Kohl over to the proper authorities. The aide dared to think that he might be drawn in to Hitler's inner circle. At the very least, he would be allowed to serve tea at secret gatherings attended only by the very most elite.

"*Jawohl*," said Strasser, saluting Kohl. Strasser turned and nodded to the aide who nodded back. Strasser brushed past the aide and left. The sound of his large, heavy boots against the stone floor retreated down the hallway.

"That will be all," said Kohl to Heinrich, nodding for him to leave too.

Heinrich stopped where Strasser had stood at the threshold and turned back. Kohl leaned against the cold stone wall of his room, his eyes staring up at the ceiling, his throat vulnerable.

He thinks so little of me, Heinrich thought, contemptuous. *He knows so little of the threat I am to him. If I had a good knife, I could lunge forward and slice across his jugular, silencing him before he knew what had happened.* But the time was not right and he did not have such a knife. In fact, he had never used a knife except to cut his meat at the table.

Kohl leveled his eyes and glared at Heinrich. "What are you still doing here?"

Heinrich bristled. Though he knew better, though he knew that he should immediately turn and leave the room without taking even another breath, his compulsive nature got the best of him. "Where will they go, the prisoners?" he asked.

Kohl's nostrils flared as he slammed a fist against the wall.

Heinrich knew he had overstepped his bounds but gloated. Kohl's poor attitude toward orders from the Fuhrer certainly heralded his downfall.

Kohl gritted his teeth and looked into the fireplace. "Do you really want to know?" he said.

"I suppose next we'll be ordered to empty the towns below of the filthy Jews," said Heinrich. "I, for one, would be glad to participate in such a task."

"That task has already fallen to others," Kohl said, raising his eyes to look at Heinrich. "Only some, men able to make the march, will be sent up here as prisoners. Are you such a coward that you would relish herding women and children to their deaths?"

Heinrich bit his lip so as not to show his delight. Kohl had risen to the bait and openly questioned the orders of the Reich. Still a lot of good it would do at the moment. Heinrich wished there had been witnesses but still added this latest indiscretion to the list in his mind. He did not answer his commanding officer, and instead lowered his eyes to the floor, feigning shame at having been called a coward. Yet another act of disrespect that Kohl would someday regret. "Will that be all, Herr Kohl?" he asked.

Receiving no answer, Heinrich turned to scurry off. His thoughts were already jumping ahead to his next move to bring down Kohl and hope against hope, raise himself in Kohl's place.

Kohl, though, as if out of nowhere, placed his large hand on Heinrich's chest before he made it to the door.

Heinrich's heart leaped in his chest. He had never fooled himself that he, or many men, would be any match for Kohl in hand-to-hand combat.

To Heinrich's relief, Colonel Kohl asked a question. "Where is Herr Gemlinger?"

"They radioed one hour ago. He will be here well before dawn," said Heinrich, glad that his usefulness was already overshadowing his infraction. It would not do if he lost his life or his position with Kohl before he caused Kohl's downfall. If he lost his position, he would have to worm himself back into a position of trust with a man of at least Kohl's rank, then prove himself all over again. Only then he could make a move to forward himself by turning on his new commanding officer. If it was his life, there was his mother to consider. He was her only means of support. Better to snivel, waiting patiently for the right moment to bring down Kohl.

"Good," said Kohl. "I am growing tired of waiting for this charade. Make sure that our guest is ready to perform when he gets here."

Heinrich saluted and left the room, closing the door behind him. Kohl looked down at the telex still crushed in his fist.

"Fools," said Kohl to no one and threw the crumpled telex into the grate. The fire leaped at the paper, which became ash in a moment.

THE JEWISH QUARTER OF PRAGUE, THE YEAR 1589

Through the barred windows of the cell, the old Rabbi Loew could see the sky lightening as dawn came. *Yes*, thought the old Rabbi Loew, lying in the filthy straw of the cell where he had been thrown. *Yes, I have been vain in my words, talking here and talking there, with this person and that person, failing to penetrate the lies to the truth.* It had all been very well to be *schmoozing* with the *goyim* and philosophizing with the *yids* at *schul*, but the time had come for action, and being an *alter kocker*, an old fart, he had failed miserably. He did not move, waiting for death, which was about two days away at the end of a hangman's noose, barring a miracle.

Two other Jews shared the cell with him. Poor Yizhar, the candle maker, who was curled up in a ball in a corner, sniveling in his sleep, who had been arrested and sentenced to death first, and Gidi, the *goniff*, the last to arrive, and the only one of the three of them who actually deserved to be imprisoned.

Gidi, the *goniff*, was a thief and a good one. For years he had made a living climbing into rich people's windows. Now he was in jail for something he did not do, also caught with the body of a dead Christian child like the old Rabbi Loew and hapless Yizhar, and was going to die for it. Gidi was no saint but he did not deserve to die — none of them deserved to die. But Gidi did not weep and moan. He did not weep and

174

moan like Yizhar. He had been in plenty of situations before and knew that in a pinch, God often came through. And if not, well, Gidi had enjoyed a good long run of breaking the law, and if it was going to end like this, so be it. Gidi soon feel asleep like Yizhar with the exception that Gidi slept like a baby, enjoying his night as if it was his last.

The old Rabbi Loew could not sleep, all he could do was think. He had hoped to pass on into Eternity—*fargeyn in der eybikayt* – from an ailment known as eating one too many *afikoymens*, in other words, dying of old age, the joke being that the *afikoymen* was the last piece of matzoh eaten at the end of a Passover seder. The old Rabbi Loew had hoped to pass at least one more Seder with his daughter Evie. He was not so old that old age would kill him before that. Were Nature allowed to take its course, he was sure he had a few more Passovers in him. At the moment though, he had a pending and imminent date with the hangman's noose.

As the old Rabbi Loew tossed on the hard floor, the straw sticking him in the face and making him itch, he thought of how matzoh was white as the driven snow piling up outside. The idea that it was made with the red blood of anyone, let alone the blood of a Christian child, was belied by its white appearance. It was a white cracker made of refined flour and water—nothing more, nothing less, not even yeast. But, thought the old Rabbi Loew, a logical argument about the color of matzoh was not going to win anyone over, not anyone who was looking forward to seeing three Jews hang before church on Sunday. And once the three of them died, it would just prove the point. He could hear the *gentile* women teaching their children, "Why of course the Jews make their matzoh with the blood of good Christian babies. We hung three of them last Sunday morning for doing just that." It was as circular as a snake biting its own tail.

The old Rabbi Loew did not stir even as the afternoon sun began to climb. Still he could not come up with a solution. His stomach growled and he longed to be home to light the candles one more time for *Shabbat* and for Evie's cooking. He hoped he got to see his Evie one more time before he died. He loved her so. He did not worry about her. She would be better off without him making trouble for her. She was a resourceful girl, even if she was a girl. Maybe someone would offer to marry her, maybe out of respect for him and in his memory, and now that he was gone, she would accept, as a woman could not really live alone. He was already thinking about himself and the two others in the past tense, when he heard the raised voice of a woman. It was Evie.

He pushed himself back up on his knees, and tried to gain his footing. He wanted to shout to her to be calm, that he was okay, when the cell door swung open and Evie was thrown inside. For God's sake, didn't she have a brain in her skull? The girl was born with a *lok in kop*, a hole in her head! Now she would be hung too. She threw herself into her father's arms. He buried his head in her neck and let the tears flow.

THE TEMPLE AT ZEBRAK

The good rabbi untied his two plow-horses and led them under the willow tree under which, just days before, his son Isaac and Rachel had stood debating whether a woman could become a *rebbe*. But Rabbi Yakov could not and did not know that. All he knew was that he had to rescue his son. His heart could not tolerate the loss of Isaac. His community could not tolerate the loss of Isaac.

Lightning struck in the sky and sent a bolt of grief and fear that gripped his chest with pain. He fell back struggling for breath and leaned against the willow, looking upwards through its budding branches as the ground shook with a thunder that sounded like judgment. His mistakes crowded against him like ghosts, not the least of which seemed to be his sending his son Isaac to Zebrak in this time of murderous occupation. The lightning and the thunder he took as the spirit and voice of *Yahweh*. But he answered them. "What would you have me do, *Yahweh*, would you have me give up?"

He knew he was being tempted by the boldness of his plan, by the arrogance of his plan, by the magnitude of his plan, as Adam had been in the garden. If he were successful, it would be remarkable, he would be remarkable, but no, he would have to remember to give the glory to *Yahweh*.

The young people who stood on the threshold of adulthood at the age of Isaac and Rachel were all that stood between the Nazis and the success of their plan to wipe out the Jews. The children too young would not remember enough. The adults shackled with bitterness and grief would wilt with despair. His Isaac and this Rachel were the future. Together with others they would find, Isaac would be able to piece together the wisdom of these awful days that would save the future of the Chosen, and the world. He must rescue his Isaac. God would forgive him for his crazy plan even if it flew in the face of humility, even if it manipulated the forces of Nature and the All That Is.

All that stood between Rabbi Yakov and the wilting despair that gripped his heart was his crazy plan. It was the only thing he knew that would create a future in a time of such darkness. It was the only thing he knew to do right now, now in the time of great, interminable, intolerable, immeasurable darkness.

As if in answer, a bolt of lightning struck higher up in the forest. He saw the flash and the flame against the mountaintop, and after, heard the deafening thunder, so close. If it was an answer, he did not understand it. Maybe it was just to say, "You are taking a risk."

"Tell me, *Yahweh*," he shouted to the sky, "tell me something I do not already know!" He patted the bark of the willow tree that he leaned against. I will know soon enough, he thought to himself, and pushed himself upright. He took a deep breath of resolve and walked to his cart where it stood near the burned-out wall of the sanctuary, gaining will with each step.

Rabbi Yakov had been a strong young man. He called on the reserves that remained in his waning body. He placed a shoulder against the front of the cart and pushed it backwards through the mud. Miraculously, it moved. He pushed again.

As he worked, he wept. His tears mingled with the rain and his sweat. He was so drenched inside and out that the hard and steady rain no longer mattered.

When the cart settled against the stonework that was the remaining foundation of the sanctuary, he stopped, wiped his brow as if he could dry himself, and went back inside the Temple.

Inside the sanctuary, Rachel heard Rabbi Yakov yelling at the sky and shook her head. "Yes, *meshuge*," she thought, "but harmless." When he came back in, he stamped his feet and shook himself like a wet dog, but to no end.

"Would you like your dry clothes?" she asked.

"When we are done," he said.

178

Rabbi Yakov helped Rachel right the remaining prayer benches. She was glad for his help. "My father told me the story of the Golem when I was very young," she said. "I have told it many times to the children of the village."

"How did your father tell it?" he asked.

"In 1589 a notorious priest, Taddeush, whipped the villagers of Prague into a frenzy against the Jews. Distraught, the old Rabbi Loew prayed to heaven for a direction that would help him avert a massacre and save his people."

"Rather formal."

"My father was a serious man, Rabbi."

"Yes, but full of heart."

Rachel had to stop to wipe the tears out of her eyes.

"Are you okay?"

"I am fine," she said.

When all of the prayer benches were righted that could be righted, they laid planks from the broken benches, scorched doors, and other stray lumber that had fallen from the walls across them. In that way they created a makeshift slab, a giant operating table of sorts.

Rachel brought lit candles to surround it. She brought out more candles and lit them around it. Rabbi Yakov carried in from his cart the clay that he had brought from the banks near his beloved Prague. He carried in armfuls of the mud, cradling them to his chest and laying them gently on the table, as if each armful was a child. When Rachel had lit the last candle, she also began to carry in the clay as best she could with her injured arm. Soon she was as wet and muddy as he was. When they had moved all of the clay from the cart onto the boards, they stepped back and looked at it.

"I hope this is enough," Rabbi Yakov said. "I have no experience at this." He picked up a handful of clay and looked at it.

"Neither do I, of course," said Rachel. "What will you start with?"

"Start with?" he said. He looked at the clay in his hand and the clay on the slab. "I suppose, what, the body?" He shrugged. "Yes, good idea. Then we can make the head and limbs to match."

Rachel nodded with a smile that surprised even her, a smile, as dead as she felt inside. There was a prayer for her. She could live again.

Rabbi Yakov pushed the clay in his hand back into the larger mound. With both hands, he began patting and smoothing the huge mound. Rachel joined him, putting aside parts for the limbs and head, and within a few moments the two, the rabbi and the woman who would be a rabbi, were grunting and sweating with the effort. "He has to be big, a superman, to scare off even an armed soldier," said Rabbi Yakov.

When they had a breadth of shoulders that satisfied Rabbi Yakov, he suggested they begin work on the limbs. Rachel nodded and pulled clay to her side of the clay body. She began to build an upper arm adequate to surpass that of any man. As she worked her way down, an ample elbow and lower arm began also to emerge from the clay.

"When we become adults life becomes so serious, yes?" Rabbi Yakov shaped a second arm on the other side, glancing over at Rachel's work and mirroring it. "And sometimes life will do what it can to crush us, but the old stories that we learned as children are always there when we need them." And when they completed the arms, they began to work on

180

the legs. Neither was a sculptor and the mud was rough, but the intent emerged in the form. "Where we are vague, *Yahweh* will fill in the details," said Rabbi Yakov.

Rachel nodded her agreement and asked for more of the story. "Please," she said, "It feeds me and gives our strange actions a design. Can you imagine if people were looking in on us? 'Yes, the Nazi army has passed through the *shtetl*, but the two of them stay and play with mud.'"

"Like children."

"Like crazy people."

"Crazy with love," he said looking into her eyes, testing to see if she loved his son. She looked back at him without wavering.

"Crazy with faith," she said, again inspired by the Gottesfurcht rabbis and their trust in the greater good and the greatness of God.

"Thank you for that faith," said Rabbi Yakov. "Left alone, I might falter." Now tears welled in his eyes. "I do not know if I can live without my son."

"Continue," she said.

He obeyed, "The old Rabbi Lowe received the answer to his prayers as an order from *Yahweh*. The order appeared in Hebrew fully formed in his mind. '*Ata Bra Golem Devuk Hakhomer VeTigzar Zedim Chevel Torfe Yisroel.*' Translated it said, 'Make a Golem of clay and you will destroy the enemies of your people.'"

"Doesn't it sound too easy?" said Rachel.

"We will find out."

After the arms, they worked together to shape a head. When the rough form was there, Rachel stood back. Rabbi Yakov stood by the head and buried his thumbs into the clay where he estimated eyes would be.

"What else, Rabbi?" said Rachel. "Are we finished with the molding of the clay?" The closest act to this one that she knew was the kneading, shaping, and braiding of the dough for the *challah*, the bread for the *Shabbat*. But the *challah* was only expected to come to the table warm from the oven, to be a blessing and an offering, and to be torn apart and eaten after prayers. A *challah* was not expected to come to life, flex its strength, and change the world.

Rabbi Yakov stepped back too. Together he and Rachel surveyed the big clay body they had molded, and made such adjustments as occurred to them, putting off the inevitable test. She fussed with the fingers. He stretched the clay, lengthening the arms to extend his clay man's reach.

Rabbi Yakov returned to the story about the old Rabbi Loew, the famous rabbi of sixteenth century Prague who had overcome even the powerful priest Taddeush who sought to destroy, even exterminate, the Jewish people. "The formulas were given, but deciphering them had to be done by Rabbi Loew himself. Worse, he had to use the *Shem Hameforash* – the true name of God which only a few holy men in each generation are allowed to know."

"You will be using the true name?" said Rachel.

The older Rabbi Gottesfurcht looked up at her. "Yes," he said.

"The very name of God," said Rachel. Not God or the Lord or even *Yahweh*, but the very name, which she, an avid rabbinical student, did not even know. She wondered if her father had known it. She believed he had. She wondered if he had invoked it in his silent awareness as he died, in order to save her life.

"The power it unleashes could turn against the man who uttered it. Even for a holy man, creating life is forbidden," said Rabbi Yakov.

"It could be justified if many lives would be saved by doing so?" said Rachel. She pushed the hair back from her forehead with the back of her wrist. Other than a few places on their bodies, she and the rabbi Yakov were now coated with clay. It seeped even under her bandage, into her wounds.

"That is why I pray that my motivations are pure enough," said Rabbi Yakov.

"And if they are not?" said Rachel.

"Then we may not live through this night," said Rabbi Yakov. "Or worse. We'll know soon if we've incurred the greater Wrath."

TOCNIK CASTLE

A long black Gestapo staff car, flags of the Third Reich flying on each fender, began its ascent through slippery weather up the mountain upon which Tocnik Castle presided. A thin man with a face like a falcon, Otto Von Gemlinger, Gestapo station Chief, rode in the back seat. He looked out the window, though in the dark there was little that could be seen of the countryside. He imagined the ignorant peasants shivering in their beds who had been so easy for the Reich to overtake.

As he looked out the window, full of contempt and boredom, the rain began again. He watched the rivulets form and race each other down the glass, and laughed to himself. He was looking forward to his encounter that night at the Castle. It was promised that he would get more information from the infamous Kronski with which he could assist the Fuhrer and curry his favor. He laughed. Soon the Fuhrer would rule the world and Gemlinger planned to be right at his side.

KRIVOLAT FOREST AND THE TEMPLE AT ZEBRAK

Armed men tromped through Krivoklat Forest, weapons gripped tight in anxious hands. They did not use the road that wound through it, but instead made their way through the trees. They could ill afford even a chance encounter with Nazi soldiers. The success of their plan depended on secrecy. Branches swatted at them, roots tried to trip them, the rain had begun again, but the men had a purpose from which they would not be dissuaded.

Kronski emerged from the foliage first. He held a Mauser bolt-action rifle, lifted from a store of Nazi weapons at the cost of a guard's life and lent him by the freedom fighters. He had reached the banks of the Moldavka River. Cseba and the other men from the Catacombs were behind him. Kronski saw the willow tree and noticed the two plow-horses tethered to it. He raised his hand and Cseba and his men stopped.

"Wait here. Spread out. Make a perimeter. Stay hidden," said Kronski. Cseba nodded to his men and they moved out into position to take best advantage of the cover afforded by the foliage.

Kronski forded the River at his narrowest point, and crept up toward the Temple at Zebrak, following the wagon tracks left by the older Rabbi Gottesfurcht's cart. He came up behind the empty cart and the burned-out wall. He cocked his rifle, stepped across the threshold of ruin into the Temple, and – *schling!* – found the blade of a rusty sword held across his neck.

Kronski turned his head slowly and saw a mud-covered girl at the other end of the antique Cassock cavalry sword that her father had kept, perhaps for such a day in hell. Kronski smirked and leveled his rifle at her. "I win," he said.

"You could lose your head," Rachel said.

Rabbi Yakov, standing deep in the shadows, recognized Kronski. "Wait! Rachel, he is a friend," he said, lowering the split plank he had chosen as his weapon when he and Rachel had heard footsteps approach.

"Friends don't point rifles at each other," said Rachel, not lowering her blade.

"Just swords?" said Kronski.

"Who said I am your friend?" said Rachel.

Rabbi Yakov tossed aside his plank and stepped between Kronski and Rachel, and lowered both of their weapons with his two hands. "Rachel, this is Isaac Kronski, the man that my son was mistaken for," said the older Rabbi Gottesfurcht.

"Charmed," said Kronski. He gave Rachel a nod.

"Drop it," said Rachel.

Kronski, a grin on his lips, staring into Rachel's big, brown eyes, laid down his rifle on a bench. "I don't suppose you're much of a swordsman," he said.

"Why? Are you planning on testing me?" she said.

"What is this?" said Rabbi Yakov. "We are friends here. Are we not, Kronski?"

"Yes, of course. I am the least of your worries."

Rachel narrowed her eyes, "You admit to being a worry?" She raised the rusty sword to his throat and took the lapel of his rough coat between the index finger and thumb of her free hand. In doing so she saw a chain around his neck. "What is this, a crucifix?"

She pulled out the chain, finding a Star of David. She released the chain and lowered the sword, taking a step back.

Kronski shrugged, hooking a finger in his pants. "Check me. I am told my father did the *bris* himself."

"You don't look like a rabbi's son," she said.

"Neither do you," said Kronski, grabbing her wrist. She slapped his face, hard.

He wanted to throw her up against a wall. She was harmless but her beauty and fight stirred him. He wanted to press his loins against hers. From behind him came Rabbi Yakov's voice. "You are a rabbi's son? Where is his *shul?*"

Kronski released Rachel and turned to face Rabbi Yakov.

"His *shul* was in Poland like I told you, *Rebbe*," said Kronski.

"And what are you doing here?" said Rachel.

"I've got the men of the Prague resistance with me," said Kronski. A look of concern crossed Rachel's face. "Don't worry, they're concealed at the edge of the woods."

Rabbi Yakov pulled at his beard. So this Kronski had found his way into the Resistance and had rallied them to his cause. He was nothing if not resourceful. "You found your own way to ingratiate yourself or did you have other introductions?"

"When help is not forthcoming, I always find my own way," said Kronski, picking up his rifle.

Rabbi Yakov knew that among the men waiting for this Kronski in the woods there would be those who would be familiar to him. Besides those who were taken and those who were killed, men disappeared from the *shtetls* of Prague every day. No one asked where they went. "What is your plan?" he asked.

"We'll wait until just before dawn and then we're going to rescue the captives held at Tocnik Castle. That would include your Isaac," said Kronski, moving further into the sanctuary. He stopped before the huge candlelit form made out of clay laid out before the remnants of the ark that had held their beloved Torah. "Rabbi, what exactly are you doing here?" he asked. The rough sculpting was in the shape of a man—a big man, an eight-foot tall man. Kronski prodded it with the tip of his rifle's bayonet, "What is this?"

"A Golem," said Rachel.

"The Golem?" said Kronski. His eyes widened but he contained himself.

"A Golem," said Rabbi Yakov. "He saved us once. He can do it again."

Kronski walked around the giant clay man. When he reached the feet again, he looked up the length of the Golem to its face and laughed, "You're not much of a sculptor, *Rebbe*."

"This isn't a time for jokes," said Rachel.

Kronski ignored her. "That's your big plan, old man? A child's fairy tale to save your son?"

"How many men will die doing it your way?" said Rabbi Yakov. "And who is to say you will prevail?"

"If any man dies, they will die a hero," said Kronski.

"I don't need a hero," said Rabbi Yakov. "The ceremony calls for two other people. I need a rabbi's son, someone with rabbinical blood coursing through their heart and soul. Are you going to help me?"

"No," said Kronski. "I will not help you with this game. What I will do is rescue your son. That should be enough."

Rachel interceded between the two men. "I will help you," she said. "I have rabbinical blood enough in my veins."

"This I need to see," said Kronski.

Rabbi Yakov took the sword from Rachel, saying to her, "This Isaac, this Kronski, is reluctant. Perhaps he is afraid or fears himself lacking. But dear one, whatever else we need will be supplied by *Yahweh* Himself."

"*Yahweh* has assured that I am here. Why assume a short supply?" said Rachel.

Isaac Kronski made himself comfortable on a bench against the wall out of the way of the rain that was coming down now through the gaps in the roof. He threw his arms back behind his head, the better to watch, prepared to be entertained.

CHAPTER SEVEN

THE JEWISH QUARTER AND CITY
OF PRAGUE, THE YEAR 1589

That night Evie and Rabbi Loew spent the Sabbath,
together, with Yizhar and Gidi, the *goniff*, in the jail cell—
not exactly the last *Shabbat* that the older Rabbi Loew had
hoped for when he looked into the future at his passing from
this world. Water was substituted for wine. Stale bread was
substituted for Evie's *challah*. Only in their minds' eye could
the hapless cellmates taste Evie's golden braided loaves made
with fresh eggs and slathered with fresh churned butter.
The light of the guards' lantern served for candlelight, soon
snuffed, leaving them all in the pitch dark.

Yizhar and Gidi generously allowed Evie to *daven* or pray
with them, even though she was a woman, seeing as how
they had all been thrown together and it was their second to
the last night on earth. They *davened* until they could no more,

and one by one lay down to fall asleep, leaving only the old Rabbi Loew who called on all of his reserves, ardent to leave no stone unturned with his Maker, particularly when so close to death. Sometime after midnight, before dawn, while the old Rabbi Loew's lips and tongue continued to move in prayer but his brain slept, his heart brought forward to him this vision in a dream.

In the dream of the old Rabbi Loew, The Book of Creation, or *Sefer Yetzirah*, opened before his inward eyes and the golden characters inscribed there danced before him, as sinewy and seductive as any woman ever sprung from womb. The very secret of the Genesis of the world was revealed to him. The old Rabbi Loew was quite impressed, but not willing to settle for anything less than the answer to the pressing question on his still moving lips which was how he and the others, and other Jews after them who might be unfortunate enough to be charged with making the matzoh from the blood of *gentile* babies, could get sprung from jail and live out the Passovers allotted to them according to the natural order of things.

The golden characters of the *Sefer Yetzirah*, were only too happy to oblige. They drew together all at once, a herd of butterflies, an orbit of delight in a darkness associated with sorrow, conferred briefly, fought back the darkness before dawn that filled the cell with their dazzle, grouped and regrouped, arched as a team flying up toward the slab ceiling, soaring in a dive toward the straw floor, and came back grazing the very tip of the old Rabbi Loew's nose on the upswing, reorganizing themselves before his very eyes, inches from his face, to spell out the following phrase in Hebrew, "*Ata Bra Golem Devuk Hakhomer VeTigzar Zedim Chevel Torfe Yisroel*," which translated is, "Create a golem out of clay who will destroy all the enemies of Israel."

190

Having accomplished what they came for, the golden characters bowed to take their leave of the old Rabbi Loew. He panicked though, complaining that inadequate information had been imparted to him. The characters gathered around him and twitting like doting aunties, assured him that he would remember them and know the rest when the time came. Then at once, they vanished like the shimmering golden dust that settles on the world during a glorious dawn, and indeed it was such a dawn. The world itself was in concert with this message that had been delivered to the old Rabbi Loew who now fell sound asleep, against his will, and slept fast as a warm suckled kitten. Had his will had its way, the old Rabbi Loew would have taken a moment before rest to scratch out the magical secret words in the stone floor of his confinement so that he could study them and commit them to memory with care, but such an opportunity was not granted to him.

Still, when the old Rabbi woke up the next *Shabbat* morning, the rays of the late morning sun streaming in on his face, his concerned Evie patting the feverish sweat from his brow, he found that the characters were as clear to him as they had been the night before. "We are saved, *maydelach,*" was all he would say, with a smile on his face, trusting without knowing that somehow God would present the opportunity to make the Golem that would save his people, sometime before he, the old Rabbi Loew, would be hung by his neck until dead in less than twenty-four hours.

The old Rabbi Loew's cheerful mood, however, was not contagious and failed to reassure Evie, Yizhar, and Gidi, who observed that the old Rabbi Loew was down with a pneumonia and fever that could kill him, but for the fact that he was sure to be executed first. Evie was grateful, however, weighing her father's mood against her own dread, knowing that whatever the cause, his delirium was a blessing. It freed her up to be with her own sorrow. She tried to ask her friend Jesus for help, but instead thoughts of the young man who looked like favorite Jesus kept swimming in her head. She remembered what he had looked like, standing on the cobble stoned street of Prague proper, munching on a bun of her crown-of-thorns bread, winking at her. Yes, his magnificent blue eyes had winked at her! Her virgin limbs warmed at the thought.

To prevent herself from further distraction, she turned her attention back to *Yahweh*, thoughts of Whom sobered her up and returned her focus. She did throw in a request to God, however, that not only did she not want to die the next day in the town center, she especially did not want to die a virgin. Being on the precipice of her mortality and viewing the rocky ground below, she now realized that whatever the cost, she wanted to experience the full range of the earthly delights that He had set at her table before returning to Him and the hosts of Heaven.

The old Rabbi Loew remained confident though, despite the morbid mood of his cellmates. Every so often he even laughed out loud, a great belly laugh that echoed off the stone walls.

Sure enough, just as the Sabbath came to a close with the setting of the sun, and not a moment before, because God too needs at least one full day off from work every week, a young *gentile* woman wearing black from head to toe, slipped into the building.

Timid and weeping, she sought out the Magistrate who was busy planning the execution of not just one, but four Jews, with the added curiosity of one being a woman, the next morning. The Magistrate was obsessed with the details. A big crowd was expected and law enforcement needed to be organized and available to stand ready to enforce crowd control. It had happened before that an ill-fated prisoner had been ripped limb from limb by an over eager crowd before his hanging could get started. His panicked screams and the fierce gush of his blood as one by one his limbs were ripped from his body, like the drumsticks from a cooked goose. This had so terrified his youngest daughter, shattering her innocence, so that even now she would not attend a good hanging as a proper daughter of a Magistrate should, and hung back from him when he wanted to give her a hug. Such a gruesome event was not going to happen again on the Magistrate's watch. The hangings would be civil and humane in the great town of Prague as long as he was in office.

At that moment the Magistrate was nibbling on some cheese. He had told his wife that he would be too busy today to be home for Saturday lunch, so she had wrapped some meats and cheese in a cloth and sent a bottle of his favorite ale for his midday meal. He could not resist the temptation to snack from it as he sat at his grand desk, mapping out the procession for the next morning. He drew out routes showing which guards would take which prisoners in which order along which paths. Next he would personally test each noose for strength and function. Later he would interview the executioners one by one to make sure they were clear on protocol. It would be a busy day.

Still, the Magistrate need not have been so concerned because the young *gentile* woman, veiled and dressed down to the last stitch in black, grabbed the Magistrate's hands in both of hers and confessed that the dead baby that had been thrust into the hands of the old Rabbi Loew two nights before had, in fact, been her child who had died of the same pneumonia that had caught hold of the old Rabbi Loew, and not at the hands of a Jew seeking blood to make his Passover flatbread.

In short order, with the old Rabbi Loew out and about and vocal enough to make a stink about the whole affair, the two other young mothers of the two other dead babies were sought out and located. With a little arm-twisting, they too were able to see clear to confessing the part they had played in setting up the Jews, and using the corpses of their dead children to support their lies. Once they had confessed, they all needed to see the Priest for absolution and to arrange for their children to be interred in a second, more final burial ceremony before their little, overused bodies thawed with the oncoming Spring.

There was a great rejoicing in the Jewish Quarter. The Jews of Prague vowed to have the best Passover ever so glad was everyone to receive back into their midst the old Rabbi Loew.

Yizhar was glad just to live, and took up the habit of kissing the ground and weeping at the sight of the open skies. Yizhar's two oldest daughters were overcome to see their papa again, crying now with joy at the drop of a hat. His youngest daughter was delighted to have her *Tate* back and snuggled up against him so constantly that he could hardly walk for tripping over her. Even Yizhar's wife managed to be happy, things not being so bleak in their marriage as she had painted them. After all, they did have three lovely daughters, two of whom were now ready for suitors. It helped that Yizhar's celebrity status was greatly enhanced, and his candles sold now as soon as they could be molded, with most willing to overlook any problems with their wicks.

Gidi, the *goniff*, while tempted to slip back into the shadows, took the opportunity to make public vows that he was turning over a new leaf, finding an honest trade and seeking an honest wife. He went so far as to steal into the Magistrate's home and return the candelabra that was the favorite of the Magistrate's wife, polished and gleaming, so grateful Gidi was for his new found future. So happy was the wife, Gidi was spying on her through the window, that he thought to take up the work of a polisher, working his way from home to home removing tarnish, as he worked to take the tarnish off his soul.

Evie was glad that she returned in time to help the neighbor's cat birth her kittens. She found now that she rejoiced in the simplest things, such as the seeming return of her father's sanity. As predicted by the shop owner, on Monday morning early, she returned to the shop with a basket of new baked breads for sale as if nothing had ever happened. Neither Evie nor the shop owner found a need to say anything. Life seemed to pick up just where Evie had left off, except that she began to make plans in secret to discover what was this God-given thing called love. She poured a passion into her breads that was sensual and earthbound, such as would lure a blue-eyed bread thief.

Not everyone in Prague was happy, however, with this cheerful outcome.

Taddeush, a Czech priest who had staked his career and risen in popularity based on his willingness to take up the cause of driving the pestilent Jews out of Prague, sat alone at a table in the corner of the tearoom. He drained an ale, muttering to himself. He slammed a palm against the table, vowing not to give up, and shouted for the serving girl.

"Another," he said, not looking up at the flushed young woman who wiped her hands off on her blood stained apron. She had been butchering the carcass of an old sow, past her prime, clearing the entrails and putting aside the small bits to be chopped for pie. She ran in straight away upon hearing herself summoned by the priest. Those of the church were often generous, and why not, it was alms they were spending, not the sweat of their backs. She had not bothered to clean herself up, both so she could be quick but also because she was going back to finish her dirty work as soon as she had met Taddeush's needs.

"Will you have something to eat with that?" she said pleasantly enough, but the priest lost in thought, did not look up. Yes, he was well aware that he had floundered for a while early on in his career, having not much to distinguish himself from other, more established and more popular priests. But when he settled on the cause that was his calling, he found a natural talent at rousing the miserable who sought a scapegoat for their unhappy lives. After awhile he came to believe from the bottom of his heart that his beautiful city, the city of his ancestors, was marred by the dirty, foreign element that had been brought by the Jews two short centuries before and that they practiced dark mysteries born of Satan. Having been handed such a cause, no doubt by the Lord Himself, he was both bound and determined to never give it up.

You could never trust Jews, they were so wily, he thought. How on earth had they convinced those three poor young women to come forward — those unfortunate mothers of the three babies who the Jews had drained like mosquitoes to death for their *matzoth*? They had been mesmerized, hypnotized by forces of evil. He owed it to his country, his sovereign and the common people alike, maybe the world, to never give up.

How had those four escaped the noose less than twenty-four hours before their execution? Unheard of, irregular, wrong. Was he, humble Taddeush, alone in all of Prague the sole protector of all that was righteous and holy? Yes, that was it, the Magistrate was corrupt, and perhaps he had become possessed of the Devil!

The damned Jews were infiltrating all of society. Just that morning he had bought a bread shaped like a crucifix. It seemed sweet and beautiful, very seductive. He became ill when he found out that a Jewish girl made the bread. How could she? Was it some joke? Was there some toxic elixir that she had planted in the breads as a bitter joke against the good Christians, some potion that would poison their thoughts to favor the cause of the wayward Jew? It was good that he had vomited and so purged himself back to Grace.

It was just as he said, no matter how the Jews seemed, they could not be trusted, not even to die. They could never be trusted to tell the whole truth. They were always plotting something. How else could they rise so quickly? These thoughts and others raced through his head, borrowed from his sermons and magnified so that what had first been fabricated, now tortured him. He had been mortified when he stood at the Town Center and heard all the gushing. The old Rabbi Loew had in short order become quite a saint. A new approach was necessary, a new plan. He gnashed his teeth and thought.

Whatever his next approach would be, it would require going to authorities beyond the Magistrate. It would require going above to those who could put him in his place. And to those below who would disobey him. He lifted his eyes from his empty mug, noticing for the first time the presence of the serving girl. He saw the red blood on her apron, the fat of her cheek, the gap in her teeth. With the back of one bloody hand that still held a carving knife, she pushed a stray strand of hair off of her forehead, leaving a streak of gore across her sallow skin. Her awful affect inspired a new plan to begin unfolding in Taddeush's mind, something genuine, direct, and lusty, a purge, and a bloodletting. No more stewing in silence, or waiting for the dawdling will of God to condescend to action.

The serving girl for her part was tired of waiting. "I'll just bring the ale," she huffed, turning to leave and adding under her breath a sardonic, "Your Holiness." She did not waste herself any further, knowing better than to expect a coin for her troubles from this cleric with the pinched face and lack of manners.

Evie's two sisters and two brothers, and their husbands, wives, and children, welcomed Evie and her father, the old Rabbi Loew, back to life with an unforgettable meal cooked in their father's kitchen. While the food was amazing, miracles worked with turnips and onions stolen from their winter larders against hopes for an early spring, it was not the food alone that made the night remarkable. It was the sense of *mitzvah*, of having been snatched from death, and there being a great pull to rejoice and give back to the world to mark the miracle in the moment. For herself, Evie could not get the bread thief off of her mind. As for her father, the old Rabbi Loew, he could not get the Golem off of his mind.

After dinner, Evie sat with her sister, Leah, watching her nieces and nephews play, sipping tea and nibbling on sweet *kichel*. "So, Eve," said Leah, "If you don't mind my asking, what was it like in jail?" Evie looked at Leah, wondering what she was really asking. Her sister led such a domestic life that Evie wondered if she even detected a hint of jealousy for Evie's adventures.

"It was cold, and I longed for you," said Evie, taking her sister's hand. "*Tate* went near crazy and I wondered what it would be like to die in front of all of those *goyim*, eager to see my neck snap. I wondered if it would hurt. And do you want to know something else?"

"Yes, of course," said Leah.

"The morning before they threw me in the cell," said Evie, "I laid eyes on the most beautiful man I have ever seen."

"Evie!" said Leah, "This is such exciting news! Perhaps there is a marriage in your future! Who in the *shtetl* would not want to marry the last available daughter of the amazing Rabbi Loew?"

Evie squeezed her sister's hand and leaned in to whisper to her. "Leah, he does not live in the *shtetl*."

"A gentile!" said Leah.

"Hush," said Evie. "Not everyone needs to know."

"Such *mishigas*," said Leah. "This bread business of yours, nothing but *tsores*. Nothing but trouble! I have never been outside the *shtetl* and look how happy I am." Indeed, Leah had a son and two daughters, a doting husband with a decent business who cared for the three of them, and a humble home to call her own.

Evie grabbed Leah's hands, and made her look into her eyes. "I cannot help what is in my heart."

"More like between your legs," said Leah.

"I can't help it, can I?" said Evie, squeezing her sister's hands. "I've never felt like this before."

"So our lives are different," shrugged Leah, ready to change the subject.

"You have felt this!" said Evie. "You know exactly what I mean."

"Tshh," said Leah. She looked into her sister's eyes. "Well, maybe."

"When, and with who?" asked Evie.

"Never mind," said Leah, blushing.

Leah and Evie sat for a moment, holding hands. Evie could tell that Leah was visiting another time and place in her mind. "Tell me more, said Leah, leaning in eagerly, a girlish look on her face.

At the end of the evening, the old Rabbi Loew and Evie stood at the threshold kissing the tops of the children's heads and the cheeks of their parents goodbye. Leah left last, kissing her Evie on both cheeks and gave her a hug. "Be careful," was what she whispered in her sister's ear.

As the old Rabbi Loew and Evie stood waving and watching Leah and her brood walk away, the old Rabbi said to Evie, "Okay, now we get down to the real work."

Evie, trying to distract her father from what she knew he was thinking, said, "Yes, for my *mitzvah*, I will plant a new orchard. I will buy the seedlings with my bread, and plant them with my own hands, and those of any who want to join me, this summer. It will be free to all, *yidden* and *goyim* alike, rich or poor."

"That's for when the storms have past, Evie," said the old Rabbi Loew. "What about now?" And Evie shriveled inside knowing what her father meant.

"*Tate*, I beg you, no," said Evie.

"It is time that the Jewish people found their might in this world, that they might live free of fear," said the old Rabbi

Loew, a wild and far away look in his eye. "It will be my legacy."

"You don't know what you would be unleashing," said Evie.

"You mean what part of God? His Wrath or His Wonder, His Beneficent Bounty or His Terrible Glory?" said the old Rabbi Loew.

"Yes," said Evie, knowing he had not heard what she had said, and not wanting to hear his rap about Moses and the Plagues or David and Goliath, or any other of the plethora of stories that her father had at his command. She was tired and wanted to fall asleep in her own bed and dream about the bread thief, his wholesome face and lithe body.

"Maybe it is the will of God," said the old Rabbi Loew. "Maybe the only question is, are you in or are you out?"

Evie was, of course, in. She was not about to allow her elderly father to embark on such a *cockamamie* adventure all on his own.

This priest Taddeush was not without connections. After pulling a few strings, he managed an audience with a prominent warlord favored in the Emperor's court. His purpose was to present the plan that had dawned on him, his mood black with discontent, that morning in the alehouse.

Standing in the grandeur of the Castle hall where the Emperor gave audience, Taddeush privately scolded himself for ever doubting. Indeed, the Lord Our God was great, and smiled on his faithful. Otherwise how could as impoverished a child as he had been ever risen to become the great Taddeush from whom Emperors sought counsel, he thought, forgetting to remind himself that he, Taddeush, had manipulated circumstances to have the meeting, not the other way around.

The Emperor Ruldolf the Second himself was overall indifferent to the Catholic Counter-Reformation. This had allowed a large number of scientists, mathematicians, and intellectuals to assemble in Prague without interference from the Church. The gathered luminaries included many prominent alchemists who busied themselves with the transformation of mercury into gold and other crowd pleasing stuff and well as inquiry into the deeper matters of life and its creation.

As much because of the indifference of the royal court as anything, a flowering of Jewish culture was permitted. This flowering gave the old Rabbi Loew leave over the many years of his life to publish his many great works. The Jews also found an economic freedom that allowed Evie to find a market for her breads in even the proper quarters of Prague and gave careers to the brilliant financiers Jacob Bashevi and Mordecai Maisel who eventually paved the streets of the *shtetls* of Prague and built the High Synagogue in the Jewish quarter of Prague which stood for centuries into the future. Still the permissive state of affairs under Rudolf was not without its opponents, the priest Taddeush being one, as were other lower members of the government who were wedded to the past. And it was not as if Jews had suddenly become popular. It was more that they were ignored.

And at the very same time that Taddeush stood before the Emperor Rudolf the Second and pled his cause, the great astronomer Tycho Brache was laying out his latest diagrams of the heavens which far more fascinated and pleased Rudolf than the skinny priest in rumpled clothes that knelt before him. The voice of Taddeush was like the whining of a gnat, distracting from that to which the Emperor was drawn. He waved his hand much the same as one would dismiss an insect. Taddeush, mistaking the moment, was overjoyed.

Thus it was that without either Rudolph's consent or opposition, the warlord set upon the Jews with a renegade fury all his own, summoning up soldiers from far and wide who longed to have a little action at night and sweep the country of Jews, by death or exile, the first being preferred. Nighttime pillaging, burning, and looting of the *shtetls* became an accepted pastime until, also without Rudolf's either consent or opposition, the old Rabbi Loew and his daughter Evie completed their preparations.

It was a dark and stormy night. The heavens clashed overhead while below, the old Rabbi Loew, his two students, and his daughter Evie *davened* over the inert clay body she had shaped. At what he felt was just the right moment, the old Rabbi Loew invoked the golden letters that had made the golden words that had danced for him in his jail cell in a manner so intoxicating as to rival the dance of the seven veils of Salome, daughter of Herodias, which led to the unfortunate end of John the Baptist.

That having been done, the old Rabbi Loew looked over at his daughter, Evie. Her once long hair hung limp and dirty to her shoulders where she had sheared it off with a knife. Her mouth hung open at one side. Her eyes were rolled up in her head. An unfamiliar acrid smell hung in the air. His students were alarmed.

Meanwhile, Evie sat at the feet of God. His Room pulsated gold light and the walls wavered, dancing in and out, as if a luminous womb. The room was curtained, or rather shrouded in diaphanous veils, or she did not know what. She stumbled as she worked to stand and meet her Maker. As He reached out a great Palm to steady her, the first thing she noticed, ironically, was that he really was Indescribable. Still, through all the Hubbub of the veils, curtains, masks, and shadows that superimposed Him, were they of his Creation or ours she wondered, He gave the distinct impression One who wore an ancient Crown, lopsided against his bald pate. His Eyes were enormous. They were unblinking and penetrating in their Gaze, and closed in Meditation, both at the same time. His Cheeks were both sunken and round as apples. His Chin was at once as pinched as the Magistrate's chin when he sat in his chamber stroking it to a point, as rounded as the larded chin on Yizhar's wife, and as squared as the chin on her well chiseled blacksmith. His Lips were both thin and fat. As He worked his Tongue to speak, it loomed in the air as if an independent spirit, and his cavernous Mouth swallowed the room. Evie knew she had lost her mind and all ground of Being. Her brain seemed to drift inside her skull, afloat and useless.

His Hand reached inside her chest and spread apart her rib cage, which she realized she had held tight and locked for some time. Like a bird, her heart flew out of its cage and filled the room, which she realized was His great Heart. As did His Heart, so did the room beat and pulse because it was actually an Organ of the Almighty, pounding out Truth and Love as constant as the planets or the stars, ever and always, before, during, and after The Word that had made all from One. She gasped.

That having been said, or rather, not said at all, but instead experienced, there would have been nothing more to do or say, perfect Loving having taken the day and night, and made them its infinite Own, except that God wished to speak. "Evie?" He said.

"You know my name?" said Evie.

"You among all are known to Me. I see you when you're sleeping. I know when you're awake," He said. "I know Everything."

All Evie needed now was a question. She was with God. She could ask Anything she wanted, but for once her mind was unavailable, stewing in its own cosmic juices. She could not form either a thought or a question.

Then suddenly it all popped into focus, and her personal God, the One she had always dreamed of, popped into focus. Evie's God was comfortable and available, like her father, only He was there for her and her alone. It was ironic that He, her God, had less to do than her father, the old Rabbi Loew. He had no congregants to counsel, no Temple to run, no political concerns to address with the *minion* or the Magistrate, and nothing to study, write, or disseminate. Evie's God had no agenda at all. He was completely, wholly and always available to her and to address her concerns. She wondered why she had ever felt alone.

The more Evie sat with Him, because he drew her up a cushion and bade her rest, the more she found God to be large, comfortable, and easy in Himself. He wore a robe like a Muslim, held by a rope that He tied around his considerable Waist. Her God dressed much as she imagined Jesus did when he was a Rabbi in the Promised Land, right down to the fact that God wore sandals and his Feet were dirty as if from scuffling around in open shoes thought the marketplaces of Marrakesh. In fact, Evie thought, had the *rebbe* Jesus survived to a hearty old age, she imagined that He would have looked much like

God did, right here in front of her. No wonder her Christian customers called Jesus, the Lord. Now she got it.

But her thoughts kept coming fast and furious. What if everyone could sit with God? What would the world be like if everyone sat with God? And when they did sit with God, would they experience what she did or a mirror image of themselves? Or would they experience one of a multitude images caught in a mirror shattered—all of the fractured pieces twinkling in the snow, melting together like an Infinity of snowflakes, each refracted in a drop of rain, in the many strands of light that made up a sunbeam, the stains of pure energy that woven together made a rainbow.

It was more than she could encompass. Her head was spinning. She wondered if she could stop it long enough to allow her to be present with God. He certainly was Present with her. She was beginning to feel her meager tolerance for the Almighty waning and a growling in the pit of her stomach, a hunger for the taste of mortal food, chicken *schmaltz* spread thick on rye, the first strawberry plucked in June, an apple wrested from a tree at the time of *Succoth*. She felt like bad company, always wondering when it would be polite to go, while sitting at the table accepting tea and cakes.

Just as she was about to keel over in a dead faint, He reached out a mighty Hand and caught hers, holding her. As His Power flowed up her arm she revived. She was greatly relieved to find herself still in her body, her lungs breathing and heart beating. Secretly, as if there were secrets before God, she had been worried that she was there before Him because she was dying and it was her own personal Judgment Day. To die a virgin would have irked her throughout Eternity, she was sure of it.

A tightening began under her skirt that at first mystified her. A bolt of Power soared down through her body and then began a return run up her spine, improving her hunched over posture immediately. There being nowhere left to go in her body, she arched back, surrendering to His Other Hand which caressed her waist. The Other Hand was slow and self-assured. It slid itself over her breasts and her pleasure parts, and then even those parts made more simple, such as knees for bending, and ears cupped for hearing. She surrendered herself to Him completely, and He did not disappoint. After his Finger, she felt His Tongue reach into her middle ear and the wet of His Saliva coupled with the Chill of His Breath made her shiver with ecstasy. He Touched every cell in her body and all was Known. By the time He had ungirded His Loins, which managed to be both circumcised and uncircumcised at the same time (she made a mental note to ask Him how He did that), her legs were open and release was certain. He planted that glorious Magic and fruitful Serum from which All Life Was Created, and she knew Pleasure beyond bounds. She was unable to contain herself and shrieked with pleasure, and those shrieks having been formed, took wing out and slipped out beyond the veils. She listened as they disappeared out into the Universe, echoing and soaring for all Eternity, and sighed.

And still His Hand clutched her hand and His Other Hand clasped her waist, keeping her from falling. She would have fallen from the splendor of the Surrender she now knew, had He not held her still. She had let go and let God, and nothing would ever be the same, she was sure of it.

But she began to notice a searing pain in the palm of her hand that was still clutched in His. Biting her lip, she vowed not to complain. He had already vowed Never to let go. It was part of his Agreement with ancient Noah, the deal being sealed with a simple Handshake and a Rainbow, both of which were a walk in the park compared to what Evie was beginning to experience. She panicked when she remembered the grim Torah stories that her father was so fond of. She was no Jonah but the stories of the Torah made it clear you could never know what the Almighty might have in Mind.

In the next moment, she forgot her vow and she wished she had never been born at all because of the searing pain in her palm. She bit her lip, as she struggled to get free of God's all powerful vise-like Grip. He had not forgotten her though, and gave her a Wink and a Nod. Her terror mounted. Her teeth broke her skin and she tasted blood. Something began to form in her hand, stolen from her as the rib had been taken from Adam. All parts of her gave to the charity to which God called her. As she gave and gave, in her hand it formed, first of golden light and then of metal, she came to understand but it did not lessen the pain. From the corner of her eye, she saw the angelic *Elohim* part the veils and gather, the Hosts of Heaven being unable to contain their impish curiosity.

In Time, which seemed both Infinite and Standing Still, the metal came to be an amulet. When it was complete, it cooled. And when it was cool, God Himself began to crumble before her very eyes, as if He was an ancient ruin caught in a earthquake. He froze as the fault lines formed all over his Form, or rather, the Form selected for Evie's audience. Bits and pieces of Him began to fall away in chunks, starting with the Tip of his Nose and his left Earlobe. The pieces got smaller and smaller as more and more cracks appeared in Him, until finally He slid into Ashes which fell like snowflakes and piled up around Evie's feet.

She looked to her hand that had been held by God and found an amulet the size of her palm, a shining golden Star of David. As she watched the Hebrew word *emet* meaning *truth*, appeared, engraved in the Star by the great and now again invisible Engraver. She clasped it close, not blind to its importance, and with her other hand, she knelt down and scooped up a handful of the Ash and tucked it into her pocket.

When Evie stood again, she found that she was back in the attic of her father's home, face to face with her awestruck father and his dumbfounded students, their jaws dropped. They had witnessed the amulet appear in her hand and her revival, as she collected herself and unaided stood. They parted, finding themselves suddenly in the presence of a woman rather than a mere girl, and allowed her to step between them. She swept past them to her sculpture. Her flesh fingers entwined with its fingers still made of clay, and she raised the amulet the better to stab it deep into its chest, up and under where the ribcage would have been, where his heart would have been, had the Golem been a human. The students of the old Rabbi Loew gulped and stood back, just barely remembering to recall the secret name of God within their hearts, as the clay turned to claylike flesh and the Golem arose. The old Rabbi Loew closed his eyes and gave a prayer of thanks.

"Shalom, Golem," said Evie, greeting the guest. The Golem nodded awkward, fresh in its body. She released his hand and he blinked in wonder. He reached out and touched the blood on her lip with one of his great fingertips. He put his finger in what was his mouth, savoring her taste.

The old Rabbi Loew, praying, heard the doorknob turn. When he opened his eyes, his Evie was gone.

TOCNIK CASTLE

Isaac, the younger Rabbi Gottesfurcht, lay sleepless in his Castle cell. He too heard the rain begin again. He thought of the prisoners outside who had already been wet and shivering in the dank night air before the rain resumed.

Shouting in the courtyard brought him to his feet and to the window. The guards were getting the prisoners to their feet, lining them up, and shouting orders that he struggled to overhear. He could not make out what it was they were saying. Some prisoners could not stand. They were shot. "Drag them away," shouted the guards to the other prisoners.

Shivering, Isaac clung to the bars of his window, determined to bear witness. Though it was night, he began his morning *daven*, coming to his favorite psalm. "Give thanks to *Yahweh*, for he is good, for his loving kindness endures forever."

His knuckles turned white and tears welled in his eyes. "Give thanks to the God of gods, for his loving kindness endures forever. "

The tears began to pour, "Give thanks to the Lord of lords, for his loving kindness endures forever."

As he recited, it came to be that the refrain, "...for his loving kindness endures forever," sounded over and over, at first by him, and then without speaking. He bathed in tears until they would not come anymore. A great hand gripped his body and squeezed the breath from his chest. His fingers slipped from the bars on the cell window, and his body curled to the stone floor in a faint. He woke to a vision.

Isaac found himself in the middle of an oncoming storm. Rainwater pooled on the dirt roads of the medieval village in which he stood. The pools caught the moonlight that pierced down through churning clouds. Candlelight flickered inside the hovels that made up the village or *shtetl* where the Jewish people of Prague had then lived, centuries before Isaac's day.

He peered inside a thatch-covered home, and from the prayers intoned he realized that the Jews were celebrating the second night of *Pesach*, their Passover Seder, breaking the *matzoth* of water and flour and eating dishes symbolic of freedom from ancient slavery.

A light rain fell. The rumble of distant thunder heralded the storm that was to come.

Isaac walked on and entered the Temple, the stone-built *shul* where centuries later he would live and pray with his father, Yakov, the older Rabbi Gottesfurcht. As Isaac, marveling, walked through the Temple, he came to what he knew to be the rabbi's quarters.

From within, the old Rabbi Loew of history, the very Rabbi Loew who was said to have made the Golem, lifted his head as he made his prayers over his family's Seder dinner that celebrated the liberation of the Jews from their slavery in ancient Egypt. The familiar symbolic foods of ritual were on the table. The bitter herbs, a green onion dipped in salt water to revive memories slumbering in ancestry — the tears of the oppressed and the Red Sea that parted to liberate them. The honeyed *charoset* made of chopped apple, cinnamon, red wine, and walnuts, symbolizing the mortar used to cement the edifices ordered by the Pharoah. A roasted egg rested in a bowl. Because of its shape no one can say where an egg begins and where it ends. An egg was a new birth like the season of Spring, but it was also a symbol of mourning as eggs were the first things served to mourners after a funeral. A lentil soup boiled in the pot hung over the cooking fire.

Wind blew in through the cracks of the building. A flash of lightning lit the smooth faces of the old Rabbi Loew's family – all of his children and grandchildren. Somehow Isaac knew this Rabbi Loew as if he were himself. Isaac knew that when the old Rabbi Loew's wife had died three years before of cholera, he had asked his God, "Why not me?" And Isaac knew that since that time, the old Rabbi Loew had yet made himself useful, both to his family and to his congregation, and that many miracles, large and small, had unfolded within the Jewish Quarter. And Isaac knew that the old Rabbi Loew was glad he was alive now with his family, to eat at least one more *afikoymen*, the last *matzoh* at each Passover Seder.

"Rabbi Loew, why is there lightning?" asked one of his young grandsons. The boy was sure to become a rabbi, thought the old Rabbi Loew. He asked questions from when he woke up in the morning until he fell asleep at night.

"To dispel darkness and give us courage. When it is light outside, isn't it easier to be brave?" answered the old Rabbi.

"Yes, *Rebbe* Loew."

"Yes, during the day there are less monsters under the bed," said an older sister of the questioning boy. The boy blushed and looked down at his empty plate.

"Yes, the only real monsters are the monsters outside," said a cousin, a boy whose beard was just coming in.

"We don't call them monsters," said the old Rabbi Loew. "We call them mysteries. We puzzle the mysteries until they are solved, until peace befalls the world and the birds are free to sing."

The old Rabbi Loew lifted his hands and began to sing with the children, the Adir Hu. "Mighty is He, mighty is He! May He soon rebuild his House. Speedily, speedily, and in our days, soon. God, rebuild! God rebuild! Rebuild your House soon!"

A roll of thunder came, this time mingled with the sound of horses' hooves pounding muddy thoroughfares. No one in the medieval village owned more than a mule. The sound of horses meant strangers.

But the old Rabbi Loew sang on with the children, now clapping his hands, "Distinguished is He! Great is He! Exalted is He! Glorious is He! Faithful is He! Faultless is He! Righteous is He! Pure is He! Unique is He! Powerful is He! Wise is He!" intertwined with the chorus, reminding God not to forget to resurrect his great Home on earth.

"King is He! Awesome is He! Sublime is He. All-powerful is He. Redeemer is He! All-righteous is He! Holy is He! Compassionate is He! Almighty is He! Omnipotent is He!" The song ended with a shout from all gathered around the old Rabbi Loew, "Rebuild your House soon!"

The shout of the children was answered by the greatest roll of thunder yet that evening, that Pesach.

"The thunder warns those who live by provoking fear that when the time comes, they will be judged by *Yahweh*," said the old Rabbi Loew. And in his mind and heart he sent up a prayer asking that the horses and their riders pass by on their way to somewhere more important than his lowly *shtetl*, adding, as always, that he be reunited with his daughter, Evie. Send her home this night, Oh Lord, he thought. Send her home safely, he added.

Lightning flashed, more thunder followed. The storm was getting closer. The galloping became louder. His youngest granddaughter, another curious one who loved both questions and their answers, tucked herself against his side. He gave her shoulder a squeeze, then knelt to speak with her, holding her smooth tiny hands in his wrinkled rough ones. "Are you afraid, *kinderlakh*?" he said. She nodded her head. "Fear has no shape or purpose, except to distract us from faith." He never hesitated to speak as an adult to children. Better that the children caught up with the words than a chance for wisdom be lost. From a little child, his Evie had been wise beyond her years.

The old Rabbi Loew believed in words. He knew with all his heart that words had magic and power that, if diminished, robbed the world and made it flat. The ancient texts attested to their magic and power. In the beginning was the Word. On the fifth day of Creation, we were but Mud. But on the sixth day, God shaped the clay into His own image. He breathed a Word into His clay, and so God created Man. Words had spoken faith into existence every day of the old Rabbi's life. Prayer preceded every action in the *shtetl*. He knew that there were ways to call the earth that were so sacred that it had to stir, so ancient that they preceded even time.

The old Rabbi Loew kissed his youngest granddaughter's forehead and stood up. She hung by his side, clinging to a corner of his jacket with her small fist. But at the next peal of thunder, she ran back to her mother, Leah, the old Rabbi Loew's other daughter. The beauty of the two of them, illuminating by the following flash of lightning, their arms wrapped around each other, near broke his heart. There was beauty in simplicity, just as there was beauty in wisdom.

"There is Nothing to be afraid of," said the old Rabbi Loew. "God holds us in the very palm of His Great Hands. His angelic minions are ever at our beck and call." Evie, had she been there, would have corrected him, saying that not only did God hold our hands in His, that we held His Hands in ours. She would have said that there was Everything to be afraid of, Everything to tremble before, and that only in so trembling would That Everything dissolve into Nothing, and would Fear, that pitiful facsimile of living, dissolve into Love. That was what she would have said, but she was not there. She was not there to protest on this sacred night. He prayed again for their reunion.

The old Rabbi Loew turned back to the Passover table. Intoning the *Pesach* prayer, he dipped the green onions on the Seder plate twice in a small bowl of salted water signifying the tears of oppression. It reminded him of the tears he still cried for his wife. She had been so beautiful he had wept under the *chupah* when they married. He had become swept up in their life together, the love in their happy bed and happy home full of children, then grandchildren. It had lent so much passion to his work. Now he knew only dust in his mouth where her kisses had once fallen. He took this experience as another lesson from God, but that did not make it any easier. As a young man he had prayed for a life like his, a life that was full and stretched out into a ripe old age. But with such a life, loss and pain were inevitable. Isaac was overcome with sorrow.

More thunder, a flash of lightning, still more thunder. Horses snorted, their hooves churning the earth outside. Any children dozing in their parents' lap startled awake. The men jumped to their feet. The galloping had stopped. The old Rabbi Loew slapped his palms on the table. "A *beyze mehume*, an evil riot," he said. "Everyone must hide."

A neighboring village had been wiped out by a riot of soldiers the night before. The old Rabbi Loew knew because an escaping Jew, a man bereft of home and family, had taken refuge in the early hours of that morning in the Temple. The man had told the old Rabbi Loew this story of his escape while the Rabbi made him a cup of tea. When the soldiers had come, the man had run out into the night to try and save his home, family, and village by putting out the flames lit by the soldiers' torches with mud scraped up from the ground. As it turned out, the man was overlooked by the marauders while his children were slain. It seemed to the man that in leaving him alive, he had been overlooked by God. The old Rabbi Loew handed the man a hot cup of tea and intended to console him, and correct him in his misapprehension of God. But after attempting to hold a cup of tea with his trembling hands, the man had thrown the cup down. It had shattered where it fell and he stumbled back out into the woods, mad with grief, to look for his dead children.

Even with the news of ever approaching horrors, the old Rabbi Loew had decided that the *shtetl* would continue to celebrate their Passover as always. Maybe the soldiers would pass by their village. But if they chose to come, there would be no running from the will of God.

The people of the *shtetls* lived peaceful lives, preferring to live without weapons. Jews without weapons were tolerated. And though they were weaponless, if the soldiers chose to come, there would be no running from the will of God.

Besides, there was nowhere to go. Starvation and cold made the forest uninhabitable. The very young were the future of the people. So if they were weaponless and the soldiers chose to come, they would stand their ground. And because there could be no running from the will of God, the old Rabbi Loew had made his preparations.

Inside the Temple, the old Rabbi Loew bolted the doors and his family members dove into hiding. Outside the Temple, the soldiers on horseback lit the thatch atop the hovels of the Jews with their torches. The slogans of hatred shouted by the soldiers mingled with the protests of men and the cries of women and children. Flames and damp smoke rose into the dank sky.

Finding the doors to the Temple barricaded the soldiers were not stopped. Amidst shouting and orders, and pounding on the door with their huge, strong fists, some soldiers sent off found and returned with the trunk of a fallen tree. The sound of the soldiers running back and forward, pounding the tree trunk against the doors again and again echoed inside the Temple, was eclipsed only by the clap of thunder and burst of lightning that followed right on its heels. A heavy rain began to fall, hissing against the flames but not extinguishing them.

"Rabbi, will we die?" asked the old Rabbi's grandson, as the old Rabbi Loew helped him into a cupboard.

"Whether we die is the will of *Yahweh*, not our will or even the will of the soldiers," said the old Rabbi Loew to his grandson. The front doors to the Temple broke down behind him. The old Rabbi Loew turned to face two armed horsemen, bristling with weapons, standing in the sanctuary, looking at him.

Outside, their Captain shouted to his men, "Bring out the murderer!" The horsemen grabbed the old Rabbi Loew and dragged him outside before a horrified crowd and the Captain, an armed warrior who seemed a giant sitting up in his saddle, his overheated breath and that of his horse becoming steam in the chill, wet air.

"What do you want of us?" said the old Rabbi Loew. He and his daughter had once escaped the polite society of the public noose, but he knew that unaided, he could not escape the wicked unleashed rage of this dark and stormy night.

"Judah Ben Bezalel! You must pay for your crimes!" answered the Captain.

The old Rabbi Loew, son of Bezalel, looked at his people, huddled against cold and fear. The skies poured rain. If he died that night, at least he wanted to die with courage and defiance in his heart. If they all died that night, at least they could die with courage and defiance in their hearts. Because there was no running from the will of God, and because to die with courage and defiance in the face of evil was the best way to die, he straightened himself up as best he could while held tight in the soldiers' grasp. "What crimes?" he said, looking the Captain in the eyes.

"Murder," said the Captain.

"I haven't killed anyone," said the old Rabbi Loew.

"Then you dare deny you use the blood of Christian children in your unholy rituals?"

"We spill no blood for the Seder. We are a people of peace."

"Silence!" shouted the Captain. "This isn't a debate." Other soldiers gathered, their horses snorting and stomping, encircling the crowd, pushing the villagers even closer together. The embers of the burning village snapped and hissed in the falling rain. The flames still grew higher. The soldiers held the old Rabbi Loew in a grip unnecessarily tight.

"If you leave now in peace we promise not to follow," said the old Rabbi Loew.

"Are you threatening me?" said the Captain, with a snort of laughter.

"Of course not," said the old Rabbi Loew. "All we ask is that we be allowed to live out our lives in peace assured of safety in our miserable *shtetls.*"

"Are you mocking me?" said the Captain.

"I wish I were, but I am not so wise as to be a fool," said the old Rabbi Loew.

The Captain dismounted and stood before the old Rabbi Loew. "We know the truth about you," said the Captain, spitting his words into the old Rabbi's face. "You whimper as if weak and spawn evil in your secret hours."

"All of this?" said the old Rabbi Loew. "And you have come just for me? Do you think this old body has such super-human strength to resist?" The Captain drew his saber. "Do what you want with me, just spare the rest. I will be your murderer if you like!"

"I will slay you whether you agree or not, whether you confess or not," said the Captain. "We know about your lies."

"Judah, no!" cried a woman in the crowd. The Captain, laughing, turned and threatened her with the saber. She gasped and drew back against the flanks of a horse, its nostrils flaring.

The Captain turned again to the old Rabbi Loew. "Kneel," he said.

"We bow for no one," said the old Rabbi Loew. He cleared his old throat and began to chant the *Ha-Gomel*.

The Captain nodded. The soldiers holding the old Rabbi Loew bent him to the ground. The old Rabbi Loew twisted his head to the side and struggled, shouting the Hebrew prayer known as the *Ha-Gomel* so it echoed to the outskirts of the *shtetl*.

"Blessed are You, Oh Lord, Our God, King of the Universe, who bestows good things on the unworthy and has bestowed on me every goodness!" chanted out the old Rabbi Loew. Rather than being dampened by the rain, his voice carried, reaching the far edges of the *shtetl* and into the nearby woods, causing a stirring.

The *Ha-Gomel* was a prayer of thanks to be said when saved from disaster. The Captain and his men did not know it but the use of this prayer at this time was unusual and even inappropriate. Any Jew who survived the night would say the *Ha-Gomel*, wracked with both gratitude and grief. At the moment, though, the disaster was in progress. The outcome was not established. It was not the right time to say the *Ha-Gomel*.

As awful the moment, the gathered Jews paused in their anxiety to wonder what was going through the old Rabbi Loew's mind. Tomorrow the survivors, if there were any survivors, would make this prayer. But tonight? In the middle of this? There was no explanation but the old Rabbi's perfect faith allowed him to surrender with gratitude to the great will of God even in that awful moment for those who would not perish, for those who would be saved. Otherwise, the intoning of the prayer now made no sense.

The old Rabbi Loew raised his voice even louder, urgent that he be heard. The other Jews who dared joined him, until all the Jews chanted the *Ha-Gomel*, understanding now from the old Rabbi Loew that whatever befell, there would be survivors, their faith awakened, even in the midst of perilous cold fear.

The Captain did not even know Hebrew but chuckled at what seemed to be a feeble effort to invoke divine intervention. "God is not on your side," the Captain said, placing the tip of his saber at the old Rabbi's neck.

The old Rabbi Loew looked up, locking eyes with the Captain. The Captain met and held the old Rabbi's gaze. The Captain tensed for the kill and raised his saber. But as he began to lower the blade, an unnatural chill, having nothing to do with the cold for he wore the finest coat of hide and fur, froze him inside and out. He found himself engulfed in a shadow blacker than the night.

Looking up, the Captain saw that the shadow fell on the wall in front of him, in form like a man. The shadow, cast by someone or something standing behind him, danced eerily in the unsteady light of the flames that rose from the burning homes behind him. But whoever or whatever cast the shadow did not dance but rather moved toward him slowly without hesitation. As the form approached, the shadow grew upward, vanishing only in the bursts of illumination caused by flashes of lightning above, but ever reappearing.

The old Rabbi Loew prayed on, intoning the *Ha-Gomel* louder and louder, starting again when it reached the end, drawing forth the guest. The Captain would have ordered him silenced, but his men were all agape. Many had dropped their weapons. The Captain resisted turning around. He could not show his fear to whoever cast the shadow. But as he watched the faces of his men, he began to wonder if what they were gazing on was even human.

As a child he had heard the dark stories of his medieval era, stories of grim retribution for simple human error. In that first moment, as the tables turned, he wondered about the stories the Jews might tell one another, perhaps tales of monstrous retribution against those who would attempt to slack their thirst for the blood of newborn babies. He wondered whether the Jews might have a Protector, if not from Heaven, then from Hell.

But as the second moment came on the heels of the first, he wished that he had not been responsible for the slaughter of so many. He confessed to himself that somewhere inside of himself he suspected, even knew, that the Jews were innocent of the slaughter of babies for their *matzoh*, knowing that he had justified his wrongdoing only because his murderous work had provided for the support of his family in uncertain times. He wished within himself for a merciful God. Within himself, he threw himself on God's mercy. He wrung the sorrow from his soul, and listened to the fear that swelled his heart up against his ribs so that it throbbed against bone.

And in the third moment, the moment of his surrender to his fate, he waited until the shadow was dead upon him and he could delay no more. He wheeled around to face whoever or whatever had cast that magnificent shadow, and discovered that it resembled a man only in form. In the darkness that followed, the ground shook with thunder.

TOCNIK CASTLE

Isaac woke from where he lay on the stone floor of his cell in Tocnik. Two guards towered over him. They grabbed him beneath each arm and without ceremony or explanation, they dragged him down the hall and threw him into an interrogation room.

From the floor where he fell, he saw a tooth, its root stained dark with dried blood. The windowless room had a smell of pain and fear. In the tradition of his ancestors, rather than kneeling, he stood and prayed, swaying as he *davened* on his feet, for all of the prisoners, including him.

In his mind he sensed the black night calling in dark and shifting clouds. In his heart and from his lips, he *davened* his favorite psalm. "…Give thanks to Him who by understanding made the heavens, for his loving kindness endures forever. To Him who spread out the earth above the waters, for his loving kindness endures forever." In his mind he sensed the moon and the stars, and even the sun that every day made its return. "To Him who made the great lights, for his loving kindness endures forever. The sun to rule by day, for his loving kindness endures forever. The moon and stars to rule by night, for his loving kindness endures forever..."

No particular outcome was assured, he reminded himself, overriding both the obscene hope and the more rational fear that rose from within.

KRIVOLAT FOREST

Cseba and the other resistance fighters squatted in the brush at the edge of Krivolat Forest, gripping their rifles in their hands. Raindrops struck the leaves and ran in rivulets. The plow-horses at the willow tree stomped nervously. Aaron, the youngest of the fighters, still a boy by rights, gripped his rifle the tightest. He was hunkered down alone, gazing up through the trees at the Castle. Iphraim, the explosives expert, approached Cseba.

"Cseba, what are you carrying?" he said.

"I have an apple and a hunk of cheese," Cseba said.

"Give me a piece of cheese." Cseba broke off a piece from the cheese and gave it to Iphraim, who then handed it to Aaron, who accepted it gratefully. Cseba handed Iphraim another piece and took one for himself.

"What are we waiting for?" asked Iphraim.

"Kronski. This is his operation," said Cseba. "He wanted to stop at the Temple." Cseba shrugged. He took a bite of his apple and handed it to the man next to him. The men passed the apple around, each taking a bite. Other men took out the small stores of food they had brought, a handful of walnuts, a dried piece of meat, a corner of bread, and shared with the others. "I don't know what his business is but we'll give him a moment. Perhaps he draws courage from worship. For me, I find *Yahweh* everywhere, and nowhere at all. I don't need a temple, not in this mess of a world."

The apple reached Cseba again. He took the last bite, broke the core in half, and threw it to the plow-horses. He wondered where the farmer was that owned them. The Nazis did not bother with plow-horses. Their vanity was for stallions.

THE TEMPLE AT ZEBRAK

Rachel poured water from a pitcher into a basin, splashed water on her face, and washed her hands until they were clean again. When she was passable, she returned to the temple sanctuary where she helped Rabbi Yakov, the older Rabbi Gottesfurcht, who had bathed in the icy river as best he could, put on the good rabbinical garments that he had brought with him from Prague.

Kronski tended to his rifle. "You're wasting your time, *Rebbe*," he said.

With Rachel's help, Rabbi Yakov shrugged on his black coat. In what seemed like another lifetime, his wife had sewn it for him to wear on special occasions when he performed his sacred duties at *shul*. Rabbi Yakov tenderly unwrapped his best *tallis* and Rachel helped him drape it over his shoulders.

"Have a little faith," said Rachel to Kronski, helping Rabbi Yakov smooth down his hair before he put on his best *yarmulke*.

"I've had faith in God. Tonight I'm putting my faith in my 7.9x57 millimeter cartridge," said Kronski.

Rachel turned to Kronski and watched as he polished his rifle. The barrel gleamed in the candlelight. "You are deluded then," she said.

"Everyone I've known and loved has been killed," said Kronski.

"And this is how you choose to remember them?" said Rachel.

"I've seen what faith can do. And I've seen what our enemies can do," said Kronski.

"Now you will be reminded of what our God can do," said Rabbi Yakov. Kronski and Rachel turned to see Rabbi Yakov, standing at the head of the cold wet sculpture of the Golem, looking down at the creature created by himself and Rachel for this occasion.

"We need four elements – fire, water, air, and earth," said Rabbi Yakov. He looked at Rachel. "You, Rachel, are water. Your love of your father flows from you."

Rabbi Yakov turned to Kronski. "You are my fire – you burn with hatred for your enemies."

Kronski looked away and shifted on his feet. He had faced many men but this *rebbe* made him uncomfortable. What if this *rebbe* could do what he set out to do, here in the middle of nowhere, with not much more than awkwardly shaped river mud? Neither the *rebbe* nor the girl were artists. "You may have my fire. I'm going outside to check on the men."

Rabbi Yakov nodded and Kronski left.

"It is better this way, no?" Rabbi Yakov asked Rachel.

Rachel nodded.

Rabbi Yakov spread his arms wide. "I am the air, for with my breath I say the words that will bring life." He turned upward and looked through the burned out roof into the night sky and the stars shining as the clouds parted. Raindrops splashed on the face of the man of clay and ran like tears down the cheeks that Rachel had formed. "And here is the Golem. Facing Heaven, made of Earth."

225

Rachel watched as Rabbi Yakov drew out the copper box that he had taken from Rabbi Loew's grave. "And with this star..." he said as he opened the box and pulled out an ancient sculpture of the Star of David, a palm's width across, molded from a metal that shined like gold, engraved with the Hebrew word, *emet*. "...not from the sky, but from faith and truth, is the circle completed," He leaned over the Golem and pressed the Star into the center of its chest. He stood again and said, "Rachel, follow me."

Outside, Kronski avoided the men and found a place on the embankment overlooking the river where he felt obscured. He threw stones at the water, the plunking sound lost in the rain. He took his knife out and carved aimlessly into the bark of a tree. An owl landed in a branch above him, the blood dripping from the squealing rabbit that it carried. He watched the owl crack the limbs and rip the flesh of its prey. But he remained bored and annoyed even though he was not with Rachel and the older Rabbi Gottesfurcht. Their lunacy was sandpaper on his soul. And why should an old man have the attentions of such a beautiful woman? Futile and foolish, both of them. Looking up at the moon, he sighed. He checked his watch, a long ago gift from his father. It was time to go back. To arrive at Tocnik Castle at the right moment was essential to the success of his mission with the men of the Prague resistance, and the time to leave and continue up the mountain was drawing close.

Back outside the temple, or rather, temple ruins, he rolled his head to stretch the kinks from his neck, and biting his cheek to keep from guffawing, entered.

Rabbi Yakov and Rachel were walking around the gigantic clay sculpture. From right to left seven times, they had walked around the gigantic body, as the Rabbi Yakov intoned, "Lord God, King of the Universe, forgive us now as we invoke the Name that which must not be spoken in the name of that which is right and that which is just..."

Kronski leaned against a wall and pared his nails. His impulse was to throw the old rabbi against the wall, smash the foolish clay sculpture, and take the girl and teach her the rough lovemaking that was his style. But the old rabbi and the girl were almost done.

He would politely say his goodbyes and lead the men of the resistance away.

He knew the anger in his soul was not healthy, that it was eating him alive, but it also gave him drive to accomplish a lot, in the real world, not the world of fantasy the rabbis lived in. He did not know what to do about it, other than to do what he did, and revel in the power that his larger-than-life drives gave him.

TOCNIK CASTLE

Overhead angry clouds boiled, building in intensity, moving faster and faster. Thunder broke closer and closer, and lightning flashed, striking the ground near the Tocnik Castle.

The black Gestapo staff car approached as a line of prisoners shuffled down the mountain. The car slowed and the rear window rolled down. Gemlinger watched the weary prisoners as they passed at the side of the road. He smiled. "*Fahren Sie An,*" he said to himself, nodding. He rolled up the window as the car continued up the mountain and pulled into the entry of the Castle.

Inside the Castle, Isaac, the younger Rabbi Gottesfurcht, was surprised by the appearance of a table and chairs. A servant laid a tablecloth. Teacups on saucers, sugar, and cream were brought, along with cakes, meats and cheeses. This was not standard in the interrogation room. He was sure of that. He could not remember when he had eaten and drunk last. While tempting, the baroque grandeur of the provisions lain out on the rich tablecloth made his stomach turn. He also wondered whether, if he took a piece of bread, he would pay with his life.

THE TEMPLE AT ZEBRAK AND KRIVOLAT FOREST

When Yakov, the older Rabbi Gottesfurcht, had finished intoning the sacred words, when he and Rachel had finished circling the clay body that was intended to become the Golem, nothing happened. He was not struck dead by the heavens, nor did any life stir in the mass of clay on the slab. He, Rachel, and Kronski stepped in closer.

"Nothing," said Rachel.

"What were you expecting?" said Kronski.

Rabbi Yakov stared at the lifeless hulk. "I don't know, I..." he started.

"A miracle? Is that what you wanted?" said Kronski. "The time of miracles is dead, old man." He patted his rifle. "This is the way we are going to free the prisoners. This is the way we are going to free your Isaac."

"Have you abandoned the religion of your fathers?" said Rachel.

"Abandon is such a strong word. Though not being Jewish seems like a good idea right now," said Kronski. "Perhaps you should take a vacation from it. As if we could."

228

"Are you trying to provoke us? Because this is neither entertaining or funny," said Rachel.

"I don't find any of this funny, Rachel," said Kronski. He grabbed her wrists and pulled her close. She could feel the sweaty warmth of his breath on her ear. "I could help you cross borders. You could be safe," he said.

She pulled away from him.

Rabbi Yakov stepped between Rachel and the freedom fighter. Conflict rose in him. This Kronski was so steeped in cynicism that Rabbi Yakov's instincts rebelled against him. But maybe Kronski was right, and maybe he was their only hope. Still Rachel needed to make her own choices. Let everyone choose what they did, the will of *Yahweh* would prevail.

Kronski, looked from one to the other and shook his head. He knew a lost cause when he saw one — that was a specialty of his. He looked up through the open ceiling of the ruined building, checking again the position of the moon. "It is late, I need to go," he said. And he did.

Kronksi passed the willow tree and two plow-horses, and met Cseba and his men at the edge of the Krivolat Forest. The men stood as he approached, stomping their feet against the cold. Cseba stood his ground, both feet planted, an eyebrow raised. "What was going on in there?" said Cseba.

"Nothing," said Kronski. "Nothing but sorrow." The steady dripping of the rain was getting on his nerves. Even when it was not pouring from the sky, it fell from the leaves that had caught it. Rain had never bothered him before. "Let's go," he said.

Cseba studied the annoyance in Kronski's face. He wanted to ask more questions of Kronski but more, he wanted to move. When he was moving, if he was moving fast and hard enough, he did not have to wrestle with his nerve.

Cseba looked to his men, and nodded. The men shouldered their weapons and blended back into the woods, making their way up toward Tocnik Castle. As they trudged upward, through the filter of the trees they could see the Rail Depot on the mountain. The first of the prisoners arriving on foot from the Castle grounds were being herded onto a railcar normally reserved for cattle.

Rabbi Yakov stood over the motionless heap of clay shaped like a huge man. He shook his head and sighed.

"It was beautiful, surely Yahweh heard," Rachel said.

Rabbi Yakov raised his hands and studied the clay that had worked into their crevices and under his fingernails, searching for his answer. While his son was in danger and there were dead to be buried, he had indulged himself in a child's project, playing with river mud, a waste of time. That Kronski, awful in his bleak aspect, was right.

Rachel looked at her own muddied hands. In the vacuum left by the loud and aggressive Kronski, a morbid silence had overtaken the Temple. The drip of rainwater into the puddles in the Temple through the opened roof was rhythmic and dismal. She felt her unfinished grief for her father rise in her throat and call as if from a distant shore. She longed to drown herself in a lagoon of sorrow. She searched for something to say to the older Rabbi but came up empty. "You tried," she said. The words sank into him like a knife.

She turned away and sank to her knees, burying her face in her hands, not caring that the mud on her hands was working into her hair. She tried to sob but the tears would not come. Her body convulsed trying to release the pain that she knew would never her leave her again. For the rest of her life, she would mourn the loss of her father.

A burned part of the roof, now water-logged, fell, crashing behind them. In her mind's eye, Rachel saw the temple that her father had labored to build falling cinder, brick and board, until there was nothing but ruins. "There was the Temple at Zebrak, built by the Jews," the local *goyim* would say and spit on the spot. A secret few would pass the site with sadness in their hearts but would not dare to speak their minds. Now her tears came, harder and harder, and her body shook as the droplets of water that fell from her eyes mingled with the rain that fell in from above.

Rabbi Yakov also heard the crashing but did not turn around. He stood over his clay project, shaking his head and weeping for his lost son, and the others, so many others. He raised a fist and drove it into the side of the man-shaped mud.

TOCKNIK CASTLE

Kohl was waiting on the steps when the black Gestapo staff car glided to a halt in front of him. Gemlinger climbed out and surveyed the Castle. Behind him, prisoners still lined up to march down to the Rail Depot. Kohl came down the steps, saluting. "Herr Gemlinger. It is an honor. I trust your journey from Aschaffenburg --"

Gemlinger interrupted him. "-- was tiresome. One million people in Lower Franconia, with only one Gestapo office for the entire region."

A prisoner collapsed disrupting the march. Gemlinger watched with interest as a guard took the prisoner aside, shot him, and shoved his body off the edge of the mountain with the heel of his shoe.

Gemlinger turned back and let his attention fall on Kohl. Kohl felt the pierce of Gemlinger's look. When Gemlinger looked away over the valley below, Kohl was left with a cold feeling in his heart. Kohl found it comforting that he could still be so chilled. It meant that he must still have a soul.

"I will be frank, Colonel, your psychic guest is my ticket to Berlin. Where is he?" said Gemlinger.

"We have gone to no end of trouble making sure that he would be here for you," said Kohl. He knew that it never hurt to let his superiors know that he had taken pains on their behalf. Often they assumed, sometimes correctly, that being in the field in occupied territory was no more than an excuse for going on a never-ending drunk.

THE TEMPLE AT ZEBRAK

Rabbi Yakov turned away from the heap of man-shaped clay and toward Rachel where she knelt. He waited until she had wrung out all her tears. Time meant nothing now to him. He had proved his obsolescence. When her back stopped quaking, he put a hand out onto her shoulder. She wiped her tears away from her reddened eyes with the back of her sleeve. She looked down at her sleeve and saw the mud there.

She stood, threw her head back and laughed, allowing the now pouring rain to wash through where there once was a ceiling and cleanse her face. She whirled, giggling at the sensation of the cold fresh water on her raw cheeks. It was eerie but the older Rabbi had seen it before, the extreme of emotions brought on by unthinkable, unbearable loss.

As the rain ebbed, she stepped back under the roof that still stood and shook her head, sloughing off the rain as would a wet dog. She made the action unthinkably, unbearably beautiful. His son must have fallen for her, perhaps in an instant. It was no consolation to imagine the meeting of these two young people and how they had felt — it only exasperated his sense of loss.

"May God spare you any part of the consequences of my foolishness," he said.

Rachel stopped. She had forgotten that Rabbi Yakov was there. She picked up a flickering candle so she could look into his face. She did not know what had come over her. Her giddiness drained away. As she looked back at the older Rabbi's care-worn face, she could see the younger Rabbi Gottesfurcht in his father. Her Isaac. The same kind, intelligent eyes and determined jaw, informed by their choice to spend their lives willing all things good into existence. They were the rare kind of person who risked everything for faith, honor, and love. And if they failed, they took responsibility. It was impossible not to admire such a man. She wished that Isaac were still here. That he were still alive.

"I stand by you, *Rebbe*," she said. "I believe in your ways."

"Do you think that's wise, Rachel? I seem to be given to vanity, foolishness and the sacrilegious."

"Your faith will bring an answer yet," she said.

"Will it?"

Rachel took a deep breath. This time when she looked around the Temple, in her mind's eye she saw it rebuilt, better even than before. "Isaac would want us to hold fast to our trust. Isn't that what you taught him?"

"Come, you need to find food and rest," said Rabbi Yakov. "I will stay and pray for the best outcome for this Kronski."

"You'll freeze. I know where there may be some blankets," she said.

"I'm fine," Rabbi Yakov said. But Rachel managed to shepherd him out of the sanctuary. They did not notice that the fist print in the side of the man-shaped mud had begun to fill in.

THE TEMPLE AT ZEBRAK

The first Awakening came in Eden. *Yahweh* had labored for five days and was preparing to wrap it up so that He could rest on the seventh day for His Sabbath. But there was something missing from this Earth, this planet of his rendering that gave him so much joy. He delighted in the birds that swooped through the air, and in the atmosphere, which was also of His Creation. He loved that He had created oxygen, a simple atom that filled the skies of Earth, and that combined with nitrogen and other minute gases made air for the birds to fly. The same oxygen, combined with hydrogen, made water for mammals to drink and for the fish to swim in. The fish were shiny and brilliant, and reveled in their leaping and flashing. And He was proud of the Thirst that He had created in mammals that would teach them both Desire and Fulfillment.

The Earth was a beautiful puzzle that He had assembled, each piece passionately committed to doing its part. After He had watched it run for a few hours, He breathed a sigh of relief. It did not implode, and it seemed that it would run in perpetual motion, or at least for a very long time. He considered moving on and starting his plan for another New World, but then turned back. Maybe His compulsive urge to create was born out of loneliness. Maybe instead of turning to yet another new project, maybe what He craved was someone else to be present to the Ecstasy that was Earth. Someone who would be unconditionally grateful for the miracle of Creation. Someone who would gather at the gallery of Creative Expression that was Earth and be an audience for His Art. And so He set to work, on that sixth day, learning how to breathe a new kind of awareness into clay, and so create a friend in His own image rather than in the random images of the flora and fauna. He was excited. For once, He would get to experience for Himself, through his Creation, what it was like to walk upon His Earth.

The Golem knew all of this without thinking, in every particle of soil that was infused with the Divine Word, and so Life. He was back again on Earth at his Creator's behest. He began to breathe the air. Soon he would be able to watch the birds fly and see the fish swim. If he had a heart, it would have leaped with joy. The first prototype may have been Adam, but the Golem was God's latest model. He lacked a vivid intellect, the better not to shut God out.

TOCNIK CASTLE

Isaac turned as the door opened. Gemlinger, followed by Kohl and two guards, walked into the interrogation room. "Where is he?" said Gemlinger.

"Right there," said Kohl, pointing at Isaac. Gemlinger was not a complete idiot, was he? Gemlinger was wondering the same thing about Kohl.

"This is not Kronski," said Gemliner.

"What?" said Kohl.

"Where is Kronski?" said Gemlinger. "And who are you?"

"I am Isaac Gottesfurcht. A rabbi's son."

"What do you know of the underground resistance?" said Gemlinger.

"Nothing," said Isaac.

"This is not the man I came here to meet," said Gemlinger.

"Not…?" said Kohl.

"Yes, you and your incompetents have brought in the wrong man. *Scheisse*. The Fuhrer will not be pleased," said Gemlinger.

"We will immediately secure the correct man," said Kohl. He was pretty sure that he could blame this on his aide, Heinrich. Though Gemlinger was displeased, this could be a good opportunity to get rid of a problem, if addressed properly. "What should we do with him?" Kohl asked.

"Kill him," said Gemlinger. Kohl nodded and the two guards grabbed Isaac by the arms.

"Wait, how do I know that you are who you say you are?" said Isaac, willing himself to stand straight and not squirm. "If you are, I can be very helpful. I can be the one you are looking for. Even better!"

Kohl instructed the guards. "The bear pit."

"I can be even better!" said Isaac as the guards pulled him out of the room.

THE TEMPLE AND THE VILLAGE AT ZEBRAK

The large mud limbs slipped off the table. The feet stepped down in the slush. The head reached up through the ceiling. It was a sight to see. Only there was no one there to see it.

Whatever thing that was edible and left in the *shtetl* had been thrown into a pot over an open fire for whoever remained alive. It was one of the miracles of community. Steaming chunks of potato, carrot, turnip, and other roots were brought up by ladle, and parsed out into cracked wooden bowls. Rachel accepted two bowls and handed one to Rabbi Yakov. She encouraged him to pull out the chunks with his fingers, and suck the warmth from them before swallowing. The fire hissed whenever a spray of rain found it. But the pot protected the fire as the fire heated the pot. So the *shtetl* survived.

Time was off kilter, and no one in the village felt the impulse to sleep. Rachel was driven by a fear that if she lay down to rest, her grief would find her and eat her alive.

Carrying a dripping tallow candle with one hand, and sheltering its flame from the drizzling air with the other, she returned to the sanctuary to continue its restoration. Rabbi Yakov followed her down the muddy path to the Temple. But rather than entering, Rachel stopped short at the threshold allowing her candlelight to fall inside. "*Rebbe?!*" she said.

Rabbi Yakov stopped behind her, concerned. He stepped around her and entered the sanctuary. The flickering light from the candle that she held cast his shadow dancing on the empty slab.

The Golem was gone.

Stepping out of the broken Temple into the moonlight oriented the Golem within those two great creations, Time and Space. Ashes to ashes, dust to dust. Many had died since his last Awakening, and their bones and ash had mingled with his soil. He felt into his own matter and learned that over three and a half centuries had gone by since he had last walked the earth. He felt the anguish and sorrow of the accumulated beings who had sloughed off their bodies, leaving their remains to become loam. He wondered about Death but did not understand it.

All he knew about his present calling was that there was Evil afoot that had to be quelled, in favor of the living who might otherwise suffer it. He placed his Faith in *Yahweh* who had created the Earth in seven days, and had thus created him.

That gave him his compass, and he had started through the woods toward the Castle on the mountain.

The Golem felt the muscular effort of his stride against the climb of the mountain and sang inside. The round moon shone on him in patterns filtered through the leaves. Cold as it was, the birds excited by the season and the coming dawn could not sleep. Their bird song and the promise of fresh blossoming smells of Spring met his awareness and made joy. The branches of the trees scratched his sides but he did not feel them except as a tickle. He did not bleed. Any wound healed right away. The rain and dew could not melt him. Even as the rivulets ran down his muddy body, tattooing him with their trails, he was instantly restored. The wetness of the night gave him a sense of renewal, a baptism in the celebration of the Lord, the *Yahweh* who brought him forth.

The secret of the Golem was that he was Thought, not Form. He was comprised of Word, not matter. As far as he knew he was invincible. And had he known he was not, he would not have cared. He had spent his centuries asleep filled with the longing for these living moments. He would have died for them.

A rhythmic quaking echoed the woods with each of his heavy steps.

TOCNIK CASTLE

Drizzle fell but the night clouds parted, slipping across the face of the moon. There seemed to be a never-ending supply of Jews. The courtyard should have been emptying as the result of the processions of prisoners down to the train station and the use of the fine new oven that had arrived on the train. Yet the courtyard was alive with dirty, groaning, restless bodies.

One man crossed the courtyard alone, Heinrich, the aide to Colonel Kohl. The sound of his smart footsteps, disciplined and in time, made by his well-shod feet, pleased him.

Heinrich was surprised to see two guards dragging a single Jewish prisoner out from within the Castle. He turned and headed back into the Castle to see if Colonel Kohl needed his further services under the circumstances. Perhaps there had been trouble, some revolt that he could resolve.

At the base of the stone wall, the two guards dragging Isaac, reached under his armpits and raised him to his feet, then pushed him, flailing, up to the top of the wall. Isaac could not reach the guards with his fists but managed to do damage with his elbows, landing blows to the ribs and a blow to an eye socket that would result in a black eye. As the guards raised Isaac up onto the wall, he got a glimpse at the ground twenty feet below in the dry moat. There, casting long shadows in the moonlight, the giant bears, starved into service, foraged for their next meal. The guards meant that meal to be Isaac. Though Isaac had wanted not to protest and give the guards that satisfaction, he screamed out as they pushed him and he fell to the ground below.

The guards leaned over the wall and watched Isaac land in the bottom of the dry moat with a heavy thud. The giant bears got the scent and lumbered toward him. Isaac lay motionless on the ground, trying to get his wind back, trying to get his bearings, and hoping to have the resources to find a way out. The largest bear let out a low growl signaling to the other bears that he meant to be first. The other bears parted in deference as he moved toward Isaac, sniffing the air. Isaac tried to move but his battered body was not recovering. His mind darted around in panic. A prayer rose from his heart but his mouth could not articulate it.

The guards turned to each other and smiled as the largest bear approached Isaac. The dry dirt of the moat was littered with the gnawed bleached bones of other useless prisoners, and the guards meant to confirm this kill too and not miss the entertainment. It was a choice post that allowed them to watch a man, a Jew, torn limb from limb — the guards had earned it by exacting numerous brutalities on the unwanted and unarmed with great enthusiasm.

But before the bears could do their work, from behind the guards, a shouting came from the gate. The guards turned their heads but could not see anything. The sound of a rifle shot cracked the air, then another and another. The guards grabbed their own guns and left Isaac to his certain death among the bears.

As the guards ran toward the gate, their Gewehr 42 semi-automatic rifles drawn and ready, the ground began to shake with a rhythmic thunder. But the storms of Spring and their electrical displays had subsided, if briefly. And the shaking of the ground did not resemble an earthquake or an avalanche. Danger was portended but its source was unknown. The guards could see ahead of them to the sentries who had left their posts, scattering and running in circles as if they had no place to go.

One of the guards was embarrassed to find himself involuntarily hanging back. As a child his mother had taken him to a concert hall. The symphony meant to mimic the sounds of war. The loud building rumble as a choir of kettle drums rattled the hall had terrified the boy. This sound of the shaking ground had that same effect on him now, though he was a grown man with experience in the horrors of the world. He himself exacted terror from others. Still, he had the impulse to call out for his mother even though she was now dead.

The guards arrived in the courtyard baffled. A few of the more stalwart sentries stayed on the battlements and shot their rifles over the gate in the direction of whatever was approaching, but as the earth shook, one by one they were thrown back off their posts, and lay where they fell, writhing broken-backed, helpless or dead, on the ground. The sound did not stop. Rifles were being loaded and pointed at the gates. But the hands that loaded and pointed them shook with fear. The easy taking of the countryside had prepared none of these soldiers to face an undaunted and resilient aggressor. And not just a band of German soldiers was at stake. The easy confidence in the supreme power of the Reich was being shaken.

The quick silence that followed was stranger still. The breath of the soldiers caught in their throats. The moonlight that had broken the clouds formed a halo. Overhead the droplets of Spring rain clung to their tree branches and put off falling to earth. Underground, the plant shoots that had broken through the shells of their seeds paused in their reaching for the surface. All of nature stopped, the world stood still.

Then the front gates to the Castle began to shake as a force was thrown up against them from the outside. Any guards nearby ran to lean their weight up against the heavy wooden doors with all of their strength trying to stop whatever was outside that wanted entry. But it was no use. The timbers creaked and groaned until the gate exploded inward. The guards were thrown back to the ground. They scrambled to their feet and started to fire their submachine guns at the giant figure standing in the shattered gateway.

The towering supernatural being looked down on the small brutes in their little black leather belts and boots. If he had been wry, he would have laughed. If he had been compassionate, he would have sorrowed in their choices. But he was neither. He was the wind, the sun, and the sky, as molten into rock, as broken into sand, as powdered into clay, as moistened into mud, as breathed into being. His great shape had arisen in the flickering light of the Eternal Flame that burned still and would burn forever in the synagogues of the world. He was The Golem.

Bullets slapped into his body and sunk into the clay. The holes left the bullets filled in and smoothed over as if they had never been. The Germans stared in awe. Their bullets, for once, had no effect.

The Golem stepped forward. With one swipe of one mighty arm he batted the front line of German soldiers off their feet. Any who dared get in his way was thrown aside. The ground was littered with broken men. But as other waves of soldiers came out of the Castle to challenge the Golem, they learned to step aside and so survive untouched.

The Golem meant no random harm. It was there for a purpose. To Live and let Live was the opposite of Evil.

Isaac lay crumbled face down in the bed of the moat, stunned from his fall. He groaned as he regained consciousness. His whole body ached. He turned his head to the side and spit gravel. He pushed himself up with his hands. Rocks and dirt stuck to his face. He would have brushed them off but saw the bear lumbering toward him, just scant feet away. He let out a yell, somehow finding it within himself to scramble to his feet. But the bear was too close. He tried to imperceptibly back away as he felt the ground for a stick or rock. He found nothing. An instinct reached to Isaac from across the century, from the roots of his tradition, and he began the *Ha-Gomel*, "Blessed are You, Oh Lord, Our God, King of the Universe, who bestows good things on the unworthy and has bestowed on me every goodness!"

The bear was amused and made almost curious by the heart song of the tender little man as it readied to pounce. He did not prefer a steady diet of the flesh of mortals but he ate what he was given. In the forest, he had enjoyed a variety of both flora and fauna, including the crisp and sweet of berries and leaves. Here he lived on a steady diet of the most debilitated of humans, rigid with fear. Always as he rose and before he ate what was thrown to him, he remembered the fresh tastes that he was born for. His heart was filled with longing for his home, for the feeling of the breeze through his fur. He longed for the taste of the fresh mountain springs. He longed for the splash of the river against his great thighs. He longed to bathe his spirit in the place he belonged. He filled with such memories and offered up gratitude for the escape they offered him in this desolate place.

While the bear hesitated, languishing in his memory, unwinding his simple prayer, Isaac also prayed. He used Hebrew words and sought to invoke the benevolence of the Creator. Isaac backed away from the bear and reached down. Issac grabbed a handful of gravel and, finishing his prayer, he threw it.

In protest but without injury, the bear opened its wide yaw, revealing a mouth full of yellowed fangs. He shredded the air with his great roar. His claws began to swat as he lunged toward Isaac. The bear's reverie broken, his heart wrenched with anger at men for taking him from his home and dropping him into the dry hollow of the moat where he lived as a slave. He could and would eat any man offered him, as a horse would not hesitate to eat a bale of hay left in his stall. He had not reckoned on Isaac, and had no reason to believe that this tender little man would be different.

Isaac, facing two tons of feral fury, stepped back. He did not prepare to die because there was no such thing. A man could not prepare to die other than by living a good life. He had done that in his few short years. He had been a good son and member of his community. Now he would be the best warrior he could.

Isaac bent to grab more gravel, looking steely into the bear's eyes. As he crouched, *something* blotted out the moonlight, drenching the barren landscape in an even deeper gloom. Against instinct, Isaac ripped his awareness off of his immediate threat, the great bear, and looked up to see something even more astonishing. A shadow, shaped like a man but far wider and taller than a man should be, hovered above him, standing on the stone wall that encompassed the moat. The bear who should have had nothing but focus for Isaac, his next unwilling meal, was also distracted and glanced up. The sound of the Golem as it flew though the air, leaping up off the wall and down into the moat, was a great *whoosh*. The sound of the Golem as it landed was a great *thoomp*.

Isaac was thrown backwards, landing face up against the ground. For an astonished moment he looked up, blinking as the constellations of stars and the round face of the moon hid behind the heavy clouds that blew in over them. He caught his breath and lifted his head and in an even more astonished moment, Isaac saw the great Golem.

Isaac forgot the bear. He scooted back onto his haunches and rubbed his eyes. There before him was the

244

great mythological being of his childhood, a monstrous manifestation of God's love for his people and a proof of faith. Not only had he taught his students about the Golem, he had sketched the Golem over and over again as a boy, and debated with his schoolyard peers what it would look like if it really existed until they laughed and turned away.

Isaac remembered in a flash of recognition that as a boy he, himself, had often been called a *golem* – a word which meant not just monster but also dreamy fool – among his crowd of more practical friends. Isaac was obsessed with questions of theology that veered off into the high flying realms of imagination. The other boys had their feet firmly on the ground. It was no wonder that they found him weird. His friend Absolon liked to run and wrestle. His friend Jason worked in his father's butcher shop. His friend Reuben liked to sit with his grandfather and carve animals out of wood. But Isaac's father was a rabbi, and that put Isaac's head squarely in the clouds. He believed in the Golem as much as anything. He knew the Golem to be as real as the fine taste of his grandmother's apple strudel. Between debates about the nature of the Universe and the hand of Divinity in it, he dreamed of sailing the seven seas, grappling with behemoth sea serpents, slaying fire-breathing dragons, and coming face to face with the Golem.

And here and now, even with Isaac as a solemn adult caught up in a grim time of war, the Golem did not disappoint. To see a rough giant sculpted of clay come to life – its chest moving in and out as if breathing, its eyes guiding its way as if having vision – was the fulfillment of a wish long wished. Often as that weird boy who had lots of bravado, Isaac had wondered in secret whether he would *faln in khaloshes*, fall into a faint, at the sight of a Golem. But Isaac was neither afraid or horrified. He was only filled with wonder. "Wow," he said under his breath. "Great *Adoshem!*"

Isaac wished that his father was there with him to witness the Golem. The older Rabbi Gottesfurcht, the good *Rebbe* Yakov, would simply nod, trusting as he did in the miracles wrought by *Yahweh*. His father saw a miracle in everything.

Isaac wished that Rachel was there with him to witness the Golem. It would end all debate between them. All that would be important would be the miracle, the mystery, and the surrender, and the love that twined between them. Little did Isaac know of the part that his father and Rachel had played in bringing the Golem to life.

Isaac also thought of the upturned faces of the boys he taught as he had told them the story of the Golem. If only the boys were here now, he thought. But then he thought again and was glad they were safe from the horrors of Castle Tocnik. He sent up a prayer from his heart that the boys were safe from any horrors of their own and that his own neighborhood in Prague was still whole.

And as all of this went through his head, he scrambled back for refuge, away from the Golem and its ursine opponent.

The great man of clay faced the great bear. The bear roared at the intruder. Air chugged through his nostrils as the bear urgently sampled the unfamiliar scent of the clay man. The Golem smelled like the earth itself, which was no enemy to the bear. The bear swayed back and forth, measuring his instincts for a course of action, and waiting for the Golem to give a sign of submission.

But as The Golem rose to his full height, the bear was clear that the Golem was an adversary, almost matching the bear in size and stature. The bear was not used to meeting anyone or anything equal to him and he did not like it.

Bellowing, the bear charged forward. The two goliaths hit head on head with a *wham* that again moved the ground. The bear reeled back stunned while the Golem stood his ground. Rain began to fall.

The lesser bears had blended back. They stood on their haunches and swayed at a safe distance, grunting and studying this turn of events. For the moment, hungry as they were, they too had lost interest in Isaac. Their world order was at stake. They jostled and shoved each other, testing to see who next would face the Golem if the greatest bear failed.

As the bear and the Golem circled, the clouds above burst. Rivulets of rain streaked down the Golem. As the rain grew heavier his surface heaved and writhed as the streamlets drawn by the water filled in and were drawn again.

The bear was built to withstand rain too, but his greasy fur became slick and wet so heavy was the rain. He remembered his meal, the tender little human who waited for him, and became irritable at the Golem for distracting him. He became irritable at the Golem for being incomprehensible. He became irritable at the Golem for resisting his superior ursine might. He became irritable at the Golem when he should have feared him.

The distracted bear sniffed the air and caught Isaac's scent. He spotted the human cowering in the shadow of the moat's wall, and with only one of his bleary eyes on the Golem, headed toward Isaac.

The Golem lowered his head and charged the bear, knocking him back off his hind paws before he could reach Isaac. But the bear's length brought his head to Isaac's feet. The bear seeing himself almost in reach of his prey reached his front paws up over his head and batted at Isaac. Caught by the back of a great paw, Isaac was thrown against the base of the stone wall of the moat and fell unconscious.

The Golem threw himself on top of the bear. The wily bear was winded but he had learned to wrestle as a cub in the den. He shoved off against the ground with his rear paws, and so threw off the Golem and stood.

The Golem recovered too quickly for logic. A reasonable expectation from his size, girth, and composition would be that as mighty as he was, he would be clumsy and slow to stand. But Golem and bear were once again both standing and facing each other.

The bear snarled and swiped his six-inch claws through the abdomen of the man of clay. A lesser adversary would have been done, in moments bleeding to death. But the Golem only looked down at his wounds and watched as the slashes sealed themselves up.

The bear stole the moment to look back over at Isaac who lay unconscious. So did the other bears. Hungry, salivating, and grown confident with opportunity, they began to crowd in. Protecting his prize, the behemoth bear growled at his lesser peers and waved them away from Isaac where he lay.

The Golem again lowered his head and charged the bear, pulling back one massive fist, which swelled to a block of gray stone. The great bear turned and charged. The Golem swung. Its fist *slammed* into the bear. Two tons of grizzly was blasted off his paws and sent flying back like a giant rag doll.

The great bear lay still on the ground at the feet of his clansman, as if an offering set before the other bears. The Golem looked at them, and they looked at the giant clay man with the stone fist. They backed away from the fallen leader of their pack and headed for safety on the other side of the moat. The Golem turned from the bears and found the one he had come for.

From the safety of a distant parapet of the Castle, Colonel Kohl, Gestapo Chief Gemlinger, and their closest lieutenants watched the battle conclude between bear and pseudo-man, their mouths agape. The soldiers who had tried to defy the Golem lay scattered across the Courtyard, groaning or dead. The rest of the soldiers were hidden in whatever recesses of the Castle were open to them, as if the Castle would protect them from the great grey creature. No man dared to offer first aid or rescue to their comrades while the man of clay was still on the Castle grounds.

Down in the moat, the Golem, the weapon of his stone fist returned to clay, trudged over to Isaac who, still unconscious, lay half in a growing puddle, newly falling rain washing over his face. The Golem slipped its great arms under Isaac's limp body and picked him up as if he were a sleeping child, needing to be carried off to bed. Successful in battle and sensing now that he was being watched, the Golem cradled Isaac to its chest and looked up at the German officers and their men in their high parapet.

Though high and far away, Kohl and Gemlinger felt the chill of the Golem's icy stare and ducked down out of sight. "*Gott in Himmel,*" said Kohl. "Dear God in Heaven."

"What on earth is it?" said Gemlinger.

The Golem turned away from the parapet, and landed a kick, *be-thwoom,* in the wall of the moat. Shattered stone flew.

The stunned Nazis in the Castle parapets dared to raise themselves up just high enough to gaze over a ledge and watch the Golem head through the destroyed wall of the moat and down the mountainside away from the Castle and into the woods, carrying their prisoner, Issac, the younger Rabbi Gottesfurcht, in his arms. The Golem was escaping, which was just as well for the Nazis who were unprepared to meet him, let alone defend themselves against him.

When it had disappeared among the trees, Gemlinger put down his field glasses and turned to Kohl. "What is it? We must know what it is!"

"I don't know," said Kohl, but he suspected it was the legendary Golem, protector of the Jews. Over the centuries, the Golem had become the subject of the dark bedtime stories that warned of the Jews and their goal of supremacy. Thus, as a child he had been warned to be wary of Jews. He had thought the Golem was ridiculous. He had thought Jews, scrawny, pale, and underwhelming, were nothing to be afraid of. Perhaps he had been wrong.

"It's getting away! After it!" said Gemlinger. It was the Golem. He knew it too, though he feigned ignorance. Forget the Jewish underground, *Herr Hitler* would be beside himself to be possessed of the original *ubermensch*, a super human creature who could not be conquered.

"But half my men are --" said Kohl.

"I don't care! I want that thing back! *Jetzt!*" said Gemlinger.

Kohl rubbed his forehead. He had already jumped ahead in his mind to wondering what kind of weapon would stop such a monster and to knowing that they did not have such a thing. However, it dawned on him that the Golem was something of a solution for another type of problem he had.

Kohl nodded to his aide, Heinrich, who had turned up again that night despite having been dismissed. Heinrich, in turn, nodded to the storm trooper next to him, intending to stay behind with Kohl and Gemlinger, but Kohl corrected him. "This is a matter of great importance," said Kohl to Heinrich, "And as my most trusted man, I need you to go with our men and pursue the creature and recover our prisoner."

"But surely, Colonel, you and Herr Gemlinger will be needing my services, as the Castle is short of men," said Heinrich. Kohl heard the whimper in Heinrich's voice and was revulsed.

"Do not return without the monster and that wretched Jew! For the Reich!" With that Kohl saluted, dismissing his aide.

Heinrich, for his part, though he longed to protest further, surrendered to his fate. If he was able to survive and return with the Golem, with or without the Jewish prisoner, surely he would be a hero—a hero with more clout even than Colonel Kohl.

But Kohl doubted it. He doubted the aide would be back at all. In fact, he was certain he would not see this sniveling worm again in this lifetime. Despite the astonishing and adverse turn of events of that night, he breathed a sigh of relief.

KRIVOLAT FOREST

Kronski and the underground fighters of Prague moved up through the woods. Tocnik Castle loomed ahead of them. They caught closer and closer glimpses of the Castle through the trees. They heard a great crashing through another part of the forest accompanied by a rhythmic shaking of the earth. From their distance, it seemed half-plausible that such shaking was caused by thunder or artillery, or both. Still it lent the night a supernatural aura. Closer though they could hear shouting in German and the occasional crack of a rifle shot as a group of German soldiers stumbled down the mountainside in scattered squads. The Nazis lacked stealth and the need for it, unlike the resistance fighters.

Still Kronski urged his freedom fighters on up toward the Castle. The commotion was at an ample distance. And the noisiness of the Germans in the woods made them simple to avoid. Little by little the soldiers of the Reich streamed downwards and past or around the band of Jews who dared to fight for their freedom. For their part, though the fighters were not discovered as they trudged upwards, the unexpected disturbance in the forest followed by stillness unsettled them and gave them a sense of foreboding.

"What's going on?" asked Aaron, the youngest.

"It's quiet now," said Cseba. "Whatever it was, had nothing to do with our approach."

Aaron, striving to be a man, struggled within himself to allay his fears.

"It is no matter," said Kronski, clapping Aaron on the back. Aaron was a good boy, thought Kronski. He realized that he wanted to see Aaron survive this mission. He jerked his hand back from Aaron's shoulder as if from a hot stove. The key to his success in this war was his ability to remain removed from those around him — to do what he had to do, and remain unattached. If he allowed himself to bond, he opened the door to tripping over sentiment. He pitied those with loved ones still alive in these times. If one had to love, best to love in retrospect, from a distance, thanks to the great intercessor Death. Then one could not be bought or sold.

Kronski turned and looked ahead as if into the future. The men behind him looked too, but saw nothing but darkness and trees. "We have to get up the hillside to the guard post," Kronski said. "There are only two sentries but after them there are seventy meters of clear killing ground to the Castle's front gate." Despite their discipline and dedication, a shudder went through the men. They looked at each other.

"Cseba," said Kronski, calling the squad's leader to his side.

Cseba stepped over to Kronski. "Yes?" Cseba said, biting his lip, not wanting to show any emotion. His experience informed how he acted in front of his men. He needed them to be bold and unwavering. He knew they would follow his lead, and so acted accordingly.

Kronski continued, "We'll take the sentries out silently, knives only. When we reach the gate, we'll use the charge." He turned to Iphraim, the explosives man. "Charge ready?" Iphraim nodded, patting his canvas rucksack.

Aaron looked around at the older men, trying to discern their level of concern. He decided to risk his question. "How are we going to cross from the sentries' post to the front gate without being seen?"

The men turned to Kronski who replied, "We're not all going to make it, but some will." The men turned to each other. "We're fighting for the countless lives this wave of hate is planning to destroy. And anyone who wants to turn back can do it now."

The forest was full of the music *pat pat, pat pat* – the sound of rain dripping from through its many branches. Ahead of the fighters, a tree that had been split and blackened the year before by a stray lightning strike was bathed in moonlight. It had opened the ceiling of the forest by falling, but its split stump was showing new life. Lichen laced the trunk. Slender branches reached up from within its ruins, tipped with leaf buds ready to unfurl when the time was right. Reassurance could be pulled from these signs of renewal, from each other, and from the promise of their mission. They began nodding to each other.

Cseba watched and when all the men had signaled their agreement, he turned to Kronski. "We're with you," said Cseba.

Kronski smiled. He had a good smile, broad and friendly, when he chose to use it. "Good," he said. "Let's go." He led the men around and over the stump before they stepped back into the darkness of the woods. Further ahead, as the foliage began to slim, he slowed. And when he stopped just before the clearing, the men stopped behind him.

On Kronski's signal, the first line of the squad of resistance fighters, knives in their teeth, burst through the last of the trees and out from the cover of the forest. The terrain was uphill, barren and rocky, littered with sawed-off tree stumps. The Nazis kept the approach to the Castle clear-cut. The fighters crouched low and scrambled upward, swift with strong intent. As they crested the hill, they heard the sounds *chunk, chunk, chunk* as searchlights flickered on, blinding them.

Kronski and the others squinted into the light. German soldiers sat behind tripod-mounted submachine guns aimed at them. "Halt," said a German voice. "Drop your weapons. Raise your arms in the air." German soldiers emerged from the trees that lined the approach, cocking their Mauser 98 bolt action rifles, pointed at the freedom fighters. A rush of wind and rain swept up the hillside, chilling the men who were trying to will themselves invisible.

"Germans, *shist!*"

"We've been ambushed!"

"They were waiting for us!"

Kronski narrowed his eyes. "Run," he said. "Run!"

Iphraim hooked his arms back to adjust his rucksack of explosive charges. He looked back to see if any of his comrades were still coming. He was tempted to make his run on the Castle gates, German soldiers or not. If he was going to die, let it be for a purpose. "Iphraim, run to me!" said his old friend, Nahman, the wine merchant, from back behind the tree line, holding out his hand

The submachine guns opened fire. The sounds *budda, budda, budda* filled the air. At least half of the resistance fighters were cut down in the first salvo.

Iphraim glanced ahead. None of those ahead of him still stood. He turned and ran back for the tree line.

"Get down!" shouted Cseba, crawling belly to the ground, back to the forest.

But Iphraim kept running. He reached out his hand to meet that of Nahman, the wine merchant. Just before his hand met that of his old friend, just before he crossed behind the tree line, he was caught in machine gun crossfire. The charge in his rucksack ignited and exploded, sending flames and his viscera in a wide arc. The trees caught fire. The forest became a Hell.

Nahman, the wine merchant, was emolliated where he stood waiting, leaving a fiery silhouette etched against the night, his hand still reached out to his old friend. His second to last thought was that he should have been more suspicious of the vagabond and his foolish plans. His last thought was concern for his comrades, living and dying. He had come to regard Iphraim as a brother in life, and now they had died together, reaching hand to hand. Tonight they would enter the Valley of Death. In an afterlife, perhaps the *shamayim*, they would be reunited with each other and their families. With his last breath he prayed they would be at peace.

Kronski and the few survivors scattered into the dark woods. They melted into the shadows, slipped up against the trees, and wedged themselves into the crevices made by their gnarled roots, making their way back down the mountainside.

Wave after wave of German soldiers ran past them shouting *"Dort sind sie! Scieben sie sie!"* "Shoot them, shoot them!" the soldiers exhorted each other, firing at random. The soldiers were unafraid of the wretched Jews who had been betrayed by one of their own. The soldiers used the kills as a distraction, to give them a sense of confidence, even if false. The soldiers saved their fears for the Golem, both of the monster itself and because they had been ordered to bring it down or face a firing squad on their return. The Jews fell easily, like fish in a barrel. The Jews that broke confidence and ran were easily cut down. The numbers would be good that night.

Searchlights from high on the Castle walls swept through the forest, their beams falling eerily between the trees. Kronski rued that his breath might be visible in the chill night air and prayed that he not be shot. A young upstart of a soldier would be excited that he had found a Jew trying to hide, cowering behind a tree. It would make his kill all the more thrilling. He heard the shouts of the Germans running past, and the moans of the underground fighters who lay dying of their wounds. He took comfort as the rich smell of the forest loam rose up, met his nostrils, and began to overpower the acrid smell of gunpowder. He dropped into a low crouch, crawling back out of the range of the lights.

"You there," said a familiar voice from behind him.

Kronski turned, ready to give orders. He was amazed to find himself held at gunpoint. "Cseba, what are you doing?"

"Don't move, they'll find us soon," said Cseba.

"Are you crazy?" asked Kronski in a hushed tone.

"I said, don't move. I'll turn you over. You can labor instead of die," said Cseba.

"You, Cseba?" said Kronski. "You?!"

"Yes," said Cseba. "Yes."

"You betrayed us to the Germans?" said Kronski. "Why?"

"Look around," said Cseba. "They have already won this war. To oppose them further only brings more death."

"What did they promise you?" said Kronski.

"That my family will be spared," said Cseba.

"And you believed them? You fool," said Kronski.

Cseba ignored him. "Over here!" he called out to a passing group of German soldiers.

Cseba turned back to Kronski. "I would do anything to protect my family. I have done that anything," he said. He resented Kronski's silence, which he took to be judgment. "Just think what you would do to have your family back again!"

In the darkness, it seemed to Cseba that Kronski winced. A wave of compassion passed over Cseba. He let Kronski blend back into the night. Cseba had turned in enough men to earn his bounty—his own safe passage, the safe passage of his family, the smiles of his children. A second thought occurred to him though—maybe he should not let Kronski get away.

Cseba turned back to the German soldiers and waved, impatient now. "Over here, I said!" The German soldiers finally spotted Cseba. They waved back at him, and looked to each other, laughing as if at a private joke. The leader of the German soldiers raised an arm, and with a nod, pointed at Cseba. A burst of machine gun fire tore into Cseba. He crumpled to the ground. The German soldiers moved on.

Kronski crawled back to the bleeding man and dragged him aside. Kronski crouched over Cseba. The two men were protected from being seen by a clutch of low shrubs.

"My family, my children," said Cseba, gasping for breath.

"In the hands of the Nazis, they would be good as dead — in fact, they would have been better off dead," said Kronski, loosening Cseba's collar.

Checking Cseba's wounds, Kronski determined that at the rate that Cseba was bleeding, he had precious few moments left.

"*Mine Gott*," groaned Cseba. The dying man whimpered, struggling against his fate. His last exhalations rose to a keening wail.

The forest filled with the baying of hounds loosed by the Germans to round up the last survivors.

Kronski grabbed Cseba's gun and struck him with the butt to silence him before darting away, subtle as the shadows.

When Kronski reached the edge of the woods, he crawled down to the edge of the riverbank. He paused, put his lips to the water, and drank. Quenched, he crouched up on his haunches. He looked both ways. Alone, he took his first deep breath of the night. He dipped his hands into the clay along the bank. He felt the twigs and pebbles in the soil and let them sift out, and drop through his fingers. Lifting the mud to his face, he smeared his forehead first. He felt it dry and adhere to his skin. He felt part of the earth. He felt alive. He was alive. Camouflaged, he made his way downstream.

THE MOLDAVKA RIVER

Rabbi Yakov and Rachel stepped out of the temple into the night, looking for any trace of the manlike sculpture that was no longer laid out inside. In better times, they might have suspected the mischief of children, carting the great man outside limb by limb, clod by clod, and setting him up leaning against a tree or sitting on a rock. But all of the children were dead or in the arms of whoever could comfort them against their trauma. In these strange times, the most reasonable answer to the mystery was that a miracle had occurred.

Rachel picked up the footprints first, places where the weight of the Golem had pressed into the soft earth down by the riverbank, where she and her Isaac had stood the afternoon of the wedding. She wondered if she would ever be able to go down by the river and not think of the young *rebbe*. She hoped not. The prints were filling in with river water, rainwater, and mud, and losing shape. But they were staggered as if made by a great striding man.

"Rabbi, look," Rachel said. "Do you think these could be of the Golem?"

The older Rabbi Gottesfurcht knelt and was able to place both his hands, palm down, inside a single print. Feeling the earth in the bottom of the print squish between his fingers, he laughed. "Yes, yes! Thank you, *Adonai!*" he shouted, on his knees, arms up stretched, embracing the night sky. Rachel tried to lean down to look too, but slipped into the mud. Together they fell back on the riverbank and laughed looking up at the great moon.

"It's true then, it's true, the great legend of the old Rabbi Loew," said Rachel, so taken with the moment. Tears streamed down her cheeks.

"That was no story, no legend, no fairytale, but the great *Yahweh* and His Elohim at work," said the older Rabbi Gottesfurcht.

A sound of popping in the distance sounded like fireworks at the Castle, which was only fit for their celebration. They laughed in waves, as the realization of the miracle struck the shores of their being. What the Golem would do now that he was brought to life, neither knew, but it did not seem to matter then and there. The miracle was enough.

But then an explosion sounded and the highest part of the forest burst into flames. Rachel and Rabbi Yakov were sobered. Recovering their footing, they looked up the mountain in awe and slipped, most naturally, into prayer.

KRIVOLAT FOREST

The Golem knew where he was going. He held the unconscious body of the young man he had come for in his arms as he strode down the mountain, through the forest. The German soldiers pursued them, led by the aide Heinrich, as ordered by their superiors, Gestapo Chief Gemlinger and Colonel Kohl. But other than follow behind and keep up as best they could, the soldiers did not know what to do. They had no idea how to stop the great monster or wrest from it the prisoner it carried.

A Nazi broke from the pack of soldiers and ran up to the Golem. He kept pace behind the Golem with his rifle in hand, and at the best moment he could find, jammed the bayonet into the Golem's side. The great clay warrior backhanded the soldier with a *whack,* and so sent the soldier flying. The soldier's body slammed up against the great trunk of a four hundred year old tree, and landed on the forest floor. It was not known whether he breathed his last when the Golem's hand struck his body or when his body struck the tree, but he was dead by the time his body hit the ground.

The senior Nazi soldier shouted to the others, "Stand back! Keep your distance!" and they did. The other Germans, including Kohl's aide, stopped in their tracks. For the first time Heinrich thought seriously about deserting his beloved Reich. There was nothing he or his companions could do to stop this thing. That much was obvious.

The Golem kept his stride without missing a step. The dead Nazi's rifle stuck out of the Golem's back, only falling covered in clay when it brushed a tree as the Golem moved along, intent only on his purpose.

The sound of a scraping footfall followed by the sight of a straggling man making his way down the river caught the attention of Rabbi Yakov and Rachel. He was caked with dried mud. The *rebbe* and Rachel looked to each other. This was not the Golem.

"It's not him," said Rabbi Yakov.

"I know," said Rachel.

"Him? Who were you expecting?" said the mud caked man.

"Kronski?" asked Rabbi Yakov. He supported Kronski under one arm, and Rachel supported Kronski by the other. In this way, the *rebbe* and the girl led Kronski back to the Temple.

"What happened?" asked Rachel.

"I've been running from the Germans all night," said Kronski. "We tried, we failed. We didn't even get to the Castle."

Rabbi Yakov and Rachel, themselves covered with their own river mud, remembered the sound, which in their exuberance, had sounded like fireworks. They remembered the explosion and the fire on the mountain. They had failed. Their Golem, an escaped rogue monster, was now out roaming the earth without purpose. And now it was clear that Kronski too had failed. Their Isaac, the younger Rabbi Gottesfurcht, Rebecca's love and the older Rabbi's only son, was lost.

The three fell silent as they made their way back to what was left of the *shtetl*. They supported each other up the slippery riverbank, crossed the grassy field, and entered the broken Temple. There, the older Rabbi Gottesfurcht and Rachel helped Kronski to a bench where he sat, slumped over with his head in his hands.

THE TEMPLE AT ZEBRAK

Neither the older Rabbi Gottesfurcht nor Rachel had the will to ask Kronski more than he was willing to say. When Kronski was ready, he would tell his story. But his return empty-handed, without Isaac, the younger Rabbi Gottesfurcht, made for a heaviness that contrasted with the dazzling moonlight that streamed in through the ruins of the Temple.

Life was a series of contrasts, thought Rachel, sometimes coming in such rapid intervals as if to make sure that you did not know yourself anymore.

"When you are ready," said Rachel to Kronski. "You'll need dry clothes, something to eat and drink. Those who are left in the village can help you." She wanted him to leave, to go into the *shtetl* and find help at the home of a different survivor, anyone but her. He had failed to bring back her Isaac. Her father, her Isaac, her world, all hope, extinguished like a candle. He had failed to bring back her Isaac.

Kronski nodded but did not leave the temple ruins. If he would not leave, she would. She would go find the home of the elderly woman, a friend who would make her tea and offer a shoulder on which she could cry. But before she could move, a shadow blotted out the moon.

The Golem stepped into the Temple and gently placed the unconscious form of the young Rabbi Isaac Gottesfurcht on the slab where, just awhile before, the Golem had been brought to life.

"*Mein Gott!*" said Kronski, regarding the Golem. "I don't believe it!"

"*Yahweh* did it," said the older Rabbi Gottesfurcht. "We just asked."

The Golem stood unmoving. He was without motive or need. He waited for Divine Inspiration. And while he waited, he took in the Temple, saturated with blood, rainwater, and prayer. He allowed the fullness and the sorrow, the love and the pain, to become a part of him.

Rabbi Yakov stood at his son's side, holding his hand, the warmth of which was reassuring. Rachel took Isaac's other hand. She felt for a pulse and nodded to Rabbi Yakov when she found it.

Rainwater dripped from the roof into the puddles on the Temple floor. The black sky started to fade to light.

Isaac's eyes opened. "*Tate?*"

Rabbi Yakov squeezed his son's hand and wept. "I did not know if I would see you again." He embraced his son, and helped him sit up. Isaac then stood up by himself. His wholeness amazed him.

And then Isaac saw Rachel. He drank in her soft brown eyes. "You live."

Rachel took his hand. "I do, and so do you," she said.

"In the middle of Hell, I had a dream," said Isaac. "The dream was that the Golem saved me. And now, here we are. Could this be an afterlife?"

Rachel looked up behind Isaac. Isaac turned his head to follow her gaze and saw the man of mud standing in the room behind his father. His jaw went slack with wonder. "God in Heaven, it is the Golem. The very Golem?!"

Wild-eyed and exhausted, Isaac looked from the Golem, to Rachel, to his father, and to Kronski whom he had never met. "And who is that man?" said Isaac, trying to focus on Kronski as the room began to swim. Rabbi Yakov caught his son and helped him lean up against the slab.

"Maybe something of the stew is left?" said Rabbi Yakov. Rachel nodded and left.

But as Isaac stood, blood began to run from the side of his mouth, his ears, and his nose, in fine rivulets at first, but building until Isaac fainted and his father had to lay him up upon the slab. Rabbi Yakov panicked inside, this was not something a doctor could fix, were there a doctor available.

The Golem observed with a distant curiosity and felt the father's concern. He reached out a great hand and laid it on Isaac's abdomen. At once, the bleeding subsided. And when Rabbi Yakov dipped a cloth in water and cleaned the blood away, it seemed as if the bleeding had never been.

The Golem felt the call of the river. Kronski followed him outside.

Rabbi Yakov waited with his son, slipping his arm under his shoulders, and cradling him that way. He remembered when his son was an infant and he would cradle him in his arms.

Rabbi Yakov knew that what came next would be important. For himself, he was full of gratitude but drained of will. Whatever came next would have to be the will of his son and his God. He prayed the two were intertwined.

When Isaac fainted, he woke to himself. It was an odd feeling to be free of his body and awake to something much larger, as if he were built of stone. He remembered that man's origins were from the clay of Mother Earth, and with that memory he seemed to seep into the ground, or rather pour like rain. He traveled down through rock, slab, and boulder until he met the red hot core of a planet sent to fury and quake when the basic tenets of all existence were at stake.

Love, larger than the feeling between two beings, had built up to the atomic from a much finer level. From such atoms, life would spring. But Love being threatened by Fear and its false anecdote, Hate, the inner core of all existence bubbled and baked. Fire tumbled over rock and cinder. Great hot explosions of molten fire burst and broke.

It was there, at the center of the planet, that Isaac met his Anger, lost and alone, stewing like a school child sent to think things over in a corner. His Anger had thought, though, and was now done thinking.

Isaac approached his Anger timidly at first, like a man coming upon a wild embrace, not knowing if it meant to strangle or adore him, but once recognizing it as his own, he held it to him. There locked, great sobs emerged, breath was taken gasping, and they became one.

As Isaac rose again to the surface and back to consciousness, he retook his body, and built his muscle, sinew, blood, breath, and bone of iron and rock. He was ready to live again, and live thereafter as he had never before lived in his life.

When Isaac opened his eyes again, there was stew that Rachel had brought. When he finished, he turned to his father and said, "I am thirsty." Rabbi Yakov found a chipped glass that the rain had filled with water and held it for him. It grieved the older Rabbi to see the hollows around his son's eyes, but he also sensed something new in Isaac, something vital, mature, and determined that he had never seen before.

"Once the Nazis decided I was useless, they wasted no time," Isaac was saying. "He saved me. Still, if I had not seen the Golem here with you, I would have thought my recollection of his intervention only a fever dream. *Tate*, tell me, I always thought the Golem was --"

"A fantasy? A fairy tale?" asked Rabbi Yakov. "No, the Golem is a last refuge."

"And who is the other man?" asked Isaac.

"A friend," said Rabbi Yakov. "But we've got to get you on your feet and back to Prague."

"On my feet, yes," said Isaac.

"We will tend to the dead before we go," said Rabbi Yakov.

"And the living," said Isaac.

"And the living," said Rabbi Yakov, "but for now rest." And Isaac did. He fell into a sleep, and his father watched over him, and over his Rachel who napped, wrapped in a blanket, in the corner.

Outside the sky was beginning to lighten with the approach of dawn. The Golem stood at the riverbank feeling Isaac, the younger Rabbi Gottesfurcht, dreaming his world. He watched the pink sky reflecting off the water as it ran past. He felt only as humans felt and borrowed those feelings, without understanding them. Still though, he was pleased that this young *rebbe* was sharing in his truth. If he could have felt lonely, he would have longed for his understanding of strength and soil to be reflected in other beings, and now he had it in this Isaac, the younger Rabbi Gottesfurcht.

Kronski knelt and washed his face off in the river. The clay cracked and fell off in pieces. He rinsed his face again and again, until the stubborn residue of clay against his skin was gone. The ripples he cast disturbed the Golem's pink sky.

Kronski stood refreshed, his face reddened from the brisk cold of the water. He walked around the clay giant a few times, studying him.

The Golem ignored Kronski, and instead watched the river return to the calm rush that was its nature. He watched the hues of sunrise deepen on its surface. God, he loved this experience of being alive, this river, this sun, and this sky.

Kronski joined Rachel where she sat on a rock watching the Golem. "Impossible," Kronski said, interrupting her peace.

"He told you it was possible," said Rachel.

"I thought he was crazy," said Kronski.

"You didn't have faith," said Rachel.

"I haven't had faith in anything for a long time," said Kronski, looking at Rachel and drinking her in. She looked away. He put out his hand, tucked it under her chin, and forced her to look at him. "They will follow this thing here. This place is not safe."

Rachel glared at him. He dropped his hand. She stood and walked back toward the ruined temple. He shook his head and followed her. She was defiant and foolish, like someone who had not learned the meaning of death. In this day and age, her principles would catch up with her, he was sure, and she would pay the price for her arrogance. He meant to talk some sense into her.

The Golem felt a blossom fall onto his shoulder from the tree branches above. He reached up, pinched between what would have been his thumb and forefinger, and dropped it into his great hand. He fell in love with it in an instant, and felt the breaking of what would have been his heart.

As Kronski stood on the threshold of the temple, he looked back over his shoulder and saw the Golem holding the little flower. He narrowed his eyes.

THE TEMPLE AT ZEBRAK

As he re-entered the sanctuary, Kronski watched Rachel go to the other Isaac who stood with his father.

The younger Rabbi Gottesfurcht, the other Isaac, the Isaac that Rachel loved, stepped toward her, welcoming her approach. In the midst of the ruins, he reached out and touched her delicate hand.

In easier times, his father, Rabbi Yakov, might have condemned the intimacy of even simple touch under strict application of rabbinic law. But then and there, cradled by the walls of the ruined temple that still stood yet, the rules be damned. Rabbi Yakov glanced aside and privately rejoiced.

"We should be leaving," Kronski said. "None of us are safe here, including your Golem."

"He is not my Golem. He is the Golem. He does not belong to me," said Rabbi Yakov.

Kronski shook his head. "Why do you mince words with me?" he said.

Rabbi Yakov was abashed. This Kronski was a friend, working for the greater good, in his own way. He had suffered great hardship but had been ignored since Isaac had been brought back safe through other means than his.

Rabbi Yakov put an arm around Kronski. "Will you help me get my wagon ready so that we can return to Prague?" he said.

Kronski did not shrug him off.

Isaac, overhearing his father talking with Kronski, turned to go with his father to help him prepare his cart.

Rabbi Yakov held up a hand to stop Isaac. "No, please stay with Rachel and help her gather whatever she wants to take," he said as he left the sanctuary with Kronski. Kronski took one last glance back, and then the two men were gone.

Rachel stood with her arms crossed, looking around the sanctuary. Isaac glanced around. He saw the pooled water on the floor, and the benches, some broken and burned, some righted and salvageable. He walked to where the Torah had been housed and picked up shards of the ark that had held it. He looked up to the roof and saw the sky. "What would you like to take?" Isaac asked her, repeating the words of his father.

Rachel bent down and picked up a soggy piece of parchment. It was a shred of her Torah. She held it to her lips. Tears came to her eyes.

Isaac turned away. Outside the birds sang their early morning songs and hopped on the branches. A few short days ago the birds had sounded happy. Now they sounded bitter and scolding.

What better could I have done? he thought. *I was unarmed. I spoke up against the Nazis. Where were you, Adonai?* His scorn for God embarrassed him, but in the wake of so much hatred and death he could not feel the gratitude for his survival that he should have felt.

"What would you like to take?" Isaac asked again.

"Nothing," said Rachel, and sighed. She heard the birds too. "My father's house is gone."

Nothing to take, thought Isaac. *There is nothing that I would take either, except you.* "Come, let's go then," he said, a hand on her elbow to guide her toward the door.

"But I won't be going," said Rachel.

"My father would like you to come with us," said Isaac.

"I must stay here and find a way to rebuild this house, to make it a home again for my village of Zebrak," said Rachel, opening her arms to the damaged synagogue. She pulled her arms back in and wrapped them around her, closing her eyes. She prayed for God to guide her as to how to do it, as a shepherd would a sheep. She felt broken and lost.

It would not be a simple project under the watch of the German soldiers stationed up in the Castle, at least some of whom would take it as a great lark to visit her sanctuary to check on her progress. It would become habit. They would visit every night after downing buckets of beer and destroy what she had done. And then the next day she, like Sisyphus, could start her project anew, that is, as long as she had her freedom.

She wondered how she could replace the Torah that had been destroyed. She wondered if and where the Torah makers still survived. She wondered if she could make her own Torah if she could not find a scribe.

Isaac cleared his throat. Rachel opened her eyes and turned to him. "Or you could..." he began, but faltered, falling into the depth of her eyes. He had never seen such eyes before hers.

"Yes?" said Rachel.

Isaac paused, pouring over her features. This girl, this woman, was beautiful and smart. All the more reason to take a chance, reasoned Isaac. But he had to approach this with wisdom. He weighed possible strategies.

"Your plans are wise and full of love and devotion, but maybe it would be wise for you to move to another home," said Isaac.

"Really?" she said.

"In another town," he said.

"What are you thinking?" she said. "Somewhere safer?"

"There is no safety anywhere in these times, but maybe there is somewhere you could be better taken care of," he said.

"It is very kind of your father, but --"

"It is not just my father who would like you to come with us. I would like you to come with us. We will take care of you," he said.

And I would care for you, she thought. "I would be welcome in your house?" she said. *I would be your housekeeper and cook. What else could I do to make myself useful? Here I am better needed — there is no other rabbi.*

"Yes, very welcome. In fact, most welcome," he said.

"You are so kind, my father would be grateful to you," she said and leaned in to press her cheek against his to show her gratitude but instead Isaac caught her, pressed his lips to hers, wrapping her in his arms.

The handsome, outspoken young rabbi had caught her by surprise. She intimidated most men and knew it, and had come to count on that power for her freedom. In his arms though, under his sway, she melted and kissed him back.

When they drew back, one from the other, she intended to say, "But I intend to stay here, in my village, the village

271

of my father." But caressing the soft white of her long neck, he had moved to the pale of her shoulders and so took her breath away.

She wrapped her fingers into his hair and let him press her up against a wall that remained. In her wildest dreams she never meant it to be like this, here in the cold, burnt Temple of her fresh dead father, but love was never the design of a simple human, but instead sparked by the Divine and unpredictable.

MOLDAVKA RIVER

The blossom caught the whisper of the breeze, wafted from the Golem's palm, and landed in the river. He watched it take to the eddies and swirl away downstream. He closed what would have been his eyes and let the first morning rays penetrate his being.

"Hello," said the little girl. The Golem opened his eyes and looked down. "Hello, my name is Sarah," she said poking his arm. She pulled back her finger and looked at the residue of clay left there. She drew back when she realized she had left finger holes in the him. She watched mouth open, as the places where she had poked, filled in and smoothed over.

The little girl had a round face, pale and smudged with river mud. She had woken at dawn. Being unable to sleep in a strange bed, she had wandered down to the riverbank where she and her friends had often played. It had been explained to her that many of her friends were dead now and that her parents were dead now. She did not quite know what that meant yet, but whenever she went to look for them, she could not find them and it made her sad. Sometimes tears rolled down her cheeks. She could not feel the tears except the blur before she blinked and the taste of salt when they rolled over her lips and she touched them with her tongue.

The tears and the emptiness, and the knowing enough to know she did not know, were new. The familiar riverbank made everything seem better. And now she had met a man all made of mud. Some people were nice and some people were not. He had not said anything but he seemed nice. "I'm Sarah, who are you?" she said.

Some people could not talk, and were never ever able to talk. She wondered if the man of mud could talk even though he did not say anything. There was one boy in her class at school, Yussell, her good friend, who did not talk much but when he talked, he liked to talk a lot. He liked to talk with her. Yussell liked to catch frogs, like her, but he also liked to let them go, like her. Some boys did not let the frogs go and the frogs died. But not Yussell. When Yussell talked, she talked with him. When he was quiet, she was quiet with him. When Yussell fell in the Temple, she fell down next to him and was quiet with him. He had not talked since the night the soldiers came with their guns to the Temple. When, years later, she realized that in dying Yussell had saved her life, she cried for him again. He was that kind of friend. When even more years had passed and she was married and had her own children, she planted a tree in his name in Israel.

The Golem wondered at the little girl. She was so little he could hardly see her. What he could see — the top of her head and the tipped up features on her face — were sweet, mud splashed, and sprinkled with sun. He reached down and picked her up, the better to see her. Yes, she had pink lips and a chin that jutted out above a neck like other humans. And like other humans and him, the Golem, she had two arms, two legs, and a torso. He liked the design of himself

273

and humans—it spoke of a grand design and the Designer. It made him feel connected and he liked that. He had figured out that everyone wanted to be connected and that no one wanted to be alone. Even men who went out to kill went marauding in groups.

The Golem liked the little girl. He liked the sound of her voice, sweet like the chirping of a bird. He liked not being alone. He missed his good friend from centuries past, the old Rabbi Loew.

The Golem held the little girl up so that he could look into her face with his big yellow eyes. She was named Sarah. She told him so. She looked into the face of the Golem and blinked. When she blinked, so did he.

Sarah knew, as anyone would know, that this big clay man was different. A glint of gold over his heart caught her eyes. She found that her little fingers could dig into his chest. She pulled at the gold and unearthed the Star of David, engraved by God, lodged where his heart should be. "Pretty," she said.

She would have puzzled out the spelling of the word, but in the next moment the Golem fell flat backward like a tree felled in the forest. With a shriek she fell unhurt on top of him still held in his arms.

Sarah, wide-eyed, looked in the face of the Golem but he did not stir. She slid from between his arms, dropping the Star, though what a prize that would have been for her. She turned and ran back to the *shtetl*, looking over her shoulder at the solemn clay corpse only once.

Inside the Temple, Rachel toyed with her hair, wrapping it back on top of her head. She felt the warmth of her body, awake in a new way, in the way of a woman who belongs to a man. He too belonged to her, he had told her himself. She did not know what to do with any of this belonging, him to her, or her to him. For now, he was outside with his father and Kronski, preparing to leave. She had stayed within the damaged and defamed temple, sorting her thoughts, restoring her resolution to stay and now, to convince him to stay with her.

Hearing the great thump and following shriek down by the river, Rachel stepped outside into the sunlight. At first she saw nothing. Then she saw the great mud arms in the air as if still holding something up. Coming closer, she slipped down the river bank and found The Golem, inert on his back, his eyes open as if gazing at the sky. Spotting the golden Star of David on the ground, Rachel stooped and picked it up. It was as remarkable as anything she had ever seen, barring the Golem himself. She played with it between her fingertips. It caught the sunlight as if it were the sun itself.

She heard the crack of a rifle shot. As she looked around, she slipped the golden amulet into her pocket. She scrambled back up the river bank and tried to blend in behind a stand of willows. But she was seen.

"You, there!" called out a man's voice.

Nazi soldiers emerged from the woods on the opposite bank of the river, rifles leveled and ready.

"*Die fraulein, halt!*"

Rachel ran back to the ruined temple. "Isaac! Rabbi!"

"What is it?" said Isaac, as she threw herself into his arms.

"Nazi soldiers, from across the river, they must be surrounding us now!"

"And the Golem?" asked Rabbi Yakov.

"He lays by the river, as still and cold as when we first sculpted him."

"His work was done when he brought our Isaac back to us," said Rabbi Yakov.

"What do we do?" said Isaac.

"I'll tell you what we do, we fight," said Kronski, gripping his rifle.

"And die?" said Rabbi Yakov. "Here and now, after all we have been through?"

"With all the more there is to do?" said Isaac, thinking of all of the prisoners in the Castle, and the encamped persons whom the Reich deemed undesirable, imprisoned all over the continent.

Hidden behind a broken wall, Kronski peered out. "They aren't coming for us," he reported back. He waved the others forward. They came up and looked out over his shoulder. They saw the Nazis shouting at one another as they surrounded the inert Golem, weapons drawn.

Kronski, followed by Isaac, Rabbi Yakov, and Rachel, stepped out of the temple into the sunlight. Nazi rifles turned and focused on the Jews. Kronski held his rifle, lowered by his side.

The Jews watched as some of the soldiers knelt by the Golem to lift him. What they discovered was that a few soldiers were not enough. Only when the soldiers had gathered many in number were they able to lift the great stone body.

Heinrich, triumphant in his moment of glory, directed a troop transport truck to back onto the knoll overlooking the river. The Golem, lifeless, was carried by the soldiers from the riverbank, up the knoll, and loaded onto the bed of the truck, intended to transport up to forty soldiers at a time. The Golem's feet stretched out far beyond the back of the truck bed. The soldiers began to secure the Golem's body to the truck by rope.

"We have it now!" shouted Heinrich, the aide to Colonel Kohl, announcing the obvious.

"They have him," said Rachel.

Isaac slipped his hand in hers and squeezed it.

Heinrich, drew his pistol from his holster and came over to the four Jews. He took away Kronski's rifle and waved the pistol in the face of the Jews. "In the truck. *Schnell!*"

"What need have you for us?" said Kronski to Heinrich.

Heinrich's eyes narrowed, but Rabbi Yakov muttered to his companions, "We must stay with our Golem, come on," and so all of them, Rabbi Yakov, Rachel, Isaac, and Kronski, raised their hands in the air in surrender and walked toward the truck.

Isaac jumped up first, and standing up in the truck bed next to Golem, helped Rachel, and then his father, up beside him.

Kronski took a last look around, took a last breath of the fresh air of freedom, and scrambled in next to Isaac.

"This is good," said Kronski, when the truck started.

"Good?" asked Isaac.

"They haven't killed us," said Kronski, "yet."

"Yet," echoed Isaac as the truck pulled away from the temple at Zebrak.

TOCNIK CASTLE

What had once been a great banquet room still boasted faded tapestries on the walls and royal carpets used to the tread of boot-shod feet. On the banquet table was laid the body of the Golem.

Colonel Kohl stood at attention. Herr Gemlinger examined the monster. Heinrich, Kohl's aide, stood back and fidgeted. Strasser and another guard watched the door.

Gemlinger poked a leather-gloved finger into a bullet hole in what would have been the Golem's abdomen had he been human. "Clay, a man of mud."

"This could not have been the thing that attacked us," said Kohl. "It was alive."

"The Jews must have switched it," blurted out Heinrich.

Kohl gave Heinrich the usual glare but Heinrich noticed that only Kohl had responded adversely to Heinrich's idea. From now on, Colonel Kohl was not his master. Heinrich would communicate only with Herr Gemlinger. After all, he, Heinrich, had retrieved the Golem, not Kohl.

Kohl noted Heinrich's impudence. Once a fool, always a fool, he thought.

"We followed it down the mountainside," said Heinrich. "It was alive. Only when we came upon it in the presence of the Jews did it become like this."

"What do you make of this, Kohl?" asked Gemlinger.

Kohl kept his hands clasped behind his back and his stare straight ahead. "I have no interest in mysticism. I know weapons, their range, and their power. But this?" While he spoke, he was careful not to meet Gemlinger's gaze.

Gemlinger nodded. "Perhaps, but I think you may be looking at the most incredible weapon you are ever going to see."

"This? This is not the real Golem," said Heinrich.

"You have brought me a fake?" said Gemlinger, glaring at Heinrich who felt the hand of Death on his shoulder. Ice ran down his spine.

"What my aide means to say is that this may be a joke, a ruse by the Jews," said Kohl. "It is difficult to believe in a living mud monster."

278

"We should find out, don't you think?" said Gemlinger. "Have your aide bring in the Jews."

Heinrich, still recovering, was unaware that he had been spoken to.

Kohl nodded to the guard and Strasser who left and returned, with the latest group of Jews rounded up by the Nazis of Tocnik Castle — Kronski, Rabbi Yakov, Isaac, and Rachel.

"Ah hah," said Gemlinger. "If it isn't Isaac Kronski, the Paranormal Pole, Jew Extraordinaire, delayed in transit but here at last."

Kronski tipped his head forward in a perfunctory bow. Strasser shoved him forward toward Gemlinger.

"Please, you are the expert here," said Gemlinger. "What animates this man of clay?"

Kronski shrugged. "Magic."

"I've studied the folklore of your people, Jew. I know what this thing is, this Golem, this monster, this *uber* weapon."

Kronski studied his shoes. "Then you may know more than me."

"All good German parents tell their children of it, to give them nightmares," said Gemlinger, his voice rising as he addressed the Jews, "To warn them of the perils of a world shared with you people!"

A chuckle burst from Heinrich.

"This is funny to you?" said Gemlinger. "You are sent after the Golem and you bring back river mud?" He turned to Kohl, "Get him out of here."

Kohl nodded to Strasser who grabbed Heinrich by the back of his well-pressed jacket, and threw him out of the hall.

"Make it work," barked Gemlinger at Kronski. "Make it work!"

"I cannot," answered Kronski. Gemlinger glared at Kronski. Kronski met his gaze.

Gemlinger motioned to Strasser with his chin. Strasser pushed Kronski back in line with the other Jews.

"You are not the only Rabbi's son here, Herr Kronski," said Gemlinger.

Gemlinger paced over to peer into the face of Isaac, the younger Rabbi Gottesfurcht. "Not as useless as I originally thought, are you?" Isaac did not flinch.

Gemlinger moved down the line to Isaac's father, Rabbi Yakov. "This creature served you. It saved your son. Now you will make it serve a new master."

"How do you know that I am his father?" asked Rabbi Yakov.

"No more delays," snapped Gemlinger. Do it now!"

"I have no such power," said Rabbi Yakov. "I know no more than the same legends you have read. The will of God is the same for all of us."

"Perhaps I can jog you to remember how you made the Golem come to be," said Gemlinger.

"How?" asked Kronski. "By torturing us?"

"I was not speaking to you," said Gemlinger and nodded to Strasser. Strasser kicked Kronski, causing him fall to the floor.

Kronski looked up. "We're telling the truth. You cannot make us do something we do not know how to do."

"Torture is a crude tool used by crude men. Men like the Colonel, here, and his man, Strasser. They would use a hammer to open an egg. I am Gestapo. We are not so barbaric."

Gemlinger beckoned the other guard away from the door. "Bring her forward," he instructed. The guard grabbed

Rachel and dragged her to the feet of Gemlinger. "You will watch as we torture her."

"No!" said Isaac.

"Rabbi Yakov, tell them what they want!" said Kronski.

"Tell them nothing," said Rachel. "You cannot let them have power over a creature like this!"

"They will do it," said Kronski. "They will torture her and worse."

"I have nothing to tell," said Rabbi Yakov. "Bringing the Golem to life was not an act of hocus pocus. It was an act of faith. I am not some flim-flam charlatan like you, Kronski!"

Kronski's dark eyes flashed, but Gemlinger interceded. He was not interested in a fist fight between an old Jew and a younger one. "Then teach me faith," he said to Rabbi Yakov. "I want to be a man of God like you and command the elements."

"*Yahweh* will not permit it," said Isaac.

"We will place this in God's hands and see what comes to pass," agreed Rabbi Yakov, ignoring his son.

Heinrich, having been ousted from the banquet hall of the castle, paced restless in its entryway, not knowing what to do to regain his right to observe the resurrection of the Golem. He knew the Gestapo Chief, Gemlinger, would have no problem exacting the cooperation of the Jews. That was what the Gestapo did, exact cooperation.

Strasser stepped out of the hall and sent Heinrich for candles. Heinrich ran to the kitchen and grabbed three civilians who he took to be servants. Together Heinrich and his entourage soon entered the banquet hall in which lay the Golem, carrying boxes of tallow candles, borrowed from the Castle sanctorum.

The youngest servant ducked his head when he entered, so as not to be recognized by Kronski. He was Aaron, the youngest member of the Prague resistance. He had learned the hard way that it was not always clear who and who not to trust. He had been found cold and hungry in Krivolat Forest by a slender young woman and her partner, a tall young man, both gypsies, and the three had come to the Castle hoping to exact revenge for the ambush of the night before and other atrocities, past and future. Little had they expected to be delivered to the hub of the action. After lighting the many candles and placing them about the hall with good, if eerie, effect, they stood at attention, as good servants should, waiting and watching for opportunity.

For the second time in two days, Rabbi Yakov conducted the holy ceremony to create a Golem. Daylight outside darkened as heavy storm clouds gathered, yielding lightning and thunder. He and Rachel circled the Golem. Kronski again was fire. This time Isaac was the element earth and in that way, the Golem made of clay would not have to stand alone as he had before.

As Rabbi Yakov reached the conclusion of his ceremony, it came time for him to repeat the name of God, not just the word God or *Yahweh,* but rather the sacred name that was not a single word, but rather unfolded like a psalm. Rachel remembered that the *rebbe* had said that the power it unleashed could turn against the man who uttered it, if his intentions were not pure. Her heart leapt in hope when Gemlinger insisted on uttering the sacred name of God after Rabbi Yakov, repeating it as if a child learning catechism. Heinrich mouthed the words along with Gemlinger, and also Kronski who knew that such words would give power to those who dared speak them. But however much the lightning and thunder sounded outside, *Yahweh* did not choose to strike the Nazis dead. When the last syllable was spoken and disappeared into air, everyone in the room stopped breathing in anticipation. The silence and expectation nearly overwhelmed the sounds of the storm outside that dashed against the Castle. And when it was clear that nothing was going to happen, that the man of mud was going to remain comatose, it was Kronski who stepped forward. "Enough," he said, as drew the pistol from Colonel Kohl's holster, leveled it at Rachel and fired.

Rachel slumped to the floor and Isaac cried out her name. Guards grabbed Isaac and Rabbi Yakov, preventing them from going to her. Kronski turned the pistol on them. "Now, who is next?" he said.

"You, a rabbi's son. How could you do this? How could you do this to your own people?" asked Rabbi Yakov.

"My people?" laughed Kronski. "I'm not one of your mongrel race, holy man. Only my father had some Jew in him, some small drop of blood that has now been washed clean by my allegiance to the Reich. I have been forgiven my wretched past."

"You used us, all of us."

"Every rabbi I met, except you, bent over backwards to help me, because they believed that I was one of their own. None saw through me. Acting skills and some gutter knowledge of your religion was all that I needed in order to infiltrate your underground."

"I told you that I knew nothing of the underground, of the resistance."

"True, but you have given me a greater gift. A great weapon to give to Hitler. I do not need to enumerate the rewards of power and wealth that will be mine. You can well imagine."

"It is useless now," said Isaac.

"We'll see," said Kronski. "Take them outside."

Gemlinger nodded. Rabbi Yakov and Isaac were dragged outside, against their attempts to free themselves and help Rachel. Kronski and Heinrich followed.

Soon the banquet hall was empty except for the dying girl. Rachel, for the second time in almost as many days, lay on a blood soaked floor. But this time the blood was hers, and she knew the wound was mortal. She was surprised at the calm that accompanied that revelation. With the arrival of the German troops, she spent many sleepless night afraid of death. But now, when it was here, there was no fear. In fact, she attained a clarity of thought she had never experienced before. And with that clarity came both a memory, and purpose. The memory of the *Mogen David* in her pocket.

And its purpose.

Rachel lifted her head and pulled herself forward. With great effort, she gripped the polished leg of the wooden banquet table and she pulled herself up. The strength in her body was already gone. That she was moving at all was driven only by her purpose.

She pulled her torso up over the table's edge and rested there for a moment against the cold clay hulk that lay upon it. She could have died here, so close, the Golem's lifeless form an earth and mud pillow for her final sleep, but her bloodless fingers found the golden amulet, the great Star of David in her pocket, and withdrew it.

"As above, so below," she said, and spoke the name of God, although so little breath remained only the Almighty could have heard her. Raising the amulet in the air, she stabbed it into the great clay chest, at the point that would have been his breastbone, had he been human, before she fell back, unconscious.

Out in the courtyard, Kronski glared at Gemlinger. "Get on with it!" Kronski barked. The rain poured down, its fresh smell muted by ash.

Gemlinger turned to Isaac who was held by a guard. "Unlike Herr Kronski, I am neither impatient or unreasonable, young Rabbi," said Gemlinger and pulled out his pocket watch. "You have one minute to save your father's life."

Isaac looked up to the hangman's scaffold that had so chilled him at his first arrival to the Castle. There, a guard slipped the noose over his father's head. Nazis herding shuffling and sopping prisoners stopped to watch. Their prisoners huddled and kept their eyes on the ground.

"Give them nothing," called Rabbi Yakov to his son.

"I have nothing to give." Isaac looked to Gemlinger. "More time, please, more time."

Gemlinger looked down at his pocket watch, "Twenty seconds. Fifteen seconds."

Isaac pleaded, "But I do not know how to make a Golem, only he does."

"And you expect me to believe that?" Gemlinger looked back to his watch. "Ten seconds, nine, eight, seven..."

An explosion came from behind. The assembled Nazis and their prisoners lifted their arms to protect themselves from a shower of stone shards. The Golem had revived within and broken out through the Castle wall. The prisoners scattered as the Nazis whirled around and opened fire on the monster.

Gemlinger did not forget about Rabbi Yakov who he believed controlled the Golem. If the old rabbi was dead, maybe the Golem would listen to him. "Kill him! Pull the lever!" called Gemlinger to the guard on the scaffold. That guard reached for the lever that would open the gallows.

Soldiers on the ground advanced on the Golem, emptying whatever weapon they had in him. But the Golem with single intent plowed through the soldiers. Their bodies flew in all directions. He reached the scaffold and smashed it into pieces with his enormous clay fist. Rabbi Yakov and his guards fell with the scaffold, buried in the gallows' debris.

Gemlinger raced to the front gate of the Castle and jumped into a troop transport. "Out of here, *schnell!*" he shouted to the driver, but the Golem grabbed the rear of the truck and lifted it off the ground. The front wheels ground into the mud and sunk deeper and deeper until the engine died. Gemlinger looked back out through the window at the Golem, and realized his only hope was on foot. He leaped out of the truck and ran for the interior of the Castle, but the Golem cornered him against a wall.

Looking up, Gemlinger felt as he had not felt in years— the shame over his frailness that he had felt on the schoolyard, the shame over his frailness that he had felt in the shadow of his father, a hulking welder who belched beer and beat his mother, the shame over his frailness that he had felt when he looked into his mother's eyes and knew that he could not save her. He closed his eyes and waited for death, huddled shivering against the cold stone wall.

Looking down at the little man, the Golem saw an Evil that he had not witnessed before. He had never met a human so bent on the eradication of so many, on an eradication of his natural self and his natural soul, on the eradication of all that was whole and of this earth. He stood and smelled the air, and felt the affliction of this iciness in the world, how it had infected whole nations of what had been humanity. And what the Golem felt was new to him, it was Anger, an anger at a God who would allow this to be. He felt alone. He raged with loneliness. But through his sorrow, he heard a song, and realized that he was needed.

Gemlinger felt the shadow pass and heard the footsteps of the Golem as he thundered away. He opened his eyes and saw that the Golem was gone. He laughed and laughed again as he had never laughed before when he realized that the Golem had not killed him and would never kill him. As his Hitler had promised him, in this moment of facing down his fears and standing for the Aryan Nation, he had become Invincible.

Led by Aaron and the gypsies, the prisoners took the opportunity of chaos and the inspiration of the Golem, and revolted against their capturers. Their Nazi keepers ran from the mud monster, not wanting to be next.

But Heinrich, who had also dared to speak the sacred name of God, smelled the air and became infected with the same awareness of his Immutability that had seared through Gemlinger. Knowing himself invincible, he became rank with realized power. He jumped up on the nearest stone wall and began to shout. "Soldiers of the Reich, no harm can come to you, for you are the great among Great, the world surrenders and spreads her legs, even God trembles before you and dies a weeping death rather than stand in your path with His Hideous exhortations of Love and Compassion, for today you stand Supreme and all must bow who stand in your path!"

Heinrich wondered at the revelations that spilled from his mouth. He wondered why he had not thought of these things long before. He rued the time he had wasted. He reveled in his Lordship.

Below, hungry bears gathered and caught his blood-hot scent.

Kronski heard the lumbering footsteps of the Golem cross the Castle parade grounds and turning, thought it fortuitous that their paths had so neatly crossed. He wondered at the power, at the Immortality, that now coursed through his body, undeniable like steel. He thought to wrestle the monster down barehanded. Instead though, he shoved the stick grenade he had ignited for this purpose into the clay creature's back. The Golem whirled around. Kronski threw himself to the ground as the clay man exploded, showering the grounds with clumps of mud. The Star of David medallion clattered on the cobblestones, but Kronski had already gone to his next target.

Isaac struggled through the rush of bodies, soldiers and prisoners driven by fear and opportunity, at last reaching the ruins of the scaffolding. He pulled away the broken beams of wood and freed at last his father, Rabbi Yakov, battered and bloodied. Isaac slid his arm under his father and pulled him to his feet. So the two men embraced and together had one thought, Rachel.

"You go, son. You go now to her," said Rabbi Yakov. Isaac turned to run, but Kronski stood in his path.

"Ha, look," said Kronski training a pistol on Isaac. "You are Isaac and I am Isaac. There was only ever room for one of us, and I, the better, will be that one."

"Let me go to her," said Isaac.

"You see, Rabbi, the time of fairy tales is over," continued Kronski. "The time of the *Uber Mench* is now."

"She will die if someone is not there to staunch the blood."

"She is dead already," said Kronski. "Are you so stupid to think that she could have survived that wound?"

"Then just do it. I have nothing left to lose." Isaac closed his eyes. When he heard Kronski cock the hammer, he would leap on him.

Kronski laughed and reveled in his victory. There was no one he hated more than Isaac, the simpering Jew, except maybe himself. This revelation caught him off guard, but then he overrode it. Once the Jew was dead, he, Kronski, would be free. Free to be Immortal, free to get the girl, free to rule the world and mold it into a shape for his pleasure.

But as it was, clay ran in rivulets toward the golden amulet that lay on the cobblestones. And that clay congealed and reshaped until it had formed again the shape of the Golem, growing until it towered over Kronski, behind his back.

The hairs on the back of Kronski's neck stood up. He whirled around and fired his pistol. The Golem, again! The great clay man picked up Kronski and tossed him aside. Then the Golem turned to re-enter the Castle through the hole in the wall that he had blasted through. Isaac looked to his father.

"Go, son, go to her," said Rabbi Yakov, rubbing his neck.

"You'll be okay, then?"

"Yes, of course, the worst is past."

Isaac jumped through the rubble. When he reached the Castle wall, he looked back and waved at his father, then followed the clay man inside.

Kronski picked himself up, stunned but still alive. He laughed realizing that moment that the Golem would never kill him. In fact, he knew that, having intoned the sacred name of God, he had become Immortal.

Seeing Rabbi Yakov unattended, Kronski trained his pistol on him. "Come with me, old man," he said. "We're going to Berlin."

The Golem knelt beside the body of the girl. He stroked her hair, as beautiful as in life, but her skin was white and cold. He tore off a wad of his clay body and placed it on her wound. Isaac watched in awe as the wad of clay turned red, drawing up the blood that she had spilled. The clay then turned back to gray as her blood flowed back into her body. The river mud turned white and dry, and crumbled off. The skin beneath was smooth where the bullet hole had been. Her lungs heaved with a violent breath.

THE TRAIN STATION ABOVE ZEBRAK

Unaware of the chaos that raged up at the Castle, guards were loading prisoners into the freight cars. Those already on board peered out, dead eyed, between the slats of the wooden grate that restrained them.

Kronski jumped out of the long black staff car in which Gemlinger had been driven to the Castle. He pulled Rabbi Yakov out of the back of the car and shoved him up the steps that led into the front car of the steaming train.

"Move it! Get this filth on the train," shouted Kronski to the guards.

Gemlinger emerged from other side of the staff car. "That is an order!"

"We are not ready," said the guard. "We still have prisoners coming down from the Castle."

"I am Standartenfurer Von Gemlinger! I order you to start this train moving!"

"But the prisoners," began the guard.

"Forget them!" said Kronski. "Or disobey at your own risk."

"Lock them up!" shouted the guard. With that the soldiers padlocked the freight car doors closed. The prisoners who remained looked at each other in disbelief as the guards ran past them and hopped on the train.

"It's a trick," said a prisoner.

"They'll shoot us down if we run," said another.

But the train whistle blew and the train began to shudder out of the station.

The cry, "Run!" rose from among the prisoners and they ran away from the station into the forest.

The wheels of the train slipped on the rain-slick rails, then caught. The locomotive began to move forward.

Gemlinger moved forward in the passenger car and pounded his fist on the side of the train. "*Schnell! Schnell!*"

"You seem in a rush, Herr Gemlinger," said Rabbi Yakov. He looked out the window at the freed prisoners running into the woods, swallowed up by the darkness beyond the lights of the rail station. "And it looks as if you have missed a few."

"A few Jews and gypsies will not matter in the big picture. I have a greater prize for the Fuhrer." Gemlinger relaxed into a seat. He spoke to Kronski as though Rabbi Yakov was not there. "The Gestapo has developed interrogation into an art

291

form. When we get the good rabbi to Berlin, he will tell us how to create a beast of our own."

"I'll die first," said Rabbi Yakov.

"You'll die after," said Gemlinger.

Kronski laughed.

"What is so amusing?" asked Gemlinger.

"I'm just imagining the look on your face when you try to explain this all to our superiors. Even better the look on their faces."

"Quiet! We'll see how you make jokes when the Gestapo gets my report. This was your assignment. Consider this your failure."

"We're not in Berlin yet."

"You're going to read my future, Kronski?"

"I've already seen it."

The train stopped short, throwing its passengers to the floor. Gemlinger got to his feet. "What was that?"

"Don't you know?" said Rabbi Yakov.

Gemlinger threw open the compartment door and shoved the two guards out. "To the engine!" He looked back at Kronski. "You, watch the Rabbi."

"Why?" said Kronski. "Is he going to do a trick?"

Gemlinger ran out of the car.

In the locomotive, the engineer opened the throttle wide but the Golem was pushing against the train. Straining, the Golem slid on his feet, but then, drawing strength from the ground, pushed back. As he held the train in check, mud extended from his fingers, slid up the sides of the train and into its open windows. The mud trailed down onto the floor and slid along from car to car until it found what it was looking for. Reaching up, the mud climbed into the furnace that fueled the train, poured itself over the burning embers, and smothered its fire. With a shudder and a wail of steam, the locomotive lost the fight to the clay giant and died.

The troop transport truck, freed by the Golem and commandeered by the Jews, was pulled up beside the train. Isaac, Rachel, Aaron, and the gypsies jumped out.

Seeing the eyes peering out from the freight cars, Isaac ran up beside the train trying the padlocks without luck. "Locked, how can we…?"

The Golem, though, seeing what was needed, punched through the sides of the freight cars, reducing them to splinters.

"Oh, like that," said Isaac. He and the others helped the prisoners out of the freight cars. "Out! Come on, quickly! Help each other." As they disembarked, the prisoners noticed the Golem and turned to stare. "Run!" said Isaac, and they did.

In the locomotive the engineer and the brakeman stared at the dead engine. Gemlinger appeared at the compartment door. "Start this train!"

"We lost our steam," said the engineer.

"I don't care! Start this train!"

"But that thing, look…" started the brakeman, pointing into the mud-quenched furnace. Gemlinger turned and shot him, blasting him back out of the engine compartment.

"Firing her up again now," said the engineer, and began cranking levels frantically. Gemlinger climbed up on the coal tender and headed back toward the passenger section of the train.

Kronski lifted the venetian blinds over the windows with the muzzle of his pistol. He saw people running and heard shouting although he could not make out the words. "I don't hear a lot of shooting. Why do you think that is?" he asked.

Rabbi Yakov had no answer.

"Well, good luck, *Rebbe*," said Kronski.

"Good luck?"

"A good actor knows when it is time to leave the stage."

"You're leaving?"

"Yes."

"And you're not killing me?"

"No need," said Kronski, opening a window.

"Wait," said Rabbi Yakov. "I cannot let you do that."

"Do what?"

"I cannot let you get away," said Rabbi Yakov, standing. Kronski laughed and climbed outside.

Gemlinger dropped down from the coal car to a step between the train cars. He leaned out, his pistol in hand, and saw Isaac and the others helping the slower prisoners, weakened or older, out of the freight cars as the Golem smashed the last of the freight cars open. Gemlinger aimed the pistol at the back of Isaac's head, but the Golem placed a giant gray hand against the back of the last car and shoved forty tons of steel forward. Gemlinger lost his balance and fell to the tracks beneath the train just as the engineer pushed a throttle forward that took advantage of the momentum created by the Golem. The train started forward again. Gemlinger, trying to crawl out from under the cars, squealed like a pig as he was crushed beneath the moving wheels.

Kronski climbed up onto the roof of the train. Seeing him, Isaac followed. Kronski jumped from car to car until he was at the back of the last freight car. He turned back to face Isaac. "You are going to kill me now, Rabbi's son?"

"I am not just a rabbi's son, I am also a rabbi."

"And that means?"

Isaac grabbed Kronski by the lapels of his coat and shoved him back. Kronski fell off the back of the train into the huge gray arms of the Golem. Isaac climbed down the railing at the back of the car and jumped down onto the ground as the train picked up speed. The Golem lowered Kronski to safety.

"Once again, I am not dead," said Kronski. "Only the ruthless can win at war. Your Golem is useless."

Kronski, feeling a tug at his leg, looked down. The hand of a *dybbuk*, a demon plagued by its own sins, was reaching up from the ground. It was joined by another, and then yet another. The three *dybbuk* rose up from the earth, twining themselves around Kronski, hellfire licking off what would have been their bodies. Their faces were human, but long and wretched with regret and yearning. Their bodies were human but twisted and translucent, resembling smoke. Kronski screamed as they yanked at him and grabbing, pulled him down into the earth. Then all was quiet.

"It's over," said Isaac to himself.

"Not yet," said Rabbi Yakov, appearing behind his son, with the young boy, Aaron, and the gypsies. They all looked ghostly in the pale light of the moon overhead. The clouds had parted. Wind whipped over the railroad tracks. The garments of the humans flapped on their bodies, dancing. The rear lights of the train waiting up ahead burned like embers.

Rabbi Yakov put one arm around Isaac and the other around Aaron, and together, flanked by the gypsy man and the gypsy woman, they walked back toward the caboose. The Golem followed.

TOCNIK CASTLE

In his chamber, Kohl prepared to die. With the help of Strasser, he put on the jacket of his full dress uniform and buttoned it up. He allowed himself to imagine that he was going to meet his family at the villa, that they would spend the summer by the lake, that he would see his children grow to be adults. But he knew, his post having failed, that he was doomed in the Reich. His family would be better off without him. If worse came to worse, they could change their surname, cross borders, cross oceans. He was too well known within the ranks of the Army and the Reich. Strasser, dressed in full gear himself, helped his Colonel up on the chair and slipped the noose around his head. Colonel Kohl nodded to his friend and comrade Strasser, grateful for all his years of service, and his service in this final hour. Strasser took the chair away, and watched the life choked from his commanding officer. Satisfied that Kohl was dead, he drew his pistol, put the barrel in his mouth, and shot himself.

The night was clear. The last of the sunset was fading. The grounds of the Castle seemed empty now. Everyone else had escaped, through death or on foot. Heinrich turned where he still stood on the wall and looked to the hungry bears below. He found himself attracted to them. They were fierce and strong. He felt their hunger like his, his hunger for power. He jumped down and turned to them, looking each in the face, eye to eye, like a man. When they moved toward him, he did not run. He fed himself to them. After all, he could not die. He was Invincible.

CHAPTER NINE

EASTERN EUROPE, 1945

THE OBERSALZBERG

A new valet assisted Adolph Hitler and his mistress Eva Braun in packing as they prepared to leave the bunker beneath his Austrian mountain home, the Berghof, from which he had planned to rule the world. The new valet had risen from the ranks, gaining the attention of the supreme leader of the Reich by mimicking his toothbrush mustache and comb-over. When Hitler sent his long time valet away on a mission of secrecy, the new valet was next in line and thus asked to step in.

"Hurry, Eva, British planes are bombing the mountain. I'm told French and American ground troops are on their way." Hitler called for his dog, "Blondi!"

"They'll destroy the gardens," Eva sighed.

"I will get you new gardens, in Switzerland."

"It's so cold there."

Hitler placed his hand on her cheeks, taking her face in his hands. "It's only temporary, *mein Liebekin*. From there we will go somewhere warmer. South America. We have friends there."

Hitler went to the dressing table. "This is only the beginning," he said as he opened a decanter and poured her a glass of brandy.

She accepted the glass, grateful, and took a sip. He reached into his pocket, pulled out a small bottle, and shook a capsule out into his palm. He handed the capsule to her.

"What is this?" she asked.

"Take it, darling. It will help you feel better."

She did.

Hitler turned to the new valet. "And you, your good services will not go unrewarded." Hitler slipped off his jacket and handed it to the valet.

"Thank you, Herr Hitler." The valet began to fold the jacket in order to slip it into a suitcase.

"No, no, put it on," said Hitler. When the valet hesitated, Hitler added, "It is a gift, a reward for your exceptional service to the Reich, and to me."

The valet blushed, overtaken with the generosity of the gift. Under orders he dared to slip on the jacket. If only all those who had doubted him could see him now. Hitler himself helped him straighten the jacket and button it.

Hitler stood back. "It's a good fit."

"Heil Hitler," saluted the aide.

Hitler smiled. "Let's finish packing."

Eva Braun slumped to the floor.

"Help her," said Hitler, closing his suitcase.

The valet leaned over Eva and drew her up onto the bed. When she did not respond, he felt for her pulse but he could not find it.

"Loosen her collar," ordered Hitler. The valet leaned in and fussed, trying to open the fine pearl button that kept the collar of Eva's blouse tight around her pale neck.

Hitler leaned over the devoted valet with a Walther PPK pistol and emptied a round into his temple. The valet fell onto Eva's body.

Hitler slipped the pistol into the valet's hand and closed his fingers around it. Hitler threw his hat down on the bed next to his former lover and his new but former valet, picked up his suitcase, and left.

The Golem stepped in front of Isaac and Aaron, and turned his right hand to stone. He struck his stone fist through a door making an entry big enough to step through. The three made their way down stone corridors until stone gave way to beautifully appointed but empty quarters. Finally they came upon the bodies of a man and of a woman in a bedroom decorated to echo Versailles.

The Golem flared his nostrils. From the bodies rose the most awful stench of Evil. The stench permeated everything. But the one whom the Golem had sought was not there.

"Hitler," said Isaac, recognizing the likeness. He kicked the heel of the man's boot to make sure he was dead.

"And who is that?" asked Aaron about the woman. She was beautiful enough, he thought.

"His lover, or one of them," said Isaac, who thought that now he heard the shouts of men outside clambering onto the top of the mountain. The exchange of gunfire sounded close by.

The Golem had not moved at all. "He is dead, yes?"

The Golem did not have the ability to speak, so he did not answer.

"So it ends," said Isaac.

Aaron nodded.

"It's time to go back," said Isaac. He tugged on the arm of the man of clay. The Golem did not move. "Rachel," said Isaac. "We need to go to Rachel. Don't you agree that it's been too long?"

The Golem seemed to sigh. He pulled away from the two bodies, the one of a man and the other of a woman, and joined Isaac.

Ahead was the sound of tables being upset and china being smashed against the walls. Isaac ran toward the sound followed by the Golem. It was Aaron, remembering his family. Isaac grabbed Aaron and held him close until the tears came.

Relief washed over the three friends when they stepped back out into the fresh air. Looking to the green valleys below, they began their descent down the mountain.

Their war, for now, was over. But the Golem turned back to look over his shoulder several times. Isaac wondered at this strange behavior. It was as if the Golem was uneasy. The Golem, who did not seem to feel.

Not long after, the surviving soldiers of the Third Infantry Division reached the Eagle's Nest. They ran into the main hall with its enormous red marble fireplace and high beamed ceilings. They met armed resistance but soon their bullets were tearing through the remaining Nazis, and the pilfered art and bric-a-brac that had been collected here. Blood stained the expansive oriental carpet that had been a gift from the Emperor of Japan, as the Allied forces pushed further into the building.

The American soldiers raced down a narrow stone corridor, dragging with them an injured Nazi. "That's it," he verified.

"Blow it!" said the commanding American soldier, a sergeant with a wife and kids at home, miles and miles away, across sea and land.

One of the infantry men produced a charge and blasted open the door that led into the bunker. The men poured in, rifles raised and ready. The sergeant led his men forward until he came upon two figures, a man and a woman, Hitler and Eva Braun. He knelt and felt for pulses. "Dead."

"What the hell happened here, Sarge?"

"I guess we won. Oh my God, we're going home."

CHAPTER TEN

THE JEWISH QUARTER, THE YEAR 1589

"Shalom, Golem," Evie had said, greeting the guest as he arose, having entered the body made of mud which she had shaped for him.

Every cell in her body told her that the attic and her father could no longer contain her. She unlocked the door and flew down the stairs before her father and his students knew what was happening.

She smelled the cold of the dawn before she leaped out into it. No longer a domestic creature, she had more in common with a wild deer or a sharp-eyed crow than her kindred. With fierce unthinking abandon she scaled the gates at the end of the Quarter and fled into the forest, protected by the earliness of the hour from contact with humankind.

The dawn rose sweet and fragrant. Evie drank deep from the cold river from which banks some days before she had stolen clay with her father. Her hair trailed in the water as she leaned in. When she rose, she threw her head back and shook her hair free. Frost formed at its tips. She was adorned in rime. Her father had his hands full with the Golem. She was on her own.

MOLDAVKA RIVER

Evie weaved through the trees, letting the sunlight and shade hit her and savoring their differences. She slipped off her shoes and left them behind. She let her bare feet slip in the mud of the riverbank. She let her bare feet know the grit of the rich loam under the trees. She breathed deep, not hungering for food or shelter. She thought she would rather starve to death than go back to her father's house.

When the last rays of sunlight began to fade, she began to shimmy up a tree. She was surprised to find out how easy it was to climb once she had cleared the lowest branch. It was as if God had built her a ladder and called it a tree. When she reached the dizzying top of the tree, she settled into the crook of a branch and hugged the highest stretch of tree that ended in the sky. Wrapped in a blanket of velvet darkness, she fell to dozing, rocking gently in the breeze.

In her dreams, troubled souls came to her and confessed the wrongs they had committed during their lives on the whisper of the wind in the branches. Some were secret sins that washed over into the way they had lived their lives – men who longed to abandon their nagging wives and demanding children, wives who had husbands they had wished dead. Some were adulterers, thieves, blackmailers, and murderers. Some had broken the Kosher laws, some had broken the sacred Sabbath. She understood them all. She loved them all and absolved them all. Life itself was a sacred path, challenging to live, impossible to master, a path to be traveled barefoot, strewn with broken glass.

The half moon rose late. When she woke, its shimmer was on everything. She slipped a hand into her pocket and allowed it to gap open. Slow and lazy, the Ashes of God danced out of where she had held them warm against her body. They orbited her head. All a glimmer, the Ashes began their ascent, carrying with them the spirits of the troubled souls, who, having been heard and loved, were content to meet their Lord. The Ashes and the Souls rose through the night sky, spiraling up toward Heaven.

She leaned back, mouth wide open, and watched as they swirled up and up, slipping out of the sky through a gap in its ceiling. She got the sense as if the world was just a pocket in the garment of a bigger being who also had a pocket, just as she had a pocket in her smock. She imagined pocket after pocket, opening onto bigger and bigger Universes, until finally the Ashes, and the Souls they held aloft, would reach Heaven itself and restore themselves as God. As above, so below. As below, so above. She sighed, and slipped back to sleep.

When Evie dreamed again, it was of her ordinary life. Her father, the old Rabbi Loew, had his hands full with the Golem. He did not worry for her. He believed she was with her sister Leah or at their neighbor's house, perhaps helping the neighbor's cat care for its kittens. Evie dreamed herself licking off each kitten and then lifting her blouse and allowing the furry little balls to nurse at her many breasts. She noticed that she looked quite natural in a soft coat of gray, black, and white striped fur with sweet pink skin beneath where the fur parted. And she knew it was true that if she were a cat, she would be a tabby.

And when her kittens were done nursing, she stretched her feline body, feeling the purr in her strong sinewy muscles, already thinking again of a rendezvous with her favorite tom. Pictures in her mind of his rough might stirred her to passion, so she set off from her nest of warm fuzzy babies, deep in the unperturbed sleep of contented infants, and slunk out into the night.

Out under the half-moon lit night, the cat who was Evie crept passed the Temple and came upon the old Rabbi Loew, out walking while other humans slept. Dappled with moonlight, bathed in luminescence, he walked hand in big clay hand with the Golem monster. It was eerie indeed to see the small, pale *rebbe* hobbling along, side by side, large hand in tiny hand, with the undead Giant. The old Rabbi Loew was teaching the ungainly and awkward Golem how again to use his feet, how to find a gait in this world that everyone finds awkward upon re-entry. In order to do so, the old Rabbi Loew had to rethink the whole process of walking. He had learned how to move his feet, one step after the other, so many decades before, hand in hand with his mother. In accord with human nature, once he had mastered ambulation, he had forgotten how. With each step he took with the Golem, he was reminded of the wonder of life and of the many gifts that *Yahweh* strew before humankind, only to have those gifts taken for granted.

Evie recognized the pious look on her father's face. With her keen cat ears she could hear the yammer, yammer, yammer of his all too familiar thoughts. Once again he was in a spiritual mood. She scowled a cat scowl and yowled a cat yowl. The Golem turned his head and set his yellowed eyes on her, and tripped. Her father glowered at the cat and used all his might to steady the greater mythical being.

Her father said to the Golem, "Don't worry, *boychik*, it's just a cat." The story of her life, she thought. She arched and hissed.

"Shoo," her father said. "Shoo!" Showing him, she shot off into the night. As she neared the end of the road, she slowed to a saunter, turned her head, and flung a look back at her father and monster. Preoccupied with their next step, neither the *rebbe* or the Golem noticed her.

And then she was gone, loping off into her whiskery night. Her night senses thrilled her. She smelled the blood of rodents and angled her ears back the better to hear their tiny teeth and tiny paws working their night moves. Everything worth knowing was at play. The world of humans was slow and plodding, sound asleep.

THE JEWISH QUARTER OF PRAGUE

Bringing the Golem to life had given the old Rabbi Loew a new lease on his own limited days on the planet. He felt like a kid again and had not thought about sleep in over two days. But now as the morning hours dawned, a ray of sun streaming in through the kitchen window and pooling at his feet, he needed rest and felt it, but his daughter Evie was gone. She had not gone to her sister's home or the neighbor's house. No one knew where she was. And there was no one else he trusted to spell him with the Golem.

"She'll be back," the old Rabbi Loew said to himself. He sat on a stool and watched the Golem move a broom back and forth on the floor. It was not sweeping, it was just moving the dirt around, but in time perhaps the Golem could be taught how to sweep a floor, and many other things.

As he sat, thoughts came to the old Rabbi Loew. *Maybe my Evie has told her sister to hide her.* He did not want to think that. *Maybe instead of asking her to help him make the Golem, he should have been finding her a husband.* But he did not think it would have made a difference one way or the other if he had found her a husband. No matter what he had done, she would have done what she wanted. *She must have wanted to help me make the Golem. Then why did she leave me?* His thoughts multiplied like tadpoles in an abandoned bucket of rainwater. They swam against the sides of his skull and annoyed him. They were appropriate and inappropriate, and altogether annoying. His subconscious mind took the easiest way out and sent the old Rabbi Loew a tension headache. He stood up to get a drink of water. For what seemed the thousandth time, the Golem stepped on the old Rabbi Loew's left foot, the one troubled by arthritis.

"Fool!" said the old Rabbi Loew. The Golem stopped, making matters worse because where he stopped was on old Rabbi Loew's foot. "*Klutz! Shnook!* " barked the old Rabbi Loew which only made matters worse. The Golem reacted to being yelled at by his *rebbe* by freezing like a frightened rabbit.

The old Rabbi Loew pushed and shoved at the big clay body, and finally rocked the Golem back a smidge allowing the *rebbe* to slip his foot out from under. "You big damn *shlemiel!*" said the old Rabbi Loew nursing his foot. The Golem looked at the ground. If he had emotions, he would have been ashamed.

As the pain subsided, the old Rabbi Loew sighed and shook his head. "Come," he said, and led the Golem, still carrying his broom, over to the cooking fire.

The old Rabbi Loew felt it best to keep the Golem under wraps for now. He wanted more time to acclimate the Golem to the world. He wanted more time to acclimate himself to the world. Evie had been almost right. Having a Golem in his home was almost more than the old Rabbi Loew could chew. But he would get it right. And he would find his Evie again, make peace with her, and bring her home. And then together, at just the right time, they would unveil the new Protector to the world and all would be made right.

For now he just wished the Golem could cook or wash dishes. He was hungry and the kitchen was dirty. But even an attempt to get the Golem to stir a pot, a monotonous task usually left to women, was a disaster. The old Rabbi Loew took a turnip, a broken carrot, and a potato, which he had cut in pieces – he did not trust the Golem with a knife – in a pot. The old Rabbi Loew poured water from a bucket over the vegetables and put the pot on the fire. When the water began to boil, the old Rabbi Loew threw in some buckwheat and took up a big wooden spoon. He stirred the pot a few times to make sure the grain did not stick. Then he took the broom from the Golem, leaned the broom against the wall, brought the Golem over to the pot, and handed the Golem the spoon. But the Golem did not understand his task, and could not repeat a continuous circular motion. His circles grew misshapen, and his strength brought the pot clattering upended on the floor. After the fourth attempt, the *rebbe* did not find new ingredients for the porridge. He just scraped the spilled ingredients up off the floor and put them back in the pot. Then he put the pot back on the fire and handed the spoon again to the Golem.

"Keep trying," the old Rabbi Loew said to the Golem, and turned to leave. The old Rabbi Loew kicked the stray turnip that had fallen on the floor from the first cooking batch. The sorry turnip rolled up against the wall and ricocheted back, coming to rest against the Golem's great foot. The old Rabbi Loew trudged upstairs to try and get a nap. He fell fully clothed into his unmade bed and allowed his eyes to close. No sooner had he begun, for some strange reason, to dream of the neighbor's cat, he woke to the smell of smoke.

The Golem looked at the big wooden spoon. He blinked his eyes. The spoon did not change. He worked to ascertain its meaning but all he got was the echo of the word, "spoon," in what seemed to be his head. He did not understand the spoon or its purpose, or the pot or its purpose, or the fire or its purpose. He had a purpose but he was not serving it here in the old *Rebbe* Loew's kitchen. He left.

MOLDAVKA RIVER

Evie woke the next morning with a start. Rain struck her face. She leaned her head back and caught it in her mouth. She was cold, wet, and alive. She worked her way down, branch to branch, until she felt the ground under her feet.

A bread crust, a wrinkled apple from the winter's stores, and a hunk of moldy cheese, waited for her in a hollow of the tree made by its roots. She looked around, wondering if she had a benefactor. Evie decided that it was not necessary to know, and that it was not necessary to eat. She was full with God and had not wanted to come back to earth, a mournful planet of crumbs and sorrow. She wondered, without fear, what it would be like to starve to death. She started up the riverbank, heading deeper into the dark and tangled woods.

Feeling a familiar tug at her bladder, Evie slipped into the underbrush and slipped her underwear down off her *tush*. Squatting, she released her yellow pee into the dirt. Steam rose, as if the ground were saying *thank you* for her warm rich urine. The earth was smart. It was people who were stupid. The honesty of her answer surprised her. Maybe it fell to her now to go back and enlighten people, or at least other women. She could start with the women and then they would whisper the truth to their men so it seemed to the men that it was their own idea. The truth was that people took life and death far too seriously. God did not seem to care if people lived or died, and maybe there was a reason for that. Maybe He was preoccupied with something else – the great Infinite, Creation and Destruction, Bliss Without End, Wholeness, something to do with Wholeness... Her thoughts wandered back to the wrinkled apple, moldy hunk of cheese, and the crust of bread that she now regretted leaving behind.

As she was ready to stand, she heard footsteps crunching leaves and branches. She pulled up her undergarment and pulled down her skirt, then sat on her heels, hugging her knees, hoping herself hidden.

Her intruders were the bread thief and two other young men from the town of Prague that she did not recognize. The bread thief was as beautiful as the day he had slipped a hand into her basket of holy baked goods. His eyes were as blue a blue as she had ever seen. Out hunting for squirrel, they had followed her curious footprints.

"Look, a wood spirit," said the tallest and widest of the bread thief's friends, pointing at her. All of them were surprised to find a girl in the woods. Evie allowed her eyes to dart from one to another, and tried to shrink as small as she could. It was no use. They were fascinated by her.

"No, it's not a wood sprite," said the bread thief's shorter friend. Evie sprung to her feet and made to bolt, but the tallest and widest friend leaped on her, pinning her to the ground.

"Not a wood sprite at all, it's a Jew," said the shorter friend. Standing back, he spat into the dirt.

Evie struggled, panting. Her captor, the tallest and widest friend, held both of her hands over her head in one hand and brushed her hair off her face with his other hand. "It's the one who kills babies," said the captor, laughing.

"No," said the bread thief, leaning over her. "It's the one who bakes breads." Evie looked up into his very blue eyes framed by his blonde hair, set against the treetops and pieces of the very blue morning sky.

Evie woke in the nighttime. Once he had discovered her in the woods, the bread thief had come every day to see her with his stolen morsels of food and his lovemaking, until one day he didn't. When he didn't come the next day or the next day, and more days after that, she came down with a sorrow that wracked her body with fevers and chills. The old gypsy woman with the missing teeth had found her and dragged her to her wagon, covered her with blankets, and poured tea down her throat. They had no words in common except the sorrow in their eyes.

The old gypsy woman tried to keep Evie, but she would not lie still. Swooning or not, Evie sat up. The wrinkled apple, the crust of bread, and the hunk of cheese sat next to her, together with a cup of steaming tea. The old gypsy woman urged Evie to eat. Her ripped undergarments hung drying above the sheltered campfire. The old gypsy woman had done her best to beat the blood and semen from them on the rocks as she washed them in the river, but Evie was forever stained. Evie got to her feet, backed away from the campfire, inconsolable, and began to run. Rain was cascading from the sky in sheets.

The next evening as the light began to fade the Golem found Evie in her church on the corner, near the town center of Prague proper. She knelt, hugging herself, wet and shivering, her clothes torn, her hair a tangle with madness, before the burning candles, looking up into the blue eyes of her Jesus, the statue with the wavy blonde hair and blue eyes who wore nothing but a loincloth. The Golem slipped his great arms under her and lifted her to his chest. She fell silent, closed her eyes, and leaned against him. He turned and lumbered out of the church. The mouths of the townspeople that he passed hung open, agape at the sight of the giant made of clay, not believing what they saw. The word of such a vision, of course, flew.

THE JEWISH QUARTER

After the old Rabbi Loew had taken the burning pot outside and quenched its fire with rain and dirt, he looked around for the Golem. Now his daughter was missing and so was his Golem. He, the great Rabbi Loew, could find neither of them, or the compass of his own life. His great plan seemed meaningless now. The Golem was clumsy and stupid, his daughter was angry and lost.

The old Rabbi Loew sat down on a bench in the kitchen and tried to pray, but instead he let his frustration overtake him, and then his tears. The day began to fade and he realized it was Shabbat. His Evie had not cleaned a kitchen, or made a *challah*. No chicken was cooking in a pot bubbling over the fire. His life was empty. As he began to pray, he heard the front door open and met the Golem with his Evie on the threshold. He threw himself on the Golem and hugged him, even with Evie in his arms. The Golem knew that he was home.

The old Rabbi Loew led the Golem up to Evie's room, and together they placed her in her bed. The Golem stepped back and watched from the threshold as the old *rebbe* drew the blankets up over Evie and kissed her cheek. She murmured and curled on her side into a fetal position. The old Rabbi Loew stepped back and stood by the Golem. They watched Evie draw breath in and out in her sleep.

Then the old Rabbi Loew took the Golem by one of his great hands and led him up the stairs to the attic. The old Rabbi Loew helped the Golem onto the table where he was made. As the first shadows of the Shabbat began to fall, the old Rabbi Loew drew the star of David amulet out from the Golem's chest and the Golem fell inert into a rest as deep as God made. The Golem was grateful.

The old Rabbi Loew leaned against the wall a moment and watched his great monster to be sure that he slumbered without condition, as if dead. If something is not alive, can it die? wondered the old Rabbi Loew. He was glad that the Golem had not resisted being rendered back to clay on the Sabbath. He was glad that the Golem was grateful.

The *rebbe* had feared that if the Golem defied the Sabbath, he would be so severed from Yahweh that he would be made an immortal monster. In time, men would be distracted by his super abilities and his immunity to death, and come to worship him, as men long before had worshipped idols. And if the good *rebbe* was clear about one thing, it was that the Golem was no Divine Being worthy of being slobbered over. If anything, the Golem was a fool, a good fool, but a fool who could not be unleashed on the world except under the most stringent of conditions, a fool not unlike himself, the old Rabbi Loew.

313

The Golem did not move even a hair's breadth. Feeling secure to leave the clay body, the old Rabbi Loew pocketed the golden *Mogen David* and went downstairs to tend to his daughter, his dear and precious Evie.

THE TEMPLE AT ZEBRAK

Rabbi Yakov gave a short tug on his reigns and his horses, familiar with the destination, stopped. He let his horses free of the cart to graze the fresh blades of grass that broke the surface of the thawing earth.

"*Rebbe!*" called the voice of a young girl, Sarah. She had grown taller since he had seen her last, just weeks before.

Behind her, the good people of Zebrak, Jews and non-Jews alike, had worked to restore the outer walls of the temple with mortar and whitewash. Piece by piece, thanks to the *rebbe's* daughter, Rachel, the temple was raised again. But now that the war was over and the occupiers had withdrawn or been led away, its outer aspects could finally be completed.

Rachel had begun leading services there in the hull of the building as it became whole, until finally she had become not just the daughter, but also the *rebbe*. Still, her lifetime identity as the *rebbe's* daughter stuck, and perhaps it always would.

Rachel herself stepped out into the sunlight holding the hand of a two-year old boy, cherubic blonde curly hair, like the very Elohim. "*Zayde!*" he cried, upon seeing his grandfather and let go of his mother's hand reaching up.

Rabbi Yakov grabbed up the child and held his cheek to his. "Zachariah, how's my big boy!"

Rabbi Yakov carried the smiling boy over to the cart and lifted the tarp. He reached in and pulled out a wooden duck, carved and painted by a friend in Prague, specially for this young man. Zachariah grabbed the duck, and kissed his *zayde* on his rough cheek, and slid down out of his arms. Examining his prize, he said, "When comes my papa?"

Rachel kissed Rabbi Yakov on the cheek too. "Have you had word?"

"Not yet," said Rabbi Yakov, "But I would expect..." He trailed off, interrupted by the rustling of the woods and the sound of unnaturally heavy footsteps.

Isaac appeared at the edge of the woods, Aaron lingering behind him, both tired and ragged, but alive. Isaac's eyes met Rachel's. She ran to him and he swept her up in his arms.

"Zachariah, come meet your papa!" called Rachel.

But Zachariah screamed and ran inside the temple.

He had never seen a Golem before.

"Racism is man's gravest threat to man — the maximum of hatred for a minimum of reason."

–Abraham Joshua Heschel

About The Authors

John Fasano is a journalist and artist with more than twenty years experience in feature films, the Internet and prime time television as a writer, director and producer. His feature work includes the genre films *Another 48 Hrs.*, *Alien 3*, *Darkness Falls*, *Universal Soldier: The Return*, *Black Roses*, *Sniper Reloaded* and *Tombstone*. His work on television includes *The Hunchback* (for which he received a WGA nomination for best teleplay), *F/X The Series*, *Mean Streak*, *The Legend Of Butch & Sundance*, *The Hunley*, *Murder at The Presidio*, *Saving Jessica Lynch*, and *Stone Cold*. His Godzilla illustrations can be seen in *G-Fan* magazine.

Roni Keller is a poet, screenwriter, and novelist published in both Great Britain as well as the United States. She writes with her dog, Cooper, at her feet. He has many interesting ideas for film and television but has never completed a book himself. He blames it on the squirrel in the backyard. Look for her next novel, *The Torturer's Daughter*.

CPSIA information can be obtained at www.ICGtesting.com
Printed in the USA
BVOW050638061011

272893BV00001B/6/P